Janessa
Hope you
Enjoy

Richard Coby

12/2014

miss you

I love you

enjoy

15/5/2014

A Monumental Journey 4

Beyond Understanding

Richard L. Cederberg

authorHOUSE®

AuthorHouse™
1663 Liberty Drive
Bloomington, IN 47403
www.authorhouse.com
Phone: 1-800-839-8640

First published by AuthorHouse   3/29/2011

ISBN: 978-1-4567-4206-5 (e)
ISBN: 978-1-4567-4207-2 (hc)
ISBN: 978-1-4567-4208-9 (sc)

Library of Congress Control Number: 2011902808

Printed in the United States of America

Dedications

Michele Elizabeth Cederberg

My gifted wife, best friend, fellow dreamer and talented photographer - you have helped me navigate through some of the toughest, mind-bending, drag you over the rocks, challenging seasons in my life. Thankyou! I am convinced that good things come to those who hope and pray and steadfastly press forward together in faith.

For that moment my love
You became a bridge
Between my heart and my quill
Between my mind and my actions
You became the impulse
That gripped me in firm encirclement
It was you Michele that I was shown
As a loving vision
Along jagged peaks and valleys
Amidst wildflowers purple
And trees deprived of life
It was you Michele
That became the wind in my hands
It was you Michele
Imparting vitality to insensate dailiness
It was you Michele
That I saw bathed in sunlight
And for a day together
You reached over and took my hand
To take me soaring with the Eagles

Excerpt from the poem: "It Was You Michele"
Richard Lloyd Cederberg
2006

1

Garrett Richard Cederberg (my son), and Aedin and Hunter Cederberg (my grandsons)

Garrett ... you continue to be a muse in my life. Your struggles, your hopes and dreams, your manner of expression, your unflinching fortitude as a young father, and your marvelous gifts, have influenced me steadfastly in the creation of one of my favorite characters in the MJ series. You will always be loved and in my heart!

Aedin and Hunter ... "Grampa and Gramma with the Jeeps" look forward to some cool adventures with you both someday.

Nicole and Dustin Rhodes

My niece and nephew from marriage; two young people who will surely reap much good in their lives if they are doggedly disciplined, stay centered on their callings, and remain united to their One True Source.

Sean Custeau and Lilly

Sean, you are a living testament of God's grace and mercy, and also a living example of the life-changing power of a Mother's love and prayers. It is my hope that Light, Wisdom, and Understanding, will imbue you, and your daughter, for all the days of your time on earth.

Foreword from the Author

I fancied the heavenly firmament as a cache of infinite musical notes. And, as I was mulling this, I questioned what may happen if I viewed the heavens through a transparency etched with the lines of a musical staff. The prospect intrigued me so I set about to fashion a template to carry out this curious undertaking. When my task was at last completed I waited for the perfect evening and, at the opportune moment, I held the large sheet up against a clear night sky.

To say I was utterly beguiled would be an understatement.

At once before me, aggrandized by tercets and triads, compositions of incredible depth began appearing in a supernal opus flowing forward. Magnificently lush extended chords, and polyphonic complexity, appeared every time I moved the sheet. In purity a wash of minuet and motet blossomed as the stars became notes stacked in suspensions and harmonies of minor fifths and sevenths.

Was this a sampling of the music of the third heaven?

Could it be that an enlightenment of astrophysical symphonies were suspended in the vault of heaven that, when interpreted, could unlock mysteries, and open distant portals, to places never before seen or heard? Was it possible that healing balms could be produced from these musical inventions that were capable of soothing broken hearts, and changing the ego-centric panoramas of arrogant humanity?

Entranced now in sheer loftiness, and with a temporary gift of heightened auditory acuity, I slowly moved the transparency across the sky and listened, enthralled, as Centaurus became a cantus firmus, and Leo Minor a seraphic capriccio. Moving to the north, the Corona Borealis played out as a madrigal of the sweetest simplicity, while Leo Major roared in perpetuum mobile. Moving collectively together in contrapuntal base, the Gemini Twins danced in an exoticism of far off lands, while Cassiopeia became an oratorio of genteel luster. With the grandeur of a Turkish Sultan, Pegasus celebrated with a lively blending of double-reed instruments, triangles, bass drums, cymbals, bell-trees and trumpets. In bel canto Andromeda sang in purity, whilst Picis Austrinus became a chaste passacaglia.

I was stunned.

With every movement of the transparency another motif of harmonic brilliance spilled forth in this majestic mingling of glimmering stars and celestial bodies. For mortals this was a gift beyond anyone's ability to comprehend, a gift beyond one's power to apprehend, a gift certainly *Beyond Understanding.* Here was a true wealth of possibilities that invited all seekers, brave enough to look up and touch the hem of it, a chance to dream and create.

Richard Lloyd Cederberg

Author/Poet

Prologue

"You are a Vildarsen then?" He growled in the old language.

Anders nodded and moved within swords length of the man. Despite his ghastly countenance Anders remained unaffected and met the Seers gaze with no emotion. I was stunned at Anders strength of character and thanked God for his friendship.

"You wish to free the dog Granmar Grettig?" The Seer continued.

Anders remained silent for several moments and then replied in soft tones: "It seemeth wise to do so!"

Out of the blue Rolf was with us. Hunched over and watching keenly, he slowly moved behind the Seer and began growling; the sound made my flesh crawl. As their eyes met Rolf bared his teeth. The Seer appeared restless. Having also emerged from the CSAT, Captain Olaf, Rorek, and Jonah were now standing in a semi-circle behind us with their weapons at the ready. Helga assured us that she had everything in her sights. Unsure, the Seer signaled at Thurid. Looking directly at Anders again he reached into his tunic.

"Who are these ye summon Anders, son of Utgard?" He growled.

With an unwavering expression Anders moved closer and calmly met the seer's gaze.

"Dost thou fear me god?" The Seer taunted flippantly as Anders coolly gripped his sword.

"Ogre, if thou stand in the way of this league," Anders countered, "this very day my blade shall send thy wretched soul to hell!

"Thou speaketh haughtily," the seer roared. "Thinketh I fear thee?"

"Think what you will ogre, but do *not* think your countenance troubles me." Anders warned with blazing eyes. "On my father's name Utgard, thou shalt gaze into the pit of Niflheim this very day!"

When the seer drew his sword a strange chant began and all the others drew theirs also. As if drawn by magic, Thurid's men moved forward towards us like zombies. Garrett tapped my shoulder. With a curious peace in his countenance he pointed towards the longboat. There I could make out Granmar Grettig and his family in the cage; all were on their knees praying.

Part One

In the Realm of Ancients

One

A Clear Victory

Anders brought his sword to bear. There was no concern, whatsoever, in his countenance. His eyes were unwavering and emotionless as he stared at his opponent. The Seer was a strongly muscled warrior who possessed great sway with those around him. The most frightening difference between the two, in my opinion, besides the great disparity in physical size, was the fierce piercing eyes of the Seer and the loathsomeness that oozed from every pore of him. Never before had I seen Anders in the frame of mind he was in.

A wild swing from the Seer caught the Norseman's sword and knocked him down. Anders sprang back to his feet undeterred and, after grinning toothily, and nodding, a calculated lunge knocked the Seers sword from his hand. Laughing cavalierly he picked it up and, when he was erect, his face twisted disdainfully and he hissed: "Luck will not save you from my blade god; I will gut you on these rocks and put your head on a pole."

Anders smiled and coolly responded: "Today will prove to you, Seer, and to all those mindless you enslave with black art, just what an over-rated blowhard you are."

A gauntlet had been thrown down. Outraged the Seer lunged towards Anders with evil intent. Anders countered effortlessly and slapped the Seers face hard as he went by. This infuriated him and, after roaring angrily, the battle exploded. Within seconds the fierce clanging of swords was echoing noisily in the grotto as the two men fought a vicious, but intelligent, game of human chess. It was mind-boggling, the ferocity they employed; thrusting, and parrying, and countering the savage blows of the other, and then springing back at the ready, seemingly with unlimited energy, to begin the attack again. This went on for fifteen awe-inspiring minutes and then, suddenly, the momentum changed. Anders sword fell from his hands and he slumped forward with his hands on his knees. In the distance I heard a woman screaming; I knew it was Angelina. I was shocked to my core. Was Anders exhausted? Was he wounded? Not knowing what else to do we reached for our weapons to protect him. When he saw what we were planning he turned and grinned.

"Do you need any help?" Captain Olaf asked in English.

Anders shook his head no. I didn't understand. Even if he *was* employing a kind of subterfuge how could he let himself become so vulnerable and still remain so calm and focused.

Taken back now by what appeared to them as an act of cowardice; Thurid's men began ridiculing Anders. Within seconds a strange chant began. For awhile the Seer just stared and then, with a twisted sneer, he started laughing in a gut-wrenching derision. Again Anders turned and smiled to let us know that his ruse was playing out. After the Seer had added his guttural voice to the chant he then turned towards the Norseman and postured menacingly. It was like watching a movie. Anders kicked away his sword, and moved back about ten feet with his head bowed. Plainly claiming victory in the contest the Seer thrust his sword above his head. Immediately the chanting stopped; Anders played into it masterfully. Genuflecting on one knee he proclaimed: "Thou art a mighty warrior Seer with the strength of Hercules."

The Seer laughed uproariously and then asked of the others: "What should I do with this wretched god?"

"Kill him kill him kill him," a frenzied chorus came back.

We were shocked at the evilness of it. In arrogant confidence the Seer turned his back on Anders to gloat. It was a foolish mistake. At once, and as silently as a thought, Anders leapt across the distance that separated them and then bounded up as gracefully as a cat and kicked him ferociously on the side of the head. The Seers sword clanged noisily to the floor.

"Gotcha butthead," Anders shouted with a wide grin.

"DUDE … RIGHT ON," Garrett screamed in delight, "now wack that stinkin' grease turd."

All Thurid's men stepped back in astonishment. I couldn't believe my eyes either; surely the force of the kick would have rendered any man senseless, but this brute was still on his feet. Stumbling like a drunkard the Seer began rubbing his temples to clear the cobwebs; blood was trickling from his ears.

"Now let's see what you're made outa," Anders growled aloud as he moved around in front of the man.

When he saw Anders his eyes opened wide and in blind rage he started swinging fiercely with his fists - and he swung again and again and again - but to no avail. Anders side-stepped each blow deftly and, when the Seer finally faltered, he dropped down to one leg and, in one powerful rotating motion, kicked the side of his knee. The hulking man stumbled backwards. Moved mightily by Anders brilliant move, we all began cheering. Lessened, now, by mounting frustration, and blinded by rage, the Seer let loose a long string of foul curses; it was obvious that he had lost his center of focus. Smiling broadly Anders never lost a beat. With all his senses attuned he pounced, as gracefully as a leopard at its hapless prey, and landed a devastating blow beneath his chin with the palm of his hand. Immediately Anders snatched up the behemoth and swung him in an arching circle over his head and brought him crashing down. The Seer landed with a sickening thud on one of his shoulders and I heard a loud snap. Thurid's men gasped. Never had their champion been manhandled in a way such as this. Empowered by the Holy Spirit Ander's had soundly defeated the Viking Goliath; an evil necromancer had fallen at the hands of a warrior half his size.

A rush of elation surged through me and I felt like crying and laughing and screaming all at the same time. If ever I'd been exposed to the stuff heroes were made of, or the stuff of legends, it was on this very day, when our intrepid friend, and crewmate, became bigger in my eyes than life itself. Similar to Homer in the Iliad, or of Odysseus in the Odyssey, or even of the legendary Hiawatha and what his awe-inspiring powers did for the Algonquin Nation; Anders the Norse Vildarsen had prevailed against the mighty Seer with tenacity, skill, strength, cunning, and brilliant subterfuge.

Snarling now like a wounded animal the Seer sat up. I thought it strange that not one, of Thurid's men, had come forward to help him. It seemed as if all of them were afraid or just didn't care. When he tried to move his arm he cried out miserably and a fearful expression washed over him. Roaring for assistance several of the others finally, and cautiously, inched forward to assist. When they were gathered around him he shifted towards Anders and, in arrogant defiance, bellowed: "Mark thy destiny in blood Anders, son of Utgard, of the clan Vildarsen, may Odin deliver thee from the jaws of my final vengeance. This day shall never be absolved from my remembrance. We shall meet again someday and, if it be Odin's will, be assured of this; I will have thy hair upon my belt!"

Anders was unmoved and, after pulling the loose hair from his face, he moved closer and starred fully into his eyes.

13

"I have heard thy arrogant words and accept the challenge. I, too, mark with zeal that day if ever we shall meet again. Be assured that the Most High Christ hath declared a victory (this day) for Anders the Norse upon thee and thou have been lessened in the struggle."

"Lessened, god, maybe, but not defeated." The Seer countered with impudence. "I will have my vengeance upon thee."

Anders smiled and returned: "Keep the blade sharpened ogre and one eye lidless in sleep. Thou knoweth not the time, or the place, if ever we shall meet again."

Groaning in pain the Seer stared sullenly at Anders as the others dragged him off. When he was no longer in sight Glammad turned towards the Norseman.

"Great son of Utgard," he began with a deeply affected air. "Thou have fought with bravery and cunning to be sure. Today I mark thee as the gilded offspring of Thor himself and ask, in thy newfound sublimity, if thou wouldst suffer me a challenge; a final request."

"Speak forth Glammad." Anders shrugged his shoulders.

"I choose to show mercy to Anders, son of Utgard, for I know in weariness doth he wax feeble from this dread battle."

Anders chuckled deeply. When Glammad saw that he was unshaken his eyes flared in rage and he pointed towards Garrett.

"I challenge that one," He hissed in prideful indignation.

Clearly understanding Glammad's body language, Garrett roared back: "You wanna piece 'a me you barf bag?"

Incensed, Garrett threw down his sword and ripped off his t-shirt. Flexing his muscles, he challenged the braggart to a contest of rough and tumble fisticuffs. Thurid's men seemed shocked at Garrett's fearless response.

"Come on cheese-ball, you ain't got the guts to tangle with me," Garrett continued cheekily. Garrett moved nearer Glammad and stared directly in his eyes. Not knowing how to respond to the fearlessness, Glammad's face turned ugly and he began spitting out a string of ancient curses.

"Come on big mouth, make a move," Garrett mocked him.

I could clearly see, from the wash of expressions chasing across Glammad's face, that he despised being taunted by someone younger. Sneering angrily he finally threw his sword aside and prepared.

"This shouldn't take long," I heard John chuckling.

Despite the fact that Glammad was a resilient fighter Garrett emerged unscathed and the victor. When he'd finally backed off, gasping and bloodied, from Garrett's unrelenting onslaught of fists; he seemed mortified with what had happened to him in front of the other men. In a rage Glammad pulled out a knife hidden in the belt of his tunic and lunged forward to stab Garrett. Having never taken his eyes off him, Garrett side-stepped the ill-fated attack just as Helga's long rifle cracked sharply. I couldn't believe Glammad's stupidity. Saucer-eyed he collapsed to his knees gasping for each breath. Despairingly Garrett looked down into his now bewildered eyes and asked aloud: "Why didn't you just let it go?" But there was no response; he had no chesty words left to retaliate with; it was the last craven act he would ever attempt. With a wheezing sigh the once arrogant defiant man slumped forward in a pool of his own blood and his spirit left him.

The SES uncloaked immediately and the rest of the crew rushed ashore to help. Thurid's men cried out when they saw this happen and all of them, in great dread, with whatever they could carry, fled along the shoreline towards the far side of the grotto. Soon every one of them had disappeared into the mist and rocks.

"What a stinkin' fight - sheesh; we wacked ten of um and wounded four others," Garrett shook his head in wonderment.

"They took their wounded Captain, but they didn't take any of their dead," John declared, "what should we do, leave um?"

"There's no way we can bury these bodies in rock Captain," Anders declared. "We could incinerate them with a wide-beam laser."

"Yah baby, crispy critters," Garrett laughed.

"It's a good idea Anders, but no, it just doesn't sit well with me."

"Alright sir – what do you suggest?" Anders asked.

"Let's weigh them down and throw them in the water."

"That's a great idea boss, like a burial at sea," Garrett agreed. "I'll start looking for some rocks we can use."

"I think its best. The water's deep and the currents will take them out to sea, but men, before we do anything, let's free those poor people." The Captain pointed at the family on the longboat.

"Aye Captain, good call," John answered.

Two

Freedom for the Family

Eight skeletal arms reached out as we neared. When John had severed the straps binding the door, four souls stepped out into the light of a new beginning. With deep humility they acknowledged John, and then our champions, Anders and Garrett, (whom they bowed deeply to) and then the rest of us as they filed past. After disembarking the longboat the family gathered near the water, joined hands, and began speaking in a language that I'd never heard before. Listening closely I realized that each was speaking something different but somehow it all blended together seamlessly into one unified powerful sound.

"Dude," Garrett poked me in the ribs, "I've heard this before; they're praying in tongues." Jonah nodded in agreement.

It was in the next few moments that I realized firsthand just how languished these people really were. Never before had I witnessed physical deprivation such as this. It seemed no matter where you went on this planet the depraved nature of man, and the atrocities arrogance inflicted upon the innocent, was the same. Something strange happened when they came near Lizzy and she reached out to them. The man spoke sharply and each of the family backed away; they would not let her touch them. Crying out, moments later, the little girl broke free from her father and ran back and hugged Lizzy about her waist. I could hardly believe what I was seeing. In shame the man hung his head and the woman and the boy began weeping miserably. I was shaken to the core watching this and the floodgates opened in me. Never before had I witnessed a thing like this. Finally, as if all had been given a revelation at the same moment, the family calmed and stared quietly at the ladies. Roxanne began detailing to them the examination they would be getting and how Lizzy would treat their wounds. She explained that they would be receiving new clothing, and that they would be fed and housed until they'd recovered. They appeared stupefied. To allay this Roxanne assured them that we were also believers in the Risen Christ, and that we were their friends, and that they had nothing to worry about. Hearing this changed them; a cloud of desperation seemed to lift and joy started glowing in their countenances. A miracle was unfolding.

"John, Anders, Jonah," the Captain motioned, "let's establish a defensive posture for the evening. I don't trust those men."

"I don't trust them either Olaf," Jonah agreed.

"They could come back - revenge you know," John added.

"Get the family aboard the SES then," Captain Olaf ordered.

"Aye aye sir," everyone chorused.

Guardedly the family passed over the gangplank towards the entrance. Inside Lizzy directed them back towards the room set aside specifically for this. In wide-eyed fascination they took in everything around them. Inside the room Lizzy carefully examined their wounds as we watched. When she was done she turned and shared her preliminary prognosis.

"They're all malnourished Olaf. Thankfully the majority of the wounds are superficial and the staining on their skin will be gone in two or three showers with strong soap."

"That's good to hear," the Captain sighed.

Motioning him closer she pointed out the areas damaged on their bodies and explained: "Here on the man's and the boys head and legs, here above the woman's breasts along the musculus pectoralis, here on the young girl's torso along the top of the gluteus muscle, and also on the back of her neck, these wounds are deep and infected Olaf. I'm afraid these people were abused and beaten often; especially the boy."

"What can you do?" He asked with concern.

"They'll need a topical anesthetic before I can remove the dead flesh. After that I'll clean them thoroughly, and then I'll under-stitch and suture the deeper wounds; they'll require antibiotics for ten days. It'll take several weeks of rest and quiet for them to fully recover."

"Hmm ... do we have the supplies?" The Captain asked.

"We do;" Lizzy nodded, "we're fully stocked medically.

The Captain motioned to continue. It became evident, as Lizzy removed the last vestiges of their rags, that the family was uneasy being naked in front of us. Given this she asked everyone to leave except Roxanne whose fluency in their language was necessary to comprehend the questions and answers that would be exchanged during the examinations.

"Everyone out then," Olaf hurried us along. "Let the doctor do her work. Dear if you need anything . . ."

"Thank you Olaf," Lizzy smiled appreciatively.

When everyone was in the control room Olaf suggested that the ladies prepare a meal for the family, one that was easy to digest and wouldn't take too much time to prepare. After mulling for a moment, Helga suggested sweet barley chicken soup, warm buttered bread, and Lizzy's healing herb tea.

"We'd like some of that, too, if you don't mind," the Captain smiled. "I think we could all use a good meal."

After the family was showered and shampooed, hair had been trimmed, and all medical procedures had been completed, the family sat down to the same delicious warm meal we'd eaten several hours previous. After devouring the meal they stood and stretched, belched several times quite splendidly, and then all four of them reclined on the floor near the table and fell sound asleep. Captain Olaf motioned at Lizzy to bring some blankets.

"That floor is hard dude," Garrett shook his head.

"They've slept on granite for over three years," Helga sighed, "Somehow I don't think they mind."

"They belch better than you man." Anders teased Garrett.

"Is that a fact," Garrett snorted. "Check this out freak-flag."

Gulping down as much air as he could, Garrett let a monster rip that bounced noisily throughout the vessel. Anders was impressed; as were we, but even that magnificent guttural sound couldn't stir the family from their deep slumber.

Three

We Commune with Whales

The next morning

Our time in Oski's Grotto had finally come to an end. We were underway again and I was indeed happy to be moving on. Half a mile out into the great sea, Garrett and John noticed that the opening of the grotto was beginning to obscure very quickly in the mists.

"What the heck," Garrett snorted, "it's like the cliffs are closing."

"Let's get a closer look with the binoculars' little brother." John suggested. "Gabriel, look at this and tell me what you think."

I was stunned. The opening was gone. And even after peering through the binoculars intently, we still couldn't see where we'd come out from along the cliffs; it had simply and utterly vanished.

"OK, this is weird; we should tell the Captain," I suggested.

"Nah ... don't bother Gab, we've got work to do," John answered. "Garrett, you and Helga check out the sea for vessels, or any kind of activity, and give Captain a report."

"I'm on it dude, thanks for the reminder." Garrett rushed off.

Using the PMRI to scan a hundred miles around us, Helga and Garrett established that there was no activity along the observable shores, and that there were no other vessels anywhere on the Great Sea. Given this, the Captain concluded that we could travel on the surface without using the CSAT; each vessel parallel to the other and separated about fifty feet. Everyone cheered.

It was a beautiful day. The surface of the sea was tranquil, the atmosphere unperturbed, and the air was fresh and oxygen rich. As I considered our surroundings, I came to the conclusion that if the granite dome had not been above us, and if we could have eliminated the whitish glow, that seemed to emanate from everywhere, we could have easily been on Lake Baikal in Eastern Siberia, or on any of the Great Lakes in America; Huron, Superior, Michigan, Erie, or Ontario. If these massive lakes comprised forty percent of the fresh water on the surface, I wondered how that percentage would increase if this vast subterranean sea, and the Ghost Mountain Sea, was added to the equation.

Five miles out both vessels came to a standstill as Rorek and Olaf ran concurrent tests on all the systems and discussed a route. Instead of going north towards Torfar-Kolla, the Captain informed us that we would be heading south-southeast towards three openings in the granite dome about seventy miles away.

"Let's keep um at five knots slow and steady," the Captain instructed when we were underway once again; we're certainly in no rush. By the way, the professor commended us on our rescue of the family. He also encouraged us to take as many pictures as we can."

After voyaging forty miles, Olaf's voice crackled on the radios: "We've got company folks, and they're quite big. If you're topside use safety tethers, no exceptions. I'm sure this will be quite an experience for us. Take as many pictures as you can. Be careful too; these are *not* dolphins or mantas!"

"Aye Captain, we will," Helga responded.

Seconds later, the Captain's mysterious message became all too clear; dozens of shadows began appearing in the water around the vessels. A wave of fear washed over me. Were we being attacked? Fitfully I snapped my safety tether to the railing and watched as enormous blackish mounds rolled up on the surface.

"Look there!" Anders pointed.

"Thar she blows dude!" Garrett screamed.

"Look at the size of that baby!" Anders eyes opened wide.

About sixty yards off the starboard bow a creature, similar looking to a blue whale, breached the surface. When the momentum ended it twisted around and came down with a gigantic splash. Within moment's dozens of the same species had joined in.

"Holy crap," Garrett shouted excitedly, "they're everywhere man. What are they Norse?"

"Whales dude, really big whales!"

One after another they breached up and then crashed down with loud smacks that echoed over the once placid waters. The sea was stirring now with their playfulness and waves soon began pounding the vessels. Rorek assured us that there was no danger of the SES capsizing, and that we would remain perfectly stable in the water. Feeling safer now, and quite enthralled, we decided to stay above and watch the show. Around us the sea was teeming with activity and, at times, a dozen or more creatures breached up at the same moment in close proximity; it was by far the most magnificently impromptu water ballet I'd ever seen.

"Brace for a collision," Rorek instructed gruffly over the intercom, "one of them's getting curious."

A moment later the vessel shuddered.

"Dude, that big goober just kissed us," Garrett laughed.

Twenty feet off the port bow the very same creature rolled on its side and stared at us from one large black unblinking eye. Crazily we all waved and screamed and then, when the massive mammal moved in closer to investigate, Anders rubbed it near the blowhole and began talking in the same language he'd used with the mantas. Amazingly the creature answered him with clucking sounds and a single slap of his outer fluke. Anders let out a jubilant cry. After tying his hair back, and peeling off his shirt and shoes, he declared staunchly: "I'm going in! Don't worry Angy! Captain Olaf, everything's fine, they're benign and friendly; she wants me to swim with her."

"Captain, don't let him, please!" Angelina whimpered.

The Captain reluctantly gave his approval though and, when the vessels had come to a standstill, Anders dove off the bow. Again he was immersed in his most beloved and sacred element, he was with the creatures he loved and related to, and he was where he was most at ease and comfortable in life. Anders re-surfaced near the creatures face and began rubbing briskly behind the eye; the whale moaned. It was a magnificent sound; like a low dulcet fog horn that reverberated deeply in your bones.

"Norse is somethin' else man." Garrett shook his head amazed.

"Yeah he really is," I agreed with growing dread.

The whole crew had come topside now to watch our fearless crewmate. He was talking to the creature again. And the whale was responding to Anders with grunting sounds and abrupt movements of its enormous fluke. I was spellbound; the ramifications of this were too much for me to contemplate. I was stunned by this talented mans audacity, and abilities, and the fearlessness he exhibited in everything he did.

"He's taking me under," Anders yelled suddenly.

"No Captain, NO," Angelina protested. "Don't let him do it!"

I could see that the Captain was unsure about what to do now. He trusted Anders, but compassion for Angelina was weighing on him. His eyes darted back and forth between them until finally he shouted: "Anders, it's too dangerous, I'm not comfortable with it, how do you know what they'll do with you underwater," he argued. "Perhaps you should just get back aboard!"

"Don't worry Captain," he waved reassuringly, "I'll be back!"

As soon as he'd disappeared the surface of the water calmed and a kind of preternatural stillness prevailed over the entire area. Angelina was weeping wretchedly now, and rocking back and forth; moments later she swooned and collapsed on the deck.

"Elizabeth …" the Captain shouted for aid.

Lizzy rushed to her side, but it was to no avail; Angelina was slipping in and out of consciousness. She had been consumed by a dreadful emotion; it was truly pitiful. Trying to offer ministration several of the crew huddled near her while we waited restlessly for Anders to reappear. I could see that even John and Garrett were dumbfounded with the Norseman's behavior. And I, being as removed as I was from the situation, was remarkably disturbed in spirit and couldn't begin to understand what was flooding through my heart; was it fearfulness, was it reverence?

Anders reappeared near the port stern. Wildly my heart beat as I watched this giant of a man. Screaming with unbridled excitement, the Norseman had somehow gotten onto the creatures back and was now holding onto the raised meaty edges of the six foot blow hole. It was the most magnificent site I had ever witnessed; like the legendary Captain Ahab riding on the back of Moby Dick. Valiantly I struggled with the flood of emotions pumping through me.

"John, ask Olaf about the scuba gear," Anders cried out in wild excitement. John waved back and nodded. Breathing deeply several times he tapped the whale with his right foot; again they slid down beneath the surface. Profoundly influenced by what was transpiring, John and Garrett implored the Captain for the gear and, after getting another reluctant nod; they both raced below decks and came back up with three air tanks, regulators, face masks, and fins. After suiting up, Garrett and John jumped in and swam out to where they assumed Anders would be resurfacing; moments later he reappeared twenty yards off the port stern and motioned for them to join him.

"Oh man this is so incredible;" Anders gushed excitedly as he put on the gear, "Something's making the water glow down there; you can see almost as good as you can up here. These whales are sages, and so loving, and so willing to bond; it's just amazing dudes."

"How deep is it Norse?" Garrett asked.

"Don't know little brother; we didn't go down all the way. John, are the regulators adjusted?"

"Yah, they're set." John answered.

"How much air do we have?"

"Forty-five minutes in these tanks," John assured him.

"Excellent!" Anders let out a whoop. "Alright, let's do this."

After Anders had slapped on the water several times, half a dozen whales rose to the surface near where they were treading.

"Gabriel," John motioned when he was next to one, "You can do it brother; you'll be safe. You've done this before. Don't be afraid! Olaf, can Gabriel have a tank?"

"If he wants one," the Captain waved back with a hearty laugh.

The thought grabbed me hard. And when the others had disappeared beneath the surface, with joyous expressions on their faces, I abruptly made a decision and hoped that I wouldn't regret it.

"Yes sir," I looked at the Captain, "I think I'd like to give it a try."

"Ok, if that's what you want," the Captain smiled and hugged my shoulder. "I'll get the equipment."

"Good for you," Betsy sounded reassuring, "I'm so proud of you. You're gonna have so much fun honey; you'll see."

I could see the creatures were easily three times longer than the SES, and almost twice in girth; it was like being next to a ten story building that was alive. After putting on the tank I lowered myself into the water. I felt so small; so insignificant; so vulnerable next to these colossi. Side-stroking up next to the one closest, I reached out gingerly and touched it; at once the skin pulled up and rolled in small undulating waves. It was an amazing response to something as seemingly insignificant as the touch of a hand. I could sense something akin to soft fingers communicating to me; but there were no words, just clear images and an undeniable sense of well-being coursing through me. I had no apprehensions at all. The water around me had become warm and smelled sweet and, as I continued stroking the whale's skin, I could feel energy radiating from deep within it. What was most amazing, aside from being next to something so large, was the palpable sense of peace I was experiencing. I sensed it knew my innermost thoughts, somehow, and the fears I was entertaining about descending beneath the surface. The creature was patient, though, and never once did I sense it compromising what I was struggling with. What was this link between us? For as long as I held on to the fluke it remained with me on the surface. Finally, mustering the courage to press forward, I leaned towards the creature and spoke aloud: "Ok Mr. Whale … I'm ready now." It understood me and, as I clung tightly to the enormous fluke, we slowly descended.

However life-changing last year with the mantas had been, this surpassed it, and was by far the most exhilarating and extraordinary experience I'd ever had in my life. Gliding effortlessly through the glowing water, I began to understand how miracles were always around us, and how we could partake of them if we wanted to, but mostly we didn't, because too many were preoccupied with, or blinded by, trivial matters and the pursuit of inconsequential things. I wondered how much in my life had gotten past me without me ever knowing it, and how many detours I'd taken that brought me back to where I should have been in the first place if I'd been more aware of what I was doing. Most of my life I'd dreamt about being unfettered mentally and free from fear. And I had always struggled to find the place where peace, and joy, and wisdom, and understanding, were the only impetus that guided my personal pursuits. Today what I had endeavored to experience, for so many years, became a reality to me. The moments that I shared with this extraordinarily intelligent and sensitive creature changed the core of what I knew about myself. Today I was experiencing firsthand what being in the moment without fear, and living life to its fullest, really meant. An hour later it all came to an abrupt end.

"They're leaving us now," Anders shouted as we swam towards the SES, "They're going to meet with the rest of the herd. As far as I can tell, they're migrating north because of a disturbance they collectively sense is coming."

"How do you know these things Anders?" I asked in amazement.

"Well, the one I was with told me Gab. And then two others came near and told me the same thing."

"I don't understand Anders; they don't talk."

"They talk fluently Doc, just not human."

"Where did you learn how to understand their language?"

"Mostly from swimming with the mantas and the hammerheads; something powerful happened to me the day I laid hands on them and prayed. I remember getting a lot more sensitive after asking God to open my mind to what, and who, these creatures really were. I know it sounds weird, but my spirit was flooded with a magnificent light that day, and my awareness about my calling changed overnight."

"You have no fear of these creatures do you?"

"NO! There's nothing to fear from them. To tell you the truth; it blew me away when I realized that these mammals communicate the same way as the others do on the surface."

"Are they related?"

"I believe only in Gods master plan." Anders continued. "These creatures are *not* the progeny of the sea life above, they're different, they developed in a different way, and they have no knowledge of anything other than their own world. They are the true seers down here, and they accepted us, almost as if they could see our spirits and understand our intentions. This has got to be the Holy Spirit's doing;

there's no other explanation. I'm just blown away by all this fellas; we are so blessed to have been able to do this. Today made this whole trip worthwhile to me."

"You're an amazing man Norse. I've grown today in a way that I never could have imagined. They *do* relate to us don't they?"

"Yes they do! They love us Gabriel, and they have the most abiding empathy with humans. It is so much more evolved than our own for one other; there's no comparison really. They've developed far beyond us in adaptation, and the realm of spirit, and that is why I used to travel so far to be alone with the mantas on San Benedicto. They've attained something humans never have, and I wanted to understand and try to use it in my own life."

While removing our gear, on the deck, something unexpected happened. Dozens of the creatures nosed up vertically all around us and began lob-tailing the surface with their flukes in unison. In response we all shouted back our farewells, too, and waved wildly. The ritual went on for almost a minute and then, as suddenly, and as mysteriously as it had begun, it all ended. Bellowing loudly in unison they all sank beneath the surface and disappeared.

Four

Hidden Lagoon

At lunch Captain reminded us of the importance of finding an outpost to manage the challenges we now had with the Grettig family. We agreed that lessening the possibility of impediment, or dangerous situations, was crucial to the permanence of their convalescence. It was later in the afternoon that Rorek brought our attention to a lay of land off the port bow.

"It might suit our purposes Olaf." Rorek continued.

"Let's check it out then brother," Captain answered eagerly.

The area was very different than anything we'd seen thus far.

Sunlight flooded down from a large hole in the dome, there was dense forestation, a rushing fjord between steep cliffs, a powerful river washing out into the sea, and a grouping of magnificent islands offshore of varying size and complexity.

"Remember Rolf's Isle John?" Garrett asked after peering through the binoculars,

"Sure do," John nodded, "too bad we never got back there."

"Check out the islands," Garrett pointed excitedly, "they're kinda the same - big trees and a whole lotta flowers homey."

"I haven't had flowers in some time," Betsy noted demurely.

"Maybe we can get out to those islands to collect some and do a little diving too."Anders looked over with a wink.

"That'd be great," I glanced over with a thankful nod.

A powerful river was cascading down through the fjord and, after considering the massive amount of water noisily being ejected into the sea, I reasoned this to be the terminus of a long series of waterways descending from the Eastern Mountains. Entering slowly we discovered that the water was far less agitated on the southern side; here erosion had carved a deep channel which allowed the SES to maneuver further inland without mishap. Eventually we came to a lagoon. It was an impressive body of water separated from the sea by a huge watershed of rock, fallen trees, mud, and tangled growth. It was deep enough to submerge in, the perimeter was impassable, we were hidden from any activity on the sea, or the mountains, and it was teeming with fish.

"Oh I like this John, look there," Helga pointed excitedly.

"They look like salmon, they're huge." John laughed.

"Catch those buggers, fry um in a pan, I'll wolf um down as best I can." Garrett laughed and began dancing a little jig.

"You bet we will," John and Helga laughed.

The outpost was perfectly suited to our needs. Now, a plan was required that would suit the family, the ones tending the family, and those of us with a lot of free time. After bantering about ideas for awhile Angelina's was chosen. Day explorers could venture out only as far as they could go and return in the same day. No overnighters. It was simple and quite equitable I felt; being with the Grettig's in the evening was crucial to their well-being; a special time for everyone to bond, share stories and pictures, and learn how to communicate better. During our time in Hidden Lagoon the Grettig family healed, the love between everyone deepened, and the relationships blossomed. I was convinced the Heavenly Father was looking down and smiling.

Five

Mysteries of the Underground Sea

As we were learning, the underground realm was wildly unpredictable and temperamental. Since the outpost had been established we'd experienced four earthquakes and, at least a dozen times, dense fog had completely obscured the surroundings in a heavy veil. While everything about this was nerve-wracking, the most bizarre anomaly of them all was when the sea currents would polarize suddenly. We understood now that it was this very process that nearly killed several of us in Oski's Grotto months before. It was a deep water phenomenon actuated by magnetic shifts along a fault line in the earth's crust in the center of the sea. When it began energy would radiate out violently and lash all the surrounding coastal areas for about an hour. The storm had happened twice since we'd been in the lagoon and there were always far-reaching dynamics. Fierce on-shore winds would build up and then, as far as we could see, massive waves would rise up and ravage the shorelines. It was horrifying and when those of the crew, disinclined to stay outside, retreated to the SES, the rest of us (more foolhardy or brave, I know not) would perch atop our favorite promontories overlooking the sea. There we could watch as the shoreline was buried beneath the savage onslaught. It was a most awesome spectacle. Massive walls of water would smash into the shoreline, and then suck back out and rebound against the islands with great mounds of foam and thunderous sounds. During these storms sinister vapors would form above us along the top of the granite dome. When the atmosphere was saturated with moisture great vortexes would begin swirling. Inside these awful funnels lightening danced and crackled noisily. On occasion the snaking funnels would descend towards the surface, wiggling and taunting, like great forming tornadoes and cause each of us to run, with the greatest of urgency, screaming like wild people, to the safe haven of caves in the area. Never, though, did it strike down at the surface and not once was anyone hurt.

During the second week, while we were exploring near where the sea came to its terminus on the far southernmost boundary, sonar discovered a massive canyon beneath us. Gauging the depth at ninety- two hundred feet, with a variance of only a hundred feet over its three mile length, we had discovered the deepest part of the sea to date. Given that the Subterranean Exploration Submersibles had a secure operational depth of twelve thousand feet, Jonah suggested that we go down and explore this mysterious rift.

"Let's join together first," the Captain motioned.

When Jonah had finished praying Captain Olaf gave his nod to proceed with what he was humorously calling "operation swimming hole" for the records. The vessel performed flawlessly and purred like a contented kitten after a bowlful of warm milk. We found the canyon barren, though, and somewhat boring; there was no life, plants or fish, and no special formations. The only thing we found worth recording was the dozen or more three foot holes on the bottom pulling water and sand down at an awful velocity. Olaf suggested we take photos and movies of these holes, and the surrounding areas, for our data bases before resurfacing. An hour later we began our ascent.

"It's a bit discouraging ya know," Garrett lamented.

"It is kinda'," John agreed, "goin' so deep and findin' squat!"

"Sheesh, we didn't even bump into a monster."

"Oh … be patient Garrett," Jonah chuckled, "we will!"

"Yah, we probably will," Anders laughed heartily.

Back aboard Helga and Garrett downloaded the files and put them up on the big screen. After some consideration Lizzy suggested to us that the great sea had, at one time, probably been an immense magma chamber restructured away from the central shaft during earthquakes and adjacent volcanic eruptions.

"I'm convinced it filled with water after many millennia of crust movement and drainage from the surface." She speculated.

"Whoa Liz," Garrett shook his head, "it makes sense!"

I agreed with Garrett. Her explanation *was* logical and I felt inclined to accept it despite the lack of evidence to support the contention.

During the weeks following, we ventured out on numerous occasions to explore, and also to dive near the islands. One day while we were scuba-diving, and taking pictures near one of the largest islands, a herd of bizarre preternatural creatures ventured near us. We had no idea what to expect, as far as behavior was concerned, so we all remained stationary and watched. Cautiously they moved closer to investigate us. They resembled octopi with transparent wings instead of tentacles and when they moved, or fluttered in a stationary position, they left behind, or around them, a trail of incandescent particles. The effect was mesmerizing but lasted only a short while. For some time they brooded, perhaps ten yards away, watching us intently, and undulating like silky material in the diffused surface light.

"Kinda' creepy ..." Garrett observed in-between photos.

"*Yah* they are ..." John agreed. "Be aware fellas. If they get any closer, we should move behind the rocks over here."

"You bet brother," said Anders, "don't know what to expect; weirdest things I've ever seen."

Despite our apprehensions we all remained calm and observant. It seemed to everyone that they were a mix of several aquatic creatures, or perhaps a genetic anomaly that had mutated over centuries. Aside from what we imagined them capable of doing, they remained detached and quite ambivalent concerning us. After ten minutes they slowly moved away in a cloud of incandescence and glided north.

"I wonder if the life above and below started at the same time Anders," I pondered, "and if they developed differently because of the environmental conditions?"

"Good questions Gabriel, but I don't have answers," Anders pondered. "When I was with the whales they seemed to have no knowledge of anything except their own world."

For several days after that we laid low. Mostly we organized our image files, read, wrote, watched some of the movies we had aboard, fellowshipped with the Grettig's, exercised, and fished in the lagoon. On the fifth day, because of a growing restlessness, John and Anders suggested at breakfast that we explore along the shorelines. Eagerly we discussed routes. Two hours later five of us boarded the raft, with our packs and cameras and hand weapons, and motored out towards the sea. After hiding and securing the raft, near the mouth of the river, we began another adventure. Our first two hikes took us north, in the direction of Torfar-Kolla; both were uneventful. On our third hike Captain Olaf, Lizzy, Betsy, and Helga joined us. Finally being able to get off the SES for some adventure was something they were all looking forward to, and we were happy to have them along.

"Hey, let's go that way," Betsy suggested, pointing south.

"Yah, that'd be cool," Helga agreed.

"Good idea ladies," John nodded, "we haven't been there."

Two and a half miles south of the lagoon the terrain changed dramatically. Here the beach was mostly sand, which allowed all the dead creatures, scattered along the shoreline, to be more visible. For the next mile we passed by thousands of bones, and creepy unknowns, and many evidences from the surface. There were enormous leathery carcass' of sea creatures that had washed ashore, endless piles of driftwood pushed up against the cliffs, pieces of old aircraft fuselage, hundreds of plastic bottles, aluminum cans, medical waste, and thousands of huge black shells that were unlike anything any of us had ever seen. Nearing four miles we came to a stand of (what appeared to be) dwarf pines, and also acres of succulent ground covering along the base of the cliffs reminiscent, to me, of California ice plant. In the same area the remnants of an ancient landslide had made the beach almost impassable and, directly in the middle, a dry watershed meandered back up into the mountains. Considering it was only mid-morning, John suggested that we venture back into the mountains (via this route) to see what was atop the cliffs.

"We can't go far John," the Captain fretted. "I mean we're lucky we were able to bring along the ladies today, but we still have to be back on time for the family."

"Olaf, Roxanne and Angelina will do fine if we're a little late," Lizzy assured him, "we can radio in if that's going to be the case."

"I agree sir! We have almost ten hours we can work with." John determined after looking at his watch. "We can hike up for two or three hours, explore for awhile, and then hike back?"

"That'll work, excellent," the Captain answered. "Let's do it!"

Adjusting our packs we pressed up through the rocky gorge. It was steep and challenging but, because of our consistent physical training, no one faltered or tired. Nearing an hour we stopped for water and snacked on dried fruit and canned bread. Nearing two hours we finally emerged from a gnarled stand of dwarf pines, lining the wash, into a valley filled with knolls and boulders. What we saw shocked us.

"It's a stinkin' dinosaur!" Garrett blurted incredulously.

Near a desiccated waterhole were the remains of a reptilian like creature, and it was enormous. Very close to the blanched skeleton we also discovered the remains of three eggs that had long since broken open. No one could find words; the implications of this were mind-boggling and would forever change our preconceptions of the underground realm. While Helga photographed the find Garrett used the handheld to access the computer aboard the SES to compare the pictures she was taking with what we had in our data bases. Once the program had compared the files we were amazed to learn that this creature had once been a sauropod-like animal with a very long neck, a small head, a bulky body, and a long tail. We had discovered the remains of a plant eating dinosaur.

"This is weird," Anders remarked shaking his head in disbelief.

"It sure is dude," Garrett agreed, "almost like we stepped back into the stone-age, or onto another planet."

"I'm of the same mind Garrett, but I wonder; how did they come to exist in both places?"

"Sheesh Gab, who knows," Garrett straightened up.

"I'm at a loss, too, Gabriel," Jonah sighed.

"So am I," Anders shrugged.

"The bones ain't that old." Garrett pointed out. "This thing was alive no more than twenty years ago."

"I agree, and if we're punctilious with our photos, and our notes, I'm sure that the information we gather today will be quite valuable to botanists and paleontologists when we get back to the surface."

"What's 'punctilious' dude?" Garrett looked lost.

"Gabriel I'm sure it will be valuable!" Jonah nodded grinning. "And I also agree about being *meticulous* in what we do."

"Meticulous? That's what it means boss? Garrett shrugged.

"We have a book aboard the *Heimdall* about unexplained sightings of creatures in west-central Africa," Rorek began sharing. "One of the chapter's talks about something the natives referred to in the past as *Mokele-mbembe*. The features were very similar to this skeleton. Apparently many have reported fearsome creatures in the Congo, including missionaries hundreds of years ago."

"But that's Africa boss, the climates different." Garrett argued.

"They say crocodiles co-existed with the dinosaurs, too, and those nasty things are still alive and well." Anders remarked.

"But not here man!" Garrett snorted.

"I read about that expedition." Olaf recalled. "The University of Chicago sent out a team in 1980 to research long-necked creatures reported to be lurking in the swamps and along the rivers in Africa in various places."

"I recall that too, lotta hoopla," Lizzy exclaimed. "Seems a biologist, Roy Mackal, and a herpetologist, James Powell went in to investigate what a band of Pygmies had killed on Lake Tele. They say it was huge Olaf!"

"What the hecks a herpetologist?" Garrett face contorted again.

"It's a zoologist honey that studies reptiles and amphibians."

"Cool," Garrett responded with a shrug.

"I wonder what it means," Helga mused. "Do you think the dinosaurs could have escaped down here from the surface?"

"That's a thought," John straightened. "How would they have made it through Noah's flood though?"

"Maybe we'll encounter some," Betsy chuckled nervously.

"Oh great," Garrett threw his hands up, "that's all we need!"

"What's that?" Anders chuckled.

"Pelucidar 2 and the *Heimdall* crew are gonna be dinosaur fighters too? Give me a break!" Garrett groaned. "I wanna go back to San Benedicto and swim with the mantas!"

Garrett's contention was disturbing and I noticed the ladies had begun fidgeting and looking around nervously.

Six

Sunrise

If ever there were a glimpse of heaven in this life, where all the ingredients of any given moment congealed into a rare and rapturous beauty, the sunrise on the great sea was it. For six to eight hours each day, depending on the cloud cover, sunlight flooded down through the enormous holes in the massive granite dome above us. Each day, just before the sun came, the entire landscape resembled a predawn world of mystifying shadow and low-laying mists. For several minutes, as the sun moved into position, a glowing reddish-yellow luminosity gradually replaced the eerie subterranean light. Moment's later wide swathes of warming sunlight flooded down through the holes and burst resplendently upon the surface of the sea and surrounding hills. It was stunning. Within minutes the surface mists were dispelled from the warmth and the sea began shimmering with inexplicable clarity. The first time that I experienced this I remember my heart soaring with verse; as if I'd grown wings.

I felt reborn in this ancient place
It embraced me as a newborn embraces life
In Aberdeen I had wandered in a darkened alley
And silently my life flickered in warm shadows around me
Like an oasis in barren soil I dreamed
Down shadow silent streets I searched
In the mangled hours of suffering I became a mountain
With hopes and dreams cradled against my breast
In my quest for the mysterious and elusive
I found my heart quickened only with the thought
That my life could be something more than commonplace

Seven

A Time of Restoration

The health and vitality of the family was returning and each was eager to know more about us and our calling. What we'd randomly shared over the weeks – HD movies and images of life on the surface, the major cities, modern technology, the rich diversity of Earth's flora and fauna, our beloved *Heimdall*, and the many marvelous places the journey had taken us – had offered them insights into a world they could never have imagined. They listened intently to our stories, about life on the surface, and we listened eagerly to what life had been like for them in the subterranean realm. Granmar and Arnora shared about their personal lives, the political positions they'd held in Torfar-Kolla, their children, and the stressful events that led up to their eventual banishment. We in turn shared how we'd met on the Aberdeen docks, our European adventures, crossing the Atlantic, the Shallows of Three Rocks, the discovery of Isla Socorro and San Benedicto, swimming with the mantas and hammerheads, Cedros Island, the Sea of Cortez, and the terrible battles we'd had with the evil Mortiken. They were enthralled with our stories as we were with theirs.

"We knew that Christ would send someone for us," Granmar said one day out of the blue and to everyone's amazement. "Our faith has always remained strong in His plan for our lives, and we discovered that even in our sufferings He always kept us together as a family, and always focused, on His greater plan. We are convinced this was by design, and also necessary for growing in His Grace, and also for the preparation of our callings."

"Your faith was certainly not in vain sir," I commended them. "And I stand amazed, too, and humbled at the fortitude you exhibited during your terrible banishment."

"Gabriel I agree with you completely," Jonah shook his head solemnly. "The great strength of character imparted to you, Granmar, and your beloved family, is remarkable. Believe me; I understand, very personally, how heartache and suffering can prepare a soul and mind for what is ahead."

"Boy, ain't *that* a fact!" Anders shook his head.

And though Jonah never elucidated to Granmar the true nature of what he'd said, I knew he was remembering what had happened to his sister Eloise, and Anders was remembering their beautiful cottage that had been destroyed that night in the barbarous Mortiken raid.

Eight

Brynhild Busla, the Viking Queen

In the middle of the fourth week, when the family had fully recovered their strength and humor, we departed the hidden lagoon and headed north in the great sea. As we traveled Granmar shared a story about nine oddly dressed emissaries that once had visited the city. Along with his own anecdotal color, and the occasional clarification of facts from his wife, the story centered on Brynhild Busla, the Queen of Torfar-Kolla, and how she had, through a series of events, become a sinister self-loathing woman fully given to manipulating the high court in any way she could while destroying the Kings dominion and influence.

King Braggi was filled with compassion when he'd learned Brynhild's parents had sold their child at three years of age. Because her plight had touched him deeply he decided to summon her from a far northern city. His intentions were to buy the young woman from the foster-parents and take her as his wife in the hopes of establishing a political alliance with the king in that province. The foster parents acceded to the King's plan and, at seventeen years of age, Brynhild became his beloved wife and the second most powerful person in the underground kingdom. For ten years the marriage was idyllic and the kingdom was blessed with wealth and peace. Thousands of babies were born throughout the land during this time. Sadly, though, the king and queen had not been so blessed; Brynhild was barren. The King's physician explained that the many beatings she'd endured at the hands of her step parents had taken their toll on her ability to conceive. Unable to control his feelings Braggi sent an assassin and had the step-parents secretly put to death. Though I knew it was wrong something inside me cheered when I heard this.

Towards the end of their tenth year of marriage the Queen was visited one day by nine strangely clothed emissaries, purportedly from the Eastern Mountains. No one had seen them enter the city and none of the many outposts had any reports of anything out of the ordinary. The strangers stood in the town square and, from the many accounts of it; the queen was said to have heard them calling to her in her spirit and had come to them without being summoned. They carried odd weapons and stood around her in a circle. No citizen came near, as they spoke, and no scribes were summoned to record the goings-on. After only a short time, and saying nothing to anyone, Brynhild departed with these strangers, carrying with her only one bag of clothes and personals.

For thirty-nine days she was absent from Torfar-Kolla. And during that time rumors spread like wildfire. Some were saying that she was on a quest to refresh her love of Odin. Some swore that she had gone to find assistance for her beleaguered husband who had, some weeks prior, departed on a mission of detente to a far northern city. In some of the viler taverns there were those convinced that she had fallen under the spell of evil conjurers bent on using her for vulgar rituals and copious profit. The fact remained that no one really knew why she had departed, and no one was prepared for what they would have to deal with upon her return. The citizenry was horrified that morning when she lumbered into the city like an ox. No more the enchanting waif, a once beautiful countenance had been replaced with hunched shoulders, sunken eyes, and a haughty scowl. Within days she had become a reviler of Braggi's rule, and also an opponent of all associated with his government. Something despicable had befallen the great Viking Metropolis and the royal relationship soon unraveled. Brynhild was now a gourmand of the lowest caliber, and food orgies, and drunkenness, were an everyday lifestyle now for her. The King was miserable, because of it, and would spend whole nights pacing on the balcony of his chambers under the gloom of a subterranean sky. Because of her deteriorating physical and mental state, and his growing shame, Braggi summoned the kingdoms most respected physicians to search for the potions that might end her torment. Nothing worked. The city was shaken because of the Kings state of mind, and rumors spread that a final parting was forthcoming.

In every corner questions were emerging about what may have happened to her while she was gone. Had she really visited a mystical city in the Eastern Mountains guarded by cursed giants of stone? Was Odin and Vanir involved? Could it be that they'd fashioned a treaty and had chosen Brynhild to witness the whole affair? From the northlands there were stories that the queen's stunning beauty had actually brought the stone giants to life and, because of this, Vanir had propositioned her to be his concubine. As it was, given Brynhild's abiding and outspoken love of Braggi, she had refused Vanir's offer and, in great wrath, had struck her body and soul with a curse. From the western settlements there was talk about travelers from Vanaheim that had met with the queen and had offered her a key for physical health, for children, and harvests, and the continuing abundance of fish in the great sea, but she had refused the offer. Was her present condition the result of her rebellion? Granmar told us there were spiritual fanatics in one of the southern settlements who were convinced that, because of the queen's rebellion, Alfheim was going to send legions of light elves to keep watch over the kingdom and everyone's freedoms would be impugned. Everywhere wild rumors abounded and there was no one in the whole of the kingdom that did not have an opinion about it. Everything happening now seemed to point at the possibility of upheaval coming to the underground realm. Could the once strongly unified metropolis be teetering on the edge of a major revolution? Could it be that this was why we were here? Had we been chosen to be part of what soon might be transpiring in the underground realm?

Nine

The Chronicle Continues

Arnora had been a friend to the Viking Queen and for several years she had also been her assistant and confidant in personal matters. She had lamented the fact that the queen was almost unrecognizable upon her return from the Eastern Mountains. It was as if something evil had returned in her stead; life with her now was demoralizing and boorish. But despite this Arnora remained faithful and never compromised the tenuous nature of the Queen's disposition. While inebriated one evening Brynhild spoke openly about what she remembered happening between her and the strangers. Arnora listened quietly. Brynhild was convinced that she'd been visited by gods who had chosen her to prepare Torfar-Kolla for a departure from the old ways by planting seeds of unrest. Arnora described the queen's thoughts as being fragmented at times; as if she were trying to differentiate between a dream and reality. But then there were times when what she shared struck her as being quite lucid. Because of this Arnora purposed to remember as much of what was shared as she could. One evening the queen confessed to her that a record of the meeting, she'd had with the emissaries, had been set aside secretly in a wooden box. When she admitted she was in possession of this box her eyes darted about the room as if she was fearful that someone was listening in the shadows. She whispered to Arnora that it was just beneath the floorboards, near her bed, and that no one knew about it but her. Though she'd never seen the contents, (by her own confession) Brynhild was convinced that information concerning the future of Torfar-Kolla was inside, and also directions to a place in the far Eastern Mountains called Sky Land. After that evening something changed the chemistry between the women and, in the days following, the queen became cold and aloof. Within a week Arnora had been dismissed from service and the queen never spoke to her again.

As the months passed Queen Brynhild continued to change physically and her animosity towards the younger and fairer women of the court became unbearable. She was wretched and inebriated always; a shadow of her former self waddling about in a combative frame of mind, mumbling incoherently, and always smelling like a pig stall. Once a comely woman with flaxen hair and finely chiseled features, she was now being snubbed regularly because of her ample girth and foul deportment. She'd become an embarrassment and the court was desperate to avoid her at all costs. Her heart had become a cesspool of loathing, and her bitter resentment of Braggi's rule had poisoned her mind with hatred. Trust and honor was almost non-existent now in the Viking court and the wicked Brynhild was to blame. Desperate to regain her status she was using whatever means were available to get what she wanted, including bribery and philandering with licentious riffraff in the King's inner court who were willing to help if she could further their own deviant agendas. Because of this an evil alliance came into being.

I recalled the story of Jezebel, in 1st and 2nd Kings in the Old Testament, as Granmar talked, and marveled at how this Biblical woman was similar in character to Brynhild Busla the Viking queen. In the Biblical story Ahab the King of Israel married the princess of Tyre to cement a political alliance; also between two powerful nations. Unbeknown to most, Jezebel was an evil manipulating woman who introduced Baal worship into Israel eventually and, in so doing, incited a mutual and long-lasting enmity with the prophets of Yahweh. Jezebel was long held in reproach amongst the Jews because she had introduced tyrannical government into Israel and also the worship of foreign gods. In the New Testament the name Jezebel was given to a wicked conniving woman who exerted a corrupting influence. In modern times the name had come to signify a brazen or forward woman who manipulated others to her own ends.

It seemed to me that Brynhild Busla had become the embodiment of the Jezebelian spirit and she was doing all she could to undermine her husband's authority.

Sadly the results of the incendiary conflict between the King and Queen had set into motion a backlash against many innocent citizens in the underground Kingdom. Brynhild's hateful manipulating soon became something it was never intended to be and began affecting the Grettig family because of their faith in the Risen Christ. Within weeks all Christian assemblies had been censored by the King's court and, like flowing sewage, an open vilification soon polluted the general populace with a new and hateful propaganda. As soon as it was known the Grettig's were Christian's, and not Odinist's, the queen had the family jailed and their heads shaved. King Braggi protested his wife's actions vehemently, but it was to no avail. Brynhild had somehow regained a powerful sway in kingdom politics because of her philandering with those profligate members of high counsel bent on undermining the King and furthering this new agenda against Christianity. Exhausted from social instability Braggi openly condemned the Grettig's to try and end his woes. They, and many others, were banished that day to an isolated settlement ten miles east of Oski's Grotto up the smaller of the two rivers. Brynhild had been successful in her subterfuge and, according to her; Torfar-Kolla had been purged from the criminal influences of Christianity and Odin could once again be revered.

Blindvidr was a horror. In this penal colony the Grettig's were forced to live in squalor for three long years. During their captivity the family's belief in Christ was tested severely with beatings and deprivation. Never wavering, all four of them clung tenaciously to the Christ that they had chosen to believe in and, because of this, they were drawn closer to one another in purpose by the Holy Spirit. Granmar confessed that, near the end of the third year, they'd all begun having dreams about strangers coming to rescue them and, because these dreams had increased in frequency and were always similar in content and detail, they knew something miraculous was about to unfold. It was remarkable how the crew's dreams, and the family's dreams, had proliferated around the same time. It seemed that both parties had been prepared in advance and had somehow been brought together at exactly the time that our paths would cross. At the end of the third year of captivity, longboats arrived to retrieve them from Blindvidr. The family's faith had not been in vain. It was nothing short of a miracle that these were the same longboats we'd encountered in Oski's Grotto after the underwater tempest.

The Grettig's had once been invaluable to Braggi for their intelligence, and problem solving abilities and, as he told it, he wanted them back to help him run the kingdom. After three years of finagling he had reached his limit with the counsel and those controlled by the queen. Taking matters into his own hands, King Braggi re-seized the horns of power in one day. His wife's oracle was hung in the public square, and then her personal cook was banished to a small city north of Torfar-Kolla where he would have to ply his trade in a seamy tavern for little compensation. Livid with her husband's reprisal, the Queen found it impossible now to manipulate the situation in any way that may favor her evil agenda. Braggi was a fierce man and no one would challenge his authority in the matter. He had reached his limit with Brynhild and now she was absolutely powerless. Within hours she was inebriated again and had climbed to the highest parapet in the city wall.

"Has the King gone mad," she screeched angrily to the throngs below. "Do you know what that man has done to your queen? I hate him, and I will leave him, and no one can stop me! Who among you dares to defy me? Who among you will help me regain my stature? Who I say? I am your Queen – do you hear me worms? I will give you power beyond your dreams and I will make you rich!"

No one listened. No one cared. Finally their beloved Braggi was again in control and that was all that mattered. Desperately the Queen sought assistance from her chambermaids. Concerned only with their own interests; all refused her. When she demanded help from the council all turned away. She was alone, fearful, and trodden down. When Braggi was informed of his wife's finagling he was incensed. In a rage he stormed from his personal chambers down into the bustling city square. Defiant to city ordinances - stating the King must always be accompanied by a contingent of guards in public - Braggi ascended the gallows a menacing figure. Pointing at the hapless man dangling from the rope he ordered the immediate release of Granmar Grettig, his family, and all the other Christians that had been illegally imprisoned. He established, in no uncertain terms, that if anyone, including his drunken, corpulent, seditious wife, ever stood in his way again that their fate would be the same as the astrologers had been.

"I swear this on my own Fathers name," Braggi roared red-faced.

The King had struck fear into everyone and no one moved in the crowd, or made a sound, until he had returned to his chambers.

Thurid the Mighty was commissioned the next day to retrieve all the prisoners banished to Blindvidr. When compensation was agreed upon, and the crews had been chosen, three longboats set sail on the King's mission of mercy. Despite all appearances it was not as it seemed. Their first night in Blindvidr the men celebrated and, in drunkenness, the truth became known. Braggi wanted the family back only to make a statement for his wife's philandering. It was a ploy to make a public spectacle of the queen for her sedition and foul deportment. Braggi wasn't interested in anyone's well-being, especially the Grettig's. Aside from what his intentions were, or of the seeming exculpation from the charges which had been levied against the family, there was one undeniable fact. It had been our timely intervention in Oski's Grotto that had allowed the Grettig's to be freed from their captors and Braggi's deceitfulness.

Ten

Mapping the Great Sea, Gautrek and Halldis, Back to Blindvidr for Closure, Inside Torfar-Kolla, and Garrett's lesson

For seven weeks we stayed three miles north of Torfar-Kolla. Working jointly with Granmar and Arnora we were able to map the sea (above and below the surface) from the granite termini in the southernmost quadrants, along the far western shores, and seventy-five miles north of our anchorage. We were also able to map the outlying settlements and all the paths connecting the diverse clans in the habitable regions just south and north of the city. It was a very productive time.

As we were finding out, the Grettig children were very different. Gautrek was eighteen. He was diffident, and melancholic, and drawn only to Garrett and Rolf and, at certain times, to Lizzy and Roxanne. But those were private conversations and the ladies never divulged anything. Granmar told us that the beatings he'd endured in Blindvidr had taken their toll on him and that he was very withdrawn. Garrett spoke to the Captain on Gautrek's behalf. A friendship was forming between them born from the empathy Garrett had begun feeling for the teenagers struggles and wounds. He made it known that they both wanted to get off the SES, during our mapping expeditions, to explore and hike. At first the Captain balked at the idea. Being so far apart did not sit well with him. Finally, though, after some intervention from John and Anders, he acceded, but only if they brought along Rolf, radioed in regularly, never stayed away longer than two nights, used the CSAT modules when necessary, and always stayed low-key around others. All three agreed. The first day Garrett showed young Gautrek how to organize and stock a backpack, and how to wear and wield a knife. Within hours he was thrusting and parrying and swashbuckling about like a pirate or some mystical warrior. Garrett was pleased. Gautrek gave Garrett his undivided attention and learned everything he was taught. The three of them were gone often from the SES, on overnighters, exploring the mountainsides, and caves, and inlets, and ravines, along the far northern shorelines. They learned to commune better in each other's languages, and

Garrett taught him self-defense, and many of the survival techniques he'd learned. All three fished often in a secret place they'd found up one of the rivers coming down from the Eastern Mountains and, after the first week, Rolf allowed Gautrek to wrestle with him as long as he fed him something special afterwards. Garrett's spirit was quiet during their time together and Gautrek's shyness and melancholy lessened considerably.

Eleven year old Halldis was precocious, out-spoken, and had a bubbly personality. The love she had for others flowed from her heart like the purest of water. In two days she had won over the heart of the Captain. Often she would jump up on his lap, before dinner, to cuddle and sing songs; it was a most endearing interaction. Never before had we known our Captain to melt as he did when young Halldis would sing to him, or pull at his huge moustache, and giggle. No matter what difficulties the day held, her gift would bring a light into the darkest and most trying situations. How her capacity to love had survived, after three years of captivity, was one of the most singular mysteries to me of God's grace with the Grettig family. Halldis was irresistible, and within days she'd won over everyone's hearts. Even our often cantankerous Rorek embraced her in a way that I'd never seen before. I couldn't help chuckling as I watched the two of them interact; could it be that Rorek was just a big ole' teddy bear at heart? Halldis had a remarkable ability to grasp words effortlessly. Given this propensity the ladies took time each day to teach her the English language. Soon she was communicating with us and had begun writing love poems for Captain Olaf and Rorek.

The next day we revisited Oski's Grotto. The evening before departure, at dinner, Granmar had mentioned something to us about his family needing final closure with their ordeal. Understanding this, from personal experiences, the Captain had authorized the journey. Upon arrival we moored both SES in a semi-hidden inlet, lined with fluorite columns, and cloaked them. Since the whole crew was going on this excursion we prepared two rafts to take us up the narrow river to Blindvidr. Oski's Grotto looked the same as it had the day we'd discovered it; a beautifully pristine and magical place; like the inside of a gigantic geode. Anders pointed out, too, that the longboat had been removed and there was no sign that anyone had ever been here.

The penal colony was a cavern about one third the size of Oski's Grotto. I imagined that even the guards must have felt like prisoners, at times, in a place as horrid as this was. The isolation was appalling. In the center of the settlement a waterfall tumbled from a rift and then over a series of terraces down into the river. In the dome above us an opening was allowing sunlight and atmosphere down into the granite prison. Beneath this opening a wooden structure had been constructed for the guards, and next to that was another structure for weapons and food. Trembling now, with emotion, Granmar pointed out the caves where the other prisoners had been held, around the periphery, and then he led us up to where they had been held for three years. The cave was no more than six feet high, about eight feet across, and twelve feet deep. I began trembling, too, as he explained the routines they'd been forced to do daily. It was a miracle that they'd endured this for as long as they had. After he'd finished grievous heartbreak rose up in the children and they began sobbing. Arnora put her arms around both and pulled them in close; soon she was wailing along with her children. With tears flowing profusely all three prostrated themselves on the hard rock. I watched something in Granmar snap as he watched his family. Deeply overwrought he began shaking his fists and crying out. It was a desperate sound filled with, what I could only imagine were, the last clinging remnants of his embittered soul rage. Seething anger consumed my heart as we were moving away and, after mulling what being incarcerated in a place like this might be like, there fell upon me a dreadfulness for the horror humanity forced upon one another so callously in this life. How could humankind heap such imprecations upon one another? As Voltaire had written: *"wracking and burning each other, detesting each other, persecuting each other, cutting the throats of each other"*- but for what purpose? What had happened to forgiveness, mercy, and treating those around you the way you wanted to be treated? A rancor of arrogance festered always in the soul of man and was, in my opinion, what prompted the greater share of humanity's evil. It was a cruel self-centeredness that would often deprive another of even the most basic of needs to satisfy some lust for power and control while inflicting misery on others.

When the Grettig's rejoined us, several hours later, they were remarkably joyful and their spirits were calm. I knew that a healing had taken place and I thanked God for releasing them. On the journey back Captain suggested that those of us interested consider exploring the Viking metropolis the next day. Some of the crew balked.

Inside Torfar-Kolla

On three occasions, during the sixth week, we entered the Viking metropolis. To assure our anonymity, as the Captain had suggested, we'd use the CSAT modules, and for protection we would bring along our hand weapons. As we'd learned, it was better to have them and not need them then to need them and not have them. The ladies balked once again, as they had the day before. Not so much about what we were doing as much as how we were doing it. They saw little purpose in wandering about the city like phantoms and not being able to interact. They chose, instead, to remain behind with Rolf and tend to (what they referred to as) more important matters. I understood where they were coming from. But because of my own curiosity I chose to embrace another perspective. Granted, we *would* be like phantoms. But being cloaked was akin, in my opinion, to just remaining unobtrusive in a place whose citizens would certainly treat strangers as major curiosities, or threats, if they were visible.

So we entered into Torfar-Kolla like ghosts, eager for another adventure, but the kind of satisfaction we were hoping for became, instead, disillusionment. Most of the streets were grossly filthy. And all the shops, taverns, market places, medical facilities, and clothiers looked as if they'd been constructed by amateurs. It reminded me of what you might see built near the railroad tracks for hobos and transients. Moving farther into the cities innards, along the tangled streets, nothing we saw pleased us. There was no continuity in design, and the engineering for water and waste was grossly unsafe to human health. Perhaps different rulers had placed differing degrees of importance on the infrastructure, over the years, and now that it was an ugly monster no one knew what to do with it. I concluded, given my anguished sensibilities towards such deplorable design, that this was nothing more than a farrago of misguided thoughts that brought no honor to the citizens. The inner city was a breeding ground for corrupt landlords, the inebriated, and those given to licentiousness. While observing the narrow streets, the darkened ally's, and hidden alcoves, staircases leading below ground, degraded characters, filthy eateries, tawdry women with teeth missing, and the glut of foul smelling taverns, I concluded, also, that criminal activity in Torfar-Kolla must far outweigh law and order. It must have been why most legitimate business was transacted outside the walls and along the shoreline.

On our second excursion into the city we entered in through a heavily treed courtyard along the northern ramparts. We'd observed three distinct areas of commerce, our present locale, around the large statue near the docks, and a little farther north; the shoreline was a bustle of commerce and industry today. About three hundred yards south of us smoke from dozens of smelting ovens was billowing out over the water and clinging to the lower portions of the mountains. From hamlets, on the northern outskirts of the city, fishing smacks sailed out each morning and returned in the afternoon with their catch. Directly south, along a complex dock construction, on an island just offshore, carpenters were building longboats. Arriving from the west and north vessels docked regularly throughout the day. Each of them carried a wide assortment of products to sell or barter with in Torfar-Kolla and in the smaller peripheral settlements.

Today, as we were searching in the city, something happened that may, to some, seem a trivial matter. But it ended up not being so for us and a lesson was learned by all. The incident began as such …

While walking down a particularly seamy street we were startled unexpectedly by a very loud sound. Several of the citizens, standing idly outside one of the bars, began laughing hilariously. The Captain shot a stern face at Garrett. With a sappy expression Garrett shrugged; to him it was no big deal. Seconds later everything took a turn for the worse. Several men began pointing fingers and yelling. Then a group of disgruntled men started pushing one another and boasting openly about who was going to beat the other senseless. In quick succession a group of slovenly men stumbled out from the bar and began cursing loudly at one another and spitting; soon they were punching each other; I couldn't believe it. Anders was the first to succumb to a fit of belly-laughs. Then several men stopped fighting to see where the laughter was coming from. Angered when they couldn't figure it out, they started pushing whichever person was closest, this then quickly escalated into a free-for-all with everyone in the street. It was hard to believe, and when John burst out laughing the rest of us had no choice but to join in. The Captain appeared mortified and motioned for us to pipe down and move away as quickly as possible. Many dozens were arguing now loudly, and pointing, and pushing, and punching and, because of limited space, the mob began spilling out into a larger adjacent street where dozens more men, from other bars, eagerly joined in. Most of the women, milling about, began running for cover as the fervor spread out and intensified. As we maneuvered away no less than a hundred citizens were beating on each other. The blind foolishness of this stunned me. From a few men laughing it had escalated into a wild unchecked mêlée. How could something like this happen? Stopping for a moment to look back, Anders and John again burst out in uncontrollable laughter.

Something had gripped the Captain; I had never seen him so beset with anything before. Upon our return he sat us all down to one of the strangest meetings I could ever remember. The Captain was provoked and red-faced and the veins in his neck were bulging when he got up to speak. Out of respect none of us made a sound. He stated clearly that Garrett's indiscretion could have compromised our mission, our well-being, our anonymity, and our very lives and, from this moment on, there would be no belching, or farting, in public while we were cloaked in the CSAT or any other time for that matter. Garrett was utterly humiliated and hung his head in shame. Mumbling an apology he shuffled off to his berth with Rolf skulking along behind.

Eleven

A Telling Message on an Ancient Stone

No one had heard from Garrett for two days now. After the reprimand he'd taken his backpack and had, according to Anders, hiked back up one of the rivers with Rolf to a high plateau that Gautrek and he had found weeks earlier. Despite the trepidation Anders convinced us not to worry; he was familiar with Garrett's penchant for soul-searching, and being alone, and found nothing threatening with it. On the morning of the third day Garrett returned during breakfast and apologized. This time he addressed everyone personally. Openly admitting that what he'd done had been foolish, given the circumstances, he assured us that it would never happen again. With tears the Captain embraced Garrett and thanked him and immediately harmony was restored.

Our third excursion took us into the city at the Western Gate. Just inside, surrounded by a thick stand of trees, was another walled area that no one had been in for centuries; according to Granmar this was the original city and all the entrances had been sealed. Because of a binding edict from some King in the past, forbidding entry into it, and also because of a legend that had been handed down for generations about children being born with withered limbs, and bulging eyes, to anyone who disobeyed; no one ever had any desire to break in to see for themselves what was inside these ancient walls. But even these hindrances couldn't impede the rumor mill that was always simmering in the city about it. Some whispered about ancient treasure being hidden in the tombs of the cities forefathers. Some were convinced that the longboats, that had made the original journey, were being stored there. Some were convinced that Loki vacationed there and would emerge under cover of darkness to steal children and wreak havoc in the streets. Some even thought that blood rituals were held inside the walls each month to appease Odin. As we were learning, superstition and gossip was rampant in Torfar-Kolla.

Near the smelting ovens, along the shores south of the western gate, we came upon an ancient stone that was reminiscent, to me, of the 'Mojbro' in Uppland Sweden; particularly in size, and texture, and shape. On the smooth facing surface two runes were carved deeply into the upper portion of the stone and, in the middle, a longboat was meticulously etched. The message was intriguing. *Raido* was the first rune; this signified a long journey. *Suwilo* was the second rune; and it represented the Earths sun as the focus of pagan worship. There were also eight words along the bottom, in the old language that, when interpreted, made my heart beat fast. They read: *For Magnus, Deposed Son of the Great Agar*

"Does this mean what I think dude?" Garrett whispered.

"Oh man dude," I felt a lump forming in my throat.

"Did those with Magnus build Torfar-Kolla?" Jonah was visibly stunned and began pulling briskly at his goatee.

"Is that possible?" Captain Olaf gasped.

"I think the words say it all sir." Anders returned excitedly.

For me it was very clear, and it would certainly explain why the scribes had chosen these particular runes above the dedication. The journey *had* been long and grueling, for the first Vikings, which could account for their usage of the rune *Raido*. The influx of sunlight could also account for why the rune *Suwilo* was chosen. Had the early Vikings built on this location because of the sunlight and, in thanks to Odin, practiced a pagan form of sun worship?

"I think yes," Jonah nodded convinced. "Sunlight *was* the requisite factor, I'm sure of it. I can imagine that their grain stores were just about exhausted when they'd reached this place."

"I imagine so Jonah." Garrett agreed. "No bread, no fruit, no veggies- just stinky fish musta' been gag-city every day."

"I'm sure there was little variety on the journey son," Jonah speculated. "And the fact that they'd discovered such a verdant contour of land must have really inspired them to settle."

"I totally agree, "Rorek nodded, "it must have been like finding paradise. I'm sure the first inclination for the builders would have been to dedicate their endeavors to some warrior, or a leader, which they obviously did here with this stone."

"Dead or alive too," Anders chuckled. "That's the Viking way!"

"Yeah, exactly," Jonah shook his head with a hearty laugh.

"So this is Magnus Rognvald's legacy; built upon the memory of his questionable life."

"Apparently Olaf," Jonah answered with a shrug.

"It's pretty amazing isn't it?" I asked.

"It really is," Anders replied, "but you know something ..."

"I know what you're gonna say," Garrett simpered.

"Yeah, where's the Anasazi in all of it?" Anders asked. "Didn't they come down here too?"

Thoughtfully Jonah pulled at his goatee. As of yet, we'd come across no tangible evidence that the Anasazi had ever been in the Realm of the Ancients. Was it possible that the many archaeological expeditions he'd taken to southern Utah been in vain? Had it all been only a fanciful legend?

Twelve

Astounding Information

The Grettig's admitted knowing little about the old city. They also admitted knowing nothing of the ancient legends, or of the curses, or of anything concerning the Anasazi inter-mingling with the Viking Nation in Torfar-Kolla.

"We have seen no memorials, or art, nor anything in city records that could affirm this notion." Granmar confessed.

But as the conversation continued they finally did recall one thing which appeared to have some bearing on the mystery. In certain of the older, more established, taverns there had been several legends, often shared, about an alien nation that had once been involved for almost a century with the Norse culture. As the tale was told, these aliens had vanished during the reign of some king in the distant past. Could it be this alien nation had been the Anasazi? Jonah stood up with a queer expression and started asking questions.

"Arnora, you mentioned before that Brynhild was convinced she'd been visited by gods."

"Yes, Jonah," Arnora shook her head humbly.

"Arnora did she ever clarify who they were, or expound on where she'd been taken?"

After talking over the questions with her husband she answered: "Jonah I will tell you everything the queen divulged to me. She was taken from Torfar-Kolla by those never seen before in the realm. They were most peculiar in appearance. Two were very large and ugly, and seemed out of place with the others. They could appear and disappear by touching a small disc. Their weapons glowed. The clothing, the adornments, even the facial markings were unknown to her. The queen was gone for many days. She said nothing was ever clear to her. She woke up one morning feeling like she had been asleep for many days and had no real memory of anything of her prior life. She was taken to a place she'd never seen before and did not know how she had gotten there. Blue sky was everywhere and she saw things that were very foreign to her. She was convinced that she had been taken to a place of the gods. She feared that she would never return again to Torfar-Kolla. I am convinced that something terrible happened to her during her ordeal to keep her from understanding or remembering what really happened. Why I think this, Jonah, I cannot explain. It is only a thing I feel from the conversations we had."

"Artificial memories, hypnosis ..." Roxanne muttered.

"Yah, it sounds like someone was brain-washed." Anders asserted.

"But the blue sky ... was she taken to the surface?" Helga asked.

"Sounds like it ..." Betsy shook her head.

"Appearing, disappearing, a small disc, they had something like the CSAT didn't they?" John mulled.

"Yah they did John," Rorek agreed.

"Was she drugged during the ordeal Arnora?" Jonah continued.

"It is possible, I am not sure." Arnora answered. "Everything about her changed from this encounter with the strangers."

"You're saying that upon her return she was a different woman than you knew before?" Jonah continued.

"She had changed in all ways Jonah. She had hatred for everything she could not control. She was offensive. She was confused and bitter with everyone. She did not appear as herself. She'd grown fat and ugly and had a foul smell. But in so short a time? I have heard of demonic possession; she may have been an example of this terrible thing. I remember her saying that she was given a large vial of powder that she must take to remain connected to the gods. Each day she pinched some and put it into the water she drank. Always afterwards she changed."

"The powder – was it given her from the emissaries?"

"Not the emissary's sir, a woman she'd met."

"She confirmed this to you?"

"Yes she did, she was positive. She knew her name."

"What was it?"

"She said Krystal."

"Whoa dude," Garrett jumped up. "What the heck?"

Jonah's eyes opened wide. He got up and left. This information perplexed me. For what purpose were the Mortiken, and Krystal Blackeyes in the Underground Realm? Had the queen been taken to the surface to a Mortiken outpost as Helga had suggested? And why had the witch made contact with Brynhild and given her these powders? Was it a narcotic, or a hallucinogen, to keep her from remembering?

"Gosh Captain, the complications ..."

"Gabriel ..." The Captain interrupted; his face was tense with perplexity, "we'll talk about it later!"

At dinner the Captain told the Grettig's the story of Jonah's sister and how she had become affiliated with the Mortiken leader. They listened in wide-eyed wonder.

Thirteen

Airlifted Out

Much was exchanged during our bi-weekly meeting with the professor. He listened intently as we explained what Arnora had shared with us and, when we were finished, he assured us that he would do what he could to get to the bottom of this mystery. He was also formally introduced to the entire Grettig family on the big screen. His was delighted to meet them and, after some insightful exchange, the professor assured Granmar that he would contact Regan Pendleton to discuss relocating them up to Montague Island. The family was gladdened and, when the professor shared images of the burgeoning Norse settlement, they began singing and dancing in great joy. Details for their journey were worked out in less than twenty-four hours. As it was, the Viking elders on Montague had been having dreams about a mysterious family, coming from another place, becoming part of the settlement. It was clear that God's hand was on everything unfolding for the Grettig's.

On the eleventh week, after receiving our first shipment of provisions, and medical supplies, the time for the Grettig's departure to Alaska had arrived. Gautrek and Garrett slapped high-fives and exchanged talismans they'd carved for the other. Arnora and all the ladies embraced and began crying. The sorrow was overwhelming and tears flowed. After they'd finished each of us exchanged tokens and said our final goodbyes. As they were nearing the helicopter I saw Arnora speak something to her husband. Vigorously shaking his head no he reached into his leather satchel and handed an object to Halldis. When she took off running towards us Granmar turned and shouted: "I love you all and look forward to hearing from you, thank-you for everything, thank-you for our lives, thank-you for our health, and thank-you for this opportunity. Remember Olaf, my eternal brother, Christ before all else!"

Shaking his head in accord Captain waved back briskly. Shyly, young Halldis handed the Captain a smooth wooden box.

"What's this sweetheart?" The Captain asked as he knelt down.

"Papa said dis would maybe hup you unlock tings about queen

and many udder tings in da maybe city in Ees Muntains," She shared in her new-found language.

"Thank-you Halldis," the Captain kissed her cheek. "Tell papa we will always keep you and your family in our thoughts and prayers!"

"OK Capin' I will." She beamed. "I lub you, see you, bye bye now, I lub you, bye bye Rorek, I lub you, bye bye!"

"Bye bye honey," the Captain and Rorek waved.

Back at the helicopter Halldis tugged at her father's arm and spoke something into his ear; Granmar hugged and kissed her and turned one last time.

"She wants to marry you Olaf," Granmar laughed.

After that, the door was shut and they lifted off. In the window Halldis was waving and blowing kisses. A moment later the helicopter flew over the rim of the hole and was gone.

"I'll miss that one brother," Rorek said with eyes glistening.

"I will too Rorek," Olaf answered with tears on his cheeks,

Fourteen

The Wooden Box

"What's up with the wooden box Cap?" Garrett asked after we were back aboard.

"I don't know," the Captain shrugged. "Granmar sure went out of his way to get it to us though."

"He sure did!" Garrett agreed. "Seems he forgot about it and Arnora had to remind him. Did you see that?"

"Yeah I did son."

"No denying it's a beautiful thing." Anders remarked turning it over in his hands and then handing it to Helga.

"I wonder if there's anything in it."

"Let me see Helga," John reached out, "perhaps there's a lever or mechanism that will open it."

Shaking it lightly, he peered closely at the surface and ran his fingers along all the edges and the corners. Shrugging, he handed it to Rorek and said: "I can't find anything Rorek; maybe you can."

Rorek went through the same procedure and then admitted: "I can't find anything either. Whataya think Doc?"

As soon as the box was in my hands a burst of energy coursed through me for several seconds. It was a peculiar feeling reminiscent, in ways, of what I'd experienced after picking up the Tempest sword aboard the *Heimdall*. Not fully understanding I decided to examine the box closely and then share my findings with the rest of the crew. After scrutinizing all the planes, and after precise measurements were taken, I'd arrived at a number of conclusions. A skilled artisan had crafted this magnificent box and a great amount of time had been put into its construction. It was made of yew. This was a common name for a genus of evergreen primarily used in cabinet making and archery bows. It was a cube twelve inches on all three planes; a piece of art inlaid with fine pinstripes, (possibly of hickory or maple) accentuating the horizontal edges, and also twelve round cherry-wood or walnut plugs, adorning the side corners parallel to the pinstripes and along the bottom corners. Five sides of the box were as smooth as glass; the bottom was rough. The lid of the box had twelve figures (seemingly female) carved intricately into the hard surface. The lids overall impression reminded me of Pablo Picasso's painting of five women in a brothel, entitled *Les Demoiselles d'Avignon.* This unique cubist approach had also been used by the artisan of this box, as well, to alter the twelve faces into broken planes. The garments appeared stylistic, as if they'd been given Indian influences, but not the kind we'd grown up experiencing in western novels or movies. The images created were truly mesmeric and took on a life of their own; especially after you'd stared at them for awhile.

"Jonah, does this style of clothing look familiar?" I asked with the intention of involving him. "If you will, consider this in context to the expeditions that you took in southern Utah and what you discovered there."

"It sure does;" Jonah looked astonished, "real similar to the Anasazi style!"

"And the fact that the box is dominated by twelve's is intriguing, too, I believe," Angelina pointed out excitedly.

"How so dear," the Captain asked.

"Man has used twelve in many of his own creations sir, and twelve is written into the creation by the Creator."

"Excellent point," Rorek agreed with sudden and keen interest, "and you're perfectly correct too! Twelve, spiritually, is a perfect number which has much to do with governmental perfection. The sun that *rules* the day and the moon and stars that *govern* the night do so by their passage through the twelve signs of the Zodiac which, in turn, completes the great circle of the heavens. We also see it in three hundred and sixty degrees or divisions that govern the year."

"Hey, this just came to me," Garrett interrupted. "There's twelve months in the year, twelve inches in a foot, twelve hours on a clock, twelve function keys on most PC keyboards, twelve dialing keys on phones . . ."

"Hey … twelve tribes of Israel," Roxanne added.

"Ok …. Twelve grades at school," Betsy laughed.

"Twelve Apostles of Christ," Jonah smiled.

"There's twelve volts in a cars electrical system," Rorek shrugged.

"And that box you're holding sir has twelve edges, and figures, and round plugs." Angelina pointed.

"And at this point there's twelve of us on this journey," Lizzy muttered with a revelatory expression.

"Gabriel what do you make of this?" the Captain asked.

The Captain had noticed that all of the figures right hands were extended towards another cube in the center of the scene. Only eight of the figures seemed to actually be touching the box; the other four were pointing at something in the background that resembled a maze.

"Could someone hand me a magnifying glass?" I asked.

"I'll get it honey," Lizzy offered.

Closely I scrutinized the bas-relief. It was so intricate and masterfully done that I began to question its origins. It seemed to be beyond the ability of human hands to me and, from this thought; two perplexing questions came into light. Who had really created this box, and why? The detail in the faces and along the edges stunned me; I'd never seen anything like this. The tiny carved box also had perfect round plugs on each of the corners.

"I think that the smaller box is a shadow, or replica, of this larger box guys." I muttered incredulously.

I could also see that eight of the figures were touching the box and that the other four were pointing at eleven miniscule figures in the background. There was also one figure independent from the eleven. Turning to the others I began clarifying after I'd put down the magnifying glass.

"There's nothing Nordic on this box, and there are no runic symbols. I'm convinced that it was *not* fashioned by any Viking craftsmen. I would seriously consider this to be a hybrid expression of different cultures and styles. But what they are, I have no idea; it's a design I've never seen before. I do have a hunch though sir."

"What's your hunch Gabriel?"

"I believe the designer gave us clues about how to open it."

"Whaaaaa!?" Garrett's eyes opened in wonderment.

"Yes, the cipher might be hidden in the carving."

"I don't understand son." The Captain leaned forward.

"Let's put it under the scanner and transfer the image to the plasma screen," Garrett suggested,

"Everyone can see it better then; fantastic idea!" Helga jumped to her feet. "John honey, help me!"

Using Garrett's suggestion I was able to enlarge the picture so everyone could view the detail on the HDP screen. Using the laser pointer I showed how the twelve figures were situated in conjunction to the small box between them. One figure was the closest, and each respective figure was situated back slightly from the other. Eight of the figures had their right index finger on a different circle around the edges of the box.

"I wonder if those eleven figures are representative of the emissaries that visited the Queen." Roxanne mused.

"Of course they are!" Jonah's eyes clouded. "And the other figure is probably the queen herself."

"That's a possibility you know," Garrett shrugged.

"Captain, there's a combination here; I'm sure of it! I believe that these cherrywood plugs act as buttons."

"So, we can push them in Gabriel?"

"Let's try and see! Perhaps if we push each plug in in succession and then release them quickly the box will open. Watch this!"

Gently I pushed on one of the plugs; there was clear inward movement.

"Whoaaaaa, that was cool!" Garrett exclaimed loudly.

The Captains eyes brightened. "Continue son," he motioned.

After I'd instructed the others what to do, eight of us carefully depressed the plugs, one after the other, and then released them.

Nothing happened!

"Ok that sucks." Garrett lamented.

"Wait a minute, look closely Gabriel." Lizzy pointed. "The fingers of all eight figures are on the box at the same time. Maybe we should push the plugs in and hold them instead of the other way around."

"Yes, of course Lizzy; why didn't I see that?"

Carefully we pushed the plugs in together and held them all securely. A moment later, with a slight discordant squeak, the lid released and opened. At once a foul odor enveloped the area. Garrett's face contorted as he lurched backwards. Was it booby-trapped?

"Smells like pig crap; I'm outa here!" He wailed.

"We're with you," the rest chorused and moved back away.

Fifteen

Gabriel's Vision

I realized that I couldn't move my legs; something queer was happening. Had a drug been released from this insidious box that would eventually handicap me? With no answers, and no other options, I reached out and closed the lid to try and lessen the debilitating effects. But when I had nothing of my condition changed; my disablement and the stench persisted. Distraught, and at a loss what to do, I grabbed whatever was near me as a morphing of faces and rainbow colors eddied in terrible vortexes around me. Panic-stricken I cried out for Anders help but couldn't open my mouth. Was it my time to die? Oh God please no! Closing my eyes I pleaded for the Holy Spirit's help. At once I was consumed in peace and strength flowed into me. I was stunned. Was the Creator really that close?

When I opened my eyes the room was no longer visible. I was standing now on a plateau high above the Loch Trossachs in the Scottish Mountains. But how could this be, I was just on the SES? In a sprawling meadow below me I could make out the hidden ranch of the clan leader, thief, blackmailer, and cattle trader Rob Roy Macgregor. Gripped with uncertainty I scanned the countryside for any sign of the infamous rogue. Knowing that he was a man who had the reputation of being brutal and unforgiving to everyone; I wanted no part of his shenanigans. After finally coming to the conclusion that I might be alone in this place I cut across the hillside to see where it would take me. Convinced that every sound was a potential danger, I made my way along as cautiously and quietly as possible, slipping and sliding in the gloom, but always staying attuned to my surroundings. In a matter of minutes the sprawling meadow, and Rob Roy's ranch, vanished in an engulfing mist behind me. After this a series of strange moaning sounds spooked me so I increased my pace to appear as a sojourner passing through the land just in case I was being watched. Upon gaining the edge of a very high cliff sunlight burst through the clouds in brilliant swaths and the topography and my surroundings came alive in rich vibrant colors. Looming on a hillside across the valley, high above a sprawling bog, a huge fortress came into view. Intrigued, and feeling as if I was being drawn, I at once began a precarious descent down through a series of gullies with the intent of exploring it. For many hours I maneuvered around moss covered boulders and jaggy outcroppings. Trekking across fields of loose shale and narrow dangerous paths, I gingerly traversed rushing streams, on and on, towards this thing that pulled me along with silent wooing. Around the fifth hour a brisk wind picked up and with it the arrant unpleasantness of the bog came upon me. Because of the awfulness of the stench I tied a moistened cloth around my face to try and lessen its effect. To my relief this worked and I was able to continue on without feeling as if I may vomit.

After many miles of sliding, and faltering, and falling on my rear, the valley floor was safely reached. Following a much needed respite I took stock of my surroundings and discovered that I was in the midst of a botanical wonderland rich with life. Flowers plants and shrubbery - colored brightly and green with healthy verdure - spread out in lush carpets for many miles. As I made my way through the valley the ground mist slowly dissipated and, after crossing, the fortress that had been wooing me finally came into full view. I couldn't believe my eyes. What had I done? Angrily I cursed myself. I was appalled for having come so far only to discover a thing so reprehensible. After calming down I purposed to study the despicable structure carefully to try and find some good in it. While scanning it I came to the conclusion that it had been constructed over decades by many disparate people who had never worked together in any kind of accord. I was convinced, too, that all involved in this monstrous creation had listened only to their inner voice and had followed what each had concluded to be an appropriate course of action for their own good. I recalled another fortress being constructed in similar fashion, by varying builders with differing mindsets, which shared no unified vision for a finished product, but I couldn't remember where. A strange thought overwhelmed me. Could it be that this was a picture of the Christian Church as it was presently in the world? And could it be symbolic of my own personal life as well? Intrigued, I made my way closer to find some answers.

A narrow flight of stone stairs were the only access to the main archway in the mammoth eastern rampart facing me. And from what I could see, the only way to get in was through that singular opening at the top of the narrow staircase above me. After getting closer I observed that all the walls and windows in the structure were rotting badly and that a foul odor was wide-spread near the foundations. I observed, through the archway above me, the gnarled figure of a man with long wispy hair shuffling back and forth. Despite my repeated efforts to get his attention; never once was I acknowledged. Always talking, it seemed as if he may be involved in a conversation with another person in the room and not aware of me. Who could this person be? Smitten with compassion I purposed to introduce myself and began climbing the stairs. As I did the skies filled suddenly with dark clouds and the atmosphere began crackling noisily in protest to the changing pressures. Torn in my thoughts and becoming more and more fraught, I questioned now if it was necessary to introduce myself to this man at all. What if he was a warlock- or worse? With gnawing uncertainty I conceded to what was bedeviling me and retreated back down the slippery stairs.

"COWARD," I screamed at myself, "what are you afraid of? Why do you always run away?"

There was a cave near the lowest foundation that was hidden by a stand of trees. I decided to remain here until my heart had slowed its fearful pace. While pondering my gloomy plight the heavens opened and rain started pounding the knoll above me; I was in awe of the intensity and somehow knew that an awful display of nature's fury would soon be following. For thirty minutes the storm raged and rivers began surging through the castle with a kind of mindless anger. Blackened water burst from every opening like indiscriminate striking snakes. The stench was one of a kind. Overwhelmed, and desperate, I retreated back further into the cave where I watched transfixed as everything collected over a lifetime was purged forcefully from the fortress in a cleansing deluge.

When the storm had finally subsided, I ventured back out to take stock of my environment. The castle did not appear as it had before; neither did any of the surrounding areas. All the weeds were gone, the rotten parts of the castle were gone, the blackened growth on all the surfaces had been wiped clean, and the stench along the foundations had been purged entirely. All that remained were the walls, and the floors, and the groundwork, which had once been chiseled into the very essence of the granite mountain. The occupant was standing now in one of the windows. He was naked. With confidence I moved up the stairs to confront him. As I neared I could see that his eyes were sparkling and that he appeared years younger than before the storm. When I said hello he refused to acknowledge me. Undeterred I moved past him into the room. Inside it was sparse, and unimposing, and I felt comfortable. Nothing he owned was of any worth save a small bed, two chairs, and a writing table equipped with an inkwell. On a shelf, near the fireplace, a bottle of wine and two glasses sat unopened and unused. On another shelf was a ream of white paper weighted safely from the winds beneath a brass vase. Near to that was an earthen container for drinking water, a pantry of fresh food, and, in the hearth, a warm fire was crackling noisily. In the man's left hand a sword was extended up towards the heavens and, in his right hand, a quill hung dripping with black ink. Wanting to make sense of it I purposed to look closer but was startled by a sudden and consuming bright light that inundated the room. With great gusto the man began singing and then, a moment later, he vanished from sight entirely. On the ground remained the sword and quill where he'd dropped them. Beset now, and feeling as if I may hyperventilate, I searched the room for any clues that might help me understand. As I did I began hearing a familiar voice, off in the distance, calling me, wooing me.

Sixteen

The Map

"GABRIEL …. GABRIEL … Son, can you hear me?"

An overwrought voice was tearing me from the old man's room. In the blink of an eye I was on the SES with a hand on my shoulder shaking me vigorously. Glancing, disbelievingly, about the room I responded: "I can hear you – yyyyyes!"

"It seemed you were preoccupied for a few minutes." The Captain continued. "You aren't ill are you?"

"Um, uhhhhh . . . gosh, hmmmm, well…."

"Talk much marble mouth?" Garrett sneered. "Screw your head on straight and check this out!"

Garrett was pointing where Roxanne was sitting. When I saw what she was pointing at I was instantly revived and refocused. She had successfully removed a finely milled tablet that had been expertly fitted into the top of the box. There were dozens of grooves carved all the way through the tablet and all appeared, to me, to be in random patterns. Upright on the table sat twelve little stone figures. In the leather pouches were three well preserved parchments, and laying on the bottom of the box a beautifully crafted turquoise and gold talisman was attached to a delicate golden chain.

"Can we unroll these parchments?"

"They seem pliable enough Gabriel;" Angelina answered after touching them, "What do you think Captain?"

"Of course, sure, let's do it!" He responded, rubbing his hands together eagerly. "Maybe there's something we can use."

As soon as the first parchment was unrolled Jonah carefully reviewed it under the scanner.

"Incredible," he cried out. "There's a smorgasbord of elements here, and some of the language and illustration is pure Anasazi!"

"Oh how exciting honey," Roxanne beamed joyfully. Jonah's temperament changed when the crew began applauding, cheering, and whistling his discovery.

"Olaf," he began succinctly, "I believe we should analyze these closely for a better understanding of what they are and what they say. This is quite amazing don't you think?"

"I do, and praise God for this new information!"

"I agree entirely," Rorek echoed his brothers' sentiment. The whole room resounded with a hearty amen.

"Let's do it then honey." Roxanne hugged Jonah warmly. "I'm eager to see what's on these parchments."

"Sir, while they're working on the parchments can I try and figure out what this template was designed for?"

"Of course Gabriel," the Captain agreed with a toothy grin. "Anders, you and John meet me on the bridge, I want to go over the charts we made with the Grettig's."

"Aye Captain," both chorused.

For the next several days we remained cloaked north of Torfar-Kolla near where the Grettig's had been airlifted out. Each day, for twelve hours plus, we remained diligent and centered to accomplish our work. We discovered, during the in-depth examination, a kind of elegant balance that delineated the artifacts. Eleven of the figurines were similar and one was dissimilar; each of them was exactly three inches in height and all were made of the same material. Each of the three parchments was ten inches in width and unrolled to a length of twenty-four inches exactly. Dispersed evenly, there were two hundred and seventeen words in all, and five illustrations on each of the three. Roxanne informed us that what they'd found so far was affirming Jonah's theory about the disappearance of the Anasazi Nation from the surface. The parchments were clear in that they had descended into the subterranean realm to dwell together with the Vikings, and that this curious relationship had lasted for many decades. Given this we purposed to search for more clues that may point us to where the Anasazi had actually migrated to when they'd left Torfar-Kolla, and also why some of the Viking population still had clear vocal nuances of the Anasazi language in their Nordic parlance.

An idea came to me while I was photographing the template under the scanner. Not knowing what to expect I laid it directly on top of the bas-relief. Amazed with the results I called for the Captain to join me. Could it really be this simple?

"Looks like a map Gabriel," The Captain admitted after peering intently at the discovery.

This was my thought too. The cutouts clearly revealed a series of details and shapes in the lower right quadrant of the bas-relief that appeared similar to a city. There was also, what could be construed as, a path meandering towards the upper left corner that ended near a series of odd shapes. At full magnification you could make out a grouping of tiny carved figures on the top edge of the box. These were identical to the figurines in the box. There was also, what appeared as, a very large body of water fed through a large inlet off of a river very near the figures.

"Hey boss, 'member when Granmar told us that the queen's beauty might have given life to the stone giants; do you think that was just a load a crap?"

"Garrett I don't know!" Captain Olaf shrugged. "We don't even know what the stone giants really are. We're only assuming they're literally stone giants. To tell you the truth, I don't know what to think about *any* of this. It's all kinda far-fetched!"

"That's a fact," Anders scoffed. "Maybe this map will lead us to that bloody city, though, and then we can find out for our own selves what's true and what's not."

"Honey, shush!" Angelina glared sternly.

"And tell me again what the Anasazi and Vikings have in common, and why the heck they're in cahoots?" John's tone had turned sardonic. "I'm sorry Jonah, I'm not saying anything one way or another, but it just seems implausible."

"Maybe the bloody emissaries were aliens!" Rorek snorted.

"Yeah, and maybe the queen was an alien too!" Betsy spit back.

"And who gives a crap anyway?" Helga snarled.

"Yah who gives a crap," Rorek stood up angrily.

"And now I'm supposing all this got into our hands just to confuse us and get us all to arguing?" Lizzy was clearly upset and I could see tears forming in her eyes as she got up to leave. "I've had it with this childish behavior, I'm taking a nap."

As soon as she turned to leave Garrett jumped up and asked: "Did you guys forget why we're here?"

"Huh?" Lizzy stopped and turned around.

"Didn't God put us down here to find the First Tribe? I mean aside from all the cool places we've been, and freaky things we've done, isn't that our one and only mandate?"

No one said a word. Of course Garrett was right. What was it that had irritated everyone? Were there evil spirits attached to this box as there'd been with the Aztecan knife?

"We should pray," I suggested after several moments of silence. "We haven't for awhile you know. The last time I remember was with the Grettig's. I've been remiss too, and I'm sure there's something we need to understand that we won't be able to without praying together."

"I believe so dear," Roxanne agreed. "And in light of what we're all feeling, I'm sure we need to understand things a lot better."

"You're right Liz. This box is in our hands for a reason," Jonah nodded, "and it certainly wasn't to pit us against each other. We need unity now more than ever. And Gabriel's correct, we should start praying together again; if we don't we'll fail."

"Amen, and thank-you Jonah," Lizzy smiled shyly. 'Maybe I don't need a nap after all."

"I guess we're off to try and find a Lost City then huh?" Anders asked, scratching his head and kicking at the floor.

"Looks that way dude – whatever," Garrett raised both hands in a sign of resignation. "It's time to split the SES for awhile; it's startin' to get claustrophobic."

"Yeah it is," Anders agreed. "Another adventure'll do us good. Sorry for the outburst Captain, I don't know what came over me."

Acknowledging his apology, the Captain again reinforced our conclusions and then suggested that we pray and inform the professor about our intentions.

"If we're going to do this," he pondered, "we need to decide what we're going to take and who's going."

Seventeen

Somber News

The next day the professor's dispatch arrived. We were informed that the Grettig's had arrived safely on Montague Island and had been accepted into the burgeoning Viking culture with open arms. Halldis already had been embraced by hundreds because of her bubbling personality, and Gautrek had found a group of young men that he had bonded with and was already teaching them many of the things that Garrett had taught him. Granmar and Arnora were very happy with their new home and had jobs lined up in the community.

Secondly we learned that any kind of information that may shed light on the Mortiken amassing in the Realm of the Ancients was unavailable. There was nothing on any of his global grids, but there remained the possibility that they had visited the underground realm for strategic reasons only. An investigation was in force, around the clock, to delve into the matter. The professor's team of experts was looking into where the Baaldurians may have gained entrance into the realm, and if any troops had been left behind for covert missions. He asked us to be patient, and assured us that he would do his best to get to the bottom of this mystery.

The third part of the dispatch was a somber update about the condition of world affairs. Things were changing on the planet at an alarming rate everywhere. The magnetic drought bands, first noticed in early 2005, were still devastating areas of the globe with savage unpredictability. The once concentric band, and legs, of the fierce atmospheric anomaly had broken up into pieces; most now were stationary in the ionized layers of the upper atmosphere. After a series of solar disturbances, several weeks prior, one of the bands had dropped down into the lower troposphere and was now undulating across the Northwest Territories, Southampton Island in Hudson Bay, Southern Baffin Island, the majority of Iceland, and the last place on the land mass that had any ice on the surface; the southernmost tip. The ice packs and glaciers on the North and South Pole had been melting at an alarming rate. The consequences of this were being felt in all the costal areas and islands across the planet. The Earth's oceans and seas had risen almost five feet because of this massive influx of fresh water. Literally hundreds of coastal communities had been abandoned because they were uninhabitable. The team had calculated that if the North and South Poles melted completely, that the oceans could rise well upwards of one hundred and twenty feet around the globe. The ramifications of this were unimaginable. The professor warned us also that the release of unsafe levels of methane, from the melting permafrost in the Northern Territories, could start a dramatic change in climate. In the last six months the melting glaciers and icepacks had begun altering the saline content of the ocean radically in several key areas; including the Foxe Basin, the Hudson Bay, and the Ungava Bay. Tornadoes, hurricanes, cyclones, earthquakes, floods, mudslides, typhoons, and tsunamis had been breaking all known records for endurance, strength, size, and utter devastation. Since Hurricane Katrina and Rita, in late 2005, the politics of world-wide disaster preparedness had become untenable. For fifteen years the World Health Organization, and the Red Cross, had been beset with the shifting global conditions and could not adequately achieve their responsibilities anymore. The reemergence of once controllable diseases was ravaging many second and third world countries. Both the W.H.O. and the Red Cross had struggled valiantly to remain solvent during the escalating yearly disasters but to no avail. Public interest, grants, and donations had plummeted because of internal corruption, bureaucracy, and the failure to deliver on their advertised promises to the public. Both companies had been forced to downsize so radically that they had been rendered ineffective in most key disaster scenarios. As a result, major costal cities now had their own Disaster Response Teams, (DRT'S) and these groups of volunteers dealt locally with disasters without the bungling time-consuming intrusion of state and federal governments. The idea had finally found its time and was working well in every area that it was in place. Most of the funds for these volunteer teams were being raised by donations from technology, mega-companies, local charities, musicians, authors, and also from artists, painters, and poets. With the money they were able to buy equipment, stockpile food, water, and varied medicines for any eventuality that may arise unexpectedly.

The bird flu, which had devastated parts of Asia and the Middle East, had become troublesome in parts of Europe and Eurasia. Similar to the 1918 flu pandemic, when fifty to sixty million people had perished world-wide, this mutated strain was resisting all efforts to contain it. Fear was rampant and thousands were succumbing.

Most global industrial markets were also buckling under to the schemes of political megalomaniacs, and because of the continual profit brokering by greedy underhanded leaders, most everything now had merged into mega-corporations and was being controlled by a group of sinister individuals located in Rome. In every democratic nation the middle class was vanishing, and a new global socialism, based on race and religious persuasion, was spreading. Religious wars had been raging in the Middle East for many decades, and the biased journalism fueling fiction and falsehoods was dominating the front pages of every major publication world-wide. The inter-net had become a cesspool of filth and corruption, simply because laws to govern it had never been put into place. No one knew what, or who, to believe anymore.

A persuasive, wealthy man, living in Europe, had become an international hero and, through a series of shrewd political maneuvers, and overly publicized humanitarian donations, was now swaying the hearts and minds of tens of millions in a concerted effort to become the next *Prime Potentate of the Global Alliance of Nations.* It seemed the fabric of humanity was unraveling at an unprecedented rate. Much was being eradicated, or restructured, because of new concepts about whom, and what God really was, and the social and political incorrectness of thinking otherwise.

Insidious groups located in Idaho and Montana were fueling a world-wide campaign to change the times and season's of everything societies had held dear for centuries. Their agenda was eliminating Easter and Christmas, the BC and AD in our calendars, or anything else that had anything at all to do with Jesus Christ.

The Earth was dominated now more than ever by mindless greed and hunger for power, and the majority of its peoples were living in debauchery, lust, drunkenness, orgies, carousing, and detestable idolatry. As the professor had bemoaned, it seemed the end of all things was nearer than ever.

Part 2

Through the Eastern Mountains

Eighteen

Alrek Stormwrack

When Roxanne shared the results of her research Jonah began dancing. He seemed happier than he'd been in months. According to the parchments, from the wooden box, the Anasazi and the Vikings *had* dwelt together in Torfar-Kolla and the surrounding villages for almost a century. The contents clearly revealed that it ultimately had been the influences of a charismatic man named Alrek Stormwrack that had convinced the Anasazi to sever ties with Torfar-Kolla.

Stormwrack's reputation preceded him wherever he went and he was a hero to those who knew of his exploits. Since his ascension to the throne King Vadrun had expressed umbrage at the co-mingling of the Anasazi and Northern cultures; the old agreement made no sense to him. In his early fifties, Vadrun, being at the end of his patience, and also at the crossroads of his desire to cope politically, summoned the fiery Stormwrack for help. Vadrun's intention was to establish a political alliance between the two nations that would implement the sweeping changes he desired for Torfar-Kolla. The deal was that Alrek Stormwrack would be responsible for purging everything Anasazi from the city and Vadrun would be solely responsible for ruling Torfar-Kolla. After in depth negotiations Stormwrack finally agreed to Vadrun's terms and, in the grandest inauguration ever in Torfar-Kolla's history, was given the number two position in the realm. It was a time of great jubilation, and the seven days of feasts and festivities brought many into the city from the outlying villages and settlements.

After the celebration Stormwrack entered into private negotiations with the Anasazi. No one but Stormwrack and the Anasazi elders were allowed in these meetings. There were no records made of the negotiations and what information we'd found in the scrolls in the wooden box was given to King Vadrun directly from Stormwrack.

Stormwrack made it clear that there were no hidden hostility's between the Viking nation and Anasazi. He established that much good had been accomplished between them, and that the blending of art and language had helped both nations expand their own views of life, and the intellectual need for those of disparate influences to share their respective cultures to understand one another. He assured them that the citizenry of Torfar-Kolla, and the cities government, were not discontented with them, or their distinctiveness; they were simply desirous of regaining their own cultural uniqueness in honor to the original founders of the great city. According to what was written in the scrolls the elders seemed to understand and were not in the least offended. Stormwrack suggested that the Anasazi leave Torfar-Kolla in three months with an exact day of departure. The elders agreed and details were drawn up between both parties. Relieved at having avoided confrontation (or worse) Stormwrack offered the elders whatever they required to make their exodus as smooth as possible. The elders accepted his offer and made a list of their needs.

With legendary aplomb Stormwrack had, once again, resolved another sticky political situation and King Vadrun was well pleased. Accordingly, Stormwrack was rewarded with four new longboats, men of his choosing to sail them, gold, textiles, and also an offer to remain second in command in Torfar-Kolla for as long as Vadrun ruled. Stormwrack took the gifts, chose the men he wanted, but graciously declined the position. He was a free spirit and chose to remain so. A fortnight later, with no fanfare, Stormwrack sailed northwest in the dead of night.

The day finally came for the Anasazi Nation to depart. With a splinter group from the Viking populace accompanying them, their leader said his farewells to King Vadrun. Glowing Weapon told the king that they would be searching for Sky Wolf. It was difficult for us to understand this in its entirety. Was Sky Wolf a person – a place? The parchments gave no background about these titles, only that they *were* titles. After a short discussion we decided to treat them only as appellations the Vikings had given to something that they didn't fully comprehend when the two nations had first come together. Despite our ignorance in the matter, there was still much intriguing about these descriptions; a reminder of something we'd discovered in Oski's Grotto months prior. Both were in the verse we'd found etched on the walls near the entrance:

Beware those of the Highest God

Those skulking serpents

That would dare enter

Odin's secret place

Listen now and take heed

The one-eyed master of thin air

Will prevail against thee

With differing names and many faces

In merging shades amongst the trees

He vanishes when you turn

Beware ghost men

Who pass through Wished For

To gain entry into the land of dark elves

Into the bosom of the Ancients

Glowing Weapon goads Sky Wolf

The Earth and Sea obey

Beware those of the Highest Christ God

Those who would tread upon Turf Beast

Beware, the world of the dead

During the meeting we purposed to trek into the Eastern Mountains to try and make more sense of what had been written. Preparations for departure began immediately.

A week later

On the morning of our departure Roxanne advised that we take along the talisman that was in the wooden box: "I'm not certain you'll need it but you never know. What if it's a pass of sorts?" She pondered. "Perhaps, if it is, it will allow certain privileges to the bearer if you ever do happen to discover a lost city."

Because the idea struck a chord with everyone Olaf gave his consent and asked Anders if he would carry it. Honored with the suggestion Anders put it on a stainless steel chain around his neck. During our last breakfast together, before splitting up, one of the conversations I remembered having with the Grettig's came to mind about a place they'd referred to as Himminglaeva.

Nineteen

Himminglaeva

The settlement was known as *the land of icy mists and clinging darkness's*. Located in the far northern territories (of Torfar-Kolla) many were convinced that it was populated by a cloistered tribe of Viking mystics and the secretive giants they had befriended. These mystic Viking warriors were said to have been cosseted by a higher power because they were descendants of the royal blood line from the first Rognvald voyage. Notwithstanding a lack of proof, the colorful account was widely accepted in the city as being authentic. There were factions, however, who refuted this. They were convinced that this 'bedtime story' was only an attempt to cover-up Himminglaeva's true purpose, that being an off-colony created for misfits, malcontents, derelicts, and every other rebellious type that had been purged from the city and surrounding settlements. Under cover of night three expeditions had ventured north, without the kings' permission, to discover the truth of the matter; all three longboats had disappeared, and no one involved was ever seen again. These incidents happened within a fortnight and, in retaliation; widespread unrest, and rioting, broke out in the city. In an effort to maintain stability, King Hamal, (Braggi's predecessor) issued a formal decree stating that no one would ever again be allowed passage to the northern settlement under penalty of death or worse. This was rigidly enforced, and soon thereafter the mystical far northern territories became known only as the *land of dark elves*. Jonah was quick to point out that *land of dark elves* was another of the phrases that we'd found etched on the wall in Oski's Grotto.

February 10ᵗʰ 6 am

We were splitting up once again and it was not sitting well with me. The following morning Rorek, Roxanne, Angelina and Betsy would be traveling north, past the settlements of Hrafnborg and Gondul to find, and explore, the legendary Himminglaeva settlement. Today the Captain, Garrett, Anders, John, Helga, Lizzy, Jonah, Rolf and I would be leaving the comforts of the SES to press out into the vast unknown of the Eastern Mountains. Taking along all we could - backpacks, tents, sleeping bags, CSAT modules, long distance radios, food and water, knives, hand weapons, ammunition, Helga's rifle, first aid, two cameras, one titanium laptop, and a map sketched from the tablet - we said our goodbyes and began our burdensome trek along the slippery coastal rocks towards a vale between two mountains.

When the SES had at last faded from view a strange silence descended on the team. Rolf was moaning quietly and pacing in circles and the rest of us all stood unsure staring at one another. A familiar feeling of vulnerability washed over me as the reality of what we were doing set in. With limited supplies the eight of us, and our wolfhound, were pressing forward into an unknown terrain as rugged as any we'd ever seen.

Twenty

My Tenuous Faith

After finally making it safely through the coastal rocks we clambered for hours up a steep gravelly wash. After that we traversed along a narrow path etched into the side of a sheer granite wall where, at last, we came to a large clearing that looked as if it might have been, at one time, a large pool from mountain runoff. On the other side of the clearing a less inclined gradient was leading up towards the next ridge. Captain Olaf suggested that we break before we went on. As we ate I was stricken with the idea that this was *the* most cockeyed thing we'd ever done since leaving Aberdeen. Why in the world was it so crucial for us to jeopardize our lives traversing this no-man's land in pursuit of what may well end up being only a legend? There was great risk in it and if anything went wrong we may well be trapped down here for the rest of our lives, or even worse. As I saw it, now, my biggest challenge was how to deal with the fears and what I often projected may happen? Was faith the key to peace and focus in all we did? And if we believed all the promises in scripture, and if we prayed daily for these things to become manifest, and if we believed that the Holy Spirit guided His people every moment of each day, why did those claiming Christ struggle so hard, not only to find peace, but also to hold onto it?

Garrett broke the silence and began sharing as we climbed.

"This reminds me of Lewis and Clark; member them dudes Cap?"

"Of course son, everyone that's studied history has," the Captain blurted between strained breaths. "What about it?"

"My junior high teacher, Mrs. Jensen, told us they accomplished something no one else ever had done before, sorta like what we're doin' on this journey ya know."

"Yah, you're right," the Captain wheezed.

Lizzy was listening and added: "The expedition took them from a camp somewhere outside St. Lewis Missouri all the way to the Pacific Ocean and then back; a long way and quite a feat."

"Yah it was, and because those dudes had the guts to do what they did they discovered a whole bunch of new animals and plants."

"They did honey and it did take a lot of courage," Lizzy agreed heartily. "They also charted early topographical maps of America in their adventures."

Little by little I was being pulled into this discussion. It was a refreshing departure from my own perplexing cerebrations, and had begun to allay the fearful pessimism that was trying to make my heart a place of rest. There *was* a parallel (of sorts) between what Lewis and Clark had accomplished, and what we were attempting to do now. Thinking that we may be regarded as part of a special league of explorers someday was quite a novel way to view what we were doing down here. I had to give Garrett credit for his observation and I agreed with him, but, a lot more people would have to become privy to what we were doing than there were now to be regarded as the Lewis and Clark expedition had been. Up to now the many files we'd accumulated were known only to a very select few. But I knew that the proliferation of knowledge took time. It was perfectly logical, too, given the nature of what we were seeking, that there would be danger and fear involved in what we were attempting, just as there had been for the Lewis and Clark expedition. Since the onset, we, as voyagers and explorers, had pressed towards something that no one else had ever attempted before - this of course being the aspect of our journey that was always mysterious to me - because there was a much greater purpose in what we were doing than just the gathering of knowledge and the self-gratification of being here. Day after day our faith and moxie had been tested in umpteen varied ways; this fact of course constituting the requisite for our resolve to remain unified and strong as a team because of what we'd been given to do. The unique vision of accomplishing something greater than ourselves was the spiritual part of our mandate and it must, in God's timing, be brought to an inevitable fruition. But would that season of bearing fruit ever be known to us? Would we be the ones basking in the warmth of our accomplishments or was it for generations distant?

In some deep part of me there was a thing that had always railed against my logical self-centeredness. I knew that the doing of it was more important than the glories one might receive for it. If all people ever purposed to do was quest after their own personal goals – doing so to unfurl their own banners and bask in their own resplendence; to stand before others of like mind and receive their earthly rewards and gloat because of what had been accomplished – God's plan *may* eventually be fulfilled but He would never be glorified because of humanities skewed and prideful focus on self, instead of the greater aspects of His eternal plan.

"I remember the first time I dove at the Boiler," Anders began. I sensed that he had been pulled into the conversation, as I had, as he began reminiscing. "I didn't know what to expect, and I'd only heard rumors about the place, and not a lotta fact, but I still moved out in faith to do something I felt I was called to do. When my peers caught wind of it they thought I was insane for taking the Raptor so far to do something so risky; especially by myself."

"You mean they dissed you dude?"

"Yeah they did Garrett! I thought I'd be respected but that wasn't the case at all. They all got weird towards me because of the vision I'd been given. Even Angie balked and tried to change my mind by forcing her fears on me because she just couldn't grasp the deeper aspects of what I was trying to accomplish."

"Well honey, she was afraid you'd never come back," Lizzy responded quietly, "I can understand that."

"Yah, that's right Liz. Angie finally admitted to me that she was scared I would get hurt and that no one would be there to help me. But here's the point I'm trying to make. Being bombarded by the negativity and fears of others every time I turned around began messing with my own confidence and focus; at least for awhile until I figured it out. Hey, don't get me wrong, I dearly love my wife, and I would do anything for her, but she's just not called to do what I am. We walk two different paths, but we're walking them together. She doesn't have the skills that I have and I don't have hers. She doesn't express herself the way that I do and she doesn't deal with problems the way that I do and vice versa; I'm sure you get my drift. We help each other, and support each other, and minister to each other, but we aren't each other. It's like what happened to her when I dove in with the whales; she was overcome because she was consumed only with the possibility that something dire would happen to me. Too often people superimpose their own personal fears on others as if the way they feel and perceive is the way everyone else does too. Mostly when others see that you have a gift, or an ability they don't, they often end up standing against you instead of standing with you."

"A lot of people are like that son, "Captain Olaf agreed, stopping to wipe his brow. "Sometimes you have to do what you've been called to do alone without the support of others. I guess everyone does the best they can with what they've been given. Fearing for another's safety and welfare, though, is a very real battle; it certainly has been in my life and Rorek's. Let's take a break people, I'm thirsty and my feet are on fire."

"You're right Captain, but the negativity gets to you," Anders continued after removing his pack, "especially when you're trying to pursue the vision you know God's given you. I'll openly admit that because of all the negative voices around me back then, the fears and uncertainties that I *never* used to entertain I began to. Fears about monsters, the fear of storms, the fear of the Raptor sinking, the fear of drowning, the fear of being attacked by hammerheads, the fear of not finding anything worthwhile, and the fear of people thinking I was an idiot for trying became a real battle for me."

"Fear's like leaven; it affects everything it touches." The Captain groaned as he rubbed his feet.

"Exactly Captain," Anders shook his head.

"Do you think we're doing that now Anders?" Helga frowned.

"What do you mean sis?"

"You know, fearing the unknown and defeating ourselves with our own imaginings?"

"It's a good question Helga, but I really can't say. I suppose a person would have to search their own heart to answer that. What I *can* say, though, is that it's not that way for me anymore. I'm totally down with what we're doing here. I mean bring it on, this is our life, let's live it, and let's accomplish the goals we have no matter what we encounter along the way." Intrigued with the conversation everyone had gathered nearer to the Captain and Anders.

"Personally people," Jonah began pensively, "from my own experiences, I think that some fear of the unknown is perfectly natural and healthy. It certainly keeps us aware of where we're at in time and space and also of the many decisions we make from moment to moment. Plowing into something blindly, and calling it faith, is downright foolish in my opinion. And then, of course, not seeing something to its end because we get bored or lose interest is wrong too. There has to be balance in everything. Personally I don't believe that *not* thinking something through prayerfully brings glory to our Creator. I mean scripture is filled with stories about those who decided to grab the 'bull by the horns' and do what they wanted to do without seeking God. Eventually they all failed. Look at Saul, Israel's first king; because of jealousy he turned against David and eventually fell on his own sword because of where his poor Godless choices had led him. There's nothing we can do to change the fact that people are more apt to find solace and comfort in a safe environment than they are on the cutting edge. Angelina wanted you to stay in the place that she deemed safe because of her very real fears about what may happen to you. I think that this is a natural chemistry for those that love and care for one another."

"Are you saying then that operating in faith is easier when everything is controllable and safe?" John asked.

"I believe sometimes it may be true," Jonah's brow tightened in contemplation, "but not always! Consider this; what person needs faith when everything is going well, when they have good health, and when they're blessed with all the money and material things they could ever want? God's people are tested differently than earth-dwellers are; just like we've been and will continue being. Of this I am convinced and I believe what scripture says about it quite literally."

"What's that brother?" John asked.

"That there *will* be misfortune and difficulty for God's people when they pursue God's plan for their lives. No matter what our strength of character is like, or what our faith level is, or what our skills are, or what we do of significance for the kingdom, God's people will be tested in severe and unique ways. I can attest to that! It's part of the process of becoming who we're supposed to be. In 2nd Corinthians 12:9 it says: *"My grace is sufficient for thee: for strength is made perfect in weakness."* If this is true, then it stands to reason that the Father *will* allow difficult circumstances and testing in our lives, or He may call us to do things where we confront our fears and frailties and weaknesses and have to totally depend on Him to get through. After all, we're just clay vessels that need a continual infilling of the Holy Spirit to survive!"

"Seems God wants us to press forward in faith no matter how we feel, or what the circumstances may be." Anders declared staunchly.

"I believe so, but not foolishly, *not* foolishly Anders!" Jonah stressed. "Everything we do must be accompanied with prayer and seeking God continually to reveal His will for you in any situation. Also we must seek the counsel of others of similar faith - like we've always done together as a team - because there is always wisdom in the counsel of others. Besides, you never know what God is going to do through you until you press forward prayerfully and do it."

"I agree," Anders nodded pensively, "it's a good point brother!"

"Wow Jonah, I haven't heard you preach for a long time!" Garrett grinned awkwardly. "I've missed it brother!"

Jonah shrugged. Closing his eyes, and sighing, he sat down and began rubbing his forehead. "I've been thinking about Eloise son and all that we've been through since that night when we discovered who she'd become. Lizzy do we have any more aspirin?"

"I do have some honey!" Lizzy said comfortingly. "It's not your fault that Eloise chose to be Krystal Blackeyes Jonah; who knows what the Holy Spirit has in store for her in the future."

"I know, I know; it's just that the grinding in my gut never goes away. I can't make peace with it, and the possibility that someday one of us may have to kill her ... it just ...," Jonah's demeanor changed suddenly and his face turned ashen.

"Lord willing Jonah that will never happen." Olaf reacted.

"No man, never, ever," Garrett agreed compassionately.

"Think about it this way Jonah," the Captain pulled thoughtfully at his moustache, "perhaps its Gods will for you not to make peace with it at this time. Maybe He wants to use this unresolved angst to accomplish something for His glory in the here and now. Now consider this, and I mean it with my whole heart brother; perhaps you will be the very one that someday rescues her and leads her to Christ!"

"AMEN and AMEN!" Everyone chorused loudly with applause.

"Yah, right on boss, that's a great thought!" Garrett gave a thumb up as he handed the aspirin to Jonah.

"I just remembered something else about the Lewis and Clark expedition."

"What's that Gabriel?" Jonah turned to take the canteen.

"Did you know that they discovered the Grizzly bear, the coyote, the magpie, the prairie dog, the gray wolf, red cedars, the California condor, cottonwoods, Sitka spruce and the Pacific yew on their expedition?"

"No I did not!" Jonah shrugged while washing down the aspirin.

"They found a ton more than that butt-wad!" Garrett snorted.

"Yah I know cheese-brain, but it's all I can remember!"

"Settle down, both of you, this isn't the time!" the Captain shot an angry glance at both of us. "Gabriel did you say that they discovered Pacific yew?"

"Yes sir I did!"

"Yew; how intriguing is that;" Lizzy murmured, "Olaf?"

"Isn't the wooden box made of yew?" The Captain frowned.

I knew the Captain's question was double-edged. Considering that there were no trees of that genus in the underground realm, at least none that we'd found thus far, where had the box really come from?

"Oh sheesh, another mystery," Garrett groaned.

Twenty-One

Following an Ancient Path

Our spirits soared after the conversation. Now everyone was focused and, as we pressed up the rugged inclines, our heart-rates remained strong. After walking non-stop for most of the morning we finally approached the terminus of the valley. For miles around, now, massive impassable granite cliffs were looming as our next challenge. After studying the topography through the binoculars John informed us that there was a pass about two hundred yards south.

"Looks like the only way sir," he informed the Captain. "It's that or we find a different route."

Lizzy advised that we rest and eat and suggested we mull our options rationally. As it turned out, we were anything but rational in the discussion. All we did was complain about our predicament and everything else we could think of. Clearly exasperated Jonah finally intervened. He suggested we pray for guidance instead of wasting our time in meaningless cerebrations. Sheepishly the Captain agreed.

A wave of dread rolled over me as we approached the imposing crack in the massive granite wall. Despite being thankful that we'd prayed, and that the Captain had given the ok to continue, I was still transfixed with a gnawing apprehension that this route was going to test our moxie in profound ways. After a needed pep talk from Anders, which bolstered everyone's courage and determination, we entered in with Rolf and Anders at the point. It was gloomy inside and the air was musty and oxygen deprived. As I pondered what suffocating might be like in a place like this, a sudden breeze picked up through the narrow canyon and refreshed everyone.

"Wow! This is nice," the Captain breathed deeply.

"Yah, it's cool and fresh," Garrett added.

"Weird … I can still smell seawater," Anders laughed.

Quietly I thanked God for this sign. After walking another three hundred yards, one of Garrett's stentorian belches ripped through the air; the sound soon became overwhelming.

"Good lord," Lizzy cried out.

"Garrett, please," Helga implored.

Again Garrett belched loudly. This time it was louder than the first and he began laughing like a madman.

"Garrett, no more," The Captain ordered sternly. "Remember the talk we had after that fiasco in Torfar-Kolla?"

"Oh yah boss, sorry, sorry, I forgot."

"It reminds me of ring-modulation and freaky filtering all at the same time Olaf." Jonah observed. "The laws of physics here seem different than anything I've ever experienced."

"Exaggerated sounds could trigger an avalanche," John warned. "We know nothing about this place."

"I agree! Stay as quiet as possible!" The Captain ordered.

The ladies soon were complaining about feeling claustrophobic and I began to fear that, at any moment, an avalanche may crush us like old dry leaves. Soon the passage began narrowing even more. Now we were forced to walk sideways with our backpacks in one hand. Progress was irksome, and movement was relegated to a haphazard sideways rocking rhythm. Jonah's insights, earlier, began hastening my own awareness's about the sound. Around me the ceaseless crunching of boots, the swishing of clothes, even our breathing was exacerbating whatever this strange phenomenon was. Talking was certainly problematic; invariably the sound of our voices became an unintelligible swirl of gibberish. Because of this we chose to communicate in whispers or remain silent. But even using these precautions, the phenomenon persisted. No matter how insignificant the sounds were, it seemed each of them was being amplified and distorted in some inscrutable way. The only relief came when we stood absolutely still, then the swirl would stop and silence would prevail until the next sound was made.

The farther in we went the more on edge we got. Fears of an earthquake collapsing the walls, or an avalanche trapping us, began weighing heavily. Still we pressed forward hoping for the best.

Then the inconceivable happened!

Near the third hour we were hit by a sudden shower of loosened pebbles and sand from above. My life instantly flashed before my eyes. The ladies screamed in sheer terror. Faintly I heard someone cursing as Rolf bounded ahead of us howling.

"Get down under your packs," Anders screamed over the din.

The air became choked with dust which forced us to cover our mouths to breath. The sound became enfeebling. On and on it went, this horrid scraping noise; was it ever going to end? I couldn't see the others now and had no idea how they were faring. Faintly I heard Rolf barking in the distance. Were we all going to die? Fervently I cried out to God to save us. Then, as if someone had turned off a spigot, it ended. As the noise lessened, and the air cleared, Garrett, Anders, Jonah, Helga, Lizzy, and the Captain came into view; all were half buried in a powdery amalgam of sand and pebbles. I was stunned at the scene!

"Is everyone ok?" John asked tensely.

Everyone responded yes.

"Help the one in front of you if you can reach them," John ordered. "Gabriel, are you alright?"

"I am John," I responded feebly.

"Then dig Lizzy out please," he barked.

"I will, I will," I cried back in earnest.

Within moments each of us was helping the one in front of them, which in turn allowed them to help the one in front of them. After everyone had been dug out, and we had climbed over the mess, we continued on shaken but thankful that no one had been hurt. Rolf reappeared whimpering.

"Where have you been dog?" John asked with irritation.

Rolf seemed remorseful but excited about something. Soon he was sniffing the air and then he bolted ahead barking and disappeared from view.

"Dumb mutt," Garrett muttered.

Disconsolately we trudged on. Soon the passage widened again, which helped, but the whole process seemed interminable. Everyone's nerves were shattered and I could hear Lizzy and Helga crying softly behind me.

"I thought it was over for us," Lizzy sobbed pitifully.

"I know sweetheart," Helga sympathized, "we're all alive though, thank God, we'll be ok."

Rolf's excited barking had begun echoing around us now. Curious to know why Anders ran ahead and within seconds he was shouting excitedly: "We're through guys, we're through, hallelujah, and it's a beautiful vale too."

Twenty-Two

A Taste of Eden

Great joy surged through each of us after we'd emerged from the passage. As far as I was concerned what we'd just been through was the worst thing that we'd ever endured on the journey thus far. It'd been like being underwater too long struggling to get to the surface to breathe. The others quickly dropped their gear and, after removing my pack and whatever equipment was draped over my shoulders, I felt a great burden lift from my mind and heart. Within seconds I was feeling better and all the churning anxieties in me began dissipating. The Holy Spirit had delivered us from a hellish nightmare into a kind of Shangri-la. Praising Him didn't seem enough to me though; I wanted to hug Him and cry on His shoulder. As I was giving thanks something John Milton had written in 'Paradise Lost' (his epic poem describing humanities fall from grace) came to my remembrance:

Some natural tears they dropped, but wiped them soon;
The world was all before them, where to choose
Their place of rest, and Providence their guide:
They hand in hand with wand'ring steps and slow,
Through Eden took their solitary way.

Around us colorful wildflowers spread out as magnificently as an Olympians carpeting. There were healthy trees, and abundant verdure, and the air was like an elixir. Taking it all in I began feeling as if I was being whelmed in a glorious enchantment and I thanked God, again, for our lives and this blessed miracle.

"I've never seen nothing like this," Garrett murmured at last.

"Like a taste of Eden," Anders sighed.

"Yah it is," Garrett shook his head slowly.

Near the center of the valley several rivers were entering an enormous body of water. And in the far southern and northern periphery I observed waterfalls plummeting dramatically from the high ridges. We had discovered a flourishing vale crosshatched by numerous streams and rivers of varying widths and depths and, around us; the ghostly susurrations of flowing water were like the soothing voices of angels. The lake was overshadowed by eddying mists, and all the shrubbery and trees were enshrouded in vapory condensation. It was truly gorgeous and mystifying.

"Whataya think about *this* place boss?" Garrett asked.

"I've never been anywhere like this before son." He sighed.

"Neither have I Olaf," Jonah added, "there's something special here. The air is incredible; the environment magical."

"Peaceful man, peaceful …" Garrett stretched out his arms and breathed deeply.

"I agree little brother." John chuckled. "I remember seeing a place like this once in my dreams."

"It is like a dream honey." Helga took John's hand.

Near the western end of the lake torrents of water tumbled over a wash of rocks and then down into another deep gorge that meandered back towards the underground sea. The sheer spectacle of it awed us and Helga photographed everything that wooed her eye. When we'd reached the far eastern end of the valley Lizzy suggested that we rest and eat. Anders remained restless as we did; something was eating at him. After he'd wolfed his snack he took the binoculars and climbed up a small rise to view our surroundings. Moments later he shouted back that there was another trailhead about two hundred yards to the east. Determining it would get us nearer to the ridges, in the far northeastern quadrant; we packed things up and began our ascent.

"It's a bit awkward." Anders declared after fifteen minutes of slipping and sliding.

"Yah it is," Garrett agreed through clenched teeth.

"Captain we should tether ourselves together," Anders suggested. "A fall here might prove fatal."

"I agree, let's do it."

I agreed too with Anders. At least now, if someone lost their footing, they would have the support of the others to pull them back. After tying each person together, at eight foot intervals, we climbed up one of the steepest inclines we'd ever attempted. I realized that without the training regimen we'd been disciplined to and the superb physical shape we were in that we could never have handled these kinds of rigorous climbs.

"I'm convinced the Anasazi didn't come this way." Lizzy muttered between strained breaths. "Going through the pass, and then up this, is not a way they would have taken."

"I agree dear," Jonah answered. "I can't imagine them staying anywhere except in that vale below. But how would they...."

"Not through that stinkin' crack bro," Garrett laughed. "Sheesh, we barely made it through."

"I'm sure there'd be something to indicate that they'd taken this route," I stated.

"You'd think huh?" Garrett shrugged. "Especially since there was so much stuff we found in other places."

"Yah, even underground on Cedros Island," Helga added.

"They didn't pass this way, period, end of story." The Captain stopped, gasping for breath.

"I agree Olaf," Jonah sighed. "No pictographs, no artifacts, not even a stinkin' footprint. It's as if the whole nation disappeared." Jonah's frustration and anger was warranted. Despite what the scrolls from the box said, could it be that the story of the Anasazi and the Vikings had only been a legend?

After finally cresting the ridge we made our way along a cragged spine of loose rock. The route was grueling and tested us severely. Upon gaining the uppermost pinnacle, we found a flattened area where we could finally take off the ropes and rest. The air here was invigorating and refreshing breezes made the once subtle aromas of the sea more pronounced. From this vantage we were able to view the great underground sea clearly in the far distance.

"Wow, look at that thing; it's huge!" John stared in awe. From horizon to horizon the sea stretched out as far as the eye could see.

"I wonder if we'll ever be there again." Helga pondered fretfully.

"Who knows sissy," Garrett shrugged. "It's in God's hands, right boss?"

"Yeah, He opened this door. We have to keep our faith Helga and press on towards the goal." The Captain encouraged her.

"And do we know for sure what that is?" Anders murmured.

"We're going *that* way Anders," Jonah pointed east with a half-hearted smile, "I'm sure we'll know soon enough what our goal is."

After a needed rest, nourishment, and some last pictures of the panorama, we began our descent down through a rocky watershed towards another valley in the far distance.

Rolf had been restless since we'd left the ridge. He'd been yapping and sniffing everything and he was exhibiting an unusual kind of sensitivity that none of us had ever witnessed before. As far as we could tell it seemed he was concerned now about losing sight of us. It was an endearing quirk that would prompt him, about every ten minutes, to stop what he was doing and bark back vigorously at us for attention. And only after one of us had responded to him, yelling or waving or whistling, was he released to resume exploring with his unbridled lack of restraint. It was a welcome and light moment in the day that made us all laugh.

After we'd trekked twelve miles more, and shadows had begun lengthening, Lizzy suggested we stop for the night; physical rigors were wearing heavily and her feet were throbbing. After the Captain gave his nod everyone was suddenly exhausted. Ten yards to the south of us I could see a small brook was flowing into a large clean pond. Knowing that we couldn't find a better place to sleep for the night, Captain Olaf suggested that we take a swim to relax, and wash off the dirt of the avalanche.

"I'm totally down!" Garrett stripped down to his boxers and then dove into the pool.

"How is it son?" The Captain inquired at water's edge.

"Like heaven boss," Garrett answered floating on his back.

The rest of us soon waded in to join Garrett. The water was clear and cool and the bottom was sandy. Rolf cautiously approached the water's edge and yapped to get someone's attention. When he got none he shook vigorously and then, after easing in, he began dog-paddling around us as regally as the canine king of Siam. Rolf's chesty attitude miffed Garrett so he dove on top of him and dragged him underwater. When both of them burst back to the surface, yelling and barking, Rolf feigned indignation and went back ashore where he began chasing his tail. Garrett began taunting him. Suddenly turning back Rolf lunged at Garrett's chest and forced him underwater with his paws. When Garrett resurfaced he was incensed at being caught off guard and a fight began between them. Back and forth they went, yelling and barking at each other, and after some hilarious water fights, between them and the rest of the crew, Captain suggested we set up camp and get dinner prepared. Everyone agreed.

Near the southern end of the pond the ground was sandy and level and also dappled with great tufts of the same willowy grass we'd seen along the great sea; it seemed an ideal spot for the night. When we'd donned fresh clothes and the others had been washed and hung out to dry, when the tents had been set up and a fire was crackling noisily, when chores were done and food was simmering, then all of us reclined together comfortably near the fire to drink freshly brewed coffee. It had been quite a day.

As we ate we mulled the curious topography. The mountains here were inundated with anomalies, topographical irregularities, and a superabundance of mystifying flora that resisted classification. Near the pond, out a hundred yards in either direction, were dozens of stony mounds dappled with exotic violet colored flowers drooping on long black stems. The steep cliffs, further out, were overhung with twisted growth resembling dwarf-pines. But these had long snakelike growths curling down together in dense mats on the ground; it was bizarre. Anders mentioned that never had he seen any birds, animals, snakes, or fish during the day; not even ants or flying insects. His astute observation astonished us because none of us had even taken note of this fact. Considering that so much life abounded in, and along the shores of, the great sea, I found it hard to believe there was nothing here at all. After dinner Rorek and Olaf exchanged updates on the radio and then we bid one other goodnight. Rolf chose my tent this evening to sleep in and, after licking my face, he lay down and rolled over on his back. Soon both of us had drifted off.

Twenty-Three

Was This the Entrance to Hell?

6 am

It was peaceful this morning and the pond appeared as a piece of glass surrounded by a halo of white mist. Humming softly, Helga was serving steaming coffee to the early-birds reclining near the crackling fire. Despite being fully rested I felt nagged by a strange melancholy and wanted to go back to sleep. Somehow Anders sensed what I was going through and was empathetic. Hunkering down near me I could see his soft blue eyes radiating wisdom and concern.

"Little brother," he began, "no matter how you feel, or how futile

it seems, we have to stay focused on what the Spirit has called us
to do. We have to stay focused on our responsibilities, and to one
another's needs, and on what must be accomplished, and we have to
pray together, I'm thinking, a lot more often. You know, there will
always be wars that rage, Gabriel, inside us, they're not uncommon;
everyone struggles in one way or another. Hey dude, when you feel
blue, share it, and we'll pray. He'll never leave us or forsake us man.
I believe that with all my heart little brother." Anders concern for me
was unwarranted and I felt embarrassed that a warrior of his skill, and
a man of his intelligence, could actually care enough to be interested
in my struggles. His advice this morning imparted vitality to me, and
it was his spot on reasoning that set my mind and body into motion
once again and helped me to refocus on what needed to be done.

"Thanks Norse, I needed to hear that."

"No problem Doc," he nodded, "and you know that I always got
your back don't ya?"

"Oh yah dude," Garrett laughed before I could answer. "And
make sure that he don't snatch your wallet while he's back there."

"OK butthead, one for you," Anders shot back smiling.

I recalled that day Anders had first seen the Tempest aboard the
Heimdall, and he'd realized that I'd been given a special calling. From
that moment on he'd been a good friend to me, an inducement, and
even a protector, and I respected him with all my heart. He'd also been
given insight into my complicated nature and would never hesitate
to offer encouragement when I needed it. Anders was the kind of
friend that I had always dreamed of having my whole life. A living

example, remarkably skilled, intelligent, and someone I could learn from. It seemed, at precisely the right moment, there was something from him that always helped clear up my momentary lapses. When he stood to leave I jumped up and gave him a big bear hug.

"Thanks brother," I said aloud, "I love you man!"

"Dude, when did you get so strong?" He groaned with a sly smile and a wink. "I think you cracked one a' my ribs."

"Lizzeeeeeee...," Garrett wailed, "Anders needs a body cast."

7:30am

Following breakfast we broke camp and, after the fire had been extinguished and buried, we departed in single file.

11am

For the last hour I'd been trying to make sense of all the thoughts that were bombarding me; it was like a swarm of bees buzzing noisily in my brain. When it had reached a kind of fever pitch something quite unexpected happened that completely disarmed my pitiable frame of mind. I was given a revelation. No matter who we were as individuals, or what we'd accomplished, or how intelligent or gifted we were, humans were nothing more than an augmentation of the dust and wholly dependent on the Most High Creator for every heartbeat and breath. This gripped me in its irrevocable simplicity. Even before birth God had known us and, in His omniscience, had seen whether or not we would embrace the Christ or reject Him. He saw every minute detail of our lives, before they happened, and every foolish blunder we would ever make, and still He loved us and held out His hand to us with salvation, and hope, and grace, and a plan for our lives. Scripture established resolutely that He would never leave or forsake the ones that accepted Him, (as Anders had mentioned earlier) and that He was faithful to complete the good work that He'd begun in our lives, no matter how many bad choices we'd made, and no matter how many times we'd fallen, until that day when we would be presented spotless to the Father in heaven. This understanding changed me. Now instead of judging everything in light of my own intellect, I was filled with a sense of awe and humility for the gifts that I'd been given and began praising Christ in my spirit for loving me, and giving me purpose, and freewill, and also because He had made me part of His grand and eternal plan. Within minutes my selfish attitude vanished and I was pressing forward again eagerly with joy and resolve towards the uncertain goal that lay before us.

1:20pm

Sadly the joy of my revelation was short-lived. Our path had changed again. After traversing another mountainous spine we were forced to descend along a series of switchbacks. Eventually this route brought us down into a gorge beetled with oppressive shadows. It was horrid here and the ladies began complaining.

"Let's pray," Anders suggested strongly and motioned for us to gather together. Afterwards, being bolstered, we continued into the ominous environs. After several hundred yards sunlight diminished to a ghostly grayish glow and all plant life and streams vanished entirely. But this wasn't the worst of it. The temperature now had increased from a pleasant seventy-five degrees to a steamy one hundred and twenty degrees plus. It was as if we'd stepped into a sauna. Within minutes all of us were coughing, irritated, and dripping with sweat. Jonah and Olaf began bickering about the Troth religion and why Anders cousins, Ulrik and Gudrun Bjornson, had never returned from their battle with the Mortiken. Garrett was playing his invisible drums in wild fitful vocalizations and had separated himself from us. Just in front of me Rolf was nipping at his tail incessantly as if an irksome swarm of insects were buzzing around him. John was several yards behind me mumbling about the Bay of Biscay and the deviling dive he'd done on the Shallows of Three Rocks. Just behind John, Lizzy and Helga were complaining about leg cramps and how difficult their hair was going to be to manage in this horrid heat. With pain stabbing at my neck, and sweat stinging my eyes, I had to bite my tongue to keep from joining in with the others. Somehow I was being drawn to Anders. He was at the head of the procession humming some melody as though nothing at all strange was happening. I could see that he had tied his waist length hair into a bun on the back of his head, and that he'd wrapped a wet handkerchief around his neck.

"Does that help?" I asked him. Turning he nodded yes and then suggested that we follow his example. We did.

Monotonously the day wore on and, despite the relief from the wet handkerchiefs; the sweltering heat caused us all to feel as if we were drugged. After descending another mile or so we came into a box canyon strewn with boulders and a honey-comb of caves.

"Now what are we going to do Olaf?" Lizzy lamented.

The Captain shook his head, as if unsure himself. For the longest time no one said a word. I sensed that each was struggling with their own fears. Jonah suggested finally that we pray. When we'd finished the Captain pointed at the largest of the entrances and said: "OK, we'll enter here then. What are your thoughts Anders?"

"No other options Captain, I agree." Anders responded stoically.

"John what do you think?"

"I agree too sir! I'll get the lanterns ready. We should have our weapons loaded; never know."

"Yes," the Captains eyes lit up as he readied his 357.

We entered into the most prominent of the openings. Once inside it became evident that there was nothing but an oppressive soundless gloom and unperturbed sand.

"No one's been here before," Garrett declared staunchly.

"I know son," the Captain murmured, "no one!"

"We're the first boss, and we'll be the last too."

"I know son!"

"Stinkin' caves, I hate um," Garrett grumbled.

After traversing near a hundred yards, we entered into a vast antechamber that all the other tunnels funneled into.

"Oh lord Olaf, now what?" Lizzy gasped.

"I guess it wouldn't a' mattered which one we'd taken huh Cap?" Garrett asked while scratching his head.

"Looks that way son," he answered.

Despite the gnawing in me I realized that there *was* a blessing for us here in the antechamber; the temperature was at least fifty degrees cooler than in the tunnels.

"Hey, where's the air conditioner?" Garrett laughed.

"This *is* nice Olaf," the ladies cooed. "Can we rest a spell?"

"Sure," the Captain agreed, "and how about we have a little something to eat too."

"Yeah I'm down," Garrett laughed, "me first! I need my strength cause I'll probably havta' save all yur sorry butts by the end of the day." Garrett's humor was badly timed and no one laughed.

"You can help us prepare for the others Garrett," Helga said with a deadpan expression. "And after that *you* can eat!"

"I was only kidding," Garrett shot back in defense.

"Do as she says son," the Captain ordered softly.

Garrett assisted the ladies with the preparations and then, afterwards, he ate by himself with a scowl on his face; I knew he wasn't angry with anyone except himself. The meal was delicious. Canned pork, canned bread, canned peaches, water, and the cool temperature raised our spirits. When we'd finished we made our way gingerly into the larger tunnel on the far side of the chamber and continued on. The walls were striated and coarse here and several times our progress was inhibited by piles of rock on the floor that had been exuviated from the ceiling. But even though our progress, through a pitch black tunnel, was tedious no one lost their composure. Finally we emerged onto a narrow rocky precipice; I couldn't believe my eyes. Rolf began howling pitiably and the ladies began to weep. Nothing could have prepared us for this.

"Is this the entrance to Hell?" Garrett cried out.

The murmuring began fueling my own apprehensions. Being convinced that Garrett's question was worthy of consideration; I stared out at the fate of us all. For some reason a thesis I'd written years ago in college on *The Inferno of Dante Alighieri* came to mind. The ninth line from Canto III could easily have been a signpost at this very juncture: ABANDON EVERY HOPE, YOU WHO ENTER!

Twenty-Four

Dante's Valley

Smoke was billowing up through enormous gaping fissures in the granite floor. The atmosphere was strongly tainted with sulfur dioxide and surface light was diminished, by half at least, from the two large holes in the north and west. There were dozens of menacing peaks, freakish rock formations, steaming cauldrons, and the reddened luminescence of lava streams everywhere. It was as nightmarish as anything I'd ever seen. We were facing challenges now never before imagined. On edge, we huddled together to reconnoiter and Anders suggested we pray. Jonah and Anders began praying in tongues and the rest of us sought the Spirit for direction and wisdom; we were ready for anything that God would give us to help uproot this gnawing in our guts. After, feeling clear-headed and focused, we refreshed ourselves with water and dried fruit and then girded our hearts with resoluteness for what must be done.

"Let's do this," Captain murmured as he cinched his pack tight. "Make sure your weapons are loaded and ready."

With watchful prudence we guardedly made our way down into the area that I had now coined *Dante's Valley.*

Hours later

The air was oppressive and, for several miles now, we'd been traversing a shadowy lifeless landscape and staying in sight of one another for any eventuality that may arise. Rolf was uneasy. Often, when I would stop to view our surroundings through the binoculars, I could see him behind us wandering back and forth, sniffing and growling, and then stopping at times to stare blankly. Did he smell danger? Seeming to sense my concern he approached me and, after nuzzling my hand, he barked several times and then resumed the same odd behavior.

"I'm worried about Rolf," I began sharing with the Captain; "he's been acting out of character sir; strange even. I can't help feeling that something evil may be approaching us. Perhaps we should prepare ourselves just in case?"

"Little brothers got a point sir," Anders agreed.

"Alright, we'll check it out. John, you and Anders pull up the rear with the hound;" The Captain ordered, "use the binoculars and let me know if you see anything unusual."

"Aye sir, we'll keep an eye out." John answered.

There was a curious weather pattern occurring here regularly that we'd noticed. In an effort to establish a sound explanation Jonah brought our attention to the gaping holes in the rock cliffs around us. He was convinced they acted as air ducts. For twenty minutes every hour, either from the surface or from the great sea, cool air blew briskly through the valley. Because these breezes boosted our morale, and helped bolster our waning resolve to press on, I wondered if God, in His infinite love, hadn't sent angels along with these winds to sooth us and to give us hope. The change was magnificent and encouraged us all to dance and lift up a joyful noise together, but how peculiar we must have appeared.

Wearily the day dragged on. As we were discovering the most challenging obstacles were the lava cauldrons. The sulfur smell was oppressive. Everywhere around us, flowing from fissures in the rock walls, streams of reddish molten lava were being swallowed back down along fractures in the floor. At times they were so enormous, and the temperature so oppressive, we were forced to circumvent them entirely to stay on our eastern heading.

On one of these detours we stumbled upon the remains of an antediluvian creature that we'd become familiar with. Because it was similar in appearance to the skeleton we'd discovered near the estuary on the great sea, weeks before, we were able to finally extrapolate a working hypothesis that made some sense. Helga photographed the remains from different angles and then up-loaded the files to the SES to be analyzed. Minutes later Betsy confirmed receiving the files. Since there was nothing to help us determine what the creature had died from, we came to the conclusion, after considering the pale color of the bones, that it had been dead for a minimum of two years.

"It's a bit odd don't you think?" Helga mused.

"What's that honey?" John answered.

"Why an animal this size would wander so far from food and water. I mean look around, there's nothing to eat here; it's a wasteland!"

"Yeah it *is* a bit odd!" Jonah's eyes burned with inquisitiveness. "Why in the world would it be here at all?"

"Unless there *was* sustenance here at one time I can't imagine why it would be in such a forsaken place." Anders opined.

"Perhaps it left the larger herd and came here to die!" I suggested.

Olaf's brow tightened and he began pulling on his thick moustache.

"If that's true Gabriel, I wonder where the larger herd could be presently. Near – far?"

"There's no way of knowing Captain. We have to consider that parts of the realm *may* be inhabited by herds of dinosaurs."

"Wow! Now that's a thought," Garrett said.

"Is it possible Gabriel?"

"I'm convinced Captain – the evidence supports it."

"I'll agree with Doc." Anders eyes shone brightly.

"Yeah but *why* are they here, and from where?" Lizzy pondered.

"Who knows," Garrett shrugged. "I told you we're gonna end up being dinosaur hunters on this stinkin' trip."

Rolf began growling. Then his agitation got fierce and the hackles went up all along his back. Without a word we prepared our weapons and backed together in a circle.

"Easy boy," I began massaging his neck. "Is something coming?" Rolf barked once sharply.

"Alright, good boy; keep an eye out for us ok?"

Rolf barked again, this time in a lower more relaxed tone. After another hug he continued crisscrossing back and forth in front of us and scanning the horizon. With mounting uneasiness we re-holstered our weapons and continued on through the rocks and fissures.

Later

"Captain how are we going to do this," I blurted. "How can we continue on when it's so hot and we know nothing about where we're going to end up?"

"It *is* oppressive Olaf," Jonah added. "I'm sweating more than I have in a long while, and these packs feel like they weigh a ton."

"They sure do," Helga groaned while adjusting her straps.

"I'm frustrated too folks. Believe me I don't have any answers or a magic wand I can wave. We just have to be patient."

"We should take salt tablets, Olaf, and try wrapping moist kerchiefs around our nose and mouth." Lizzy suggested.

"A good idea," Jonah agreed. "It'll keep the pollutants out of our system and maybe even help with the coughing too!"

"Excellent! Did someone bring eye-drops?"

"I did Olaf!" Helga answered.

"I could use some lass; my eyes are on fire."

"They're at the bottom of my pack, hold on a minute."

"Let's break then and stretch; the winds are due again soon."

"Right on boss; how about a snack Liz," Garrett grinned. "I'll help you guys prepare it if you want."

"Sounds good honey . . . Olaf?"

"Serve it up!" The Captain nodded. "I'm sure that Rolf could use some food and water too, poor guy looks beat."

"Hear that bubba?" Garrett threw a small rock at him. Rolf barked and then pounced at Garrett's chest with both paws and knocked him backwards.

"You wanna piece 'a me you fur-ball butthead?" Garrett roared back as he jumped on Rolf's back. Down they went wrestling.

"GARRETT," Captain Olaf barked, "save your energy!"

"OK boss," Garrett shouted up from the blur of body and fur.

"Another thing Captain; we can sprinkle water on our clothes," John suggested, "It'll help diffuse the heat."

"How much do we have?"

"We have just under twenty-three gallons." Lizzy calculated.

"Well then … does everyone agree?"

"Yeah boss I do!" Garrett jumped up when he'd pushed Rolf off his face. "We need to stay cooler, that's a fact!"

"I agree with little brother Captain," Anders winked. I could see that he had a twinkle in his eye. "And if this doesn't work for us, then I suppose the only other option is turning back."

"WHAT!" Lizzy spun around flabbergasted, "After coming this far? Young man that is certainly out of the question, I don't care how bad we feel, we are *not* turning back!"

"Certainly not," Helga huffed indignantly.

"Guys I was only kidding!" Anders shrugged awkwardly.

Soaking our shirts helped and, after eating, we continued on eastward. Along the way the lava cauldrons slowly vanished, the terrain became less bizarre, and the temperature began cooling. After descending through a steep series of switchbacks we came to a dry watershed. The old stream bed here was smooth stones and fine sand and the temperature was even cooler than just an hour before. It was a blessing beyond belief. After sniffing everything, and barking up at the steep cliffs, Rolf found a spot and burrowed down into the cool sand. Moments later he had fallen asleep. The Captain suggested we take an example and was the first to drop everything and lay down.

"This feels great," he groaned as he rolled on his side. "I'm gonna take a short nap." Laughing, all of us did the same.

Upon awakening it was pitch black. With all the lanterns lit and dispersed, Garrett and Anders went off in search of firewood and the rest of us set up camp. Soon they'd returned with armfuls of brush and then went out again several more times along the ravine to build up our supply. Within minutes a fire was crackling and the ladies had begun preparing for the evening meal. Both were singing. Everything sounded richly resonant and pleasing here. The high arching granite walls, around us, were acting like a movie screen and I watched spellbound as the undulating orange reflections of the fire danced above and around me like ghostly apparitions. I recalled the raft trip we'd taken into the Pontevedra Province and the night we'd stuffed ourselves with all the yellow perch John and Helga had caught in the bay. What a magical time that'd been. I was convinced that Captain had been correct in his assertion earlier; we *were* obligated before God, and to one another, to finish what we'd begun, no matter how we felt or how difficult it might become. Maybe now the worst of this trek was over and we would find our mysterious goal tomorrow. Perhaps we were closer than we knew and all this would end up making sense sometime soon. Though we hadn't discussed it much, I was convinced, deep inside, that none of us believed anymore that we were going to find a hidden city out here. I was convinced we were here for another reason, and whatever that was would be disclosed in Gods time. What we needed was continued patience and unity and faith to finish our course. Being alive and healthy and eager to press forward gave me a burst of hope as I ate the delightful meal the ladies had so thoughtfully and lovingly prepared. Tonight the camaraderie between us was excellent. And after contacting Rorek with updates, and praying together, everyone hugged and quietly retired.

Twenty-Five

On the Third Day

5:50am

This morning my body was languishing in a dull throbbing ache. The hard ground was taking its toll on me. Thankfully I remembered the breathing and stretching regimen Anders had taught me, last year, to rid the body of nagging pain. Within minutes I had loosened up and was flexible again. Since the pain was gone, and my mental processes had cleared, I was able to focus now on stoking the fire and making a pot of coffee. Around me a chastened glow brooded; the campsite and surrounding areas were still. The others rolled out sometime later and joined me near a warm fire crackling noisily. Smiles were exchanged but not a word was said; it seemed all anyone needed this morning was the steaming elixir of life. Draggled and droopy-headed Rolf rolled out last and laid his head on my lap. Soon he had fallen asleep again. While basking quietly in the unperturbed stillness, immersed in the cool air, drifting peacefully in our own thoughts, a sudden burst of brilliant sunlight inundated the ravine from the hole above us.

"Man, look at that!" Garrett was the first to cry out.

It was resplendent, as if heaven had opened a portal and was greeting us personally. Within seconds the suns warmth began dissipating the ground mists hovering along the canyon floor. We watched enchanted as reddish golden hues swept out like an artist's brushstrokes on the bleak granite walls. Erupting gloriously around us these myriad colorations transformed the once barren ravine into a fine pastel impressionism. When the wash of colors had evanesced, we breakfasted on our morning ration of canned pork, biscuits, raisins, and water. Afterwards, taking stock of what remained; we found we had provisions for eight days and seventeen gallons of water. Our most pressing concern now was running out of water before a new source had been located. At our present rate of consumption, barring any emergencies or changes in temperature, enough remained for four more days.

So we pressed forward carefully, taking no chances, and always keeping an eye out for one another. An hour or so after we'd left the campsite I began experiencing problems; my left foot had begun throbbing, one of my eyes was weeping, my stomach was queasy, I had a headache, and my thoughts were being gripped, once again, by a host of powerful uncertainties. These were so draining this time that I began to question the sagacity of my cohorts, what their intentions were, and what they might do to me if things ever really got bad out here. Was it some kind of mental illness? In stark utter despair I finally cried out: *Most High God, please help me rise above my many fears and this horrid creepy madness in my brain. Please help me understand where you have us now. Please, I can't do this without you; none of us can! Holy Spirit I need your wisdom, and peace, and your understanding, and I desperately need a touch from you!*

In an instant there came to my mind the many miracles we'd experienced so far on the journey and also the victories we'd been given against the Mortiken. I remembered the encounter we'd had with the fatman and his protégé; I remembered Garrett and me finding the Rognvald settlement in the Pontevedra from the high promontory; I remembered the time when we had almost died in the river on the rubber raft; I remembered the time we'd made it through the fearsome storm on the way to the Madeira Islands; I remembered the challenges we'd overcome crossing the Atlantic Ocean and I remembered, in alarming detail, the bizarre Red Dragon incident in Scammon's Lagoon where we'd been witness to the depraved depths of human madness. I was shocked by the realness of these thoughts and realized that not in any of these dreadful incidents had we been destroyed or lessened! Was this present challenge any different than those had been? God had brought us through all these, seemingly, impossible situations alive, and stronger, and more unified as a team, and we were all still pressing forward together in faith. I was stunned with what was happening, how it was affecting me, how it was changing me. In a moment I felt empowered and my thoughts became lucid and loving once again. The Holy Spirit was never late; He was perfectly on time in all things. We *weren't* going to run out of water, or food, and we *weren't* going to kill each other. How foolish I'd been to let myself be consumed by such notions. As I was rejoicing a sudden light bathed my mind in a profoundly consuming peace; I somehow knew that Christ would *never* abandon us down here. Never would He leave us or forsake us, and how often this had been brought to my awareness's since we'd begun this trek. We were here for a reason, and He was going to help us fulfill what that reason was. After grasping this with both hands I felt a surge of appreciation for what the Holy Spirit was doing in our lives and I began to sing. Something extraordinary happened then. Ahead of me Garrett was pointing east and blubbering wildly.

"WOW! Oh man, can you believe it," He cried out in a kind of rapture. "Look at that place!"

"Oh Lord," Lizzy was weeping; "We've found paradise."

In the distance sunlight was illuming a verdant topography. An enormous body of water was prominent on the far end of the valley, and there were several waterfalls cascading down from the enormous granite dome; it was a breathtaking sight. I could see the greenish tinges of flora around the water, and verdant trees were widespread throughout the outlying hills; it was like a mountainous paradise. There was nowhere else to go now; we could see the end of the realm in the distance. Had we come to the end of our trek? Filled with wonder and joy Jonah prayed and then we all sang a song together. As we were another energizing breeze picked up along the ridges, it was like a sign and it gripped us all with an overwhelming emotion.

According to the Captain and Lizzy's calculations we'd covered nearly forty miles since departing the great sea and had climbed, overall, seventeen hundred feet in elevation.

"Where do you think we are now Olaf," Helga asked.

"About eight hundred feet from the surface," the Captain replied after pocketing his calculator. "But I don't have a clue where we are in relationship to the surface."

"Rorek can help with that," Lizzy reminded him.

"Yah boss he can use the VEW program to pinpoint where we are with the GPS in Gabriel's laptop," Garrett continued Lizzy's thoughts.

"It's a great idea! Contact Rorek Gabriel and ask him to figure out where we are."

"I'll let you know as soon as I have something."

"Another thing Olaf," Lizzy pointed towards the valley, "I'm thinking that lake could be an ancient caldera."

"A caldera you say?" Olaf turned inquisitively.

"You mean like Crater Lake?" Garrett moved closer.

"Yes I do honey, that's right!"

"What exactly does that mean to us Liz?" Jonah asked.

"I don't know yet Jonah, I just have a funny feeling about it!"

"Oh great," Garrett kicked the dirt, "another funny feeling."

After passing over the spine of the ridge, we stopped on another plateau to rest. Before us a panorama of colors and irregular shapes stretched out as far as we could see. To get a general feeling of the topography John scanned the mountainside and surrounding areas with the binoculars.

"Captain, look there," he pointed at an obtuse fracture in the crumbling granite wall. "There's no traversable path down to the valley anywhere in my field of vision sir."

His report was humbling. After chasing his tail momentarily, Rolf howled and lay down. Descent would require ropes and climbing gear but we had none. As we were pondering our predicament the radios crackled noisily. It was Rorek, and he was very keyed up.

"Olaf, do you copy, *do* you copy, come back!"

Twenty-Six

A New Satellite Algorithm

"It's good to hear you," Olaf roared heartily. "You will not believe what we're looking at you old salt dog."

"Oh I think I might you young whip," Rorek returned dryly. "We can see a good part of the area that you're going into now."

"How?" the Captain asked inquiringly.

"We're looking at it on the VEW. We've been doing a pretty business here since you folks left. These girls are something else."

"Get to the point!" Olaf demanded impatiently.

"Aye then, here it is. Betsy and Angelina had a brainstorm before we sailed for Himminglaeva. They developed an algorithm that lets us peer down into the great holes. I decided to up-load the information to the professor to get his opinion. He contacted us within the hour Olaf; the man was beside himself. His engineers were so impressed that they developed the bloody software within twenty-four hours."

"Wow!" The Captain pulled at his moustache thoughtfully.

"Rorek its fantastic news, how does it work?"

"Gabriel I'm not a scientist. But as I understand it, the professor decided to use those big gigapixel cameras aboard the GRACE 2 satellites instead of taking a bunch of pictures with the wide angle lens and stitching them together for the visual information. The resolution will allow these cameras to capture images at up to 50 centimeters per pixel from five miles up. The new software has given him the ability to recalibrate the cameras with specific input. I can't explain it any better than that mate."

"It's so cool, I'm blown away Rorek!" I exclaimed.

"It is amazing Gabriel! Now, here's a bit more of what I know. Based on what's entered, the VEW will pinpoint those very same coordinates. When the satellites are in position it begins taking pictures automatically, twelve frames per second, until the target has been passed. The moment the process begins the user is alerted. That way they can watch what's happening in real time or view it all at a later date. It's a short window though, because of the speed the satellites are moving at, but still we can get anywhere from thirty to ninety seconds of video depending on the size of the hole. Another thing … even if we're not on the vessels we can still access the information on the handhelds."

"Now that's convenient! Can we make use of the program from this locale here?"

"Yes! It's a simple download Gabriel, and you can access it on your mobile phone or laptop from the address we're sending. Here it is:" profrabat@earthnet.net/VEW/algorithm/tkholes

"Most excellent, you guys are making positive strides over there." The Captain praised his brother.

"We are brother, thank-you! I'm very pleased!"

"Rorek what exactly are we seeing here in the distance?"

"It looks like you're on the last precipice overlooking the Caldera Vale, is this correct?"

"Yes! How do you know?"

"The PMRI; we're less than twenty miles from you, as the crow flies, so it's working well. We can see all of you on that ledge."

"You said Caldera Vale?" Olaf's eyes widened.

"A name Betsy gave it. I think it's appropriate don't you?"

"I do as a matter of fact, it's great!"

"Alright then, here's what we know about Hidden Valley. Betsy came up with that name for our records too. Anyway, the hole over the caldera is enormous, biggest one yet. The plant life and water is abundant down inside the area and nearer where you are we've seen the outer edges of a large bog."

"We can see the lake and the bog clearly Rorek." The Captain concurred. "Is there something about it we need to know?"

"No one knows anything. Everything points at it being part of the ancient caldera though."

"I knew it!" Lizzy beamed with satisfaction.

"We've corroborated that the great sea was once a massive lava chamber. And the holes that bring atmosphere down into the realm were once magma vents that channeled lava to the surface. I never realized how geologically active Utah and northern Arizona really were in the past. The caldera apparently collapsed into this smaller magma chamber, adjoining the great sea chamber, and created quite a unique anomaly. That valley is one of a kind; nothing like it exists anywhere on the planet. You may be encountering some pretty bizarre stuff when you get down there."

"Do you have any idea how big the area is Rorek?"

"About fifty by seventy miles, and just north of you the Green River has a tributary that disappears underground half a mile from the hole, and the Colorado River also has a tributary nearby that disappears underground about five miles northeast. We can see the Green River tributary emptying into the area you're in now."

"Green River eh, I haven't heard of that one."

"It starts somewhere in western Wyoming and flows southward down through Utah and becomes a tributary to the Colorado River."

"So where are we then?" The Captain asked.

"You're near the Dixie National Forest." Rorek answered.

"That's interesting! And where are you and the ladies?"

"We've been in Himminglaeva for two days."

"And what did you do with the other SES?"

"We've brought it along with us of course."

"What? … How did you do that?"

"I learned how to operate both vessels from one control computer. And Olaf, I can assure you that you guys will *not* be returning the same route you came by!"

"What are you proposing?"

"The Eastern Mountains are riddled with volcanic activity and, according to the professor; the whole area is becoming unstable at an accelerated rate. Something geological is happening."

"Whataya' mean by unstable boss?"Garrett looked troubled.

"Just that son, the area could come apart at any moment. I guess there's major pressure building up in the Pacific plate; so much so that the ground has begun to deform on the surface in certain areas; they're expecting something big at any time."

"Oh great," Garrett moaned. "Is there a bus stop somewhere near?

"Rorek, how are we going to get back to you?"

"You won't have to. We'll rendezvous with you in several days. The GRACE 2 readouts have shown us that the caldera is connected to a vast underground labyrinth filled with water, which includes Crater Lake in Oregon; they're both part of the same underground system. We'll be able to explain in more depth when we reach you. I'm sure you'll understand better then."

"Better understand what Rorek?" The Captain sounded perplexed. "Please tell me something we can chew on!"

Twenty-Seven

Shocking Discovery's

"Alright then," Rorek cleared his throat. "There's a labyrinth of passages between Himminglaeva and that crater in the distance. We'll be navigating through a series of flooded caverns and passageways. The SES can get through easily; don't foresee any difficulty; they're all large and free-flowing. If all goes well we'll be in the Caldera in three days to pick you up."

"That's amazing Rorek," Anders muttered.

"It is Anders; GRACE 2 discovered the route two days ago."

"Sheesh man, those satellites are savin' our butts." Garrett laughed.

"They are indeed son," Rorek returned.

"How deep are we talking brother?" Olaf asked.

"The farthest we'll be down is seven thousand feet."

"It sounds challenging."

"Yah, and scary too," Garrett gesticulated.

"It's not going to be all that bad, no one needs to worry. The professor uploaded coordinates into the navigational computer yesterday. Until we actually enter the caldera everything will be automated. He also sent us a virtual presentation to view. Believe me; we'll be fine as long as our link with the satellite stays stable. We're planning on leaving here in the morning."

"What about communications," The Captain asked.

"Aye, no problems, we've been communicating with the professor every day since you departed; he's ten thousand miles away, and we're three thousand feet underground; it's clear as a bell."

"Thank God for that!" Olaf sighed.

"What *is* Himminglaeva exactly?" Jonah asked.

"It appears to have been a prison system in recent times."

"Like Blindvidr?" Helga asked.

"Similar, but on a bigger scale," Rorek answered.

"You mean no mystic warriors or giants?" Jonah chuckled.

"No my friend, it's just a graveyard now. We went ashore the afternoon of the eleventh to investigate; not at all what we expected.

We found burned structures, old weapons, skeletons, just a mess. From what we can tell the settlement was attacked from the East."

"Seems the dissenters were correct, the Kings spin-doctors were just doing their job;" Lizzy laughed, "just an off-colony for riff-raff eh?"

"Aye lass, there's no evidence to disprove it." Rorek answered.

"Have you determined a timeline for the massacre?"

"The ladies took different samples around the site to analyze Olaf. They're convinced it happened only a year ago. But there's something else, too, we found that symbol again."

"The helmet and sword over a shield," Anders asked keenly.

"Aye, the very same Norse! We found it carved twice on a bluff overlooking the settlement."

"Now what do you suppose it could mean?" Helga questioned.

"Probably that the First Tribe was there at some point in the past," Garrett contended.

"Can't prove it, but aye, we believe so and so does the professor. There's another thing Olaf."

"There's more?"

"Aye, several things actually, Roxanne found a copper cylinder in the settlement. It was hidden away in a shallow cave; can't believe our luck. We found two more parchments; well preserved too. She's going to interpret them on our way to you."

"We'll be interested to hear what they reveal."

"We found evidence the Baaldurians were here too Olaf."

"Ach … wouldn't ya' know it!"

All of us were huddled near Captain now listening intently.

"They were there for sure," Rorek confirmed angrily. "We found talismans exactly the same as the one Gabriel found that night aboard the *Heimdall*. There were war clubs, too, and the remains of at least a dozen bodies. Four of them Baaldurian for sure; Roxanne measured them at seven to nine feet."

"Clear evidence I'd say," Olaf murmured.

"Who was fighting whom Rorek?" Anders asked.

"We're unsure about that."

"Perhaps a faction from Torfar-Kolla," Jonah pondered.

"Could be, maybe," Rorek sounded unsure.

"Hey, didn't chubby tell us there was no Mortiken activity in the underground realm?" Garrett blurted angrily.

"As far as we know there is none;" Rorek replied, "right now anyway. But according to what we found, there was recently, and it was violent too."

"Where did they come in from?" Lizzy asked.

"No one knows for sure dear!"

"Is it possible then that Arnora's story about Queen Brynhild rendezvousing with Krystal Blackeyes was true?" Helga puzzled.

"I'm finding some credence in it." Rorek answered.

"Can you speculate where they may have entered and why they're even down here?" The Captain asked.

"I can't, but the Professor suggested they may be in the process of invading the realm to set up a stronghold."

"Could that be in Torfar-Kolla maybe?"

"No brother, not there!"

"Well, where then?!"

"Perhaps farther West; the professor has a group of personal operatives investigating at present but nothings for sure yet. They're the ones that have been with him since he started the GVIN. They're speculating the scum may have used an entrance hidden in the Grand Canyon, but no one knows for . . ."

"I remember that," Jonah interrupted. "Just after returning from Lake Powell last year I remember him telling us that the Mortiken had infiltrated up the Colorado River past the city of Campo."

"Aye, I remember it too," Rorek answered.

"Apparently the Air Force was involved," Jonah continued, "and there was that media blackout. No one seemed to know anything except the professor. I thought it strange, you know, him knowing so much and everyone else knowing squat. Evidently representatives for the Mortiken were trying to manipulate the policies of the Imperial Dam so they could get into the Grand Canyon."

"It *was* a big deal; I remember that clearly," Rorek replied. "Think it has something to do with this new information Jonah?"

"I'm not sure, but it surely seems coincidental."

"Aye it surely does," Rorek agreed.

"Rorek, the parchments you found, has any of it been interpreted yet?" Olaf asked.

"Some of it has. We'll e-mail what Roxanne's done tomorrow."

"Rorek," Anders finally blurted, "in your opinion what exactly is the bottom line, as far as our journey is concerned?"

"I'm gonna let her explain." Rorek sighed.

"Hi guys! Hi Jonah, I love you all!" For some reason Roxanne's sweet voice rang clear like bells and diffused my frustrations.

"OK then," she continued, "here's what we've discovered on the parchments today. There were two longboats that left Cedros Island and returned to the Sea of Cortez, these boats had Rognvald's aboard that claimed Christ."

"Oh wow! Could it be then that those loyal to Christ and Agar deceived the others somehow?" I suggested with keen interest.

"Yes Gabriel, I believe so and I also believe that this was by design. We're sure now that Ragnarr and Borghild were responsible for the subterfuge."

"Weren't they mentioned on one of the scrolls we found in the tomb on Cedros?" Garrett asked coolly.

"Yes honey they were, on the fifth. Remember Magnus had complained that Ragnarr and Borghild's faith was steadfast and that their words burned inside him. I truly believe that the Holy Spirit used this couple to give Magnus one last chance before his death."

"So Ragnarr and Borghild built Himminglaeva?" Garrett asked.

"Yes honey, great deduction. We're convinced that they were the original architect's. And after the two longboats reached where Torfar-Kolla presently is now the real believers continued on."

"You mean they took one of the longboats and left without the others knowing?" Anders asked with a grin.

"Yes, that's what we believe!" Roxanne returned boldly.

"How cool is that dude!" Garrett slapped high fives with Anders.

"So then," Anders continued, "is it possible then that they migrated back at some point to infiltrate Torfar-Kolla to preach the gospel?"

"Yes, I truly believe that!" Roxanne returned vigorously. "And I commend you dear friend for an equally great deduction."

"They were *missionaries*?" Garrett blurted out.

"Yes honey they were! Himminglaeva was founded as a Christian settlement in the beginning. We believe it was first built and settled by Ragnarr and Borghild and those under their leadership. We're also quite certain now, too, that Torfar-Kolla was first established by those who had embraced Magnus as their leader. The stone you found near the old city was indeed a memorial."

Rolf began growling suddenly and ran ahead of us. Seconds later he was barking frantically at the edge of the precipice and his hair was standing on end. As we neared him the guttural throated bellowing of something ripped through the air.

Twenty-Eight

Saurischians and Sauropods

"Good Lord, what was that?" Lizzy cringed.

"Whatever it was it sounded wicked!" Garrett replied wide-eyed.

"What are we going to do?" Lizzy cried out.

"Yes, what *are* we going to do?" Helga demanded.

All of us stood frozen and undecided, struggling to understand what we were faced with.

"Alright then," Olaf gestured to spread out.

"We're on it sir," John responded with an intuitive nod.

"Gabriel, please keep the dog quiet!"

"I'll try sir," I shrugged with little confidence.

What was emanating from Rolf was beyond guttural; he was as rankled as I ever remember him being. After instructions were given, he whimpered and licked my face. When everyone was in position, the Captain motioned at Jonah to join him; I knew he was concerned and wanted him near.

Once again raging fulminations rent the air. It was a dreadful sound, like tearing fabric, and I was at a loss trying to understand what it was that could be in such a rage.

"Anders, take the point and find out what this is!"

"Aye Captain," he answered curtly. Like a cat, Anders scurried nimbly towards the edge of the precipice.

"Keep your radios on," The Captain whispered tensely.

"Aye sir," everyone chorused with equal apprehension.

"Olaf, do you copy!"

"Copy Rorek . . . go ahead," he whispered.

"Olaf, a herd of dinosaurs just came out of the cliffs north of you a few minutes ago. They're wading in that bog below the precipice; seems they're all feeding from it. I can hardly believe this!"

"Good lord!" the Captain sank down on the ground.

"We can clearly see your position," Rorek continued. "We'll have this connection with the satellite about five minutes more."

"Norseman," the Captains tone had become tenser.

"It's true Captain," Anders waved back. "There *are* dinosaurs down there; must be thirty; some of um big buggers too!"

"Captain, that's not just a swamp then!" I exclaimed.

"I guess not dweeb," Garrett blurted. "Think it might be their stinkin' soup-bowl?"

"It's where they *feed*?" Jonah's expression became comical.

"Yah it just keeps getting weirder don't it?" Garrett gesticulated wildly. "I wonder what's next; flying elephants. Hey maybe the stinkin' mother ship is comin' to sweep us off to Valhalla so we can spend some time killin' boar and sippin' hard cider!"

"GARRETT!' The Captain motioned strongly, "ZIP IT!"

Affected by Garrett's sarcasm, Rolf bounded away; soon he was yelping in frenzied staccato bursts and lunging at the edge.

"KEEP THE DOG QUIET!" Anders roared wild-eyed.

It was too late though; several of the herd spun around.

"Captain they've found a way up to us," Anders pointed tensely.

"How did we miss *that*?" The Captain sputtered frantically. "Rorek, can you see anything?"

"Aye; there's a shallow valley between two lesser peaks, no way to see it from your position. They're maneuvering towards you from the south. Our satellite connection is going gray Olaf. I'm gonna lose you any second! Prepare yourselves and be careful! We're all praying! I'll keep the ra . . ." The radio signal crackled and then went silent.

"Captain, they're moving quickly!" Anders pointed.

"What are they?"

"I have *no* idea," was Anders flabbergasted response.

"Gabriel . . ."

"Sir . . ."

"Do you know what they are?"

"I'll take a look!"

With my heart pounding, and knees wobbling, I stumbled out towards Anders on the precipice. My mind was a blur of thoughts. I missed my room in Aberdeen. I missed Betsy. I missed good food. I missed the SES. I missed the *Heimdall*. I missed any place but here. I wanted away from this place, but the swarm of butterflies in my gut reminded me that what I wanted was well beyond my ability to make happen. After reaching Anders he grabbed my arm and pointed. The breath in my lungs was snatched away momentarily at what I saw.

"I know what these are sir!"

"What are they?" The Captain growled.

"One group is from the order of saurischia and the other is from the sub-order of sauropoda."

"What's that?!" The Captain shot back angrily.

"Saurichians and Sauropods Olaf, they're dinosaurs." Jonah answered laughing. Astonished, he ran towards Anders and me.

"Do you know what this means?"

"YES Jonah, I do!" Lizzy cried out. "These are the same creatures they've sighted out in the Congo for the last hundred years. They're real, they're really real!"

"I know it's bloody awesome!"

"What are we going to do?" Helga was becoming hysterical as the sound of the approaching behemoths gained in intensity.

"Captain, we need a defensive posture," John suggested firmly, "and we need to establish it RIGHT NOW!!!"

With a cursory motion the Captain deferred command to John. After hastily saluting, John roared directions to us with the authority of a battlefield general: "Ladies stay right were you are; Helga, load your rifle; Garrett over there; Olaf right there; Anders, you and Gabriel here in this shallow, Gabriel call Rolf to you; Jonah stay with Olaf; everyone get your weapons ready ... MOVE NOW!"

All scattered and took up their positions. Wisely he had chosen two shallow caves and several giant boulders split asunder where we could hide in sizeable cracks and stay in view of one another. John's impromptu plan rang true. I praised God for his wisdom and recalled in a flash how remarkably he'd been involved when Rolf and I had been swept away on the underground river. The ground, now, was beginning to rumble like an earthquake.

Would this be our last stand?

Were we going to die here today on this forsaken ledge?

Moments later seven prehistoric monsters bolted noisily around a rocky overhang seventy yards to the south of us. The reality was overwhelming and the ladies screamed out in sheer terror.

Twenty-Nine

A Fight for Our Lives

"HOLY CRAP," Garrett recoiled. "Can you believe it?"

"Oh god we're going to die," Lizzy wailed despondently.

"STAY DOWN!" John screamed over the mounting turmoil.

The noise coming from the creatures was like fog horns, and the saturation, in the atmosphere, was overwhelming. It felt like an oppressive cloak, and the pressure pounded my ears ferociously. I was soon shaking, in a wretched kind of despair, and blubbering aloud; how in the world would we ever get out of this? My heart beat wildly, like a war drum, and the expressions of horror on the others faces made my blood curdle. There was no amount of schooling or special training that could ever have prepared us for this moment. It seemed as if we had been transported back in time and, for what seemed an eternity, my mind froze in fear. Because we were powerless against these creatures, (in delirium) I asked Jesus to forgive me for all my sins and to accept me into His kingdom. Out of the corner of my eye I saw and heard Garrett beseeching God with his hands in the air: "Most High Father God give us strength to overcome this. Holy Spirit we need you now, in this very moment, please, we need you to anoint us to overcome this enemy otherwise we're gonna croak!"

In they rushed. Three of them appeared as enormous lizards with gaping alligator jaws; the other four had long necks and tails and a small head with lusting beady eyes. Never confronted with such a thing, and being utterly provoked by them; Rolf leapt fearlessly towards the creatures to do battle.

"Rolfy come back; please come back" Helga wailed tearfully.

John spun around and motioned for all of us to stay calm and to breathe. He was as vexed as I'd ever seen him. No mortal could prevail against this force and all of us knew it. With a kind of grim determination I bolstered myself to meet a gruesome end. Rolf's hair was standing straight up now from the tip of his tail to the crown of his head. For a moment I found his appearance droll; as if he was sporting an enormous Mohawk. Barking and lunging back and forth Rolf taunted the creatures dauntlessly. Something seemed to snap in them, as he did, and then the strangest thing happened. All of them stopped dead in their tracks and stared silently at their vociferous antagonist; how curious Rolf must have seemed to them. The respite was short-lived. Feeling unthreatened the creatures roared savagely and charged directly at Rolf; furiously he back-pedaled to escape their onslaught. My heart sank as I watched. Would our brave friend be killed today right here before our eyes?

"OPEN FIRE!" John ordered loudly.

Helga's rifle thundered in quick succession. This worked and changed the momentum. Shaking wildly six reared back on their hind legs and bellowed in protest. Coming down hard they separated from one another and began stomping in a mad frenzy. I could hear small rocks falling from the cliff walls behind us as they did. Only one of the creatures was focused on Rolf now, and it bore down on him with evil intent. Rolf snapped. I could hardly believe what I was seeing. Blind with purpose he was oblivious to everything now except the beast. After nimbly side-stepping the creature's clumsy attack Rolf leapt up onto its back, in one great bound, and began ripping viciously at the fleshy part of its neck between the ears. The enraged saurischian thrashed about in an effort to rid itself of this troublesome nemesis. It wasn't working; Rolf was undeterred and kept ripping at the creatures flesh like an enraged lion.

"CAPTAIN . . ." John yelled while re-loading his weapon. "We have to take these things down!"

"Do what you have to!" The Captain screamed back.

The explosive sound of gunfire echoed noisily along the rocky precipice as the crew began squeezed off rounds. It was a deafening clamor that echoed thunderously along the cliff behind us. The gunfire wasn't working, though, and the creatures continued raging around us in dangerous demonstration. I wondered what it would take to kill these things, or even if we could. Piles of rock were forming all along the ledge and I imagined that at some point an avalanche may very well overwhelm us; thankfully, though, the cliffs posed no imminent danger and soon the rocks stopped falling.

"Target their eyes and near the top of the neck on the sides," Anders shouted while pointing at his own body. "They're vulnerable there!"

Anders suggestion was inspired and when Helga dropped one of the smaller sauropods, with an eye shot, I felt a surge of confidence pulsing through me once again. We *were* going to make it! Soon the other creatures began stumbling under this tactical onslaught; one by one the beasts collapsed in heaps. A miracle was unfolding before our eyes, and when I looked over at Garrett he smiled and pointed up. In my spirit I thanked God for what He was doing through us.

Within minutes all the creatures had fallen except the one Rolf was on, but because the chance of hitting our beloved canine was too great no one dared open fire. Interminably the seconds ticked by. Bucking and heaving the creature was frantically trying to off Rolf but he was *not* obliging him; Rolf was just as wild and crazed (and covered in blood) as the saurischian was now and nothing seemed to interfere with his focus. Nervously we waited for an opportunity to strike.

Through the din, some yards away, I heard the radios crackling and could just barely make-out Rorek's voice.

"Olaf . . . do you copy, are you alright?" I heard him ask.

"We're still alive!" I heard the Captain answer frantically. "Six are dead Rorek! Rolf's on top of one; we can't get a shot off!"

"Olaf, before we lost satellite I saw the rest of the herd head back into those caves north of you;" Rorek continued, "there were half a dozen smaller ones with them."

"They have newborns?" Jonah gasped.

"Aye, seems so," Rorek answered.

"No wonder they attacked us, they were protecting their young!" Lizzy was bedazed and almost sounded remorseful.

"Now this thing makes sense Lizzy." Jonah answered.

"Rorek, when will we get satellite again?" Anders inquired.

"About ninety minutes!"

As soon as Rorek had signed off, one clear blast of Helga's rifle echoed across the plateau. Soundlessly the last beast crumpled in a heap. Barking frantically Rolf jumped off and shook; his appearance was savage. Covered in blood he bore no resemblance to himself. As the animal quivered Rolf slunk around and looked in its face. For several moments the eyes of the creature stared back at him weakly and then, death came and they closed. After pawing the creatures face several times Rolf backed off snarling. A short distance away from us he lay down and stared blankly. Slowly extending my hand Rolf growled chillingly; all his fangs were bared.

"Whoa dude!" Garrett recoiled with me. "Better back off doc, doggy ain't there no more."

"Let him be Doc," John ordered. "He needs to chill. It'll take some time. Give him space until he does!"

The battlefield was a spectacle. Lying dead on the precipice were seven enormous mounds of dinosaur flesh in the last throws of nerve life. Blood was profuse and had pooled up in various places along the shelf; it was actually running over the edge and into the valley below in small rivulets in several places. Around me the exasperated faces of the crew gazed speechlessly at one another. No one moved; all of us were locked in a whirl of thoughts and emotions. What an incredible experience we'd been given, and what a victory.

"I told ya dude!" Garrett muttered wearily at last.

"What's that little brother?" I asked.

"I told you guys that Pellucidar 2 and the *Heimdall* crew would end up being dinosaur hunters."

"Yeah, I 'member that," John agreed with a half-hearted chuckle.

"How right you were," Anders nodded wearily.

"I never thought it would be battling the buggers for our lives though!" Garrett added with an affected smile. "This was stinkin' weird man, I can't believe how stinkin' weird this was."

"Thank God no one was injured." Anders bowed his head.

"Amen Norse," I agreed, "and it's only Rolfy that got bloody."

The observation somehow lightened everyone's spirit and all chuckled and murmured heartfelt amen's.

"Rolf'll clean up, don't worry; look at that mess." John pointed towards the cliff behind us, "nobody's ever going through there again!"

"That's a fact, nobody ever," Garrett shrugged, "Now what?"

The entrance was blocked completely. Hundreds of rocks and boulders were piled up at least thirty feet in various places. There was no way back, and the only way forward presented us with even more challenges. Gravely we gathered together to discuss our plight and pass around a bottle of much needed water.

"We should pray Captain," Anders suggested.

"Yes … and then we should clean the weapons," John added.

"I agree men," the Captain shook his head.

"I heard what Rorek was saying sir," John continued after we'd finished praying, "I think it would be wise for us to at least try and get to that caldera before the light disappears. We can't stay here; these things will start stinking soon and we definitely don't want to be around when they do."

"I agree," Anders shook his head, "it might well bring in other wildlife that we haven't encountered yet."

"There's water and vegetation there;" Jonah went on optimistically, "maybe even some decent fish too."

"It's a good idea," Helga agreed.

"I agree," Lizzy shook her head.

"I'd say around a mile and a half if we use this southern path." John pointed. "Whataya think Jonah?"

"I agree brother," Jonah shook his head, "we can't stay here. We have to find someplace cooler, someplace more accommodating to our needs. The caldera is the only choice we have at present."

"We need rest, and we badly need to bathe; I don't know about you, but I stink." Lizzy added with a grimace.

"Rorek won't be here for several more days. I agree with Jonah," Helga went on, "we need to find someplace cooler! I'm gonna need several days to recuperate; I'm beat and so is Liz! I'm sure everyone else is too."

The Captain nodded and looked into everyone's eyes. "Everyone agrees then, outstanding! Let's do what we need to and then let's get the heck outa here!" Everyone cheered and applauded.

"Gabriel … better get Rolf some water."

"I'll just put down a cup Cap." Garrett answered. "Poor dog's wack right now; if he wants some water he can get it himself."

"You're right son," The Captain agreed. "I'm praying he'll come back to himself soon."

When we'd cleaned the weapons, and had taken pictures of the carnage, we departed. Scowling, Rolf slunk along behind us as we made our way down the rocky path.

Thirty

After Leaving Dinosaur Ridge

As we made our way Captain Olaf suggested that we build a comfortable campsite near the Caldera when we'd arrived. The idea stimulated everyone and took their minds off the battle. On one of our breaks I climbed a hillock to better see where we were headed and where we'd been. The lush area we were entering was as beautiful a place as any we'd seen, but the view back was like something hellish vomited from the mind of a demented artist. All of us agreed, as we walked, that our trek from the Great Sea, across the treacherous

Eastern Ridges, down through the Gorge of Sorrows, and then across Dante's Valley, was one of the most arduous undertakings anyone had ever attempted.

"We better keep moving folks," the Captain instructed, "we've got a way to go yet."

"I've got some ideas for a makeshift kitchen," Lizzy said as we continued, "I'll just need some strong men to help me."

"No shortage of them here," Jonah laughed.

"Did we bring an axe with?" Lizzy asked.

"I've got one," Garrett affirmed.

"Good, I think we'll build a kitchen table then," Lizzy chuckled.

Another hour of walking brought us to the great Caldera. Now we would be able to rest for a few days. As was our way, we gathered together and prayers were offered up for our lives, and health, and also for the strength we'd been given during our difficult ordeal through the Eastern Mountains.

Earlier

Dante's Valley was basically an outlandish wasteland with the occasional outcropping of beautifully unique flora. From what we were able to ascertain, the bog was made up primarily of brownish green water, slime, vegetation in various stages of decomposition, unusual plants, preternatural in appearance and dimension, and also a host of other things that defied any clear description. Where we'd come down, near the western end of the bog, dinosaur droppings were strewn about in clumpy foul mats, and because the fetor was horrid and thick, we were compelled to use moistened handkerchiefs to keep from gagging. Continuing on, we began encountering dozens of cruddy acrid pools separated from the body of the bog. The growth near these pools was spectacular.

"This agaric growth," I pointed out, "if I remember correctly Captain, it's a kind of saprophytic organism called sulfur fungus. They're really big mushrooms."

"Mushrooms?" Garrett asked aroused from his moony musings. "Are you gonna make mushroom soup Liz? I like mushroom soup; is it time to eat already? I'll help, I'm hungry." Laughing, the others gathered together to investigate the discovery.

"These *are* sulfur fungus Gabriel, good call." Jonah gestured towards Lizzy excitedly. Soon both were scrutinizing the umbrella like caps and the gills on the underside of the six foot wide monsters.

"Certainly these are aberrations," Lizzy speculated.

"No doubt about that," Jonah agreed, "I've never seen anything quite this big before."

"Neither have I," Lizzy ruminated, "and since all these isolated pools are similar to sulfur springs, the chemical composition of the water must be responsible for encouraging this incredible growth. What do you think Jonah?"

"Unless it's an underground release of radioactivity, I agree Liz! Remember the odor at the Shallows of Three Rocks; it's very similar here too, and the sulfur tainting seems to be occurring from within the cliffs." Jonah pointed back over his shoulder.

"Radioactivity - isn't that dangerous?" Helga looked squeamish and grabbed a hold of Lizzy's hand.

"It is Helga, in the right doses. If there *is* any dangerous emission from nuclear decay it would be evident in the dinosaurs."

"They'd all be croak city from eatin' this nasty crap." Garrett cringed and pretended he was dying.

"There *would* be a lot more corpses and skeletons." Jonah chuckled. "You have to wonder, though, where this growth found its inception Lizzy."

"I would have to presume that the spores originally descended from that hole above us."

"It's a viable theory certainly," Jonah pulled at his goatee. "I also find myself not excluding the probability that the dinosaur herds may well have brought many of the spores and seeds in with them as they migrated through these labyrinths from other areas."

"You mean in their poop?" Garrett smiled affectedly.

Jonah nodded yes.

"Now that's an interesting notion," Lizzy puzzled. "I don't know how we could prove it though. We would have to trace back to where they had actually entered into the realm and find out what they'd eaten before doing so. But how in the world could we do that?"

"I believe we've found ourselves, and our contentions, in a stalemate then my dear." Jonah shrugged.

"Floatin' on a breeze or dumped down in a turd …"

"Those appear to be the only two options honey," Lizzy smiled at

Garrett. "It sure would clear up a lot though if we knew where they'd entered the realm and where they're presently congregating."

The conversation had pulled me in, especially with Garrett's colorful additions. I was certain, though, that discussing this topic to extent would only produce speculative results; there was no way that we could confirm, in our present circumstances, whether the plant life down here was indigenous, or brought down from the surface, or had been imported in dinosaur feces. Although unavailing, aside from being a rousing conversation, we continued ruminating about the migratory habits of these antediluvian creatures and how they had gotten into the realm. Some of us were convinced that since we'd found Saurischian remains, in two completely different locales, that this was proof positive that dinosaurs did occupy the entire realm in widely spread herds. I was skeptical though. The Grettig's had never mentioned anything about dinosaurs, and we'd discovered no records, in Torfar-Kolla, or in Himminglaeva, mentioning anything about anyone having ever encountered these behemoths. Still, there were many mysteries to be resolved. Was the two finds we'd discovered part of the same herd? And if yes, how far and from where did the herds travel to get to the bog in Dante's Valley? Was this the only place they fed? Were there other passageways throughout the mountains the dinosaurs used to roam about in? Did the herds have access to the surface from any underground location? Did the US government have knowledge of these behemoths? And if they did, why was it being kept secret from the general public?

Given the many questions remaining, and the many mysteries

unresolved, it was frustrating that this leg of the journey would soon be ending. If all went according to plan we'd be departing within the week. And if this was the case then we would be learning little more than we already knew. One of the most baffling dilemmas was still the Anasazi. Given what we'd learned so far, was it possible they had been eradicated by the same malevolence that had destroyed Himminglaeva? Certainly it would have been a terrible loss, but wouldn't there be something remaining of the fabled city; a remnant of the culture, the partial remains of a dwelling, a tool, a garment, a pictograph, a skeleton perhaps?

And then there was the mysterious wooden box. If it was constructed of Yew wood, and this genus did not grow in the underground realm, had it been made on the surface and then placed down here to put something into motion that we were unaware of?

A host of chilling questions gnawed at me.

Why had Granmar given us the box at the last minute and not earlier? And how had they gotten the box? And where did the family go every night after they left the SES? And with whom did they meet? Had they broken into the castle, and into the queen's chambers, to remove it from under the floorboards? And why did he send Halldis instead of bringing it himself? Was Arnora's story about the box true, or were the Grettig's just another set of hands it had passed through to get to us? Had the Grettig's been threatened? Had the box been purposely planted in our hands? Could it be we'd been duped and were pawns now in a more elaborate scheme? Were the Grettig's and the Mortiken involved in some way? Why was I the only one affected after the box had been opened? Did it have something to do with being the chosen one? Had I really been written about in Viking prophecies or had that only been a convenient interpretation? But if that was true then what about Floki Vildarsen; how could anyone ever dispute what he'd said to me just before he'd died? The Captain and John heard it too. And how could one ever explain Anders knowing what Floki had shared with me without ever hearing it firsthand. Truly, there were many unanswered questions and mysteries and I had no idea how to resolve any of it.

Thirty-One

The Rim of the Caldera

We were finding growth akin to cranberry plants in the bogs shallower waters now. It was colored in gradations of deep claret and also very fragrant; sweeter than roses or even jasmine. Intrigued with the unique qualities of these plants, Lizzy extracted a dozen seed pods and stored them in small plastic sample jars for safe-keeping while we took pictures. Perhaps at some point in the future we may find an opportunity to plant these on the surface for analysis.

After passing the bog we crossed over a shallow watercourse and climbed to the top of a rounded mound covered with tufty grass and flowers. From here we could clearly see that the flora and landscape, nearer the caldera, was dramatically different than any we'd seen thus far. The outcroppings of rocky terraces, pine trees, dense low-lying shrubs, and wildflowers gave the environment the feel of something rare and picturesque, almost as if we'd stepped through a portal into a subterranean Shangri-la.

The still water of the Caldera resembled the surface of a black mirror; the effect was truly uncanny. To understand the area better, John scanned the far environs through the binoculars as the rest of us, with guns ready, investigated the grouping of irregular hammocks surrounding us. Finding nothing life-threatening we pressed on. Nearer the rim of the caldera the aslope topography began changing again; here everything was comprised mainly of black sand and an assortment of irregularly shaped pebbles. Upon reaching the shore we found, to our great delight, that the water was quite temperate so Lizzy suggested that a swim might be in order.

"Sounds good to me, let's do it." The Captain eagerly nodded his approval. "Stay together everyone!"

The water embraced me like cool velvet. Fifty feet from the shoreline the granite bottom was deeply dimpled with dozens of depressions with sandy bottoms. It was perfect for what we had in mind. All were similar to comfy chairs and each of us found one to relax in. I chose one next to the drop-off and, when I peered over, I was quite amazed to find that the blackish water, we'd viewed from atop the knoll earlier, was really quite translucent to a great depth.

"The water's pristine." I announced to the others.

"It really is," John smiled. "If we had some gear Gab it might be nice to explore a bit eh?"

"Yah, I'd like to do that myself," Anders nodded with an impish grin. "I've been itching to get under the water again. Never know what you may find on a ledge, or in a shallow cave, or in the belly of something large and nasty."

Anders caught my eye and winked. Half-heartedly I nodded back. The thought made me shudder. Was it possible there were monsters dwelling in the depths of this frightful abysm and, god forbid, had any of them become aware of us?

"What say then men?" Garrett stood up and removed his shirt.

"Aye young warrior," Anders nodded, doing the same.

"A bloody good idea chaps;" John laughed heartily, "permission Captain?"

"Have at it ya fearless swabs," he laughed fitfully. "But don't expect any of us to join in with these daft shenanigans of yours."

"Throw your shirts over to me," Lizzy instructed, "we don't want them drifting off."

"YES MOTHER," all three chorused and complied.

Resolutely they leapt off the side, laughing uproariously, and disappeared for almost two minutes. Looking over I could see them far below me undulating mysteriously in the translucent water. My heart soared, as I watched, and the wings of my imagination unfurled. What a test of endurance it'd been getting to Caldera Vale, a unique challenge that had required both fortitude, and determination, and one that had also tested the mind and body severely. Into the valleys and over jagged granite ramparts we'd pressed on in pursuit of a legend, something hidden, and something mysterious. Traversing rivers and venturing down into desolate wastelands, all of which had seen unremitting centuries pass before them; we hunted together for the aliment that would sustain our fragile lives and for the hidden paths absolutely essential to achieve our glorious mandate. Down here, in this magnificent Realm of the Ancients, in all these unfathomable places we had discovered, the winds of chance blew indiscriminately and, as our hearts and minds were opened to the potential within us individually, experiencing together those moments where hunger and survival joined hands together in harmony, we all became predators out of necessity that flew together unhampered, and unfettered, and fearless, in pursuit of our goals.

When at last the men burst upon the surface all were chattering excitedly about sea serpents and mermaids and sunken pirate vessels. Something magical was happening. For over an hour Anders, John, and Garrett explored the caldera together while I flew on the sinewy wings of my own imagination. Once, when they surfaced, all were laughing about a cave they'd found filled with pieces of eight and a host of imaginary booty; I knew their imaginations had been freed from all shackles and they were all in the grips of a wondrous euphoria. When at last they'd had their fill of diving and dreaming, and were quite exhausted, they returned to their sand chairs to relax and meditate. In my heart I was convinced that these men were the characters of legends and I saluted them with honor and respect.

It was blissfully untroubled here. All I could hear were breezes whispering in the trees, the gurgling sound of the river, the soft hiss of waterfalls in the distance, and the gentle sloshing when someone moved in the water. Helga perked up at one point and began reminiscing about Ernesto Padilla's Inn. Soon we all were talking and laughing about the lobster feast we'd enjoyed the following year in Peniche. The ladies began planning another banquet with all the trimmings, as soon as time would allow, and we all looked forward to the joy we'd have stuffing our faces with the delectable hot juicy sweet buttery meat.

Rolf reappeared suddenly near the shoreline. I knew he'd been watching us intently from where he was hidden in the bushes and had finally somehow mustered the courage to come out.

"Come on Rolfy," we began encouraging him.

After shifting around nervously for awhile he finally slunk to the water's edge. At all times eyeballing us warily he began nosing at the surface of the water. He was a pathetic mess and must have felt terrible. Soon he was lapping thirstily and, when he'd had his fill, he started shaking spasmodically to try and rid himself of the thickly matted dry blood.

"I love you bubba," I motioned. He changed. Leaping crazily in circles he began chasing his tail and scampering back and forth along the shoreline barking madly.

"That's a boy Rolfy," we encouraged, "you can do it."

Pawing vigorously at the water's edge, as if he were digging for something, he finally ventured in and dog-paddled out. When he'd reached my side he began whimpering mournfully.

"I know boy; it was a tough one huh?"

Rolf looked up quizzically and barked.

"You were the winner though dude; 'member?"

Then, as if someone had waved a magic wand, his demeanor again changed and he began yelping excitedly.

"Helga did you bring any shampoo or soap?" I asked on a whim.

"Yeah Gab, I have both. You want some for Rolf too?"

"You bet; how did you know?"

Smiling sweetly she removed two bottles and several bars from her backpack and, after she took one for Lizzy and herself, she threw the others over towards me.

"Would you mind handing them out honey," she asked sweetly.

"Sure I will," I smiled back sheepishly.

The ladies wasted no time. Within moments there were mounds of lather atop her and Lizzy's head and, after dispersing the soap and shampoo to the others, I began the task of cleaning Rolf.

"You washin' the mutt first?" Garrett shook his head scornfully. "Why don't you let the cheese-brain swim around for awhile and take care of your own self?"

"Rolf's first today Garrett," I shot back, "and I'm willing."

"Rolf's a hero Garrett and he deserves to be pampered," Helga giggled. "You guys should wash too."

"Indeed you should!' Lizzy huffed indignantly. "And as your medical practitioner, and nutritionist, I am ordering it gentlemen.

And these clothes will have to be scrubbed; they're so ripe they could stand up by themselves."

After a good laugh the ladies relocated behind an outcropping of rocks about ten yards from us.

"We're going to strip down so we can wash our clothes," Lizzy shouted back, "I suggest that you all do the same. And mind you now, no peeking."

Grinning, the Captain assured them that they were safe. Soon the ladies were in high spirits and gushing about how wonderful it was being in such a lovely place and being clean again.

"Let's do this then," the Captain shrugged at the rest of us. "I can't remember when I've ever smelled like this before."

"We *are* kinda ripe aren't we?" John grimaced.

"Even after all that swimming I still stink," Garrett moaned.

"You always reek butthead," I laughed.

"Oh yah puss brain, well you stink so bad …."

Before Garrett finished Anders dove at him and pulled him under. When they resurfaced Anders hoisted him up suddenly and threw him out over the edge.

"I'm gonna cure your foul mood fool," Anders blustered and flexed his muscles after Garrett had resurfaced.

"You're dead meat dweeb," Garrett growled as he flailed towards the shoreline.

"Bring it on dillweed," Anders taunted and flexed his muscles.

After climbing back up on the ledge Garrett plowed madly

through the shallow water and, when he was near enough, he dove at Anders. Unfortunately for him he missed by a few feet.

"Aim much dweeb?" Anders mocked with muscles rippling.

Garrett stood back up and they both flexed and roared and then quietly scrutinized each other. Then, without as a much as a word, both of them turned with a thunderous roar and dove at John and me; down the four of us went tumbling and yelling. When we'd resurfaced something happened that I'd never seen; Captain Olaf dove at Jonah and pulled him under. We couldn't believe our eyes. Watching these two, usually reserved stoic men, acting crazy was something I would never forget as long as I lived. Today I was discovering a part of the crew that I'd never experienced before, and I was really enjoying it. I knew that this behavior was cathartic in nature and the many tensions of the grueling trek were quickly vanished. Rolf bolted from the water, after I'd finished washing him, and he began running lickety-split up and down the shoreline, stopping only to shake vigorously and bark and chase his tail. He was happy again and so were we.

After donning fresh clothes Lizzy suggested that we set up the campsite. Nodding, the Captain pointed north towards a stand of trees. The area was two hundred yards from the waterfall, nestled amongst boulders, and alive with colors.

"It's just perfect Olaf," she smiled and kissed his cheek.

At once work began; leveling sand, setting up tents, making a fire ring, collecting wood, and constructing the make-shift kitchen table that Lizzy had wanted. As we worked I realized that the woodland here had the aroma of a healthy pine forest. Mixed together with all these familiar scents were the perfumes of the delicate wildflowers carpeted lavishly over the hills. For the first time in months we were witnessing birds, thousands of them, many differing in size and type, flitting amongst the trees. Curiously they approached as we prepared the site. Circling over our heads some lighted upon our gear and began chattering noisily. Stopping to watch, several of the boldest hopped near, chirping, and when we offered them crumbs, they darted in to snatch them and then flew away. Within moments there was a great commotion in the trees, and soon after that the sky was filled with them. They must have been discussing the new food supply. It wasn't long before they'd discovered the dry stores lying out where Lizzy and Helga were preparing dinner. Fearlessly dozens darted in and stole what they could and then flew up to their perches to feast upon the treasures. Moments later Lizzy put an end to it and covered everything that was exposed.

The waterfall in the distance was truly breathtaking. Water was being routed along dramatic rifts, and down over jagged precipices before it tumbled down into the valley in thick brownish cascades.

The river was forced between spindly rock formations, which made the current fierce, and then it spewed out across a rocky plain and then into the caldera. At this point it commingled seamlessly into the pure waters and then slowly dissipated into the depths.

After dinner

With chores finally completed, and our stomachs filled with a satisfying warm meal, Garrett took to playing fetch with Rolf along the shoreline; Lizzy began humming sweetly and knitting; John and

Helga took off towards the waterfall; Jonah and Anders decided to try fishing in a large still pool near a stand of trees; Captain Olaf got out his Bible and began reading, and I, taking it all in, began writing in my journal once again. There was serenity in this camp and everyone's hearts were at ease.

Thirty-Two

The SES Arrive

Our second day at the Caldera Vale Rorek radioed to inform us about the dangerous navigational glitches he'd discovered in the software on both Subterranean Exploration Submersibles. They'd been unable to navigate underground. He brought us up to date about his attempts to secure information from Rabat and the fact that nothing helpful was being reciprocated from the GVIN. No one seemed to care, and the operatives all seemed to have a different idea about how to fix the problem. The only thing they could agree on was that the professor had been indisposed for most of the week, and that no one had an idea where he was, or when he would be available again. Olaf had assured his brother that we were all healthy and well and that our supplies would last another eight full days. Relieved with this, Rorek promised that he would report in every day until the problem had been resolved. Rorek's grim report had impacted the Captain gravely and he motioned for me to join him. He asked that I not share what I'd heard with anyone. I agreed.

"Captain, what do you make of this," I asked after the radio conversation had ended. Olaf shook his head slowly.

"I don't know what to think Gabriel, nothing like this has ever happened to us before," he sighed. "All I know is the idea of the professor being *indisposed* and *unavailable* bothers me a lot."

I, too, was bothered by these troubling notions. Why were there so many differing stories about the software repairs, and why weren't his operatives in agreement? Was it possible the professor had taken ill or something insidious had happened to him? What would happen if Rorek never came for us?"

Six days later

Being early risers Garrett and Rolf had snuck off at 5:45am on another of their (hunting frogs in the fens and mud-beds) excursions. Rolf had been pawing in the mud near where the river entered the caldera when he'd noticed a rolling commotion on the water's surface. Rolf's fur stood up like a Mohawk and he began growling and pulling on Garrett's pant leg. Soon the water had begun boiling in mounds. It was obvious that something was coming up from the depths and, not knowing what to expect, they'd run up the embankment and hid in a stand of trees to watch from a safe distance. Garrett had impressed upon me later that, given what we'd been through up on Dinosaur Ridge, he wasn't about to take any chances. No monster emerged from the dark depths of the abyss, though; instead both SES surfaced two hundred yards out. Beside himself with excitement Garrett ran up to the campsite to inform everyone of the news.

"Yo dudes, time to rise and shine! You ain't gonna believe it!" His animated kerfuffle had awakened me in an instant and I hastily pulled on my clothes.

"Garrett what's up dude?" I asked stumbling groggily towards the shoreline with him.

"Check it out," he pointed through the mists. "Praise God hallelujah and pass the chili dude, we're gettin' outa this place!"

"I wonder if they got the software problems fixed."

"Dunno dude, but I'm sure glad to see um."

"Oh yah me too dude." I agreed.

Gliding soundlessly on the mirrored surface; both SES slowly approached the shoreline. It was like a scene from a science fiction movie. Jules Verne's '20,000 Leagues under the Sea' came to my remembrance, as I watched, and I began to wonder what those hearty souls might have imagined, in 1866, aboard the steamships *Governor Higginson* and the *Columbus* and the *Helvetia* and the *Shannon* when they'd seen a three hundred and fifty foot phantasma gliding soundlessly on the open oceans. No one had any idea that it was

Captain Nemo's incredible submarine the *Nautilus*. I remembered reading that some had speculated that it may be the fabled Moby Dick down from the hyperborean regions, and some of the press thought the terrible Kraken, whose slithering tentacles could entangle and pull down the largest of ocean going vessels, had come to annihilate them. It was a time of worldwide discussion about the credible and the incredible. Thankfully, for us, this was real and not one of those times of marvelous fiction; we knew for certain what was approaching us.

"Halloooo there on the shore," Rorek's strong voice echoed in the early morning stillness, "Where should we put in?"

"There's a channel over here," Garrett pointed as Rolf barked excitedly. "Check it out; you'll be able to get within a few feet of the shoreline. Gosh boss its sure good to see you."

"Likewise son, likewise," Rorek waved back.

"Did you get the software problems fixed?"

"Good as new son and we got a system upgrade in the process."

"How cool is that?" Garrett's eyes shone brightly. "Nose up to the sand, you'll be able to jump right off the bow; it's shallow."

"I can see son, good call," Rorek acknowledged while maneuvering both vessels nearer the shoreline.

All the others had awakened now and were along the shoreline chaffering excitedly. Within moments both vessels had ground to a stop in the soft sand. All of us began applauding when those aboard moved forward near the bows with ropes. When the vessels were secured we joined together to pray and thank God for this very special moment. After a short conversation we split up into groups. Anders and Angelina vanished into the forest. Jonah and Roxanne took off walking. Olaf, Rorek, John, Helga, and Lizzy hunkered down near the campfire and began a discussion about the logistics of our impending departure. Garrett and Rolf took off along the river to continue their search for frogs and I decided to make another entry into my journal.

I was startled when Betsy appeared suddenly and sat down with me. Embracing warmly; we held each other without saying a word. Then, as if a dream had begun, sweet-scented words began flowing between us. Her thoughts were reaching into the emptiest parts of me. And what was radiating back out of my heart, for this beautiful and precious woman, was something that I'd never felt before. Not even Ingrid had aroused this kind of intensity in me. It was evident that our love had grown since we'd been apart; but how could that be?

"I missed you Gabriel Proudmore," she whispered in a resolute voice cracking with emotion. "I love you so much and I was so worried, and I don't ever, ever, want to be apart from you again."

"Oh Betsy, I don't want to either; I love you too."

Gingerly she took my hand, smiling, and led me down to a semi-secluded area where trees had piled up in clumps along the water's edge. Here we were still able to see what was going on and it put us both at ease. I was so curious to know what was going through her mind but was loath to ask for fear of ruining the magic. Both our spirits were quiet and for awhile we starred at the mirrored surface of the Caldera and said nothing. Almost imperceptibly we moved next to one another. Her leg was against mine. And after running her fingers up my neck into my hair she kissed my cheek. I was mesmerized and overwhelmed and her closeness left me woozy with a wave of goose-flesh washing over me. How intoxicating it was being so near to her and breathing in the subtle fragrance of her hair. Softly I stroked the top of her hand and up her arm. She giggled and then leaned towards me even more. Without any thought of it my hand moved up to her shoulder and I pulled her in close to me.

"I love you Gabriel Proudmore," she whispered in my ear. "And someday, when this journey is over, I want to have your children."

I was transfixed. The world had disappeared around me and all I could see was her face and hair. Softly her head fell on my shoulder and her breathing became articulated. A fire was kindling in me now, and I could tell that one was kindling in her too.

"Oh Betsy, would you really be my wife?"

"Of course I would my darling." She kissed my cheek again.

Tears were flowing down both our cheeks now. I don't know who reached out first, but both of us were suddenly locked together in a passionate embrace. As if we'd been touched by the magic of angel's wings, our lips found the others, and my mind went blank.

"Ah, young lovebirds," Rorek sighed wistfully.

"Yeah, must be nice. You miss your wife don't you?"

"I do brother, lately now more than ever."

"She was a fine woman and I miss her too." Olaf embraced Rorek again warmly. "I'm glad we're together again, it's good to see you. How was the journey?"

"The vessels ran smooth; it's amazing how these things operate. I can't tell you how impressed I am with the professor's engineering and design skills."

"He's a rare man." Olaf nodded.

"His inner circle was very instrumental in us getting here at all you know." Rorek's face was suddenly etched with stress. "As you know, it took quite a while longer than we expected brother. Because no one knows where the Professor is, at present, two of his closest associates, Hector and, uh … oh great, I've forgotten his name; anyway, they did the work for us. After the software was repaired the main-frame in Rabat experienced more problems with the satellite connection and the radios went down. We surely had a time of it stuck underwater."

"Good lord, what did you do?"

"We couldn't do anything!" Rorek's expression turned dark and gloomy. "We were stuck for two damn days. It was nerve-wracking, but certainly a miracle when the coordinates finally came through.

"Thank God for that." The Captain sighed.

"Yah … Hector and the other fella told me that they had to upload the programs from a laptop because there'd been a fire at the GVIN."

"You're kidding, a fire?! I wonder what's going on there."

"Don't know, seems odd though that they had to use a laptop to upgrade us, and even odder that no one knows where the Professor is." Rorek frowned.

"Don't understand that either. I *will* tell you though that I hate being out of touch. The boys tried a dozen times to contact you but there was only static."

"It really bothers me that his mainframe went down you know." Rorek vented angrily. "You'd think his systems would be backed up with some kind of fail-safe, especially in a situation as delicate as ours is. We're totally dependent on satellite interface you know."

"Aye, we are Rorek. I don't like it either. We'll have to talk to him when we can. I'll be very glad when this bloody phase is over."

"Aye, I feel the same way!" Rorek sighed.

"Say, was there any word from him about the *Heimdall* and when we'll be leaving this place?"

"Ach, I forgot - there was! He told me the morning you left that the *Heimdall* is on the water again and all repairs and modifications have been completed."

"Excellent! Where is she berthed?"

"North of Seattle at the moment."

"Seattle? What's his reasoning?"

"Apparently when we're done here we'll be surfacing topside near the continental shelf and docking the SES in an inlet somewhere north of Seattle. We'll be boarding her there and sailing north."

"Why north?"

"Apparently Kodiak Island has been getting visitors; they're migrating in now from all over the globe."

"It's begun then eh?"

"It would appear so Olaf. The day of many collisions seems to be hovering nearer than ever."

"God help us all then brother."

Thirty-Three

Departing Caldera Vale

The next morning

After praying, Jonah and the Captain decided it would be to our advantage if everyone was aboard one submersible for the journey through the labyrinths. At first the crew balked, because of the limited space, but then the logic of it settled in. Considering that there was much to discuss, and share, it would be far easier doing this face to face than on the plasma screens or radios.

I remained topside when the others went below decks. With the Long Distance Binoculars I retraced the path we'd forged across

Dante's Valley, along the bog, and then up to the high precipice. What a bizarre battle it had been, but what a miracle it was that all of us were alive and unharmed. I'd come to the conclusion, in the last day or so, that the only truly important thing we'd accomplished down here had been rescuing the Grettig's and helping nurture them back to health. Since we were no closer to finding the First Tribe than when we'd entered the realm, my prayer was for continued discernment and the kind of unity, and wisdom, that would bring this phase of our journey to an honorable conclusion. There were many unanswered questions, still, from our time in the Realm of the Ancients. Perhaps when these had been resolved, and fully grasped, maybe then we would be able to see what we'd accomplished here in a clearer light. Once again I thanked God for our many adventures and victories, and also for the opportunity I'd personally been given to experience life with these wonderful people that I so respected. After locking the hatch and the 'all secure' klaxon had sounded, both SES descended into the Caldera to begin the next phase of our underground journey.

Thirty-Four

Translating the Himminglaeva Parchments

The descent became daunting. Near the six hundred foot mark every remnant of sunlight disappeared which, in turn, immersed the SES in a kind of blackness that was bizarre. I'd never experienced anything like this before; it was similar, very much so, to sinking slowly in a very large bottle of ink.

"Can't see squat out there," Anders muttered with both hands shading his eyes over the window. "It's like a block of obsidian."

"It'll be like this most of the journey guys." Angelina informed us. "You'll get used to it."

"Can't we use the exterior lights?"

"NO!" Rorek snapped angrily. "No we can't!"

"Why not?" John was visibly irritated with Rorek's tone.

"For some reason," Rorek continued more relaxed, "when we're deeper than five hundred feet, and we're downloading or uploading, the exterior lights interfere with the satellite signal."

"That's weird!" John frowned. "Are we downloading now?"

"We are- we're getting updated coordinates. And I agree John," Rorek nodded. "But I have no answers; its new territory for us."

"A brave new world eh," John shrugged his shoulders.

"Yah, you could say that," Rorek responded stoically.

"Did the professor say anything about it?" Olaf joined the conversation.

"He did some weeks ago. He said it might have something to do with a rare particle emission down here and how it may react with the magnetic field around the lights."

"Oh that's great;" Garrett gesticulated wildly. "Now we're gonna look like stinkin' glow worms."

"Let's hope it doesn't come to that son," the Captain chuckled.

"That's radiation isn't it – particle emission?" Helga asked. "We're not in any danger are we- our health?"

"It's doubtful;" Rorek shook his head, "but no one's ever been down this far before in a Caldera; so I can't say for sure."

Garrett grimaced angrily and kicked the wall. "You know

something; I'm tired of this stinkin' place; I miss the *Heimdall*; I wanna get back aboard and do some flyin' man."

"It would be nice son." Rorek answered with a half-hearted smile. "All I know, for a fact, is that the meter readings have been stable for radioactivity. I think we'll be fine; as far as we can tell it's affecting only the exterior lights."

"How far to the bottom boss," Garrett asked pensively.

"About nine thousand feet," Rorek returned.

"WHOA! And then what're we gonna do?" Garrett asked.

"Well son- and the rest of you swabs listen up here too- after we leave the Caldera, we'll be going northwest through a series of large tunnels. The channels are wide and deep and it's a straight shot all the way under Nevada; no obstacles until we reach the Crater Lake area. There we'll have to navigate through a convoluted series of labyrinths that will eventually take us out into the Pacific Ocean. After that we'll head straight north until we reach the Olympic Seamount. We'll be surfacing somewhere north of the Olympic Coast National Marine Sanctuary and wait for the professor to contact us."

"Why're we goin' up there?" Garrett asked puzzled.

"The Captain'll share that when he's ready." Rorek barked.

"OK boss, no problem, its cool!" Garrett shrugged.

"Have you encountered any marine life down here Rorek," Anders questioned, "anything at all?"

"No, we haven't seen life since leaving the great sea Anders. Just junk from the surface and one plane wreck."

"A wreck eh?" Jonah got inquisitive. "Where was that?"

"About thirty miles south of Himminglaeva."

"That's interesting," he said pulling at his goatee. I understood Jonah's quandary. It was imperative now that all the facts be laid out for everyone to understand. We were all frustrated and the Captain knew it. It was an elaborate puzzle so far and little of it made sense in context to the whole. There was much that needed to be talked through and understood, and this was the very reason that the whole crew, (including Rolf) would be aboard SES 1 for the next twenty-four hours. As we were nearing the bottom Rorek informed the crew that he would be keeping SES 2 in sync-lock fifty yards behind us on the port stern until we'd reached Himminglaeva.

On the bottom we began inputting Hector's newly updated coordinates into the mainframe. When it was loaded, Rorek, Helga, and Garrett, booted up all the navigational systems on both vessels to test them. These would be solely responsible for getting us through the underground labyrinths and out to the Pacific Ocean.

Today after dinner we'd be discussing, all the new information Roxanne had interpreted on the Himminglaeva parchments. Given the significance of this, I was very anxious to see if our theories would be corroborated, or refuted, by her interpretations. After a delicious meal of baked ham, sweet potatoes, vegetables, and hot buttered biscuits, we joined together in the front of the vessel.

"Well guys," Roxanne began, "I think I finally have an accurate translation from these two incredibly telling parchments. We both agree - Jonah and me - that the content sheds a positive light on what we've discussed in previous conversations. The fact that we found these at all seems a miracle to us, as I'm sure it does for you too. Anyway, I'll read what we have; see what you guys think."

__Parchment 1__

It is I, Ragnarr, and my beloved wife Borghild:

It is we who leave this record by writ

For generations henceforth

To dispel malignant voices deceptive

In all that will be discovered in ages yet,

Great Eternal Father,

Blessed of all creation,

We, being of the First Tribe,

Warriors pursuing the path of our destiny,

Rognvald's born of the blessed Christ,

Filled with His Spirit,

Most High and Holy Lord,

Creator of all that is,

Constant companion,

Giver of life in the eternity of infinite ages hence,

Devoted followers of King Agar,

Revilers of Magnus and of the deceiver Odin,

We, Ragnarr and Borghild

Pursue in Truth what He hath now prepared for us.

Twice we have come to the throat of the unknown.

Sitting betwixt its teeth in awe,

We gaze again down the black portal

Of those which hath gone before us-

Njord- Freya- Freyr- Angrboda- Baldur-

Nerthus- Forseti- Gerd and Skadhi,

Those who departed the tomb of Magnus,

Brave souls that sailed north in eight vessels;

Where hath providence taken thee?

Daily we yearn for thy fellowship.

For the knowing we pray for word of thee.

Long nights are spent weeping for the conjugation,

But alas, we know that it shall never be.

We know you have been taken into another land,

One greater than our ability to understand.

Again we pass the noble stone arch,

Entering into the troubled waters of leviathan

We purpose to beleaguer those deceived,

Those separated from us at the tomb of Magnus;

Using Holy wisdom and trickery to conceal

The truth of our purpose.

Although at first reluctant

The others have been pacified by our ruse.

Thinking us now with them,

Convinced we follow Odin and not the Christ,

We have gained their confidence

And they speak forthright before us.

The faithful Christ hath sent us

And He will always have a remnant

In any land or kingdom He doth choose.

We have been chosen for His glory alone,

Empowered by His Spirit to keep Truth alive

Parchment 2

We have purposed to separate ourselves

From the stench of abominations,

Those who revile the Most High

And censure His Truth

Have become lifeless shadows,

Serpents as wingless birds

Singing sonnets of the dark elves,

Embracing those that will be led,

Handmaidens escorting the dead to Valhalla,

A scourge dark upon hapless souls,

The dulcet soothing of Odin's Valkyries

Repudiating all that is good;

Our souls wax weary of this treachery,

And the Christ is humiliated with their babblings.

Having grown weary of the ruse

This night we separate ourselves from madness.

Under cover of shadows we sail

North past the Eastern Mountains.

In one vessel seven couples, born of the Christ,

Ragnarr- Borghild- Thord- Bestla-

Hrosskel- Swanhild- Hamal- Nauma-

Gunnar- Helga- Ivar- Aesa- Saemund, and Olvar,

Pursue what has been promised.

We live or die in honor to our Great King.

Yet now a fortnight hath passed

Since we left the Great Sea,

And those deceived of Loki and Magnus.

And having found now a land of deep mists

Where, from the vast hole above us,

Sunlight warms the earth in daily cycles,

There is at long last peace in our souls.

Here the seasons shed their life,

The fish are exaggerated in size and character

And take no skill to ensnare.

They but leap into our hands

And fill our bellies with pleasure.

Darkness that plagued our souls,

And ails of the bowels have gone.

Having been restored we will build our homes here,

We will worship the Holy Christ,

Our children will multiply greatly,

And the Holy One will be glorified.

Thirty-Five

Unexpected Danger

Himminglaeva had originally been established as a Christian settlement and these two parchments proved it. This offshoot Viking colony had broken away from the stench of Odinism and, under cover of darkness; seven couples successfully had escaped an insidious spiritual deception. After sailing one hundred and fifty miles north on the underground sea they discovered a new land to settle in; it was the topography known to us now as Himminglaeva. Inured by fatigues and hardship, these courageous kinfolk successfully escaped all the spiritual intrigues endured on the long ocean voyage from their homelands in western Norway, the Orkney Islands, and northeastern Scotland. It was an amazing story about tenacity and the love and determination between Christian people.

We had discovered similarities, too, between the Anasazi's departure from Torfar-Kolla and the original Rognvald diaspora. At some point the Anasazi elders had decided *not* to follow the Eastern path through the mountains. The only route they could have taken then would have been north along the shores or in vessels on the sea. The geological records made mention of a devastating earthquake during the time period in that very vicinity. Based on this, it was theorized that the earthquake then could have re-structured the underground topography as it had done on the surface in Utah and Arizona directly above. Was this the reason why so much of the interior construction of Torfar-Kolla was so shoddy? Was it possible the city had been partially destroyed in the cataclysm and then re-built quickly and haphazardly? Was it possible, too, that when what the holy men had seen in their visions had been destroyed and, because of what was construed by them, then, as an intervention by their gods, that they were forced to re-invent another route to save face? Could it be that they had *not* trekked at all through the Eastern Mountains, as we had assumed, but had actually gone north along the shores of the great sea? But there was pause with that theory too.

From personal experience - which in our circumstances was far more the litmus test for us than anything else - Rorek and the ladies had sailed the SES north along the shores in the great sea and had found nothing to indicate the Anasazi having ever taken the northern route. If they had *not* gone east through the mountains, and they had *not* gone north, which route did they take? Given the fact the underground realm was circumscribed in scope we knew they hadn't taken a southern route. For many weeks we had explored the southern quadrants thoroughly, all the way to seas end, and found nothing at all to indicate the culture ever having been there. And surely they hadn't gone southwest because this is where we had entered into the realm up the Underground River and through Oski's Grotto. The only other possible route was northwest, across the great sea, but they would have needed many vessels to accomplish that. Was it possible that the recent Mortiken raids and subsequent destruction of Himminglaeva had, in any way, been connected with the mysteries surrounding the vanished Anasazi Nation? Because of all the unknowns Jonah had been in the grips of a brooding ill humor for many weeks.

"I just can't believe this," he said with wearied disdain, "there's nothing tangible that even suggests them ever being here. There's no evidence to corroborate anything except what was in that stupid wooden box. I can't believe it! We've found nothing, and Rorek and the ladies found nothing ..."

"It's *really* gotten confusing, I agree with you whole-heartedly." Helga spoke strongly in the same spirit as Jonah.

"To tell you the truth, I'm ready to throw it in about all of this," Jonah railed. "The only reason that I came down here was to sew up loose ends about my research. I thought for sure it would be resolved by now. I'm shocked that we don't have at least one lousy artifact, or a lousy workable theory to grab hold of and run with."

"I agree with you Jonah," the Captain nodded sympathetically.

"What's really confusing is why Brynhild Busla was taken, and *where* she was taken." Helga continued. "Do you suppose this whole scenario was engineered by someone else? I can't help thinking that she was taken out of the realm on a helicopter and then returned."

"Now there's a thought," Garrett threw his hands up.

"It would be impossible to know." Angelina answered coolly. "I'm certain, though, that there's no way she could have made the journey on foot and returned in that number of days."

"I agree," Roxanne nodded, "the figures don't add up!"

"Maybe somebody had to meet with her for some political reason; you know, to make a deal behind the Kings back." Garrett suggested.

"That's a theory honey," Roxanne acknowledged Garrett. "And though we can't know for sure, there still remains the possibility that Arnora's recollection of the facts could have somehow been skewed, which in turn has influenced how we're dealing with it now."

"You mean she didn't understand the facts entirely?" Anders questioned. "How could that be though if she personally worked with the queen? You'd think that she would be the one with all the accurate insider information."

"Maybe she listened to what she thought was fact and then she formed her own opinions about it," Betsy contended. "And then, based on her erroneous judgments, she shared what she thought with Granmar and then they formed their own opinions about it."

"And that's what they shared with us; what they thought was

accurate; it's kinda like what we're doing now." Garrett's face brightened as if he'd had a revelation. "So what's the difference between them and us then? They were trying to articulate something from their own perspective just like we're trying to do now. . ."

"And nobody's take is accurate," Anders gestured heatedly. "Good point little brother. So what's the point of it all then?"

"I understand what you're saying fellas," the Captain reacted after pondering what he'd heard, "and speculating about it doesn't seem to be getting us anywhere does it?"

"Nah ..." Garrett and Anders shrugged.

"How can we form valid opinions when the facts are haphazard? Seems to me we're just chasin' butterflies and goin' round in circles. If we're trying to figure something out that's already messed up, then we're just making it worse." Garrett philosophized.

"I agree with you guys, I do, but wait a minute ok," I interrupted, "there's something else here that we've all missed. It was Helga that mentioned something earlier about the whole thing possibly being engineered. I've been thinking about it. What if Queen Brynhild never came back at all? What if someone else was returned in her stead to try and undermine Braggi's authority and initiate unrest in the regime?"

"Holy crap Doc," Garrett jumped up and knocked over the chair. "That's the best idea I've heard yet. And if it's true, then it worked; that stinkin' place went to hell in a hand basket. Makes sense dude, and it's still messed up real bad."

"Yeah you're right," Anders agreed. "WOW, an imposter, what an intriguing idea."

"It's a point that I hadn't thought of," Rorek grunted; "A spiritual and political maneuver by an outside source. Sounds to me like the kind of work Krystal Blackeyes would do."

I heard Jonah groan behind me.

"Sheesh man, I didn't think about her." Garrett's face contorted.

"And her obvious loathing of the King is suspect to me too of foul play." Helga went on. "This is beginning to make more sense."

"And the fact that, upon her return, every underground city got caught up in social unrest is suspect." Angelina added smugly.

"It is Angelina, but we're going to find out a lot more if we ever find something tangible and get some answers." Rorek interjected.

"I'm of a mind to stop going on about this now," the Captain stood up and stretched after sensing Rorek's gist. "There's no way we can know anything for sure at present. It's obvious that some of what we thought was fact is not. The information we've gotten lately certainly refutes some of what we learned only a few months ago."

"Certainly has been a lot of subterfuge Captain," Angelina added.

"I agree sir," Anders shook his head.

"Like who's the woman in Torfar-Kolla now, and where did she come from, and where's the real Brynhild Busla." Helga added.

"Maybe the Mortiken took her," John shrugged. "Or maybe it was Krystal Blackeyes."

"And what about Amalek Baaldur," Garrett grimaced. "I hate that turd lick Goliath wannabe John – he needs to die!" Everyone shook their heads in agreement.

"Is it possible the Mortiken are involved in this?" Captain Olaf pulled at his huge moustache thoughtfully. "How in the world could they have gotten down here? Not from the west or from the south; there are no entrances. Didn't the professor say the only other access was where the Colorado River empties into the Sea of Cortez?"

"He never verified an underground entrance in the Grand Canyon Captain, at least not to us- only that there may be one the Mortiken used." Rorek remarked with more than a hint of skepticism.

"Do you think that he knew about the Mortiken incursion and didn't tell us?" The Captain grimaced.

"I don't know Olaf," Rorek shrugged, "I hope not."

I could see that Rorek had been deeply affected by the Captain's suspicion and for several minutes no one spoke. The question gnawed at me. The possibility that the professor had kept sensitive facts from us was disturbing. And the possibility, too, that the Mortiken were in the realm, and that Brynhild Busla had become a victim of their evil intrigues, was frightening.

"I wonder why the Holy Spirit put us in the Eastern Mountains," Lizzy pondered aloud.

"Maybe He didn't, maybe we did to try and prove something that never existed in the first place." Jonah grumbled.

"Don't be so hard on yourself Jonah." Lizzy continued. "If we've found nothing we can certainly complain about what the purpose was in going, but should we? We just need to keep pressing forward and trust God. I can think of a thousand places, though, I'd rather have explored than the eastern Mountains. There was some beauty, I'll admit, but oh goodness gracious me it was so hot and dangerous through that terrible Dante's Valley. And the Gorge of Sorrows, and those caves, and that horrid crack; I thought we were going to die. And dear Helga; we never sweat as much in our entire lifetimes. Even Garrett's hair was hanging in wet noodles; poor dear, I've never seen it that way before. Everyone was so miserable and dejected. And there's something else too ..."

"Yah," Garrett interrupted, "we almost got wacked by dinosaurs."

"Too bad Edgar Rice Burroughs isn't still writing dude," I began laughing, "He would have had a hay-day with our adventures here."

"Yah, the Pellucidar Series would have another half dozen books." John laughed along with the others.

"Maybe you guys were there just to learn how the dinosaurs migrated underground." Betsy speculated.

"But did we? And who cares about that crap anyway!" Garrett argued. "How is understanding their migration patterns gonna help us find the First Tribe; tell me that?"

Suddenly it began shaking violently in the Caldera. Within seconds the motion was overwhelming.

"What's happening," Olaf shouted.

"An earthquake; and a damn big one," Rorek grimaced. "My god, we're in serious danger brother!"

"What should we do?" Helga screamed.

"Grab a hold of something!" Jonah instructed frantically.

I felt nauseous. All the others were stricken too; the ladies were wailing and Rolf was howling. I could hear dull reverberations from whatever was hitting the hull. It was a baleful sound, like an army of frenzied demons coming for us. A sudden dreadful bursting sound outside the vessel created an explosive shifting movement inside the Caldera. I was immediately gripped with a foreboding of doom and I forced myself not to vomit.

"What was that? Olaf shouted red-faced.

"SES 2," Rorek cried out, "I think it's gone."

"Gone? What do you mean gone?" The Captain shot back.

"I think it's been crushed Olaf, but I'm not entirely sure, there was something about that sound." Rorek's face was etched with anxiety. Again the Caldera shook violently and everyone cried out.

"Take us to the surface NOW," The Captain ordered frantically, "We'll have to sort this out later."

"Aye, but I don't know about this Olaf; I've never done it before; I don't know what's going to happen. Give me strength Holy Spirit; here we go people- hang on to something . . . oh Lord …"

Through the confusion I could just make out an agitated voice crackling on the radio. It sounded like the professor but the words were unintelligible.

Part Three

Back on the Surface

Thirty-Six

Rorek's Skill Saves Us

After Rorek had blown the ballasts the vessel forcefully surged upwards. Thankfully the cone of the Caldera was very large and free from any obstructions that may act as hindrances in an ascent that was much like an against gravity freefall. Within seconds Lizzy, Angelina, Jonah, and Roxanne had passed out on the floor. As we gained momentum the g-force suppressed everyone where they were. Rolf was overwhelmed and began howling; he couldn't move. In sheer terror he evacuated his bowels all over the floor; it was awful. As we neared the surface I watched in fascination as Rorek deftly adjusted the ballast and planes from where he was sitting. He was contending with every bit of expertise to keep us alive. My admiration for him blossomed in these harrowing moments; no one on the crew could have handled this emergency except him.

"Hold on to something," he shouted, his voice cracking with strain, "it's going to be awkward. Here we goooooo . . ."

The SES breached the surface like a mad whale and rose up its entire length. My heart began pounding so fiercely that I got light-headed. After hovering a moment, suspended in midair, we crashed back down on the starboard side. When the vessel had stabilized, I scanned around me to see if anyone had been injured. As far as I could tell everyone was fine and there was no blood anywhere that I could see. For what seemed the longest time we all stared at one another in a kind of silent stupor. As we were a kind of joyfulness rose up inside me that became overwhelming. Feeling as if I might burst wide open I began shouting and singing at the top of my lungs. At first the others stared wide-eyed, but soon they joined in with me and began rejoicing. It was truly amazing what was happening. Our worship soon became consummate and, as we lifted our praise a kind of light, filled the room with peace and power. For five minutes we sang and laughed and applauded and cried out to God with a joyful noise. And then suddenly, as if by magic, my flesh and mind was quickened and all those still conscious came alive and got focused.

"Helga, Betsy, tend to the others." Captain Olaf ordered pointing.

"If you need smelling salts they're in the first aid cabinet. Make sure nothing is broken before you move anyone."

"Aye Captain," the ladies responded as they hurried to the sides of those still unconscious.

"Are the rest of you ok?" the Captain asked. Everyone responded they were. "Ok let's get busy then. Check all the systems and make sure there are no shorts or leaks. Garrett, check the mainframe, and John, please check the power couplings on the reactor."

"On it," both waved and scuttled off.

"Gabriel, I'm sorry son; it's a nasty job, but I need you to clean up that mess Rolf made; it smells awful in here."

"No problem sir," I nodded squeamishly.

"Anders, please open up the hatches so we can get some fresh air."

"Aye sir," Anders waved and scampered up the aft ladder.

As we were working the radio started crackling again. It was the professor and he was clearly overwrought.

Thirty-Seven

The Professor Baffles Us

"Captain Olaf ... do you copy ... DO YOU COPY?

The Captain responded directly: "Yes professor, we copy you."

"RESURFACE IMMEDIATELY," he cried out with great emotion. "You are all in grave danger, very grave indeed!"

"We're on the surface now." The Captain responded coolly.

"Most excellent Captain," He responded with a clearly affected tone. "Now sir, we're getting you out of there; do you copy?"

"Loud and clear professor, you're getting us out of here. Now what exactly does that mean sir?"

"It means that your work there is done sir. Please be advised that helicopters have been dispatched to transport you out. They will arrive within twenty-four hours. It's over! You can go no further! The mission parameters have been revised as a result of the catastrophic event. Do you copy?"

"I do sir, loud and clear." The Captain responded with elation.

"Now … SES 2 was completely destroyed Olaf. Please do not attempt to go back down to retrieve anything. Listen carefully to me Captain Olaf; this transition will be delicate. Leave everything behind, including all the photographic files; I will take responsibility when we airlift SES 1 out. This is of great importance; retrieve the small box behind the mainframe; it is orange and has 'Prof-Rabat' stenciled on the outside in black. Also erase the geographic grid on the mainframe and every communiqué between us that has been backed up; do you understand me?"

"Copy that Professor! But not taking the photographic files seems absurd. They're all on one small hard drive and it will be no problem carrying them."

For several moments there was silence and then he snapped back with an irritated tone: "Be assured Captain Olaf that my technicians will take care of them, there is no need for concern, please do not argue with my requests!"

"Hold on professor, we're encountering another emergency here." Dumbfounded the Captain keyed the radio off. "What is up with this guy?"

"And why is he on an open channel?" Helga grimaced.

"What a 'tard," Garrett chimed. "If we don't keep those photo files and the geographic grids we can never prove we've been down here."

"I agree with little brother. Those are our files, Captain, our personal files," Anders spoke with conviction; "taken mostly on Gabriel's camera and that dude can't tell us what to do with our own files."

"I agree with both of them sir," John declared staunchly.

"We do too Olaf," Helga and Lizzy nodded.

"Olaf, something has perverted the man's reasoning it seems," Jonah said pulling at his goatee. "Seems he's had a change of heart about us, and then there's that thing in his tone that I don't recognize; it sounds like fear, or like he's being manipulated. He's trying to hide something, I'm sure of it."

"Oh this is *just* great," Lizzy lamented.

"How did he know the vessel was destroyed?" Rorek pondered aloud. "Lighting wasn't on, exterior cameras weren't on, and all the sensors on the other vessel were destroyed instantly. He couldn't have known anything. It's something we would have had to tell him."

The Captain looked at his brother questioningly.

"Something has bothered me about the sound it made Olaf," he continued. "Implosion has an entirely different sound than explosion."

"What are you suggesting Rorek?"

"The sound bothered me Olaf. The way the energy rolled over us seemed as if the vessel had exploded."

"Are you suggesting sabotage?"

Rorek shrugged.

"Do you think that it was detonated purposely?"

Again Rorek shrugged and said: "That's what I'm thinking, but I don't know for sure."

The possibility was shocking and we began discussing it heatedly with one another. Several minutes into the exchange the Captain held up his hand for silence and then rekeyed the radio on.

"What should we do with *this* vessel professor?"

"It's about time you got back to me Olaf!" he barked brusquely. "Leave the vessel, don't worry about it. Abandon SES 1 as soon as possible and make for the highest plateaus. Make sure there is enough room for the choppers to land safely. Again I stress, take nothing with you except what is mandatory for your immediate welfare!"

"Are you sure professor?" Olaf reiterated.

"How many times do I have to say this to you Captain? Leave *everything* behind; clothes, weapons, cameras, photo files, artifacts, everything; I will supply you with everything new when you reach your new coordinates in the Pacific Ocean. I will decide what to do with the remaining submersible. Please do not concern yourself. By the way, is everyone alive and well?"

"Oh now he asks," Garrett muttered disdainfully.

"And did you notice his tone?" Angelina was clearly miffed. "How rude he's become with us."

The Captain looked over at Betsy and Helga and both nodded that all were awake now and uninjured.

"Yes professor, everyone is alive and unharmed," the Captain returned stoically.

"This is most excellent. I am relieved that no one was on the other vessel, how dreadful that would have been," he spoke with a clear air of remoteness. "Now, if you would Captain, prepare to be evacuated and also expect a critical up-date shortly."

"What's next Professor?"

"International politics are in upheaval and the financial markets are collapsing Captain Olaf. Everything has changed on the surface. First and foremost you will all be transported back to the *Heimdall*."

"Where *is* my vessel exactly?"

"The schooner is anchored just south of the Strait of Juan de Fuca, very near Tatoosh Island in the Pacific Ocean."

"Tatoosh Island ... that's really remote, why there?"

"This is not your concern. All you need to know is the schooner is waiting for you. All the new systems have been installed."

"New systems professor," the Captain balked, "what kind of new systems?"

"I will answer all your questions when we rendezvous in three days," the Professor continued with a clear tone of exasperation. "Now ... I salute you all in honor for your dauntless work under very difficult circumstances. I am leaving Rabat within the hour; may God bless and keep you courageous friends."

"What new systems Captain?" John questioned anxiously. "Does that mean now that he's bugged or mined the *Heimdall* too? What's happened to this man?"

"May God bless and keep you courageous friends?" Anders sneered. "Now wasn't that sweet!"

"Was it just me or did he sound snide when he said that?" Jonah asked. "Something is seriously wrong Olaf."

"It's like he was reading a script." Angelina observed.

"Yah, it kinda was Ang," Garrett agreed.

"Ok, we know that something's wrong, but let's not jump to conclusions until we know the facts," the Captain suggested with anger burning in his eyes. "It could well be the stress of what's happening in Rabat, but in my gut I'm sensing something else like Jonah is people; something deeper; something uglier; almost as if something, or someone, is manipulating him. But until we find out for sure I've decided that we're *not* going to follow his instructions."

"Yah right on boss," Garrett cheered along with the others.

"Here's what we're going to do," the Captain gathered us together. "Gabriel, contact your father with a double encrypted message and see if he knows anything about what's happening. Garrett, you and Helga upload everything onto our thumb-drives and then wipe the hard drive with a magnetizer; kill it, leave nothing for them. Gabriel, retrieve all your photographic files and then you wipe that hard-drive clean too. Helga, back up every conversation we've ever had with him since the Sea of Cortez and then wipe the rest clean. From here on out we are going to protect ourselves. This is between us now people. And if he wants to play games, he chose the wrong people to do it with."

"Aye, that's a bloody fact," Rorek concurred angrily. "And I hope he didn't do anything shady to our vessel."

"Don't breathe a word of this to anyone," the Captain continued. "Also know that I will be dealing personally with him from here on. If he calls or radios and you answer, refer him to me. It's imperative that I keep the continuity of what's transpiring between us going from here on out."

"It's a good idea Olaf," Jonah shook his head. "I wonder what's up the man's sleeve."

"Do you think he's turned on us Captain?" Betsy frowned.

"It's certainly a possibility based on the conversation lass. But to what extent is unknown. We can't take any chances; there's too much at stake now."

"Wanting us to leave all of our critical information behind seems out of character Olaf," Lizzy shook her head flustered. "He's never done that before."

"I agree dear," the Captain nodded. "It's a new game now, and lets all get a mindset for that."

"Olaf lets join together in prayer and get some wisdom," Jonah suggested, "we must put this into God's hands. If subterfuge has been introduced into the ranks we need to be prepared and have a strategy; only the Holy Spirit can help us do this."

"I agree," the Captain sighed.

"I hope we're not getting out of the frying pan just to dive into the fire here sir." John shrugged.

"Let's hope not John."

Thirty-Eight

A Major Planetary Shift

A frightening report came shortly after the conversation with the Professor had concluded. Hector, his committed friend and confidant, sent us the most startling of all the updates we'd ever received since the journey had begun. For the first time in the recorded history of mankind, a super-volcano had erupted, two day's previous, which had, in an hour's time, affected the entire planet and radically changed all world markets. The lives of millions of people were now in the balance, and tens of thousands were officially dead from mega-tsunamis, tidal waves, and ravaged fault lines. The catastrophic event took place in the Tuamotu Archipelago, and massive aftershocks were being felt around the entire globe. It was one of these aftershocks that had almost destroyed us in the black depths of the Caldera just the day before. All of us sat stupefied as Helga shared the dreadful news.

Located in the South Pacific Ocean, two thousand miles south of Hawaii, halfway between New Zealand to the west, and South America to the east, the Tuamotu Archipelago is in French Polynesia and an overseas territory of France. French Polynesia consists of thirty-five rugged volcanic islands and more than one hundred and eighty low-lying lush coral atolls. Simply put, the atoll is a ring-shaped coral reef surrounding a lake-like body of water known as a lagoon. The curious form has led to much speculation as to their origin. Most agree on a theory that involves a connection between fringing reefs, barrier reefs, and atolls. A typical fringing reef is attached to, or borders, the shore of a landmass, while a typical barrier reef is separated from the shore by a body of water. Atolls begin as a fringing reef around a volcanic island. Over time, as the volcano stops erupting, the island begins to sink. The fringing reef around the volcanic island becomes a barrier reef as the island gradually sinks and a lagoon is formed between the reef and the island. Over time coral growth, at the reefs outer edge, pushes the top of the reef above the water. As the original volcanic island fades away beneath the sea, only the atoll remains. The reef itself is formed from the secretions and skeletons of a variety of marine organisms, including corals, mollusks, and coralline, this being a lime secreting algae. Atolls are made mostly of limestone, of biological origin, and occur primarily in the tropical waters of the Pacific and Indian Oceans.

It was on the Atoll De Makemo that this catastrophic eruption happened in conjunction with the largest and most powerful typhoon in recorded world history. It was a devastating event that changed French Polynesia and the surrounding areas forever.

For several months five of the atolls had been expelling steam, thermal fluid, and sulfur dioxide, up through fumaroles as far south as Atoll Haraiki. At first these were considered normal geologic occurrences, but that thought process was soon amended. Four weeks before the event, birds had migrated off the atoll, and all the animal life had taken up residence along the shoreline. Three weeks before the event, the township of Pouheva had to be evacuated because of the danger the frightened animals presented to the general populace, and also, because the sulfur dioxide levels were occasionally making the air unfit to breathe. Ten days before the event all trees and flora on the atoll withered from surface temperatures exceeding two hundred degrees. Eight days before the event, and after hundreds of rumbling micro-quakes, five domes bulged up along the northern shores of the atoll during a series of 6.0+ earthquakes. Steam vents opened in hundreds of places throughout the string of lush islands.

Something major was about to happen.

It seemed now that a continuous pathway for pressure release had been established directly to the enormous magma chamber. For several days the pressure in the chamber continued dropping until a critical stage was reached and the superheated water within the magma chamber finally exploded.

The results were astonishing.

With the force of ten thousand Pompeii's the ground shook wildly while all five domes violently blew off enormous chunks of cap-rocks and expelled millions of cubic feet of ash and rock into the atmosphere. After twenty-four hours of non-stop eruptions the flank of five smaller calderas finally collapsed into the ocean with half a trillion tons of rock and debris in its wake. Within minutes it had become one massive super caldera.

The consequences were catastrophic.

A wave of frightening dimension - somewhere between twenty-one hundred and twenty-three hundred feet in height - roared out from the event as if a huge rock had been dropped in a small pond. In a three thousand mile radius, part of Australasia (this term is used to describe Oceania, which includes most of the islands of the Pacific Ocean) and hundreds of smaller island civilizations were affected by the monstrous wall of water. The Hawaiian Islands, Kiribati, Vanuatu, Northern New Zealand, The Fiji Islands, the Cook Islands, Pago Pago, and Apia, the capital of Samoa, all were devastated from a rage of tsunami's one hundred and twenty, to three hundred feet in height. Nothing like this had ever happened before in the recorded history of mankind. The report said that the typhoons relentless, hammering, 'wall of water' rains had been the key to the planets ultimate survival. Miraculously situated over the event, these torrential rains had helped to keep much of the ash from getting up into the jet stream and ultimately had saved the earth. Much of the ash was forced down in torrents of steaming muddied liquid that covered most of the islands and surrounding oceans. Everywhere it touched became a wasteland.

But it could have been far worse.

If there'd been no mega-typhoon, to lessen the proliferation of ash into the atmosphere, it may well have created a global 'nuclear type' winter and driven all of humanity, as we knew it, into early extinction. Thank God this had been averted. We were still alive, and we were together, wiser, stronger, more determined, healthier, and focused still on all of our responsibilities. Given the complex circumstances developing with the professor, I sensed there was still a great deal of work for us to accomplish in our quest to discover the First Tribe of Rognvald's.

Thirty-Nine

Airlifted Out

Three helicopters arrived twenty hours after the Captain's conversation with the professor. I could see, as the noisy machines dipped over the rim, that they were the very same HH-60 that had transported me, Garrett, John, and Anders back into the Pontevedra Province many months before. Everything was packed and ready to go and, as instructed, we were waiting on the highest plateau.

Despite getting only four hours of sleep, we'd been able to gather together all the files and destroy all the main systems in sixteen hours.

We decrypted every e-mail and radio communication we'd ever had with the professor and backed them up on a thumb-drive. And when all the transfers had been completed, Garrett and Helga made the entire system appear as if it had succumbed to a ruinous internal electrical malfunction. It was a work of genius, as far as I was concerned, and I couldn't help laughing at the subterfuge. Shunning the professor's request, to leave everything behind, we brought along clothes, backpacks, food for several days, my laptop and camera, the Himminglaeva parchments, John's titanium combat knife, all the pistols, ammunition, the wooden box, all the backup files, and the Prof-Rabat box.

As we boarded the helicopters I knew this was going to be more difficult than I'd imagined. It was like we'd failed somehow and were running away before we'd finished. What we'd experienced yesterday had changed our direction entirely. And I realized that the whole journey had been a testament to this very thing; the crew making plans, based on what we'd decided was the best direction to move in, and then circumstance changing our plans and putting us right where God wanted us to be at exactly the right time. There was a fundamental in this we needed to embrace. There were far too many things we *could* do instead of those things we *should* do to preserve the direction of our primary mandate; that being finding the First Tribe of Rognvald's. We were too easily distracted by our own desires and goals. Knowing exactly what should be done at all times was something none of us had even come close to mastering. As it was, even after hours of intense prayer, and many hours of intelligent discussion, we had still trekked into the Eastern Mountains in search of the lost city, not the

First Tribe. Was this because of Jonah's disenchantment in his ability to attain his hard fought dreams and goals? Probably! Had everything he'd suffered in the last year changed his discernment and made him more melancholy and introspective? Perhaps! Could it be that we were being deceived by our own thought processes; our own egos; or our own desires for success? I was inclined to say yes. But I wondered at what point in the journey had our good discernment lessened. Despite everything, we still had developed as warriors, adventurists, sailors, and historical professionals, and our esprit de corps was unwavering and we were proud of this. Our experiences had been exemplary, and exciting, but no matter how honorable what we'd accomplished seemed, or how it gratified the ego, it still had brought us no closer to finding the First Tribe than before we'd entered the Realm of the Ancients. This was the bottom line. Filled with emotion, I watched as the remaining SES faded from view below me. The first time I'd seen Torfar-Kolla flooded back to me and it felt as if I'd written my thoughts in my journal only yesterday. *Ten thousand yards of impressive ramparts etched an asymmetrical line against the far distant subterranean horizon. Atop the rugged stone walls, banners of various crest, shape, and color floated sluggishly in light breezes. Through an enormous gaping hole in the massive granite dome, a sudden bathing of sunlight brilliantly illuminated the city and surrounding hills. It was spectacular! Clouds began forming further inland and, as I watched, lightening randomly etched across the skies in jagged white hot traceries. It seemed Lizzy had been correct; because of a unique inter-mingling of surface and sub-surface atmospheres, storms were possible in this vast underground labyrinth. Near two rocky islands offshore, dozens of smaller fishing craft were plying their trade, some with nets, some with poles, and some with bows and arrows. Smoke from dozens of smelting ovens billowed in dense clouds along the sandy shoreline south of the city. Near the ovens, carpenters and craftsmen were busily constructing longboats and smaller fishing craft. I could also see a bustle of activity outside the enormous gates and along the shoreline. Around the base of a gigantic statue, people appeared to be bartering and doing commerce with one another. Life seemed normal here. Anchored outside the surf-line at least thirty large vessels floated motionlessly in the dark waters waiting. As I watched spellbound, the flags atop the cities ramparts began snapping briskly in sudden restless winds; it seemed a storm was fast approaching from the distant mountains. No matter how I approached this intellectually, it was difficult to assimilate what I was seeing and feeling. This wasn't a vision or some fanciful myth passed down through generations, nor was it an imaginary story shared around campfires, this was real! We had actually discovered a thriving Viking Metropolis down here in the Realm of the Ancients. The discovery was mind-boggling and overwhelmed me with the utter uniqueness of what we were doing together on this journey.*

After clearing the massive rim the helicopters veered northwest towards the Pacific coast. I was relieved that we would be back aboard the *Heimdall* very soon. Unable to imagine what may transpire for us in the weeks ahead, I fantasized that we would sail together for a while before having to decide where we would go. I could only hope that once the square white sails of *Heimdall* had billowed open, and we had once again tasted the freedom of the sea, that Providence would keep us together for as long as it would take us to gain our original goal. My greatest concern, now, was never realizing what we'd set out to accomplish. If all we'd done was destined to remain incomplete, perhaps we could still sail back into European waters together, or up into the North Sea, or maybe to those paradises we'd visited along the way. Perhaps we might return to San Benedicto Island to swim with the mantas or return to the Galapagos to continue our research. I just could not imagine the crew disbanding.

I wondered if my father had received the e-mail and what his take on the professor's current frame of mind might be. I wondered how far-reaching the destruction had been on the surface, and how Torfar-Kolla had fared during the catastrophe and the violent aftershocks. I wondered how many people had died in the realm, and how many had perished in the cities and rural areas on the surface. I wondered about Ingrid, how she was, where she was, and if she was still alive. I wondered about the financial and food distribution systems; had they been devastated? Was anarchy on the rise? How were society and the government dealing with the disruptions? What was happening in the Middle East and what was happening with Israel and Jerusalem? Were my Father and Mother still healthy and safe? Was my Father's global business still solvent and operating? Had he lost money? Had any of his tankers been destroyed? Was my account still solvent? Finding my thoughts increasingly troubled, I decided to try and sleep. Perhaps in a dream I may find the answers and some peace.

Forty

Tatoosh Island

Nearly six hours into the flight, the pilot's crusty voice came over the helicopters intercom system and jolted me awake.

"Take a look out to your left folks."

There, off the largest of a grouping of rugged islands, anchored outside the surf-line, the *Heimdall* was floating on the water like a beautiful white jewel. For a moment an overtaking emotion welled up inside me and I was covered in a blanket of goose flesh. Our floating home, now, was right within our grasp.

"Oh man, she's beautiful," I gasped rubbing the sleep from my eyes.

"Dude, what's changed about her?" Garrett asked quizzically.

"I dunno son," Rorek squinted through the window. "The cabin profile seems a bit different doesn't it?"

"Is the wheelhouse larger maybe?" Betsy suggested.

"Back to your seats and buckle in people," the pilot instructed us, "we'll be landing shortly."

Methodically the pilot circled the island twice and then descended. Without mishap all three touched down and we all jumped out. After off-loading what little we'd brought along, I watched one of the pilots reach out through the window to hand Captain Olaf a piece of paper, and also something that resembled a portable radio. Following a short exchange they shook hands and then the helicopters ascended slowly and veered southeast towards Seattle; soon all three had disappeared into the gathering costal gloom.

The weather began changing within minutes of their departure. Strong breezes, pungent with the aromas of the ocean, were gusting now over the island from the northwest; very soon the skies were dappled up with darkened clouds and the sun became obscured.

"Seems like an omen," Garrett grumbled as he pulled up his collar against the sudden chill.

"Goodness gracious I hope not honey," Lizzy sighed.

"The professor sent us a fax," the Captain shared after gathering everyone together inside the building. "It was sent during the flight; I'll read it:

Captain Olaf...

I send you greetings and sincerely hope that your flight was comfortable and that the meal was adequate. As you can see, the Heimdall is anchored offshore and in fine condition; you will be re-boarding her again tomorrow. At that time you will better understand the new operational systems and weaponry, and you will see the modest expansion we have accomplished for your comfort on this upcoming leg of your journey. I know that you are all anxious to be aboard her again. I am sure, too, that you will be pleasantly surprised with what has been accomplished aboard the vessel; nothing irregular mind you. I have made arrangements with the Coast Guard and also the Makah Indians to house you tonight in the cottage next to the Lighthouse. They were eager to be of assistance, especially when I told them who they were dealing with. Rest assured that they have been sworn to secrecy. The side door is open, the power is on, there is food in the refrigerators, and there are cots to sleep on. I hope that you will all be comfortable. I will hopefully be arriving tomorrow noon by helicopter. There is much to discuss and I look forward to being with you all again. Professor ...

"Nothing irregular? ..." – Anders jumped up with a disdainful expression. "What the heck does that mean Captain?"

"I'm not quite sure." The Captain's eyes were clearly overtaken with puzzlement.

"It seemed extraneous in the message Olaf," Helga noted.

"Of course nothing irregular would be done with the repairs and modifications - irregular?" Rorek repeated the word several times, almost as if he was savoring it.

"Let's consider the way his thoughts unfolded Captain."

"What do you mean Gabriel?"

"Well, he started out telling us that we would be pleasantly surprised with what had been accomplished, and then he mentioned he'd gone out of his way to make arrangements with the coast Guard and the Makah Indians for our safe stay here, then ..."

"They were eager to be of assistance when they found out who they were dealing with?" John interrupted with a smirk. "Come on, what a crock! What's wrong with that picture?"

"The Professor would *never* say something like that to gain an advantage Olaf, would he?" Lizzy remonstrated.

"This is really curious," the Captain scratched his head. "Gabriel, finish your thoughts?"

"Yes sir, as I was saying, being pleasantly surprised with what had been accomplished and then writing something that has us questioning the authenticity of what he's written seems antithetical. I have to agree with the others, it sounds to me as if he's trying to get our attention by being unlike himself. But *why* is the question. Tell me sir, is there any way that you can radio the helicopters and retrieve the ip address on that fax they received?"

"Can't we do that on this fancy doodad the pilot gave me? It came as a text on it and then it was printed out."

"What! Let me see that." Garrett's eyes lit up.

"It's not really a fax then." Angelina clarified.

"No, I guess it's not then," the Captain shrugged.

"That'll be to our advantage, you can chill boss," Garrett assured. "Let me access the internet and check it out."

"Alright son, will it take long?"

"Just a minute or so," Garrett answered.

"Do you need any help?" Helga asked.

"Yah, do you know how to get past this double firewall?"

"I don't know, let me see."

"Something's wrong with the man Olaf," Rorek went on, "I can feel it, but I can't put my finger on what it is; he's just not himself lately."

"He's never been like this, ever," Lizzy lamented, "he's always been on the up and up and we've never had to second guess anything."

"You're absolutely correct," Olaf agreed, "and besides …"

"Boss, here it is," Garrett interrupted, "this message wasn't sent from Rabat; it was sent from a computer registered to a company in Seattle called Global Paradigm."

"The Professor's in Seattle?" The Captain gasped aloud.

"I don't know about that boss. All I know is the message was transmitted from that computer and it's somewhere in Seattle."

Why the Professor had chosen this place for a summit was mystifying. Were we any safer here than any other place along the coast? This grouping of islands had often been referred to as the Galapagos of the Pacific Northwest because of the rare climactic conditions that existed here. Was that the reason he'd put us here? Was it the remoteness that had prompted his decision? Being an uninhabited sanctuary for puffin, sea otters, seals, orca, grey, and humpback whales, and also an ongoing living laboratory for marine biologists from all over the world; it seemed an unlikely location for people in our profession to rendezvous at. Tatoosh Island was the largest in this grouping of islands situated half a mile from Cape Flattery on the Olympic Peninsula in Washington State. It was also the farthest northwestern point in the continental United States with one of the most breathtaking views on the whole of the Pacific Coast. Something had begun bothering me. We'd been informed earlier that the ancient Makah Indian Tribe had been in possession of Tatoosh for many decades, and during that time it had remained their ancestral summer fishing headquarters. Interestingly though, notwithstanding the newly renovated hiking path, (that rarely was used) this island and the lighthouse were always kept closed to the public. So why were we here then? And why had the Professor prearranged with the United States Coast Guard, (who were in fact contracted by the State of Washington to maintain the lighthouse) and the Makah Indians for us to land on their private helipad and remain one night before we set sail the following day? Why couldn't we have just boarded the *Heimdall* and waited for the professor's arrival? Knowing full well that he never made haphazard decisions and that all the movement of people and resources in his GVIN was carefully calculated before it was implemented; I found it increasingly difficult understanding why he'd chosen this particular place. After dinner and fellowship, and also some intense group prayer, we all found a cot and fell asleep.

Forty-One

Early the Next Morning

A brisk northern wind was gusting occasionally and loose shutters were squeaking upstairs. The skies had cleared completely, and an exuberant full moon was streaming through all the skylights in intense swaths. Aside from the soft breathing of the others in the room it was quiet and peaceful in the cottage. Rolf's growling had awakened me. After measuring my surroundings for a moment I swung my feet onto the floor, stood and stretched, and tried to orient my thoughts; it was 1:47 am. Rolf sat down next to me and nuzzled my leg; he was curious why I was awake. I wondered what he was sensing. After donning my pants, and tip-toeing to one of the larger windows nearer the kitchen; I scanned the property outside. Nothing looked out of the ordinary. On the pavement there were shadows from clouds passing by, and from the swaying trees around the cottage; everything appeared normal. Suddenly Rolf got very irritated and began snarling.

"What's wrong with him?"

"Oh man you startled me John," I recoiled.

"Sorry bro; what's with Rolf?"

"I don't know; something's in his craw."

"I'll go wake Anders and Garrett." John whispered.

"No need dude, we're here" Garrett whispered back.

"What's going on?" Anders asked tensely.

"Rolf woke me. There must be someone out there."

"Let's get our pistols and take a look."

"Good idea Anders," John whispered, "coming Gab?"

"You bet," I responded dauntlessly. After holstering the weapons we quietly made our way outside.

"Don't you think we should tell the Captain," I asked.

"If there's anyone out here he'll know soon enough," John chuckled. "Let him sleep."

"Dude, its cool being on the surface again ain't it?" Garrett whispered. "The moon looks awesome; it's so big here."

"Yah it is little brother; it's righteous," Anders answered.

"Let's go check the *Heimdall* fellas." John suggested.

As inconspicuous as possible we made our way down the blacktop path towards the ocean. North of us we could see and hear two aircraft making their final approach towards SeaTac airport. East of us I could make out the low rumbling of a group of motorcycles on the coastal highway. South of us I could see the bright lights of Seattle glowing eerily through the vaporous marine layer. From where we were, on the western side of the island, I could see that the fog was now about one hundred yards offshore and retreating steadily.

"There's the schooner," Anders gasped.

"Sheesh, it's beautiful man," Garrett murmured. "There's another structure backa' the wheelhouse, we have a new winch too."

"Looks nice," John agreed, "guess the raft's got a garage now eh?"

"Man, I can feel the wind in my face dude, can't you Gab?"

"You bet I can Garrett, I can hardly wait!"

"What's that out there?" Anders pointed.

Emerging ghostlike from the retreating fog we began seeing the outline of something about half a mile north.

"Looks like another vessel," John answered.

"Look at the silhouette; looks like it belongs in a pirate movie."

"Yah it does Anders- strange," John agreed pensively.

Something gripped my guts. Could this be the vessel that we'd disabled last year in Scammons Lagoon? The thought horrified me and I forced it from my mind. When we'd reached the shoreline the four of us remained hidden in the shadows of all the thick growth near the path. From here we quietly watched over our surroundings. As I was wrestling with my fears a sudden clanging metallic sound echoed across the water from the northwest. Moments later there was another and a third after that, and then, after a moment of silence, we all heard the muffled sound of someone's gruff voice shouting.

"It's that vessel anchored north of us I think," John said.

"I wonder what's going on out there." Garrett asked.

"Weighing anchor maybe," I suggested.

"There's no light, it's doubtful" Anders stated. "Whatever they're doing they're doing it in the dark; you know, covertly."

"I wonder if they're pirates." Garrett mused.

The thought made me shiver. A moment later a huge wave thundered on the shoreline and exploded in mounds of whitewater.

"Swells pickin' up," John noted. "Good thing the *Heimdalls* anchored outside the surf-line."

While we were talking Rolf's growling increased once again and he began sniffing in the direction of the vessel northwest of us. Suddenly a flock of cormorants whizzed past overhead; they were agitated and squawking noisily. The sound irritated Rolf even more and he yapped sharply at the sky.

"Keep it quiet dog please," I begged Rolf.

After he'd nuzzled my hand, he slunk up and down the path looking around and then, suddenly, he turned and ran into the undergrowth.

"Where'd he go Gab?" John whispered.

"Dunno," I responded, "the cormorants spooked him I think."

"Hey check it out dude," Garrett pointed, "What's our raft doing tethered to that pier down there."

"To get out to the schooner later *maybe*," John speculated.

"Who do you think put it there?" Garrett asked.

"Maybe whoever anchored the schooner had to use the raft to get ashore so they could fly out on the helicopters."

"Good point Gabriel," John said, "I'm sure that's it."

The four of us found rocks to sit on where we quietly watched the surroundings. Twenty minutes went by. Rolf was gone still and all of us had begun contemplating returning to the cottage.

"There's nothing out here fellas; let's go get some more shut-eye." John suggested.

"Yah, why not," Anders agreed. "I'm tired of this anyway."

As we made our way back to the path the sound of an approaching motorized vessel startled us.

"What the heck," Garrett turned in the direction of the sound.

A moment later, Rolf bounded out from the underbrush and began pulling at my pant leg. Something had spooked him.

"Look there," John pointed at the approaching vessel, "is that who I think it is?"

"Oh sheesh man," Garrett's eyes flared angrily.

"Have we been sold out?" Anders groaned despairingly.

The rolling marine layer was several thousand yards north of us now and moonlight was clearly revealing the vessels features; in an instant my worst fears were realized.

"It's the Red Dragon," Garrett cried out in dismay.

"Little brother, run up and wake the others." John ordered crisply. "Tell the Captain everything we've seen and tell them not to turn on the lights. Tell them to get every weapon we have ready, and tell him to bring our blades." An instant later Garrett bolted up the path.

"What are we gonna do John?"

"They haven't seen us Gabriel. We're below line of sight."

"We are, yes," Anders agreed, "and it gives us the advantage of intercepting the motorboat when it lands."

"Yes, exactly Norse, if the larger vessel is unaware of us, and we can keep the smaller vessel from radioing back, we may be able to take them out, permanently disable the boat, and then get aboard the *Heimdall*."

"I like it John, it's doable!" Anders sounded compelled and his voice was bristling with energy. "Once we're aboard we'll use the CSAT and get out of here."

Five minutes later the Captain, Rorek, and Jonah were standing with us. Following John's overview the Captain told Rorek and Jonah to gather together all we'd brought from the SES and to get the ladies aboard the *Heimdall*.

"I brought the weapons," the Captain informed us when they'd left, "John, here's your knife, Anders, here's one of Rorek's, and Garrett, here's the other. Gabriel, this is the one you used underground."

"It's perfect sir-thank-you!"

"Alright men," the Captain continued with a sigh of resignation, "what we're going to do must be done covertly, agreed?"

"Agreed sir," John whispered. "Will Rolf work with us Gabriel?"

"Oh sure, he understands what's goin' on, he hasn't made a sound since the birds flew over."

"But there'll be sounds soon dude," Garrett chuckled with a low growl, "the sound of Rolf crunching their stinkin' bones."

"He'll do fine Captain; remember he was the one that alerted us to this in the first place."

"He was son, yes, and I'm sure he'll do just fine."

"We better keep our pistols holstered Captain, just in case." Anders suggested. "You never know how this might develop."

"I agree; use them only if need be. Stealth will be our advantage. Remember, if the Red Dragon becomes aware of the schooner they might try to destroy her. If that happens then I'm sure you understand that without our vessel we are out of options."

"Sir, do you think this was the professor's doing?" I asked.

"I don't know son, I certainly hope not."

Later, as the others were boarding the raft, John, Anders, Garrett, Rolf, and I departed the area to intercept the small vessel now fast approaching the island. After a short discussion with his brother, Captain Olaf scrambled along the rocky shoreline to rejoin us.

"Rorek is going to board everyone and then turn on the CSAT," he explained when he'd reached us. "He'll weigh anchor and take the schooner around that peninsula four hundred yards south. When I give him the word he'll come back for us on the raft."

"How will that be sir?" John asked.

Smiling, the Captain pulled out a small two-way radio his brother had given him. John nodded back with a wink.

"Let's do this," the Captain ordered with grim resolve.

It became very clear to me, as we crept along, that the exuberant full moon was both our enemy *and* our advantage tonight. Since we couldn't use flashlights, without giving away our position, the moon would be the light that would safely guide us along these rocky shores, but also, it could be the very same light that would give us away if we were seen in it. Staying as low as possible we cautiously made our way nearer the enemy vessel just now making landfall.

Forty-Two

The Element of Surprise

We could hear voices as we neared their position. The area that they'd chosen to come ashore was obscured from the north and south by large boulders. East of us a steep path wound up to the top of the promontory where the lighthouse was. I realized at once that this very view was on the advertising brochures; it was the renovated hiking path leading down from the heli-pad. Six Mortiken were gathered together in a loose circle arguing and pointing up at the lighthouse.

"What are they saying," the Captain leaned in close to me.

After listening for several minutes, I turned in horror and

answered his question: "It appears they have orders to kill all the visitors in the cottage sir and then destroy the lighthouse."

"That's us Captain, we're the visitors! Can you believe it; they're actually here to kill us!" John growled angrily.

"We need a battle plan," The Captain looked at John tensely.

"Captain here's what I see," John pointed at the topography. "That sandy inlet funnels down towards the path they'll use to reach the top of the promontory. There's no other approach to the cottage; the cliffs are too sheer and they're not going back the way that we came in. See there, right next to the cliffs, where the sand ends and the path starts; there, in those bushes, is where we'll hit them. They have no line of site with the Red Dragon now, or where they'll be in the inlet, and this larger swell will give us a regular supply of noise to cover any sound we make."

"It sounds good," the Captain nodded. "What are your thoughts Anders?"

"I agree with John sir," Anders nodded eagerly, "and I'm hoping that they walk in single file and not clumped together."

"Yah, true," John nodded intently, "it's a good point."

"If they *are* clumped up it will prove difficult for us," Anders continued. "They've got AK's and we *don't* wanna gang war with these pukes. If they approach in single file, we'll be able to move on each one of them individually. The element of surprise will be our greatest ally in my opinion. We have five, they have six, but we do have a special trump card with Rolf."

"Amen to that," John chuckled sardonically. "One of those poor wankers is not going to appreciate the wolfhound tonight."

A few feet away Rolf snarled and it gave me chills.

"Let's get this nasty thing done then," Olaf gestured grimly. "Stay quiet, and Garrett, no theatrics, let's just do it and get outa here."

"It's a nasty business boss, I know," Garrett answered with an unusual show of compassion, "I promise I won't be a jerk; I wanna leave too."

"These are dire circumstances Captain," John went on, "and who would ever have imagined that our first night on the surface we'd be confronted with a thing like this. We didn't start this Captain, we're just responding to a threat that could have killed us. Thank God Rolf awakened Gabriel so we could deal with it."

"Yes, amen," Anders hung his head with a sigh. "You know, I'd sure like to know how the professor plays into this. I just can't believe that he'd put a contract out on us."

"The way this thing is playin' out sure seems as if he did." John rationalized. "It's all beyond understanding to me at his point."

"Those wankers came here to take us out and destroy the stinkin' evidence, how's that for hospitality?" Garrett lamented angrily. "Who the heck else knew we'd be here? Only chubby butt! Sheesh boss, is the dude with the Mortiken now?"

"I don't know son! Please settle down! We have to pray," the Captain motioned for us to gather together. "It's the most important thing we can do now."

The hulking soldiers had turned off the beach now and were shuffled towards us. Each was carrying the AK-47 we'd seen them use in the past and all were in single file and separated from one another about eight feet. Anders nodded this was perfect and then motioned where each of us should infiltrate the line. With growing apprehension we waited for the precise moment. Rolf darted past me on the moon drenched sand; he was focused on the straggler at the far end of the procession. Spellbound I watched as his long muscled body launched effortlessly through the air like a cougar. Without a sound he brought the man down and, in one swift jerk, ripped out the front of his throat; I was shocked at the savagery and felt my stomach turning. The man writhed as Rolf stood over him; seconds later he stopped moving. Pushing at the lifeless body several times Rolf finally turned and vanished into the brush like a phantom. Huge waves had begun breaking now and mountains of whitewater were clawing regularly at the cliffs. Any sound was being drowned out by the waves. When I realized this my focus cleared and I felt remarkably confident that we would get through this dread ordeal. None of the Mortiken was aware of their comrade's grisly fate; all were still trudging along oblivious to all around them. When the five of them were directly parallel to us John motioned at us to move.

Forty-Three

Violent Confrontation

They appeared dumbfounded, as if we were apparitions. Immediately they began yammering in a strange dialect. So much energy was racing through me and my heart was pounding like a war-drum. When they'd finished whining I heard one of them suggest we *may* be the 'Ghost Warriors' Amalek Baaldur had warned them about. He admonished them next, with the greatest of urgency, that we were merciless to our enemies. I couldn't help chuckling as I caught an image of my past self - no endurance or muscles or strength or fighting skills - poring over texts and writing thesis's in college and realized how much I had changed from those days.

In regular rhythms waves were pounding the shoreline and on the wide expanse of shrub riddled beach the moon shone brightly. Garrett appeared differently to me than he'd been before other battles. His face was etched with quiet determination. He hadn't postured or said a word as he starred at the hulking man in front of him. None of us had. Something baffling happened next. All of them placed their weapons down in the sand and then moved back away several yards from them. Were they yielding to fears? Why in the world would they give up the weapons that could offset the battle in their favor? Bowing slightly they began fidgeting, and I could see their eyes darting about; surely they were looking to find some route of escape. When they realized there was none a ritualistic chant began. It soon became evident they were invoking Odin for strength. For several minutes we watched and listened, hands on our weapons, and then it stopped. For several moments both parties stared quietly at the other. In restrained fortitude each of us braced for battle. In unison they growled like animals, then they postured menacingly, and then the one in front of Garrett spit at him.

"Oh yah you ugly dirt-bag," Garrett bristled with indignation, "I'm gonna stuff Odin up your nasty butt."

Outraged all five lunged forward. Garrett quickly sidestepped his opponent and, after a flurry of hammering fists, he connected with a devastating uppercut that had the man stumbling backwards to keep his balance. I could see blood begin pouring from his mouth as he collapsed to his knees.

"How 'bout them apples spitmeister," Garrett razzed the man just before he flat-footed him in the face.

The Mortiken fell backwards, his face bloodied. Shouting his approval to Garrett, Anders ducked a punch and then blocked a roundhouse swing. With a roar he picked up his opponent and slammed him in the sand. Something snapped and the man began writhing in pain. The scene exploded. Disgruntled now, my opponent lunged at me like a wild gorilla. Posturing viciously with my knife, he backed away and immediately was knocked down from behind with a vicious reverse clothesline from Anders.

"Help the Captain Gabriel," Anders screamed and pointed.

I saw at once that he had been knocked down forcefully. The look on his face gripped me and a sickening feeling apprehended my guts when I saw the cad pick up a large rock to crush him. Impassioned I cried out to God to strengthen him. A second later he bounced back up, reanimated, and connected with a well placed right uppercut to the rogues jaw. I was shocked at the power of the Captains blow. The Mortiken collapsed to his knees, sandbagged, and then, just like Garrett had, the Captain thrust his foot down forcefully down between the scum's eyes. It was as poetic a movement as I'd ever witnessed and all of us cheered as the hulking man fell dazed on the sand. John was suddenly behind me grappling with the biggest of them.

"Gabriel," he screamed "watch out for the roots!"

After a violent exchange I heard the Mortiken cry out in pain as John's buried his knife in his shoulder to the hilt. Distracted with all the confusion, I stumbling back over the very roots John had warned me about and fell flat on my butt. One of the lumbering ogres lunged at me. Roaring, he lifted his leg to stomp me.

"MOVE ..." Garrett screamed as he bolted towards us.

In a flash I rolled out of the way just as his foot slammed down in the sand. Filled suddenly with a prevailing power I jumped back up and kicked him in the side of the knee with all my strength. The man roared angrily and, as he stumbled backwards for his balance, Garrett came down from behind with both fists between his shoulder-blades.

"How's that skid-mark," he yelled as the hulking man collapsed in the sand and fell forward on his face. Both of us nodded appreciation at the other.

"Check it out dude," Garrett pointed.

As I turned I caught a glimpse of Rolf darting into and out of the fray. What was he doing, and why wasn't I feeling fear anymore?

Suddenly strong meaty hands were on my shoulders and they began squeezing and shaking me. The pain was intolerable and shot through my whole body like darts. Mustering everything I could I somehow broke free and spun around and slashed down across both forearms and across the chest. Roaring in pain the Mortiken stumbled back as blood began pouring down his torso.

"Check out Rolf," Garrett shouted again and pointed.

I could see him dragging each AK47 out into the bushes one at a time. A surge of joyfulness and strength began coursing through me. Could it be that the Holy Spirit even used animals? Soon the dog had completed his task and with head cocked, and hair bristling, he began pacing back and forth on the sidelines eyeballing us.

"Gabriel," Garrett screamed and pointed. My much bloodied angry opponent was rallying back towards me from behind. I was shocked at how quickly he had rejuvenated and turned to respond.

Several times more we were accosted by the hulking men. Each time, though, we bounced back with unwavering determination; none of us were willing to relinquish anything to these ogres. Time after time knives glinted in the bright moonlight as we slashed out and thrust down at them. Both sides fought valorously- gaining a little, losing a little - but we always stayed centered on our opponents and the source of our strength. Slowly the tide of battle turned. Fifteen minutes into the mêlée the Mortiken began losing focus and the will to continue. Bloodied and tiring each was blubbering in desperation.

"What's wrong fatso;" Garrett taunted his opponent as he moved closer and drew his knife, "did Odin go out for a beer?"

Bellowing in anger each of them lunged forward. The attempt proved futile and one by one they succumbed to a final unified and savage onslaught from us. When my opponent finally collapsed my heart began pounding so hard I thought my chest was going to explode. Anders opponent fell next, and then John's, and then Garrett's, and then, finally, Olaf's. It became painfully evident, as I scanned the surroundings, that our wolfhound was nowhere around. Feeling as if I may vomit, I stumbled back away from the gruesome scene towards the ocean, where I washed the blood from me, cleaned and sheathed my knife, and tried to calm my racing heart. The others soon had joined me at water's edge.

Save for a whispering breeze, and pounding waves, it had become eerily quiet. Around us moonlight was casting long shadows through the trees over the dunes, and the exanimate faces of the corpses had begun to glow with an eerie lambency; the whole scene made me shudder. Feeling detached from the savagery now my mind became a blur of troubling thoughts. I realized that what I'd done had been as easy as breathing and I felt no remorse. Was there something wrong with me? Was it possible that we'd become like them? At heart were all humans capable of killing another? Through experience we'd come to learn that the only way to deal with the Mortiken was to make them fear you more than you feared them. They were ruthless killers and violence was all they understood and respected. These had been sent to murder us in cold blood and destroy the lighthouse. Why did God allow such things in our lives?

When the surge of adrenaline had lessened all of us backed off, a short distance, and again gazed dispassionately at the lifeless bodies in the sand. Something shifted inside me and, when I realized the scope of what we had accomplished, a flood of tears rose up inside me and a storm of sorrows burst wide open and overwhelmed my heart.

"It's cool man! Sometimes we just gotta cry." Garrett squatted down next to me. "What a nasty thing that was eh? Dude you were a zombie doin' your business; you sure you're alright?"

"Yah I'm cool man," I assured him, "I'm just; I don't know; I'll be alright in a bit."

"Cool dude, I'm gonna try and find that dillweed dog." Garrett hugged me and moved away.

The Captain was on the radio now instructing Rorek to bring the raft. During the conversation Rorek reassured him that the Red Dragon was still dark and unaware of what had been accomplished. They were anchored, and cloaked, on the other side of the peninsula and he would be rendezvousing with us shortly. He also assured Olaf the *Heimdall* was in prime condition.

"It's never looked better. I'm amazed Olaf," he gushed.

From what we've seen, since they've been aboard, a new diesel and transmission had been installed, bilge pumps had been replaced, there were two new capstans, the sails and servo-motors had been replaced, all the berths had been remodeled, the electronics and CSAT had been up-dated, every computer was replaced, a powerful, remote-controlled laser, the size of a shotgun, had been installed above the crow's nest on the center mast, and there was a structure behind the wheelhouse to store the raft in. Following the conversation the Captain motioned us together. Despite the update he felt distant to me and his eyes were vacant; something was wrong with him.

"John, you and Anders disable that boat and meet us at the pier."

"Aye sir," they chorused and dashed off.

"Boss, what about the bodies?" Garrett asked. "Should we ..."

"Leave um; let the birds have um;" he cried out gruffly, "I just don't care; let's get back to the pier now!"

The Captain's decision surprised me; it was unlike him to be so brusque. I would have imagined it prudent to bury them, or at least hide them, given the area, but I realized too that the possibility of the corpses being discovered any time soon was unimportant to our objectives or our well-being. As we made our way back through the rocks Rolf appeared suddenly beside me; he seemed himself again and was soon rubbing against my leg when he could. After telling him how proud I was of the great job he'd done Rolf woofed softly and licked my hand. The dull reverberations of a motor were becoming more distinct now. Emerging ghost-like through the swirling mist the raft was approaching the pier and Rorek had begun motioning for us. Moments later Anders and John came running up and boarded.

"From the SES to a rubber raft;" Garrett chuckled. "It *is* a diversity of craft we enjoy on this journey isn't it?"

"It's done then?" the Captain shot a glance over at John as Rorek pushed off from the pier.

"Aye Capn', its Davy Jones newest trinket," Anders nodded.

"Good riddance to it! Let's head out to sea, Rorek, until we can figure things out; thank you men."

"North then brother," Rorek suggested.

"Aye, towards the Scott Islands," Olaf sighed.

"Captain, should we try disabling the Dragon since we're so close?" John asked. "We still have two limpet charges."

"Not this time John, I have no intention of doing anything until we get some answers. Something's wrong, I can't get rid of the nagging inside me. We have no idea who's aboard that vessel now and I'm not about to put anyone in harm's way."

"I understand, and agree sir, everything *has* changed, yes sir, everything surely has," John nodded.

"I just need time to think and pray," the Captain said wearily.

"Perhaps we should send the ladies home Captain;" Anders suggested when things had gotten quiet. His voice was cracking from a strain of emotion. "It's too dangerous anymore sir, and there are too many unknowns. I don't want my wife, or the other women hurt; I couldn't bear that."

His suggestion was unexpected, but even more unexpected was the Captains response to him.

"I've been thinking the same thing myself;" he murmured despairingly, "we'll talk about it when we're aboard son; it may be the only way now. I'm tired, and I need to pray and think."

Deeply overcome, the Captain buried his face in his hands and began sobbing. Yielding to his emotion I began to intercede for our beleaguered leader and for all the others. As I did I strongly sensed that our journey was drawing to an end. It felt very different now than it had in the beginning. Maybe it was just me, but I couldn't help wondering if we had finally somehow reached the end of our endurance. It was no secret that much had happened to us in the last two years; good and bad, scrapes with death, and a host of things that were well beyond our ability to understand. But still we'd persevered, through it all, and had kept pressing forward in faith towards what we felt God was leading us to do. Now, though, the possibility that our gifted confidant had become an enemy was all too much to bear. Our reliance on the professor had been crucial to all of our daily affairs. He'd been our eyes and ears for many months and he'd also been instrumental in many of our major decisions. If this was really as it appeared, if it was true that he'd turned against us, for whatever reasons, how could we ever complete what we'd set out to do?

A thick fog was billowing in as we made our way towards the *Heimdall*; it was a clinging mist that chilled us to the bone. Soon we were blanketed in a salty cloak of moisture and had huddled together for warmth. I watched, enthralled, as small brooding crystals began beading up on the others faces, and at the tips of their noses, and on the ends of their hair.

Drip, drip, drip ... suspended momentarily, each fell onto our clothing, or onto the floor of the raft. I caught one to examine it. And after studying it a moment I pressed it between my fingers and it was gone. Was this a depiction of our lives; small drops of water coalescing into a greater whole, drops reflecting the beauty of supernal Light momentarily and then evaporating into the sun's heat, or absorbed into a desiccated ground, or crushed between someone's irreverent fingers? Through the swirling feathered edge of the fog I could just make out a glowing line, towards the east, demarcating the tops of the mountains; another new day was approaching.

Forty-Four

Elwin's E-Mail Galvanizes Us

Once aboard John and Anders stowed the raft, Garrett weighed anchor, and Rorek maneuvered the schooner out into the Pacific due west. The Captain explained briefly that we would be heading north towards Cape Cook along the northwestern side of Brooks Peninsula. For safety's sake we would be using the Chameleon Surface Adapting Technology and would be staying forty miles off the western coast of Vancouver Island until he'd decided what to do.

"We'll be lying low awhile," the Captain went on between sips of hot chocolate. "I'm tired guys, and this thing with the professor has thrown me off my game. We have to pray that God will give us the wisdom we need about direction and what to do. Hopefully Elwin will be sending something that will shed some light on our situation."

"Olaf," Jonah began somewhat reserved, "The time has come for Roxanne and Angelina to take their leave."

"What?"

"Yes Captain," Roxanne spoke out, "my college course will commence five weeks from today and Angie has decided that she wants to help me run the research department. The new text is published and we'll need to get copies into the university library in San Diego first. Then we'll be flying a load over to the university in Portugal and get the professors there acquainted with the Viking curriculum. We'll be overseas for two weeks setting up the department and prepping the instructors."

"Ok! Wow Roxanne; quite an accomplishment; I hope it does well. I'd like a copy of the text aboard if I may."

"Of course Olaf; we'll make arrangements to get one to you."

"Thanks so much! Should we take you back to Seattle then?"

"There's no need. We'll make arrangements to fly out from Gold River later today."

"Gold River you say?"

"Yes sir, if you can get us to Nootka, there's a pontoon service there that will fly us into Gold River. They have an airport in the township that will take us to Seattle. We can get a redeye to San Diego this evening or a morning flight tomorrow."

"Will you be leaving us too Jonah?" The Captain asked.

"No Olaf, I'm staying awhile longer. There's something we still need to resolve."

"Yah, I'd like to know that too," Garrett agreed.

"Does anyone else want to leave?" The Captain looked around guardedly. All shook their heads no.

"OK … let's get some sleep and we'll talk again later over lunch. Sound good?" Everyone nodded yes.

Sensing his brothers waning spirit Rorek offered to pilot the schooner. The Captain quietly nodded his thanks and went below. After Garrett cloaked the schooner Rorek set our heading north northeast towards Nootka Sound.

Several hours later

It was 11:30 am. Coaxed from sleep by the aromas of another of Betsy's marvelous creations, I slid off the bunk and stretched. It was a sound sleep and after only five hours I felt very much rested. Outside my berth window the halyard lines were dancing in a blustering wind and the sky was getting mottled with dark clouds; was another storm approaching? While preparing for my toiletries Betsy announced over the intercom that breakfast was ready whenever we were. Being famished, I opted not to shave, and pulled on my clothes. After running a hand through a tousled mop of hair I snatched the laptop from the desk, curious to know if Father had sent me anything, and dashed off to the galley.

"Hey sunshine," Betsy greeted warmly, "ready for some bacon and eggs and waffles and juice?"

"Oh yah you bet I am," I smiled eagerly; "it smells great."

"Did your father send anything sweetheart?"

"I'm gonna check now. I'm hoping there's something."

Once on-line I saw that there were over seventy e-mails; most of them junk advertisements and allurements for one kind of a drug or another. After scrolling through the list I realized that nothing had arrived from my Dad.

"There's nothing here Betsy."

"Honey didn't you double encrypt the last one you sent him?"

"Oh yah, that's right, I forgot!"

After pulling up the hidden file I saw the icon blinking; a message *had* been sent early the previous day.

"What does it say?" Betsy put down the plate of food and slid in next to me. After wolfing down several mouthfuls, and raving about how great it was, the file was opened and I began to scan the contents. As I was, several of the others sauntered in sleepy-eyed and hungry. The e-mail read:

Hello son – be very cautious in everything you do now! Consider everyone the enemy unless they have proven otherwise. All of your lives are in danger. Make sure that Captain Olaf knows everything that I've shared with you here.

Now, it has come to my attention that the GVIN has been catastrophically compromised. The professor's family is apparently being held hostage somewhere in Rabat and the professor himself was kidnapped and has disappeared. No one knows any more details. It happened suddenly and was carried out flawlessly. There have been no demands for his release yet and no one knows where he is. One of his operatives, Hector, (the fella that sent you the up-date and the one who's helping us with protection aboard the tankers) informed me five days ago that security and the main headquarters in Rabat have been overrun by these hooligans. Also, some weeks ago the GVIN computers were compromised by a rogue group, purportedly led by Amalek Baaldur and a subsidiary company located in the Pacific Northwest called Global Paradigm. Seems this company is a front to launder money for the Mortiken and their global affiliates. According to Hector, the faction that had infiltrated the company had been slowly compromising everything for eight months. Can you imagine that? And the fact that no one knew about it troubles me. Be advised Gabriel that the Mortiken occupy key areas now globally, and the control they have has increased enormously. In the next few days I'll compile what I have and send you a list of these areas.

From what I understand presently, the Underground Realm has been compromised by the Mortiken and large parts of Torfar-Kolla, and all the other outlying settlements, along the Great Sea, were ruined in the geological event. Yesterday I learned about this from a group of the professor's operatives that have monitored the situation covertly for him personally. Gabriel, please guard all the information and photos that you've collected down there. This is imperative; give them to no one, and tell no one that you have them!

I don't know where you are presently son and I'd be lying if I said I wasn't worried. I've heard rumors that the crew was airlifted out of the realm recently, but those reports are sketchy. I need to hear from you ASAP, your Mother and me are concerned about your welfare, as well as the crews'.

Son … I found out a few hours ago, just before I sent this to you, that the professor may be hostage aboard the Red Dragon, but no one knows where that vessel is at present. If you have any information about this let me know. Please be careful son, and give my best to the team. We love you and are very proud of all of you! Have Olaf contact me at his earliest convenience. Please use this encrypted number: 1-000-439-2789.

Again son, don't trust anyone, and please tell the others not to say anything to anyone about what you're doing. You have $600,000.00 now in your account. The card will work everywhere, but I've made it completely untraceable. Use it wisely! Mother sends her affections.

Love Dad

Those in the galley were riveted and I felt something shift in everyone after I'd finished reading. It was as if a huge emotional burden had lifted off everyone's soul and had been replaced by an indignant anger. Now, everything made sense; his strange behavior, his unusual requests, the departure from his normally structured correspondence; it was all because of the duress he was under.

"Wow, what a letter," Betsy murmured. "Global Paradigm - this puts a different slant on everything now."

"It surely does lass!" Captain Olaf pulled vigorously at his moustache. "This surely has put a fire under me. Thank God for this note! I think now that it's clear what we have to do next."

"I agree!" Anders shook his head. "But how can we find out if he's aboard the Dragon? We'll have to try and get him off if he is you know."

"I'm open for suggestions," the Captain glanced about keenly.

"Boss I know a way that might work." Garrett stood up. "The Global Paradigm computer we traced has a GPS in it; kinda like a cell phone does. If I can locate a point of origin when that e-mail was sent, it might also give us the latitude and longitude of where the computer is located when it uplinks ..."

"You can do that son," the Captain interjected excitedly.

"I can try boss." Garrett shrugged. "Helga can help me too; she's really good at this kinda stuff."

"Helga?" the Captain turned.

"We can certainly try Olaf."

"You mean if the computer's aboard the Red Dragon we can ascertain where the vessel is?" The Captains eyes were hopeful.

"If they access the internet; yah," Garrett nodded.

"Olaf, we're approaching Nootka," Rorek's voice came over the intercom. "Are the ladies ready to disembark?"

"We should take them in on the raft," John suggested. "We can't let anyone see us."

"I agree." The Captain nodded. "And Gabriel, make sure that you answer your Father ASAP. Let me know when he responds."

"I'll do it now sir," I assured him.

"John, you and Anders offload the raft, and Betsy," the Captain continued, "please inform the ladies it's time to disembark."

"Aye sir, on my way," Betsy answered.

"Rorek, how close are we to shore," the Captain asked.

"We're thirty-seven miles out Olaf."

"Are there any vessels between us and the shore?"

"There's one sixty miles north of us on a southwestern bearing."

"Alright, position the *Heimdall* three miles from shore then."

"Aye, it'll surely make it easier for them to get the ladies in – it's a good idea."

"Keep me posted then Rorek; I'll be in the galley."

Forty-Five

A Unique Opportunity

The moment had come for us to say our farewells. Parting was proving difficult, though, especially for the ladies, and it was getting a bit more emotional than I felt comfortable with. We all boarded the raft, as soon as the schooner was anchored, and took off for Nootka. We found the channel leading into the harbor easily, using one of the Captain's costal charts and, after paying a nominal fee, we tied off on a slip along the pier. Thankfully no one asked any questions about where we'd come from. Once inside the terminal, and personal belongings had been checked in, and a flight had been booked, both couples drifted into different corners. Being the odd man out I found a table on the terrace and ordered a coffee from a rotund waitress with greasy hair who smelled like the hold of a fishing vessel. This was not a place that I had any intention of returning to.

Later, when it appeared they were about to part, I moved over to offer my personal farewells to the ladies and wish them the best in their upcoming endeavors. Both women carried on about how much they were going to miss me, and how they wished I would consider coming along with them, and how they didn't want to leave at such an important time but they had to and, in-between the sniveling and tears, hugs and kisses were liberally showered on me. Trying my best to remain stoic I found myself thrown off my game completely with a heart that was being effectively ground to a pulp. Soon both women were bawling again and then they began hugging me even more. Never before had I been the recipient of such intensely mournful affections; it was embarrassing. I noticed several in the room now smirking over the tops of their papers and shaking their heads. Knowing there was nothing at all I could do to make this any better; I pulled away and ordered another cup of coffee, this time with a magazine and a hot buttered cinnamon roll, and went back out on the terrace. Finally, an hour later, Jonah nodded at me that they were ready to leave. After waving from a safe distance I turned and made my way down the wooden staircase. Both men were subdued as we made our way out towards the pier. After boarding the raft, I could see both women on the terrace waving. Anders and Jonah moved to the rear gunwale to wave back. Both of them were crying. With some reluctance I pushed away from the old dock and navigated out through the channel at a snail's pace. What was so difficult about this for them?

As I mulled the situation tears began welling up in my eyes; would we ever see them again? Maybe that was it. Maybe they were all afraid that they wouldn't see each other again. Troubled now, I asked God if we would ever see them again. The moment I'd finished a flood of peace surged into me and I heard a still voice whispering not to worry and that everything was as it should be. When the ladies had finally faded in the mist both men moved apart and began sulking. After clearing the surf line I accelerated to twenty-five knots and then radioed ahead that we were returning. Olaf told me that they'd moved the schooner two miles to the north of where they'd been.

"I'll turn on the strobe son," he continued, "you can navigate by that. Ok, it's on now."

"Captain I can just make it out northwest of us; we'll be there probably in about ten minutes."

"Copy that, see you then, Captain out."

I began yearning to be part of Roxanne and Angelina's new occupations. There would be simplicity and order in what they did and their duties would not require them putting their lives in harm's way anymore. I was convinced that Anders and Jonah were aware of this too and, despite their present brooding; I knew they were happy with the change for their wives and that they would soon be back to their old selves.

Once aboard, and after stowing the raft, we gathered together to discuss our present situation and what we were going to do. While we'd been in Nootka Rorek had inputted the exact coordinates we'd retrieved from Global Paradigms computer into the VEW.

"Looks like they're heading north," he pointed at the blinking icon on the screen, "I'm guessing towards Kodiak Island."

"Certainly a possibility," Helga answered, "but they …"

"Just had a thought," Betsy interrupted, "sorry sis; Captain, what do you think about using the algorithm we developed instead of the VEW program?"

"Of course," I jumped up excited with the suggestion, "it's more sophisticated than the VEW and we'll probably be able to see every little detail aboard the Red Dragon with it Captain. There's also the potential for hearing what's going on too."

"It has listening capabilities?" The Captain leaned forward in his chair intently.

"It does," Betsy shook her head, "and also infra-red and night vision if there's ever a need. But we cannot see below decks, or through the atmospheric anomaly, or through any kind of cloud cover. And we need clear skies and no magnetic interference."

"You should know Olaf that presently the anomaly is about one hundred miles north of us." Rorek brought him up to date. "If we're going to attempt this we need to do so as soon as possible."

"Alright, let's do it then!" The Captain looked convinced.

"Only one problem," Betsy glowered, "we've lost the address."

"No we didn't sis!" Garrett laughed. "It's on Gabriel's laptop; we loaded the software when we first found out about it."

"It's true," I smiled proudly. "I know it for memory sir: <u>profrabat@
earthnet.net/VEW/algorithm/tkholes</u> "

"I knew you were good for somethin' cheesewad," Garrett roared
laughing. "Your quick study brains like a steel trap but we gotta do
something about all the flies buzzin' round yur butt."

For several moments we all laughed at Garrett's crude humor
after which the Captain gave instructions to get started.

"There's still the possibility, Captain, that whoever commandeered
the GVIN has disabled all these programs." John suggested.

"Nothing ventured, nothing gained," was the Captain's response
to his concerns. "We'll have to find out if the Professor's aboard that
vessel first and, if he is, we must get him to safety."

"If we *can* access the program in Rabat, they won't even know
we have," Betsy continued. "Entry is encrypted to our personal
codes; we're invisible when we're inside the system; it was one of
the Professor's safeguards."

"That's good to know," Helga smiled. "There's a possibility, too,
that we don't have to route through Rabat anymore Olaf; we may be
able to access the satellite directly from our own mainframe."

"It's true Cap; we do have greater capacity than ever," Garrett
made clear. "Whatever the professor did while the *Heimdall* was dry-
docked allows us to be a lot less dependent on Rabat."

"I wonder why he did that," John pondered.

"Don't know, but we've gotta take advantage of it; what say we
get started." The Captain suggested with eager eyes.

"Before we do Olaf, let's pray." Jonah suggested.

"It's a good idea Jonah, why don't you lead."

After analyzing the new systems, we found that what we had previously understood about the virtual capabilities of the *Heimdall* had to be set aside. It was a new approach now and I heard, in my spirit, the immortal words of Sherlock Holmes: "a new game was afoot." At present it seemed we were able to process all information without routing anything through Rabat. It was as if we'd become an autonomous control center in our own unique realm of expertise; much like Air Force One was for the United States government in times of national emergency. The recently installed computers were able to control all surveillance and satellite communication without interfacing with the GVIN. Why the professor had chosen to do this was a mystery; it was almost as if he'd taken himself out of the equation. The upgrades had freed us and we weren't dependent on anyone anymore.

As the *Heimdall* sliced through chill waters towards the northern parts of Vancouver Island; we swiftly and precisely pieced together every bit of information the satellite was streaming down to us about the Red Dragon. After calibrated the audio on the software, we were able to hear all conversations above decks. We heard that Krystal Blackeyes was going to rendezvous with the Dragon somewhere along the western coast of Canada within twenty-four hours. They were going to anchor somewhere north of us near a grouping of western Canadian archipelagoes to board supplies and more soldiers that were being imported from the Sea of Cortez. What was most amazing, though, was discovering that the professor *was* captive aboard the Red Dragon; my father's information had been correct.

We were faced now with a variety of unique circumstances. First and foremost, it was our intention to rescue the professor and in the process hopefully try and snatch Jonah's sister. We were also hoping that after we'd formulated something viable, and if we could remain unassailable during the implementation of it, that the tide would be turning against the Mortiken global agenda. The Baaldurians certainly weren't the only ones capable of clandestine operations; we were too, and hopefully now we would be able to prove it. Jonah was delighted with the news about his sister and began developing a strategy with Lizzy to deal with her if we were fortunate enough to be successful in our endeavors. I realized, too, that without Krystal Blackeyes it was entirely possible that the global agenda for the Baaldurians might come to a halt temporarily or perhaps even longer. Was it possible that we could affect such a change in global chemistry?

Forty-Six

The Sinking of the Red Dragon

Later in the day

"Captain, I have the Red Dragon on radar," John reported from the wheelhouse. "They're twenty-nine miles northeast on a parallel latitude heading."

"Copy that," the Captain responded. "Let's maneuver a mile off her port, stay slightly aft John, head to wind luffing, and sails slightly loose; we'll shadow the vessel until she stops."

"Aye Captain, but won't they see us?"

"No they won't my friend," the Captain answered grinning.

"Not with the new CSAT John," Rorek explained, "The vessel is completely invisible to them."

"But the wake we're creating …"

"The effect can be extended three hundred yards now; this new CSAT is total bomb dude!" Garrett explained with his usual flair. "They can't see anything of us, not even the wake."

"I didn't know that," John answered, "I'm impressed."

During our exchange the weather picked up suddenly and within minutes the surface was heaving with whitecaps. A northern wind had fallen upon us and it had begun biting at our faces with an icy sting.

"This doesn't look good," Garrett complained.

"Windbreakers and headgear," the Captain shouted on his way up the stairs into the wheelhouse. "Gabriel, you and Anders tighten the lanyard on the forward jib; don't want it damaged."

"Aye sir," they shouted as they made their way forward.

"I'll take the wheel John," The Captain said upon entering the wheelhouse, "Please help them secure things out there."

"Aye sir," he responded as command of the vessel changed hands.

"When you're done John please come back and monitor the radios; I'm gonna have my hands full with this bloody wheel."

"Sure will Captain," John answered. "And be careful, it's bucking somethin' awful."

The storm was unpredictable and soon we were heaving stem to stern in wild seas and waves began crashing over the bowsprit and parts of the deck.

"Make sure the scuppers are open!" The Captain barked. "Close all the windows below ladies, and Anders, lock down the capstans. Garrett, secure the main door and all the inside doors!"

"It's from the Gulf of Alaska Captain," Helga explained over the intercom. "Navtex reports say it'll be a rough ride."

"Aye, keep me up-dated lass," The Captain grimaced. "And keep an eye on the radar too; I want to know where the Dragon goes."

"Copy that; they're four miles northeast presently."

All of a sudden the weather came down on us like a hammer on an anvil. It was terrifying. Within minutes the rain had begun to freeze and a layer of ice was beginning to build up on the deck and railings.

"Olaf, let's lower sails before they freeze; Rorek suggested, "We can use the diesel."

"You're right brother," the Captain shook his head. "Tell the others for me will you? I've never seen anything like this before."

"Aye, it's a wild one brother. Anders, John, Gabriel, Garrett, sails down now and carefully," Rorek ordered over the intercom.

"Aye aye," they chorused, waving as they scattered to the servo-systems on each mast.

"Is the diesel warm?" the Captain inquired.

"It's ready to engage, yes." Rorek returned calmly.

"Let's step-up screw torque as soon as you engage.

"Aye Captain," Rorek answered with an unusual show of respect.

"The new diesel will give us the power we require in these seas. I'll let you know when the transmission synchs brother."

The switchover went flawlessly and I could feel the schooner stabilize nicely in the ramping seas. We had the power now necessary to maintain our course.

Lightening crosshatched the skies and the once distant rumbling thunder had become explosive bursts all around us. It was deafening and, for a few moments, I considered that we just might not make it. Given this I began entertaining mythology in an effort to lessen a burgeoning trepidation in me. Grinning, I considered perhaps that *Aeolus*, the barrel-chested Greek god of wind was unleashing this withering blast, or perhaps *Fujin*, the Japanese wind demon, was sharing some of those terrible things he kept hidden in that great bag draped over his shoulders. But then, perhaps, and infinitely more to my liking, I considered that *Thor*, the great and mighty Norse god, was brandishing his powerful hammer against the evil Red Dragon to help us in our quest somehow. Yes, this was the reason and I began laughing and my focus returned. How the imagination would wander at times, and how utterly frivolous our thoughts could become in context to reality. I wondered, despite how colorful the human spirit had been over the centuries, in its artistic expression of those things that remained inexplicable, if it was possible that these mythological heroes weren't just angels on assignment.

The crew was focused at their tasks; this storm was testing us all. During an exceptionally brilliant flash of lightening, one that seemed to cover the entire sky, I caught a glimpse of Captain Olaf's face illuminated through the wheelhouse window. Never before had I seen our leader as determined or more focused on his duty. With eyes set straight ahead, and teeth clenched, I knew he was fighting valiantly to keep the vessel from yielding to the wooing of Davy Jones. Fiendish wind was ripping at my exposed face and the cold stabbed through my clothes like needles. On and on the battle went. There was nothing mythological about this; it was a life and death struggle. Courageously we fought to keep the vessel in harmony. But just when you thought that the conditions could get no worse the sea turned on us with an unexpected savagery. Mountainous swells had begun topping one hundred plus feet around us and wind was pummeling the vessel from the north and the west and then from both directions at the same time. Funnel clouds were appearing randomly in the turbulent atmosphere and striking down ferociously at the surface of the water. Never once though did they come near the vessel; I felt as if the Holy Spirit was protecting us in the midst of this raging weather. For what seemed an interminable period Olaf fought the raging sea with great skill and courage, all the while maintaining lateral stability of the keel as we sliced down the mountainous swells into the ominous troughs and then back up the other sides. For two hours the storm raged, but then, as rapidly as the ferocious squall had appeared, it degraded. Within the span of sixty seconds the winds had abated and warming rays of sunlight had begun bursting forth from behind dispersing clouds in a show of grand supernal glory.

"Navtex is reporting another storm system bearing down on us." Helga reported. "It's not over Captain; we're only in a lull."

"Copy that lass, keep me posted!"

However welcome this change was, the frigid arctic air and mountainous swells persisted; as a precaution everyone was instructed to continue using safety tethers. Removing the buildup of ice was tedious, and the cold was miserable and, to make matters worse, the scary atmospheric anomaly had begun undulating in the sky just north of us. I felt as if it was taunting us and laughing at our plight.

"Cox Island is off our port bow Captain," Helga reported some time later. "There's a helicopter circling the Dragon just southwest of Lanz Island; it has pontoons."

"Pontoons; they're landing on the water?"

"Aye sir, they just did. A boat's being lowered. A lotta hoopla on the vessel sir; a big fire burning on the forward bow; must be someone important." Helga reported.

"Can you see who it is; is there more than one person?"

"There's only one boarding the raft, no one else. It's a woman; blonde hair; petite; looks like the witch."

"Then it was accurate," Jonah sighed. "Eloise *is* here."

"Lord willing you two will be back together real soon." Garrett encouraged him. "Witch or not, Gods got good plans for her."

"I hope so son," Jonah sighed. "You know there's no way she can stay aboard if we do happen to rescue her."

"I know," Garrett answered somberly, "it'd be too dangerous."

"It would son, yes, so we've decided - Lizzy and me - to take her back to Pine Valley. We have a room there; it's where the sword and rubies are; we can hide her safely."

"Lizzy's going with you?" Betsy asked surprised.

"Only for a week or two," Lizzy answered reassuringly. "We're both assuming that she's pretty far gone honey; it's possible that she'll require medical help to readapt."

"She *could* compromise everything you know, how you gonna deal with her?" John seemed puzzled.

"We're not sure; we're going to pray John. It'll be me and her for awhile I imagine. We'll have to play it as it comes."

"I can't imagine that she won't be restored completely," Betsy began stabbing at tears rolling down her cheeks, "We've all prayed about this so many times Jonah."

"Can you hear anything on the Dragon Helga?"

"No Captain, there's too much interference. It's getting increasingly magnetic and I'm concerned that we're going to lose our visuals."

"What's causing it?" The Captain asked.

"It's the anomaly, it's getting closer." Helga grumbled fearfully.

"Will we go through it?" the Captains brow tightened.

"Don't know yet, but I'm convinced it's the cause of these storms."

"You suppose the next one could be worse?"

"It's possible, but I'm out of my league on this."

As the brothers were talking, the weather changed again with sudden and dramatic fury. Ominous swirling black clouds descended as violent erratic winds buffeted the vessel from different directions.

"Positions everyone," the Captain shouted tensely. "Rorek, put the transmission in second gear, we'll need more screw torque."

"Aye brother it's a good idea."

Lightening was striking savagely at the surface around us and within minute's diminished visibility had made it impossible to make out one end of the schooner from the other.

"I've never seen anything like this," Rorek grumbled as huge raindrops pelted the wheelhouse window.

"Neither have I brother," the Captain sighed. "Thank God there are no reefs here; it would be disastrous."

"Yes indeed, thank God," Rorek nodded as he ran out to help.

Several times bolts of lightning struck the bowsprit; thankfully the massive energy was being diffused out through the hull and wasn't bothering our electronics at all. Every time the schooner was hit the water around us would glow bluish white and any fish near the surface were killed instantly; the sea appeared like an apocalyptic vision. This storm was more electrical than the one previous. Despite nature's savage volatility, though, I felt no fear at all, only a gritty resolve to make it through alive so we could continue and fulfill our mysterious mandate.

"Captain, I just intercepted an SOS from the helicopter and then it went dead," Helga cried out, "they've gone down near the shore. Sir I just caught a glimpse of the wreckage; it's on fire."

"Good lord lass," Olaf responded wide-eyed.

"Good riddance to um boss," Garrett laughed wildly.

"Olaf, there's water in the hold," Rorek's voice crackled over the intercom. "It's not hull breach; one of the bottom portholes was left open. I'll get the bilge going before we start listing starboard."

"Copy that! Keep me up-dated."

"Captain, I'm picking up a distress beacon from the Dragon; I think they're floundering."

"Floundering … where lass?"

"Just west of Lanz Island," Helga continued.

"Looks like they may be sinking boss," Garrett added.

"I agree; I think they've hit a reef." Helga assumed.

"Either that or rocks boss," Garrett added.

"Oh Captain," Helga cried out, "we just saw the vessel clearly for a few seconds on the VEW screen. Part of the starboard bow is ripped away and it's on fire; they're sinking Olaf; my god the professor!"

"Olaf, waters' cleared; I'm shutting down the bilge."

"Copy that Rorek; any damage?"

"None at all; we're blessed!"

"Olaf, please, we've got to try and help." Jonah implored with tears.

"I know Jonah, I've changed our heading."

"Wonderful, thankyou Olaf," Jonah stabbed at his eyes.

"Prepare to intercept the Dragon," the Captain ordered over the schooners intercom. "John, issue everyone firearms."

"I'll hand them out now sir," John responded.

Immediately following our Captains decision to help, the storm abated, and the seas began calming. The timing intrigued me. Ten minutes later what remained of the Red Dragon came into view off our port bow. The only parts of her still visible were the masts, the tops of the cabins, and part of the stern and rudder; the vessel was quickly nosing down into an icy grave. John was on the bow now with the telescope searching for survivors.

"John what do you see?"

"A lot of bodies on the water Captain, and there are pieces of the vessel scattered everywhere. Several hundred yards port stern I see two dinghies'; there's a lone man in one of them and four in the other, and that ponytail sure looks familiar." John reported.

"Garrett, shut down the CSAT! Are they armed John?"

"It's hard to say from here." John shouted back.

The moment the *Heimdall* appeared the Mortiken began gesturing wildly and screaming to each other that we were the Ghost Vessel. A moment later they started shooting at us and at the other dinghy. The lone man disappeared below the gunwale. When the two dinghies were separated in the currents the Mortiken turned their full attention towards us and fired repeatedly.

"Helga, your rifle," The Captain ordered frantically as a hail of bullets whizzed near us. "John, take out those bums!"

"Aye sir," John waved as the others began firing.

During the first volley two fell and, as soon as Helga was in place, the others fell seconds later. The lone man stood up, when the gunfire had ended, and began waving and pointing down. Immediately the raft was lowered and Jonah, Anders, John and I roared off in the dinghy's direction. During the short ride we watched the Red Dragon's last moments. Systematically breaking apart, the vessel let out a final gurgling hiss and slid beneath the frigid Pacific waters. It was a most astonishing sight, watching this vessel die, and though I could have easily grieved the loss of something so remarkably kept, I was thankful (more) that Amalek Baaldur's prize possession had finally been destroyed; we all hated him and everything he stood for!

"It's the professor Captain," John radioed back as we neared.

"Copy that John," he answered, "it's wonderful news."

The carnage was frightening. Around us the lifeless eyes of many dozens of bodies were fixed on the sky as John maneuvered through the wreckage of this once formidable sea going vessel. Most of them, I could tell, had been horror-stricken in the last moments; desperation was frozen on every face like a grim mask. Transfixed on the scene, I recalled something from the 'Book of Heroes' in Norse mythology entitled 'Doom of Odin'.

"I find no comfort in the shade
Under the branch of the great ash.
I remember the mist of our ancient past.
As I speak to you in the present
My ancient eyes see the terrible future.
Do you see what I see?
Do you hear death approaching?
The mournful cry of Giallr-horn shall shatter the peace
And shake the foundation of Heaven.
Raise up your banner and gather your noble company
From your great hall, Father of the Slains
For you shall go to your destiny

No knowledge can save you, and no magic will save you.

For you will end up in Fenrir's belly, while heaven

And earth burn in Surt's unholy fire."

Gripped by the terrifying scope of what'd happened a surge of overwhelming compassion welled up inside me for what the Professor had endured at the hands of the vile Baaldurians.

"Please hurry my friends," he was shouting and waving excitedly. "There is no time to lose."

Forty-Seven

Saving Krystal Blackeyes

"Professor, are you well," John asked as we pulled alongside.

"I am my friend, I am, yes. And praise God this dreadful trying circumstance has finally ended; may the Holy Christ be exalted for allowing that loathsome vessel and its inhabitants to be destroyed and for putting you here at this most happy moment in time."

"You got that right buddy," Anders cheered.

"There is someone here that you know and love Jonah," The professor pointed down with a show of compassion. "I was able to pull her from the wreckage but grievous is her wounds; she is near death my friend."

Jonah crawled over the gunwale into the dinghy. Lying on the bottom, barely stirring, was his sister Eloise; the terrible ordeal had rendered her wretched. Bedraggled and bloodied from a terrible gash that started on the bridge of her nose and ending near the back of her scalp; she was in dire need of medical attention. Being aware of the criticalness of her condition, Anders radioed ahead to spell out all the details to Lizzy of the incoming medical emergency. She was stunned but assured him that they'd be ready.

With his tears falling on her ashen features, Jonah gently drew his sister up to his chest and began to rock back and forth. She was not the malefic witch Krystal Blackeyes anymore. Now only a helplessly wounded woman was lying in Jonah's quivering arms; all the evil posturing and ability to control had been taken suddenly from her. A miracle was unfolding right before our eyes. How long had we prayed for this. And now God was answering in a most profoundly unexpected way. With more love than I'd ever felt from him, Jonah pleaded aloud with the Father for her life and for her salvation. As he was I saw her eyes flutter open for a moment and heard her whisper:

"Jonah, is that you? Where am I? Where are Mom and Dad?"

Seconds later she passed out once again and her breathing got shallow and erratic. There was no time to lose. Within minutes she was safely aboard the schooner. At once the Captain ordered Garrett to re-engage the CSAT and he gave Rorek new coordinates. A hush fell in the room as the ladies prepared for surgery. Everyone on the crew except the Professor (who was sleeping) and Rorek (who was piloting the schooner) remained near to help. After testing everyone's blood Lizzy found that Jonah's and Garrett's were compatible with Eloise's. This alone was a miracle since there was no blood aboard for emergencies. Lizzy was overjoyed and, after drawing a quart from both men she and Helga (who would act as her surgical nurse) began scrubbing up. As per Lizzy's instructions Betsy gave Jonah and Garrett each a glass of orange juice to drink and then instructed them to lie down in the galley to recover. Grumbling; both obeyed. Within minutes Eloise was administered anesthesia and her head was shaved in the areas damaged.

It was hard to believe that the woman lying on the operating table was the Mortiken high witch. She was so unthreatening and petite, and so near deaths door, and so completely at the mercy of our practitioner, and so desperately in need of the Holy Spirit's intervention for her survival. There were six jagged deep cuts, and several hairline fractures, on the woman's skull; according to Lizzy's prognosis the wounds were life-threatening. As soon as Helga had removed dozens of wooden splinters Lizzy disinfected the wounds, cut away the mangled flesh, and then stitched the long gashes on her head in three different levels; deep tissue, mid-tissue, and surface skin. For hours the ladies toiled to repair the damage. And when things became critical, as they did several times, Lizzy brought Betsy in to help maintain the correct level of anesthesia and administer the transfusions while she and Helga struggled to save her. Twice Eloise flat-lined during the procedure and had to be resuscitated with the defibrillator. There was a feeling of desperation in the room during these harrowing moments and Jonah sobbed pitiably. Nearing six hours of surgery the ladies had finally finished with Eloise.

"She'll require a lot of rest Olaf," Lizzy sighed exhausted as she sipped her coffee. "She's suffered a serious trauma to the scalp and skull and also her spine was compressed between cervical two and five. Thankfully she's not paralyzed. Olaf, she may not know who she is for awhile or possibly even ever."

"It's that bad eh?" The Captain shook his head solemnly.

"I'm afraid it is, Olaf, it's in God's hands now." Lizzy answered. "She was truly fortunate that the Professor was able to pull her from the vessel, otherwise ...."

"I don't even want to think about what that would have done to Jonah's frame of mind," the Captain sighed.

"Captain I'm sure the Mortiken are going to assume that since the Dragon and crew was lost, Krystal was lost also," John pondered. "This *could* work to our advantage strategically you know."

"Yes, it could," the Captain agreed.

"Olaf, we *must* lay low awhile for her sake." Jonah pleaded.

"It *would* be wise to stay quiet for several days until she gets through the first phase of healing Olaf," Lizzy supported Jonah.

"I've contacted Roxanne and told her that we'll be bringing her home," Jonah continued after hugging Lizzy, "She and Angelina are preparing the safe room now. She's saying it'll take about three days to get what we need and then they'll be ready."

"How do you suggest we transport her?" the Captain asked.

"I was hoping the professor might help us with that when he wakes up," Jonah answered. "Do you think he can access his helicopters?"

"I don't know if he can or not Jonah. Let me check the charts ok? I'll find a place to anchor for several days; someplace that's off the beaten track and safe."

"Captain Olaf sir ..."

"What is it Gabriel?"

"What do you think about me trying to get my Father on that number he gave us? He may be able to help us with a solution."

"It's a fine idea son," the Captains eyes opened wide with hope. "Let me know if you do; I'd like to talk to him."

"Alright sir, I'll start trying now."

The Captain and Rorek immediately began poring over Canadian coastline charts. After dinner Olaf showed us the route we'd be taking towards Smith Sound, and then, how he would take us northeast in the direction of Penrose Island Provincial Marine Park between Fitz Hugh Sound and Rivers Inlet. He told us that this particular marine park was a beautiful archipelago of small coves with a labyrinth of narrow deep channels. It was an isolated topography that catered primarily to wilderness camping, and hiking, and fishing, and canoeing, and also those searching for peace. Here was an undeveloped wilderness with no facilities and absolutely no creature comforts, a pristine mosaic of God's multi-faceted and undefiled creativity. Having become a lover of all things untouched by the hand of man it sounded perfect to me. According to the charts the only settlement of note was the township of Dawson's landing, twenty miles to the east, but this would pose no threat to our anonymity.

"The anomaly is shifting north people," Garrett radioed from the control room. "All satellite functions have returned. The Doc's made contact with his Pop boss; he's on the phone right now and he wants you to come and talk to him."

"Excellent son, thankyou; I'm on my way!"

Forty-Eight

Reorienting

"Olaf, good to hear your voice my friend," Elwin began.

"Likewise Mr. Proudmore," the Captain answered. "I hope that you are well sir. Much is changing now you know."

"Yes it is Captain; dramatically so, and I'm very glad that you made it through your ordeal in the Caldera safely sir. And yes, we *are* well here, and the business is prospering. I also have something exciting that Mother and I are working on that I'll talk to you later about. We'll be praying for Jonah's sister's recovery. What an incredible turn of events Captain, and my kudos for a job well done. We can only hope and pray that she'll be swayed away from Amalek and the Mortiken ethos; he'll go on a rampage, I'm sure, when he finds out what's happened to her."

"We feel the same Elwin, but we also see the situation working to our advantage strategically."

"It could, yes; we'll know soon enough. Olaf, Gabriel brought me up to date on your present situation. How this unfolded with the Red Dragon and the witch is just amazing to me."

"It is indeed; a miracle in my book."

"You know the professor's organization has been overrun and destroyed; a most unfortunate turn of events. There is, however, one HH-60 that remains safe; Hector has it hidden if there's ever a need."

"The three that transported us to Tatoosh Island Elwin, what happened to them?" The Captain asked.

"They were shot down, Captain, over Arizona near the Grand Canyon; no one survived."

"Oh Lord, that's terrible; what about their families?"

"All were unmarried with no children Olaf. They all understood the risks. No one can be trusted in the GVIN anymore save two operatives who have worked closely with the Professor since the company's inception. The professor can tell you who they are; I don't know their names off hand. By the way, is he well?"

"He is, yes. As far as I know he's still sleeping Elwin and I don't want to bother him. It was a traumatic ordeal for him."

"I can't imagine what he went through Olaf."

"I know. I'm sure, though, that when he has a chance, he'll tell us everything about it."

"I'm looking forward to hearing the story. Captain Olaf, Gabriel told me about your present dilemma and I want you to know that I have a solution; a way to transport Jonah, his sister, and Lizzy down to San Diego safely."

"Wonderful, I was hoping you would. We feel helpless concerning this; don't have a clear direction on anything at the moment."

"Give it some time Captain, everything will reorient. There's work yet to be accomplished you know."

"I believe so Elwin," The Captain sighed.

"Olaf, my tanker, the Absinthe, is presently docked in Cordova Alaska. It'll be there three more days and then they're heading down to La Paz in Baja. I'll make arrangements with Captain Mortimer to rendezvous with you. From what I can see on the charts, he'll be able to stop just west of Calvert Island, latitude 51 degrees – 30` and longitude 128 degrees – 30`. We'll board your people at those coordinates and get them down to San Diego. I'll keep everything quiet; no one will know who we're transporting or what our business is. I'm close friends with a company in Point Loma that books private flights Captain. I'll make arrangements for a private helicopter to take them directly from the tanker into Pine Valley. I'll also clear the flight with air traffic and give it the highest medical priority possible. No one will bother them, rest assured."

"This is excellent Elwin. Jonah will be overjoyed with this news; thankyou so much my friend."

"Glad to be of help Captain. Please, as soon as the Professor has regained his strength I'd like to talk to him. There are some loose ends we need to deal with, the main one being the remaining SES. Olaf is there anything that you need, anything I can do?"

"No Elwin, we still have money from the grants, the vessel is in prime condition now, and thankyou also for Gabriel's account. We'll need to restock soon though; food and supplies was the only thing the professor was unable to accomplish. Would you happen to know a place where we can?"

"That's no problem sir. I'll instruct the Absinthe to re-stock the *Heimdall*. Please e-mail them a complete list of whatever you require so they can put it together for you. If you could do that today they'll be able to purchase everything in Cordova before Wednesday's departure. Now Captain, please anticipate the tanker arriving in five days on September seventh, Thursday, probably early afternoon. I'll have the first mate contact you when they near the rendezvous point."

"Elwin, this is most excellent."

"We're a team Olaf; I could do nothing less, and my sincerest thanks to you for taking care of my son. Please let me know when you've reached your next anchorage."

"I will sir; we should be there early evening."

"Enjoy yourselves; you deserve a break. Captain Olaf, in closing, I want you to know that the work you and your crew are doing is most exceptional. You have my utmost respect sir, in all ways. I cannot imagine what it's like doing what you do on a daily basis. You and your team are a most important and critical part of the war that has encroached upon our planet. You have accomplished much that has moved the tide favorably for us against this despicable enemy. Stay strong and focused Olaf and know that I believe with all my heart that God has put your team together, and that He is with you, and guides you at all times, no matter what you endure or how it feels. There is so much talent and ability aboard your vessel. In the weeks ahead I believe that much of what you have been struggling with, concerning the First Tribe, will come into a clear light. I am very proud to be affiliated with you Captain, and also your dauntless crew. If there's ever a need, *ever* sir, please do *not* hesitate to call me. I'll talk to you soon Olaf, God bless you my friend."

Forty-Nine

A Time of Rest and Reflection

After finishing with my father, the Captain informed Jonah and Lizzy about the new travel arrangements, and then he instructed Betsy and Helga and John to put together a list of what supplies were needed aboard. I could see tears in the Captains eyes when he passed on his way to the wheelhouse. With strength and avidity he grasped the big wheel and set course for Fitz Hugh Sound. Upon reaching speed he began singing a catchy song that I'd never heard before. The words seemed to tell a story about a Norseman who had gone through hell in search of his dreams. And though he had not yet realized them in their fullness, it was the many struggles he'd endured, in the pursuit of his dreams that had made the man stronger and more determined. The Captains strong voice filtered throughout the vessel and out over the water; soon Rorek was singing along with him with great gusto. A burden had lifted from the Captains heart; his face was glowing, the creases on his forehead weren't as prominent, he seemed ten years younger, and he was joking again like he had so often in the past. All the sluggishness of spirit had somehow been replaced with a bubbling eagerness to press forward. I loved when things like this happened. Captain suggested to Betsy and Helga that they consider putting together a celebratory dinner sometime in the next few days. Both ladies raved about the idea.

As we were entering Smith Sound, Helga informed the Captain that they'd faxed the completed supply list to the Absinthe.

"Captain we got what we needed and then some," she went on. "John put together a list of ammunition and added two dozen more limpet charges too. Seems Mr. Proudmore had already contacted them because they didn't question anything we asked for; we were assured that everything we ordered would be delivered at the rendezvous."

"How cool is that dudes?" The Captain laughed heartily.

"You got that right," Garrett shouted back from the bowsprit. "Hey boss ... when did you start talkin' like me?"

"I didn't know I was you little peckerwood," the Captain laughed joyfully. "All I know is that I feel great and I'm so doggone hungry I could eat a buffalo." Everyone burst out laughing.

After the joviality had subsided Captain began sharing from his heart over the vessel's intercom. Everyone stopped to listen.

"I want to thank you crew for all that's been accomplished in the furtherance of our mission; it is greatly appreciated. You folks have no equals in my opinion. I know that much doesn't make sense right now, and I'm sure that each one of you is struggling with a certain amount of confusion about what we've been through in the last several months, but I'm sure as we press forward in faith, and we trust God to guide us, that these many things vexing us will be resolved. I praise God for each and every one of you, your incredible skills, your teamwork, your unfailing desire to always do the best you can, your humor, your tenaciousness when it seemed hopeless; and I want you to know that I believe with my whole heart that there is no finer group of people working together anywhere on the planet. Keep up the terrific work folks. I love you all dearly!"

For several moments no one said anything. Whatever transpired between him and my Father had lifted a burden from him which had freed his spirit somehow. Was he channeling, in some way, with us the grateful sentiment my Father had shared with him? I began hearing catcalls and whistles from different parts of the vessel, and a boisterous "thank-you Captain" echoed down from the crow's nest where John was working.

"That's us to a tee boss," Garrett shouted back from the bowsprit, "the best lookin' and the most talented butt kickin' dogs in the whole stinkin' universe! Ya baby!"

"Oh Captain we love you too," Helga giggled from the galley. "Now, about the celebration dinner you requested, here's what we can do with the supplies we have aboard. How about roasted sweet and sour pork loin- five spice apricot glazed turkey breast- broccoli raab and creamy pearl onions- homemade cranberry sauce- steamed jasmine rice, and french vanilla ice-cream for desert, we also have a dozen bottles of wine too sir; red and white. What do you think?"

"You girls can do all that?" The Captain was flabbergasted.

"Sure we can," Betsy responded cheerfully, "and even more if we had the provisions."

"Wonderful!" He laughed again heartily. "And while you talented ladies prepare for this culinary extravaganza I'm going to get us to our new anchorage."

Never before had I been in this part of the world; the rugged coastlines, that had obviously taken the brunt of many fierce storms, were ravaged, and furrowed, and strewn with boulders and, for as far as we could see, wind rippled sand wound north and south like a mottled earthy ribbon. Still, despite the fact that it was a pristine wilderness, unpopulated, and untouched by the schemes of modern constructions, the indicators of human carelessness was widespread; the shores, and many western archipelagoes, appeared as junk heaps littered with driftwood and trees, plastic bottles, medical waste, giant kelp, and hundreds of huge glass floats from the Japanese fleets that fished the Pacific water's in this area.

Our present bearing was taking us up through a gorgeous inland route called Rivers Inlet; the terminus of variously sized rivers and streams cascading down from the vast, and wild, mainland of British Columbia. Most of the topography was mountainous and widespread with Red Cedars, Hemlock, Sitka Spruce, and Pacific Silver Fur. It was healthy growth and, in select areas, I could even make out where the old forest had been carpeted magnificently with velvety textured mosses and hung mysteriously with gauzy lichens. Sometime after we'd entered Rivers Inlet John shouted down from the crows' nest to inform us that we would be passing, what appeared to him to be, the remnants of an ancient Indian village on our starboard.

"Wow this is great. Can you believe it?" John went on as the schooner came alongside the village. "Take a look at how they used to live guys, so simple and close to nature."

"I feel drawn to explore this settlement Captain; can we go ashore for awhile?" Anders asked.

"It'd be cool boss," Garrett nodded eagerly. "Never know what we may find here."

"Maybe even the Anasazi eh? John smiled broadly.

"That's a thought," I laughed; "wouldn't that be something?"

"Let's do it then." The Captain returned. "Let me get the vessel leeward of that island first. Can you see any features John?"

"A large inlet on the eastern side sir, well hidden; a lot of trees," John shouted after peering through the telescope,

"What's the depth?" the Captain asked.

"I'd say thirty, forty feet sir from the color of the water, but a lot shallower around the rest of the island."

"Prepare to drop the forward anchor Garrett."

"Aye sir," he shouted enthusiastically from the capstan.

Rolf had been sullen and withdrawn since Eloise and the professor had come aboard. He was sleeping underneath Garrett's bunk now and taking his meals in the engine room instead of where he usually ate outside the wheelhouse door. He seemed confused and preoccupied with something. As soon as we were anchored Rolf bolted to the bow. Hackles up, aroused, and indignant, he stared out towards the distant woods. Soon he was growling and slinking back and forth, as if there was something ashore that demanded his attention. Considering his behavior a precursor to some impending danger, we scrutinized as much of the area as we could (through the binoculars) but found nothing foreboding along the periphery of the woods or in the water around us. Rolf's vexation increased on the trip in. Twice he tried lunging off the bow of the raft but each time Garrett restrained him by gripping tightly to his leather collar and pulling him back. It was becoming a herculean effort for him; Rolf was strong and very stubborn. Eyes fixed on the nearing woods he continued tugging at his restraint and barking frantically. After ignoring every plea to behave, Rolf finally broke free and jumped into the water.

"Wuzzup with that dumb dog," Garrett growled in irritation. "Yah, go ahead and swim off you dumb mutt, see if I give a crap!"

Once on shore Rolf looked back for a moment, shook vigorously, and then galloped off into the woods barking madly.

"Let him do what he wants," the Captain advised, "we've got to get busy. We may have six hours of daylight left; if it takes any longer we'll be spending the night."

"It's cool with me boss," Garrett shrugged, "we got the food and there's plenty of wood."

"The last time I remember Rolf like this was on Socorro," Rorek said. After jumping off the bow he pulled the raft in and secured it on a huge piece of driftwood. Garrett nodded in agreement as he tied a second line at the stern.

"Yah your right boss," he said, "That's when the mutt caught a whiff of the graveyard and led us to that chest with the scrolls. Maybe he's caught a smell of somethin' here too."

"Could be son, could be ..." Rorek returned.

"We should have our weapons ready sir," John advised.

"I agree," Anders nodded, "no telling what we might encounter."

"Alright, let's load um up and spread out."

"Cool boss," Garrett nodded and began pressing cartridges into the pistol he was carrying.

"Stay alert," the Captain ordered as he waved us forward, "and John, radio Jonah and tell him to prepare weapons also?"

"Aye sir I will!"

"I dunno Cap, it's weird," Garrett remarked after a few minutes, "it kinda feels like we're supposed to be here."

"I feel it too Olaf," Rorek agreed, "how puzzling."

"God's timing, gentleman, it's always perfect. It could be that we're here at this very moment for a special reason."

"You mean First Tribe special Gabriel?" Anders grinned.

"We'll see Norseman," I nodded with a wink.

"Look at this place," John remarked with arms spread wide. "These people were really good with wood."

"And colorful too," Anders added pointing at a faded totem.

The old settlement was built along the shore for two hundred yards and, as far as we could tell, from where we were, it spread up into the woods another fifty yards. There was something inexplicable here; something mysterious and spiritual; a kind of peacefulness that reached into the soul.

"Do you guys feel something unusual?' I asked.

"I don't have a clue *what* I'm feeling son," the Captain returned, "whatever it is it's layin' up in me pretty strong."

Eight Eagles appeared suddenly from the western woods above us. Looping lazily they began speaking mysteries to my soul. It seemed to be a sign of sorts, especially at this point in time, and for some reason their appearance reminded me of something interesting from a Poet I'd studied in college.

Looking up to that which
Defies understanding
We are challenged to
Rise above our fears
And move upward

Eastward we are drawn
Along the unknown paths,
Mountains recumbent in
Wordless sighs capitulate
Under heavens felicity

With beating hearts,

Rife with ingenuous aplomb,

We purpose to triumph over

The high toothed ridges of

The infamous Garnet Peak

Floating effortlessly

8 Eagles drift by in fluid symmetry,

Percipient above ageless granite crags,

They loop and meander sinuously

On invisible winds

Purposing to join them

We press forward,

As each footstep,

Temporary, bereft,

Deposits another grain of life

Flourishing only in memory

Remembering this brought some comfort and undergirded the thoughts churning around inside me. I had always agreed with what the poet had contended. Every step in life requires a specific decision and moves us in the direction of something, and it also requires us to rise above our fears in the pursuit of what we've seen and purposed to accomplish. I wondered how much of our lives we wasted making the wrong decisions, and taking the wrong steps and then, because of it, ending up where we never should have been. From personal experience I understood that life could become unbalanced at times and take us down the wrong paths. These detours often created serious challenges and, if we were unawares and did not employ wisdom, we could end up in a morass that would take us three or four times longer to get out of than it'd taken us to get in. I was convinced that no one escaped this life untested; everyone got wounded (in one way or another) because of circumstance and their own foolish decisions.

We were designed by the Creator to love and help one another, but far too often unsound choices created circumstances that would force us to become isolated from those around us and ineffective in our callings. Every human being was subject to this. Easily separated by whatever spirit, or force, was working against them, (envy, jealousy, ethnicity and beliefs, social prejudices, colors, pride, fear, hate, wounds) people would put up social walls and hide in an effort to survive the very forces that they had put into motion. Trying to make sense of life's many struggles many would embrace anything that they believed would bring them peace and happiness. But it would never be a wise or lasting decision. What people desperately needed was a personal, and lasting, relationship with Light and Truth. Truth was inerrant and did not create different truths for different people. Light was not some capricious mythology, or bedtime story, nor was it some school of transcendental thought, or some Catholicity of religious propaganda. Truth was not cultural, nor did it have anything at all to do with the multi-faceted creations of mankind's pathologic imagination. Light was not something that functioned for the individual's personal pursuit of acceptance and success. Truth and Light did not create confusion or hatred, nor did they dwell in any form of darkness. Truth for us was a man who had given all to redeem His own creation back to Himself! Light and Truth was the Christ! I was convinced that everyone the Triune God had created was placed completely, and without qualification, at a point in time where their lives would make the greatest impact to fulfill His will for His creation. I was convinced that the One who chose that place - where we were born, and to whom we were born, and when in time we were born - also knew the beginning from the end and exactly what our impact would be. Time was rolled out as a scroll for the One who had created time, the universe, and beyond. He was *the* omniscient, omnipresent, and omnipotent God, and *He* had given us our lives for a very special reason. Many were called in this life but few were chosen to bring glory to the One who *is* Glory and Light. In my circumscribed understanding of Truth I knew that the conclusion of the matter was simply as Solomon had seen it. Everyone should fear God and keep His commandments; this was the whole duty of man during the extent of his life on this planet. For the Triune God, the Creator of all things, would one day bring every deed man had wrought into judgment, including every hidden thing, whether it was good or evil.

This journey had become the greatest challenge of my whole life. Nothing I'd ever done had even come close. My life made more sense to me now than when I'd begun with these people so long ago.

And though we'd been confronted with circumstances beyond our understanding I was thankful that the Creator loved us specifically, and that He was guiding us daily, and that we were unwaveringly unified together in purpose, with the faith and diligence to fulfill His will, and also our mandate to discover the First Tribe of Rognvald's.

"Come on Gabriel keep up," I heard the Captain calling in the distance, "We've got work to accomplish. Let's stay focused son."

"Aye Captain," I returned with a sigh, "I'm coming, I'm coming."

Clumsily scrambling to catch up I thanked God again for what He was doing in my life and for the most incredible and talented friends' one could ever hope to have. Faintly I could make out Rolf's frenetic barking in the far distance now, and the waves crashing on the rocks reminded me of all the dreams still tucked away in my heart waiting for wings to fly.

Fifty

Inland from the Haida Village

As I struggled to catch up a still small voice began speaking. It startled me. It was as intelligible as listening to any of my crewmates talking, but they were a hundred yards ahead. It felt as if something warm was being poured over my head. Most amazingly the voice spoke my name specifically: *"Know that you are loved, Gabriel, beloved of this age, soon you will understand better. Prepare for something wonderful."* Hopelessly taken I knelt down and praised God for loving me and for calling me to accomplish something for Him with these wonderfully talented people. Suddenly I was mindful again of my physical surroundings.

"Gabriel stop lollygagging," the Captain was motioning angrily, "get a move on, we've got work to do."

There were three enormous war canoes and thirty dwellings standing near the shoreline. The settlement appealed to me in its simplicity; every structure I could see was rectangular in shape and uniformly constructed. Exterior walls and gabled roofs had all been framed with bulky cedar timbers and sheeted with roughly hewn cedar planks. Mortuary and totem poles, of varying height and diameter, were interspersed throughout the community, and in front of each dwelling carved posts brooded like ancient guardians. Symbols on the poles, once brightly colored, had all faded from years of inclement weather and neglect. Time had taken its toll on this village. Only a few of the dwellings appeared safe enough to live in; most were in various stages of decay and some had even fallen and were rotting in heaps. It was puzzling. If everything had been built from the same materials, and in the same way, why had some structures fallen and decayed while others refused to?

"Is everything alright Gabriel," the Captain asked as I approached.

"Oh sure, I'm ready sir. Sorry it took so long."

"What say we split up then," the Captain suggested.

"Sounds good," Rorek answered. "Come along with Olaf and me John, let's discuss up-grading the satellite dish to accommodate the new software."

"Sure Rorek. Here Gabriel, take one of the radios."

"Why are we splitting up again?" Garrett asked with a scowl.

"Seems like the right thing to do son." The Captain shrugged as though curious himself. "There's something about this place that I can't put my finger on."

"Feel like we're supposed to be here Captain?" Anders laughed. "Don't worry, I've been feeling the same way since we anchored."

"It's not only that Norse; I feel more than ever that a doorway is about to open for us. This whole thing that's happened with Eloise and the Professor; I dunno, it's strange, but I have so much peace."

"Check it out boss," Garrett pointed, "just as you said that the sun broke through the clouds; it's gonna clear up now."

After praying and checking in with Jonah we split up into two groups. The Captains began an in-depth inspection of the village and war canoes, and our group ventured back into the woods along a path that had somehow remained open despite all the dense forest growth around. As we walked I recalled that the Haida Indians possessed an outstanding mutualism with nature. The men were superbly gifted as woodworkers and robust and highly stylized in their artistic expressions. Most everything in their rustic world, dwellings, cooking utensils, and canoes, were made from the trees that grew around them. Even the women wore skirts woven from cedar bark. The Haida nation was known traditionally as ruthless warriors and slave traders, raiding at times as far south as California. Some of the Haida war canoes were enormous; as long as fifty feet. An early anthropologist, employed for a time with the Canadian Museum of Civilization, Diamond Jenness, described them as the 'Indian Vikings' of the Northwest Coast and I remembered that he'd caught a bit of their heart and soul in something he wrote:*"Those were stirring times, about a century ago, when the big Haida war canoes, each hollowed out of a single cedar tree and manned by fifty or sixty warriors, traded and raided up and down the coast from Sitka in the north to the delta of the Frasier River in the south. Each usually carried a shaman or medicine man to catch and destroy the souls of enemies before an impending battle; and the women who sometimes accompanied their husbands fought as savagely as their husbands."*

The culture was not overly religious. The Haida believed that mammals and fish were actually supernatural beings in disguise, and often, the sterns and prows of the war vessels were carved with grand figures resembling birds or animals as a way to showcase the artisan's skill. Religious ceremonies, and myths, were often shared between tribes, (such as the Tlingit and the Tsimshian) but they were altered just enough to make it appear as if they weren't really stealing ideas from one another. Ironically, as many outsiders believed them to be, the Totem Poles were *not* a form of idolatry; they were proclamations of prestige between tribes and of the artisans that worked in each village. Due to the European intrusion and the many devastating diseases they brought along with them, and also the introduction of alcohol, the once proud Haida were eventually, and sadly, diminished to one tenth their original size. In time the more high-profile lands of the Haida Nation were usurped by commercial fishing and logging. As we were seeing here little remained of this once gifted culture, now most of their lands, in the outlying regions, were uninhabited and the once thriving villages had been methodically swallowed by an ever encroaching forest.

Four hours later

Our hike had taken us deep into the forest. It was colorful and verdant, and the air was as sweet as any I had ever breathed. After traversing densely mixed communities of red alders, big leaf maples, and western red cedars, after walking along pristine streams teeming with sock-eye salmon, after passing by the occasional willow tree and mats of strongly scented yarrows, we were now resting near a large lake over-flown regularly by Canadian geese and hundreds of Eagles. It was absolutely stunning here.

"Captain Olaf," Betsy's voice broke the silence unexpectedly, "the professors up and asking for you."

"Put him on lass," we heard the Captain answer. "Anders, where are you guys presently?"

"We're resting near a large lake Captain, maybe seven miles from the village. Our plan is to walk around the periphery and then head back to you if that's ok."

"Of course it is. Be careful and keep me posted, Olaf out."

Hearing the professor's voice again lifted our spirits so we decided to listen in for awhile to the conversation between them.

"I pray all is well with you Captain," the professor began. "I am feeling much better and am quite eager to discuss our up-coming itinerary. There is much to share with you, and the crew, and many things of great delight are forthcoming."

"Certainly looking forward to that," the Captain replied. "I'm relieved to hear that you're well. We're all anxious to know what's been happening lately. I hope you understand Professor that we were all somewhat bewildered with your behavior."

"I am sure that you were, yes, indeed. But I am, too, equally convinced that you will be surprised to know the truth about what *really* happened to the GVIN organization and me. My dear friends the plot is thickening concerning the Mortiken and the First Tribe, and we are all in a most favorable position now in our valiant endeavors."

Despite how much that last phrase piqued our curiosity, Anders chose instead to switch off the radio so we could clearly hear what was going on around us. We had a problem to resolve that required silence. Garrett hadn't been with us for some time. Earlier, while Anders and I had been discussing the technical aspects of Viking longboat construction, Garrett had gotten listless and disappeared into the forest. Understanding his proclivity for introspection, his penchant for being alone, and his undying love of exploring, we'd decided to let him be and trust the Holy Spirit for his safety. It'd been several hours now and we'd heard nothing from him; we both were starting to get concerned.

The trail finally brought Anders and me to a wide gravel bar in the confluence of several streams. The topography here was rife with stands of alders and dense patches of wild white petaled strawberry plants and, just north of us, the resonant sounds of a large river was becoming ever more evident. As soon as we'd cleared the streams and were maneuvering around a thicket of wild raspberries, Garrett's sudden boisterous voice startled us.

"Holy crapola dudes, you just ain't gonna believe it!"

Garrett was as animated as I'd ever heard him. Turning in the direction of his voice, Anders shouted back anxiously: "Garrett, where are you little brother?"

"I'm right here Norse," was his reply.

Fifty-One

Along the River

Just north of us Garrett emerged suddenly from a stand of big leaf maples; he had a huge grin on his face and was hastening with his hand for us to hurry.

"Guess whose back?" He pointed as we neared. "Dweeb, get yur nose outa yur butt and get over here."

Rolf burst through the trees rambunctious and galloped full tilt towards Anders and me. Bristling, focused, and quite worked up about something, he began nuzzling our legs and yapping joyously.

"You guys ready for another shocker?"

"What do you mean?" Anders asked.

"I don't have a clue anymore about nothin'. I hate to say it but I think our dork mutt is pretty much a genius. I mean sheeshka la beeshka dudes, why did we stop here, and why did we pass the Haida village, and why did we want to explore it, and why did we take this specific route? Who woulda' guessed dudes that out here we coulda' stumbled on somethin' like this?

"Stumbled on *what* dude?" Anders prodded impatiently.

"Follow me guys," Garrett motioned nonchalantly. "I'll show you what dillweed found out here in the middle of nowhere."

Both our interests were kindled now. With Garrett in the lead we continued on the remarkable path we'd walked since we left the village. I couldn't help thinking it rather strange, considering how dense the growth was here, that this particular path had remained so well defined and free from obstacles. Around us the trees were dense and verdant and free from any visible disease. When the canopy finally opened Anders pointed up at, what I could only imagine were, the same eight Eagles we'd viewed at the lake. Meandering in circles they seemed to be moving along with us directly overhead. The river was very near now, and the air was becoming more enlivened with the smell of it. After turning east we emerged on a high embankment and caught our first view. About two hundred yards east of us a waterfall had split into two parts. One part was roaring over a sheer precipice and the other, separated from the first by a huge boulder, was being forced down through a narrow high gorge and squeezed out in foaming torrents. A hundred yards after that, when the sediment had settled, the river became placid and turquoise in appearance and flowed peacefully southwest towards the ocean. Carefully we veered down a steep embankment towards the shoreline.

"Check it out dudes," Garrett pointed south with a grin.

I could hardly believe my eyes. Just below us, in a large clearing, twenty yards inland from the river, rock crannogs and several dozen wooden structures were standing intact and in good livable shape.

"Someone's been here recently," Anders gasped.

In various areas rock walls had been constructed to isolate and protect plots of land, and on our side of the river, along the shoreline, logs were stacked in piles every twenty feet or so. In some of the isolated areas uncut corn and wheat were still standing that had never been harvested. An ingenious paddle wheel had been built along the shoreline, with pivoting cups to catch or not, and it channeled water along carved wooden troughs into each of the plots. The wheel had not been lifted up, or locked; it was still turning quietly with the flowing current. It became quite obvious, the more we looked around, that whoever had lived here had departed in a hurry.

"It's a Viking settlement," I finally gasped aloud.

"You bet it is," Anders cried out jubilantly, "and it's also similar to what you discovered last year in the Pontevedra Province."

"Oh yah brother," Garrett laughed and began dancing. "Now, you dudes wanna know whose digs these are; check it out!"

Garrett pointed up to a flat surface on the hillside directly south of us. Etched into a granite overhang, as bold as the day it had been done, was a sword and helmet over a shield.

"The First Tribe of Rognvalds," Anders shouted and danced

in circles with Garrett. Stopping suddenly they stared at each other quietly for a moment. Then both of them flexed their muscles and roared ferociously. The moment was magical and filled me with joy.

"Can you believe it?" Anders continued after they'd both spent some time in mysterious contemplations. "It's a bloody miracle you know. We'd better tell the Captain."

"I'll do it," Garrett replied bristling now with energy.

The conversation, however, did not unfold the way we had anticipated. Apparently as the professor listened a blank expression had formed on his face. Afterwards he told the Captain he recalled something about the existence of a settlement in this locale from the satellite surveillance that he and Hector had done months before. When the Captain pressed him for facts he'd only shaken his head, with a bewildered expression, as if there was nothing at all he could recall. There was only one thing we could determine from his reaction; that because of his recent trauma the professor had forgotten about it until he heard our report and this had sparked the memory of it. Was finding this settlement, despite the professor's forgetfulness, that important to our goals? When Rorek had pinpointed our position the Captain radioed to explain his intentions.

"We should be there shortly son."

"Cool boss, we'll be here checkin' things out."

"No Garrett! Don't touch a thing! The professor requested that you all please delay your hands-on investigations until we arrive."

"Ah come on ... you mean we can't look around boss?" Garrett complained. "No harm lookin' is there? Rolf's been diggin' steady; sheesh he's dug like five holes in the graveyard already. What's the big deal?"

"Let's try limiting your activities to just looking." The Captain instructed calmly. "He wants to treat it like an archeological find and I see no problem with that. I'm sure you know that Roxanne would've done exactly the same thing. The professor's convinced that there's something in that settlement that will change everything for us."

"Ok boss, cool," Garrett shook his head angrily. "We'll just hang around like geeks, and pick our butts, and wait for king tut to give us permission to do our jobs."

"Son, chill out!

"Whatever!" Garrett grumbled.

"You know Garrett," the Captains tone was compassionate, "Gabriel's Father mentioned the same thing in the conversation we had. He was convinced that in the weeks ahead we'd be finding things that would help us discover the First Tribe and I believe it."

"Ok boss, I'll chill, sorry." Garrett shrugged. Obviously still dissatisfied he handed the radio to Anders and then walked down to the river and began throwing stones.

"Something else fellas," the Captain perked up, "Jonah's contacted Roxanne and she's requested that we establish an uplink they can use to download the images."

"Oh sure," Anders answered. "We can do that aboard the vessel Captain. How are they by the way?"

"They're both excited about the find and Angelina sends her love."

"Cool, that's good to hear."

"Please stay put until we reach you Anders; this should really be a lot of fun to explore … Olaf out!"

As soon as the conversation had ended Rolf's barking intensified. We watched him drag, what appeared to be, a chest out of one of the many holes he'd dug near the periphery of the settlement. As soon as he'd dislodged it from the earth he began jumping around it crazily and then he took off running into the woods again barking wildly.

"Dumb dog," Garrett muttered.

Fifty-Two

What Jonah and the Professor Revealed

Captain maneuvered the *Heimdall* into the shoreline. Garrett and Anders caught the fore and aft lines and secured them on trees near the water's edge. After John had extended the gangplank we all met onshore. First we rigged a canopy and then the ladies brought tables and chairs ashore that we could use for meetings, meals, and research.

"Can you feel that?" Anders looked up at the sky suddenly.

"Feel what," Helga asked.

"The air pressure is changing; I think we're in for a storm."

"I've read about the storms up here," Rorek shared, "they say they're pretty wicked."

Several on the crew expressed concerns, after that, about the remoteness of the location. Some were bothered with the prospect of wild animal's encroaching on the camp, and possibly getting aboard the schooner and trying to fight with Rolf. In the distance we could hear his barking echoing through the trees.

"We'll be safe here won't we?" Helga fretted. "This place feels even more isolated than the Pontevedra did."

"We saw nothing threatening on the hike," Anders assured them. "Just birds and fish mostly."

"Yah, its cool here guys," Garrett reassured them.

"Should we set up the propane stoves then Captain and cook outside, or should we stay aboard the *Heimdall*?" Betsy asked.

"Cooking out might be nice ladies," the Captain answered after pondering for a moment. "If the storm hits we'll just move aboard. We should probably reinforce this canopy with extra ropes just to be safe. What about having the feast out here under the moonlight?"

"An excellent idea," Rorek laughed, "I'll get out the lighting and generator Olaf; John would you mind giving me a hand setting up?"

"You got it," John answered.

"Can I say something before we get started?" Anders asked.

After a short talk, about the fact that most wild animals avoided human contact if at all possible, the ladies relaxed and got focused on what needed to be done. During the pep talk Rolf reappeared suddenly and was now dragging the chest he'd dug up towards the camp. When it was near the canopy he started running in circles and barking and acting as crazy as I'd ever seen him.

"What a doofus dog," Garrett blurted throwing his hands up. "He musta' found loco weed out there."

"Maybe he needs Prozac," Lizzy howled laughing.

"Rolf, settle down," the Captain instructed sternly. "Maybe he's hungry. Betsy lass, would you mind feeding him?"

"Sure Captain. You want some num-num sweetie?"

With an excited yelp Rolf bounded over to where she'd begun doling out his kibbles and canned meat and water. The Captain's observation was spot-on and, when he'd begun wolfing his food, a blessed peacefulness fell over the camp.

"Now *that's* more like it," Garrett sighed.

"Before we open Rolf's chest," the Captain grinned, "Jonah and the Professor have asked to share some things. Jonah ..."

"Thank you my friend!" Jonah answered as he moved around in front of the table. I could see at once that something had changed in him; he'd been imbued with a kind of resoluteness; something that none of us had seen in him for many months. He was focused again and I sensed, too, an inflexible strength exuding from within him.

"Now, my friends, before the professor fills you in, I want you all to know that I was contacted by Bill Sondheim from the Modis Project recently. I think you'll recall we discussed this man's work right around the time we discovered Isla Socorro. Remember?"

All of us nodded yes.

"Anders this will be new to you my friend, so if you have any questions, please feel free to interrupt."

"I will, thanks brother." Anders leaned forward to listen.

"Evidently Bill's been trying to contact me for months now with an update." Jonah continued. "Roxy was finally able to contact him yesterday and she gave him our e-mail address. Bill informed me yesterday that modified versions of these Terra/Aqua (EOS-AM) satellites were sent up four months ago to replace the older systems. He's confirmed there's an increase now of activity on and around Revillagigedo Island below the Coast Ranges in Alaska, and also on Kodiak Island."

"The day of many collisions is nearing," Anders murmured.

"We believe so," the Professor stood up, shook Jonah's hand, and then took over. "During the software switchover they were able to retrieve ten years of backup files Norseman. They discovered that this very site here was inhabited less than three months ago, possibly by a faction of the First Tribe that has since gone north, we believe, to an undisclosed area in the vicinity of Revillagigedo. My friends, the habitants that lived in this settlement were, for all intents and purposes, a branch colony from the main body that traveled back and forth regularly to the main tribe and have since re-joined them. We believe this occurrence was for a uniquely specific reason."

"Do you think they'll be coming back?" Rorek asked.

"A possibility, but I am not sure." The Professor answered.

"Professor what about Montague Island," Helga asked.

"Just this morning I contacted Regan Pendleton for an update and also to share the information I have received. It was an encouraging conversation we had, to be sure, and a most blessed man he is indeed. Regan informed me that the settlement is burgeoning and healthy and intelligence presently confirms that the Mortiken are still completely unaware of this glorious settlement that God has allowed to flourish. Montague is unharmed!"

"And my father's longboat," Anders asked with keen interest.

"Completely safe Norseman; no one knows of its secret location in Cape Cleare."

"What about the Grettig's Professor," Garrett asked.

"They have been accepted into the community, they have their own home now, the children are being schooled, and Granmar and Arnora are active members in island administration."

"And you believe there is invaluable information here in this settlement for us Professor?" Rorek asked.

"I believe, Rorek, that …."

"Sorry to interrupt Professor, before you answer, can you clarify some things for us?" John's face was twisted up in puzzlement.

The professor nodded and replied: "Of course John."

"All of us would like to know what happened to the SES and the GVIN sir, and also to your family. And how in the world did you end up on the Red Dragon?"

"Captain Olaf?" the Professor looked in his direction. When he nodded affirmative all of us moved nearer to listen.

"My friends let me be as brief as possible, in an effort to avoid all emotional embellishments that may sideline us, so we may continue on with our most important work here. First, and most importantly for me, please be assured that my wife and family are tucked away safely on an island in the Azorean Archipelagoes. Praise to the Most High! They all send their love to you and wish you well."

The response was overwhelming and all of us stood and applauded this most excellent news.

"Thank you friends, thank you *so* much," the Professor continued after wiping away a sudden wash of tears on his cheek.

"Secondly, the utter destruction of SES 1 remains a mystery to me and also to my engineers. We theorized that the sudden tremendous pressure on the vessel, during the collapse of the caldera, must have somehow breached the hydrogen lines between the hull and interior cabins. We have no other explanation. Thank God none of you were aboard.

"Amen," everyone chorused as Rorek and Captain looked at each other and shrugged.

"Now, continuing, this may be difficult for you to understand my friends, but the demise of the Global Virtual Informational Network was engineered by me, Hector, Rafael, and Jonathan."

"Bloody well," Rorek gasped in amazement.

"Yes, it was allowed for particular reasons. The modifications and up-grades accomplished on the *Heimdall* were done by my order because of this ingenious undertaking, this being to allow the *Heimdall* to become the new GVIN, and also so I could reposition my trusted operatives and then disappear so as to join you aboard your vessel to continue pressing forward towards our glorious goal."

Fascinated now, we all leaned forward in our chairs to listen to an account that was completely unexpected. After chuckling deeply, with a kind of satisfaction, the Professor continued.

"To spare you extraneous details, much better suited for our eventual memoirs, let it suffice to say that it became known to me that my organization had been infiltrated many months ago by a rogue group in affiliation with the Baaldurians and Global Paradigm. We believe now that these infiltrators were sent from the Mediterranean. Certainly I kept these facts from you, as it unfolded, so as not to interfere with your crucial work. Knowing if I was to maintain the secrecy of our most important mission together, the four of us had to devise a plan that would change, to our advantage and satisfactorily, these dastardly circumstances we were confronted with. Sadly, as it was, the only way that this could happen, was to temporarily put my own life in harm's way. Know that I did this willingly and for the reasons that I just mentioned. Following the coup d'état I was taken by private helicopter to the Mediterranean to an island unknown to me, very remote and desolate, where a private flight was booked to take me to western Vancouver Island to meet with affiliates from Global Paradigm. Beside the two pilots, Krystal Blackeyes was the only other person aboard the flight; it would seem that she was on her way to rendezvous with the Red Dragon. During the flight I overheard bits and pieces of information from a string of phone conversations she was engaged in concerning her present role in the Baaldurian global insurrection. As far as I could tell she was coordinating everything, presently being carried out globally, aboard that very flight. If this is accurate, then I might conclude that she has a position of eminence and power with the Baaldurian that is unsurpassed."

"I can imagine, then, that her not being around anymore is going to create havoc with their agenda," John surmised.

"I agree with you John, yes, I would agree" the professor nodded. "The overthrow of the GVIN and the purported death of me and Krystal Blackeyes now (in the storm) certainly have made the playing field different than it was just a week ago."

"Most assuredly, and Professor did you hear anything else in her conversations that may be of interest?" Lizzy asked.

"I heard also that Brynhild Busla was being detained on an island somewhere along the western Canadian coastline."

"Oh man ..." Garrett sat up straight.

"She's alive?" Betsy gasped along with the rest of us. "You mean that horrid woman that returned was really an imposter?"

"It would seem so, yes, on both your questions. And if what I heard has any credence to it, she is being groomed as we speak as a pawn in some scheme that will be taking place in the near future."

"Do you know where she's being held specifically," the Captain asked leaning forward with keen interest. "Is there a possibility that we could find and rescue her professor?"

"Perhaps Captain, but her whereabouts are only sketchy at present. I believe though if we are shrewd, and it is God's will, that we may be able to locate her in the days following."

"You mean we could rescue her?" Garrett began wringing his hands in a way I'd never witnessed before. "We could actually have her most exquisite highness aboard the *Heimdall*?"

"Yes young man," the Professor smiled toothily, "it is most certainly a possibility."

"Oh man boss, a real queen, a real queen. Oh yah, that's what I'm talkin' about … I got first dibs on her dudes."

"GARRETT," the Captain recoiled suddenly as the rest of us began laughing in hearty fits. "Son she's still married!"

"Oh yeah, Braggi, I forgot, sheesh." Garrett sat down dejected.

"Professor, please go ahead and continue."

"Thankyou Captain Olaf. I heard also that Amalek Baaldur was slated to make an appearance on the Red Dragon sometime this week someplace on the Behm Canal east of Revillagigedo Island. I heard, too, that the Mortiken strongholds stationed underground in the Grand Canyon, and those stationed on the islands of Angel de la Guarda and Tiburon in the Sea of Cortez were now being transferred up to Kodiak Island over the next month. We have heard reports that this is being done covertly on renovated tankers."

"That's how the Rognvald's were transported to Montague."

"Yes it was Betsy, isn't that interesting." The Captain chuckled.

"Stupid wankers had to copy us." Garrett laughed.

"Please if I may," the Professor cleared his throat and continued. "There was one particular conversation that was rather curious to me, and I'd like to share what I know of it. Somehow her questions led me to believe that the Mortiken high command was under the impression that the Ghost Warriors, and the Ghost Vessel, had been destroyed underground. I was convinced though, because of how they were conversing, that the exchange was supposition and not based in any substantiated fact. But what I kept asking myself was how they would have had any knowledge of you being underground at all. You were known only to me and Hector and the Grettig's. Only we had knowledge of your mission."

"NO professor, that is *NOT* accurate!" Anders jumped up and looked him directly in the eyes. "Thurid's men and the Seer knew of us too. We battled them in Oski's Grotto, remember? They saw all of us, we conversed with them, and they also saw the SES appear."

The professor's eyes opened wide, as if he'd suddenly become aware of this fact. This was curious to me. Had he somehow lost memory of these facts, as well, from his ordeal with the Mortiken?

"You bet we battled those fat geeks," Garrett moved next to Anders in a show of solidarity. "And after we finished whackin' their greasy-haired dingle-berry butts I'm sure they didn't brag about it."

"No, they were humiliated!" Anders shook his head. "And I'm sure that when they finally returned to Torfar-Kolla that the story they told the others was heavily prejudiced."

"Yes, Anders, I agree!" Helga's eyes burned. "I'm sure their story was that they'd defeated us and not the other way around."

"I have *no* doubt!" Anders grimaced. "Professor, you should know that the Seer promised that he would have his vengeance on me and that he was going to wear my hair on his belt someday. Frankly sir, I knew it was braggadocio and that another confrontation was far-fetched, but vengeance can come in many different forms. Lying about the outcome of our battle, professor, to justify the loss of the Grettig family, and the death of their men, was probably how Thurid and the Seer manipulated their reports to the King to protect their reputation in the city."

"Bingo dude!" Garrett slapped high fives with Anders.

"That's right on brother, I totally agree!" I moved near Garrett in a show of solidarity with Anders. "And I can only imagine, professor, that from these heinous fabrications a notion may have gotten back to the Mortiken that the Ghost Warriors had been defeated."

"How, though, is the question, how," the Professor sighed.

I could see the man was disconcerted and for several moments he sat quietly starring at the ground. I could also feel his embarrassment, but I felt no compassion for him.

"You should know that the unexpected part for me was when the conversation had ended," he continued after returning to us from his contemplations. "For a time, from where she was seated, I heard the woman sobbing. She was quite distraught, and I can only imagine that she was grieving your loss Jonah. Please understand that in that moment I saw there was still a chance for her and I was taken with compassion for her eternal soul. After that she moved forward into another section and I saw no more of the woman until I pulled her body from the wreckage of the Dragon."

When the professor had confessed the hope he still held for his sister, Jonah had begun weeping. Quickly he'd excused himself and had gone back aboard the *Heimdall*, I assumed, to check on his sister and then to retire. Minutes after he'd departed the Professor went back aboard, also, complaining of a headache and his desire to sleep. We all knew he was struggling with much.

"Leave um alone," the Captain ordered. "There's nothing we can do to assuage what either are going through."

"I agree Olaf." Lizzy said with tears glistening in her eyes. "As weird as it may seem, I am really thankful that Eloise is with us. I can't help but think that even her wounds are somehow a blessing, considering the horrid circumstances she was trapped in. I believe, no, I *really truly* believe that we're all exactly where we're supposed to be no matter how strange it may seem."

"Amen," the crew murmured.

"Alright then," the Captain stood. "We have until the 7th to go through this site with a fine-tooth comb and figure things out people. The tanker will be here Thursday afternoon for Jonah and his sister and Lizzy and to drop off our new supplies and ordnance."

"How long you gonna be gone Lizzy?" Anders asked.

"Until Eloise stabilizes honey, then I'm coming back – no more than ten days, I'm thinking, maybe two weeks."

"Are you riding a tanker back?" Garrett asked.

"I'm not sure how I'm getting back yet."

"I wish you didn't have to leave Liz," Betsy moaned.

"It'll go by fast sweetheart."

"I know, but still ..."

"You'll be missed Liz, can't imagine doing this without you." Rorek added with an unusual show of emotion.

"Oh Rorek ... I love you too," Lizzy hugged him.

"What say we turn in folks?" The Captain suggested. "It's late and there's not a whole lot we can do now. It's been a long day and I'm sure everyone could use the rest. We have a lot of work to get done; probably do it a whole lot better after a good night's sleep."

No one argued and within moments all had retired to their berths. The evening was balmy so I opened my porthole window. As I pulled up the covers and snuggled in I knew, somehow, that a lot was going to change for us in the upcoming week.

Fifty-Three

A Story of Young Brynhild

Monday, the 4th of September

We laid out a plan, after breakfast, for studying the site and also for opening what Rolf had found in the graveyard. When he heard his name he began pawing eagerly at the ground near the chest. I figured he needed some sugar for what he'd done but, as I leaned down to give him a big hug; he suddenly snapped erect, began sniffing vigorously at the air, and then darted down to the river.

"He's caught a whiff of somethin' else now," Garrett shrugged.

A few moments later he bolted upriver to the waterfall and barked madly at it for awhile. After that he stopped and turned and vanished into the undergrowth.

Lizzy told us Eloise was still unconscious but her heart rate and functions had stabilized nicely. She was very happy with this report and hugged Jonah. What she had to share about the professor, though, changed her demeanor; she was clearly disgruntled and in no way was holding back her emotions. As she told it, he'd developed flu- like symptoms, and a fever of 105 degrees overnight. And when she'd instructed him to stay in bed, and to drink plenty of liquids, he had gotten indignant and rude; he'd vented angrily like a child because of her requests. Never tolerating this kind of behavior from anyone, especially patients, Lizzy told us she gave the man a tongue-lashing after which he got repentant and quietly acceded to her wishes.

"What an obstinate man he is," Lizzy lamented, "philosophical about everything and, quite frankly, he's developed an arrogance that's really unbecoming. Goodness, I know he's been through a lot, and I'm doing my best to help him, but still he goes and treats me like that. Olaf, there's something eating at that man that he has no peace with. I'm so mad with him right now I could just slap him. I had to remind him twice that you were the Captain aboard and not him."

"My darlin'," Rorek smiled affectionately and put his arm around her shoulder and kissed her cheek, "no matter what kind of an ego the man has Olaf's the Captain and that will *never* change. He's a guest, no matter what he's done with us, and if he can accept that then we'll have no problems with him. If he can't, well, then he can take a long walk off the proverbial gangplank and file for unemployment! There will always be order aboard the *Heimdall*."

"Amen ..." the rest of the crew murmured.

"Given his present situation, though," Rorek continued, "I would imagine that losing the GVIN, and all those people he worked with, has finally sunk in and ...,"

"The breach of trust with his employees has adversely affected his personality." Helga continued Rorek's thoughts.

"Yes Helga," Rorek agreed.

"And the fever, and coming off the edge of what happened to him on the Dragon, is probably what's made him physically sick." Lizzy added with more compassion.

"Yah, who knows what weird diseases them filthy Mortiken carry around with them," Garrett groaned. "They all need to die!"

"You got that right spikes," Anders sneered. "And I hope we get a chance real soon to wack some more of that filthy scum!"

Garrett and John eagerly agreed.

"Olaf," Lizzy continued, "after he calmed down he suggested that Gabriel take the position of site manager because of his training with Roxanne. He seems quite preoccupied with doing things by the book. I agreed with him so I contacted Roxy and she agreed too."

As we were talking Rolf returned and sat down next to the Captain. And even though he was bristling and full of energy he remained quiet and watchful of everyone.

"A fine man for the job," The Captain beamed proudly and then he squatted down and began petting Rolf's neck.

"Ok buddy, you ready? It's your turn now. Let's see what you've found here."

"Let's do it!" John responded eagerly.

"Gabriel, where should we start?" The Captain turned to me.

"Sir I suggest that Helga record everything with the camera, the same as we did when we opened the Tempest, and I think John and Rorek would be best suited to open the box without ruining it."

Captain Olaf beamed again and gave his approval and then motioned at Rorek and John. Both men nodded. After acquiring the tools necessary the men had the chest open within moments. Inside there were several half-rotted female textiles, half a dozen copper brooches which, according to Lizzy, were used to attach the straps of a woman's pinafore, a pair of carved ivory dice, two uniquely crafted daggers, a box full of antler bone whorls used for spinning and making linen, six beautiful gold coins, and a small leather book held together with copper eyelets.

"Not much here Olaf," Jonah admitted after perusing the contents.

"The book might have something useful, the coins may be worth something, the daggers we should probably keep as souvenirs, but everything else is pretty much junk in my opinion."

"What do you suggest Gabriel," the Captain turned to me. He was beaming again as he had been for most of the day.

"Captain I agree with Jonah. And I suggest that we photograph the entire contents of the book. We can upload the files to Roxanne for analysis; her interpretive skills are far more adept than mine sir."

"Alright son," the Captain smiled. "How about we set up a make-shift studio under the canopy to get the work done?"

"I'll do it boss," Garrett volunteered.

"I'll call Roxanne to let her know; I think she's home today." Jonah waved as he made his way aboard.

The process didn't take long. Several hours after uploading the files Roxanne responded with what she'd discovered. Eagerly we all gathered around the plasma screen to listen.

"Hi guys, hope all is well," she began. "We're doing really well here, and things are progressing nicely with the colleges. Angelina is running errands today so she won't be here for this. She went to check on the Raptor and make sure the company was doing the maintenance that they're being paid to do. She sends her love to all and told me to tell you Anders that she misses her 'inky dinky doodle'."

"Huh?" Garrett spun around. "What the heck does that mean dude?" Anders sank down in his chair and refused to answer Garrett.

"We'll both be flying over to Portugal Friday the 7th to deliver the textbooks and then we'll return on the 9th in time to rendezvous with Jonah and Lizzy." Roxanne affirmed.

"Sounds like perfect timing, and it's really nice to hear your voice lass; you look beautiful and rested," the Captain smiled as we all applauded. "Did you find anything of use in the book?"

"I did Olaf, yes! And it seems to be a part of a larger composite. There are markings that lead me to believe that this just may be the first in a series of three books. Here's the gist of how it reads: "It would seem Brynhild was born to an aristocratic family in a position of influence in the Kings court, but for reasons unknown she was repudiated at the age of four and given to another family of lesser status. Although poor and cruel these people had, somehow, found favor with Brynhilds'parents so, after a deal was agreed upon, she was taken to be raised in a repressive household. At the age of six the child was relegated to being a servant and daily was assigned menial tasks to satisfy her cruel foster-parents. Despite her deplorable existence the child's physical beauty blossomed. When she was ten her foster-parents, fearing blame would fall upon them for doing evil to the young girl, kept her clad in rags and smeared her face with soot so that no person would ever see her true beauty, or gaze upon her in wonderment. For seven years this ruse worked. Still, Brynhild's spirit was indomitable and she shared her story with as many people as she could when they passed by on the byroads. At some point, around sixteen years of age, she began having dreams nightly which only strengthened her resolve to be freed from her tormentors. The foster-parents were approached one day by the emissary of a king from the far south and they were made an offer. That's where it ends guys."

"It's about Brynhild Busla, I'm sure of it." Helga blurted.

"I'm thinking the same lass," Rorek agreed with equal fervor.

"Remember what Granmar and Arnora told us that night on the SES?" Helga continued.

"I do," Betsy replied round-eyed, "and it correlates with what Roxy just shared with us."

"Yah it does;" Helga gushed excitedly, "somehow King Braggi

found out about Brynhild, maybe from one of her many conversations with those passing by, and he sent an emissary to make a financial offer to her foster-parents to save her."

"Oh how romantic." Betsy gushed.

"Discovering this book out here in the middle of nowhere is certainly more than just happenstance Olaf," Jonah postulated.

"I agree brother," the Captain chuckled.

"I wonder if the other books are somewhere near." Anders pondered. "It'd be nice to know the whole story you know, might give us clues about where she is presently."

"Oh man," Garrett sighed, "it's startin' to sound like a Cinderella story and I like it big time dudes. Saving her seems like something we should be doing, just like we did with the Grettig's."

"But where in the world would we even start?" Lizzy asked.

"She could be anywhere son," Rorek argued.

"But wouldn't that be something if we could find her and rescue her?" Helga sighed.

"Yah, that'd be cool, and if we do, I got first dibs," Garrett smiled mischievously.

"Son, she's probably in her late thirties," the Captain calculated, "a bit old for you don't you think?"

"Who cares about that boss; she's gotta be a fairytale babe. Can you just imagine it, me and her, entwined in love?"

"Son, I just don't think it's going to happen," the Captain chuckled.

"Ahhh Cap … you guys are a buncha party-poopers."

Fifty-Four

The Supertanker 'Absinthe' Arrives

Thursday, September 7th

Our rendezvous, just west of Calvert Island, was confirmed by Captain Mortimer at 12:45pm. We were informed, too, that another brutal storm was moving down from the Gulf of Alaska. Because of how this enormous swell may endanger the *Heimdall*, being in close proximity to the tanker; he suggested that we batten down everything beforehand, just in case the storm hit while he was off-loading the goods and, also, so that when the work was completed we could find shelter inland as quickly as possible. Olaf completely agreed and assured him we would be ready.

It was exactly 1:30 pm when the Absinthe' emerged, like some ghostly apparition, from the sea mist and came to a standstill three hundred yards off our starboard bow. There was a bustle of activity on the main deck as her crew prepared for the exchange. Captain Olaf had his game face on and the moment he'd maneuvered the *Heimdall* into position, a crane began off-loading crates onto a large area that had been cleared behind the bowsprit. Just north and west of us the sky had become a swirling dark tapestry etched continually with vivid lightening. Thankfully the sea remained placid during the entire exchange. The whole crew worked feverishly stowing the supplies below decks in the storage lockers and refrigerators. Thirty minutes later, when everything was stowed, Jonah, Lizzy, and Eloise, were craned aboard in a special enclosure designed for emergencies in high seas. After some tears, and hasty goodbyes, all of them were whisked below decks. Then, when the crane had been secured, and was covered with a tarp, the tankers air horn sounded and the massive ship began moving away.

"Farewell to you Captain Olaf," Mortimer bellowed through a megaphone from the port rails amidships. "I'll make a call to Mr. Proudmore and bring him up to date. Be advised sir, the storm is nigh upon us. The radar has it twenty minutes out; it'll be a rough ride; Godspeed to you my friend!"

Olaf waved back fervently and quickly mounted up into the wheelhouse. Everything now was in God's hands. Hopefully we would make it back to safe haven before the massive storm hit.

Part Four

A Great Viking Prophecy is Fulfilled

Fifty-Five

First Contact

We raced back to our anchorage near the settlement. Given the possibility of tidal surges Captain Olaf turned the schooners bow west and, when he felt it was safe, the fore and aft lines were secured and both anchors were dropped. While battening down, or covered with tarps, everything loose or vulnerable, terrifying black clouds began swirling above us. Within moments the storm bore down on us mercilessly. For awhile I watched through my berth window; the blending of hammering rain, booming thunder, flashing light, howling wind, and swaying trees, made the environment outside seem surreal. It quickly became torrential and visibility was lessened to about ten yards. The fact that these people had endured such storms not only filled me with a profound respect but also a gnawing trepidation. During flashes of lightening I began observing what appeared to me as human shapes moving amongst the trees and around several of the structures in the village. Rationalizing that the environmental conditions were playing tricks; I fetched the binoculars to try and prove true what I thought I'd seen. For awhile I strained to see through the binoculars and saw nothing. But then, just as I was about to convince myself that I'd seen only the movement of trees, I clearly again witnessed two muscular men with long hair standing on the shoreline looking directly at the schooner. Aghast, I recoiled from the window to make myself less visible. What in the world were their intentions, and why were they here; especially during such a storm? With curiosity compelling me now, (far more than my fears) I focused the binoculars near the same area and clearly witnessed a group of men moving around the crannogs. An arousing thought gripped me, could it be that these men were affiliated with the First Tribe? I knew the Captain would want to know.

"Captain Olaf!" I whispered on the radio.

"What is it?" He responded within seconds.

"Sir, there are people in the village." I informed him.

"Come on Gabriel; in this storm?"

"Sir, I've seen them twice, I am *not* imagining this."

"Alright son, alright … John, Garrett, Anders, topside, check this out; be careful!" the Captain advised.

"Aye Captain," all three answered.

"Let's take pistols and modules," the Captain went on.

"Have them sir," John responded.

"Loaded and ready brother," Anders affirmed. John turned, nodded, and then asked the Captain: "Do you want us to go ashore and confront them sir?"

"No John, establish visuals and then get back below and lock the door." The Captain returned.

"Aye sir," all three chorused.

"You don't think they'd try to board us do you Olaf?" Rorek pondered with a fierce expression.

"If they do they're in for a rude awakening," the Captain bristled. "Helga, you and Gabriel see if you can get any images to analyze."

"Aye sir …"

"Professor, do you have any suggestions?"

"No Captain Olaf! You have acted wisely and I would have done nothing differently," he assured him with a look of pride. "Is there anything I can do presently to help?"

"Stay here and help us monitor what's going on outside," the Captain smiled back with a hint of reservation.

"I am at your disposal," the professor maintained with a clear show of respect. "I am eager to understand what we are faced with."

"Didn't expect that reaction," Rorek whispered when the Professor turned away. The Captain shook his head in agreement.

Cloaked in the CSAT John, Anders, and Garrett exited the vessel stealthily and spread out along the larboard rails.

"Gabriel was correct, we do have company Captain." John voice was lessened in the din of the storm. "I count ten men."

"What are they doing?" the Captain queried.

"Two are just starring at the vessel and the others are removing tools or weapons from the crannogs and putting them into wooden boxes."

"What kind of weapons?" The Captain's brow tightened.

"Don't know sir, can't see clearly."

"Do they seem inclined towards us?"

"Not in my opinion sir, they just seem curious."

"I agree," Anders added, "it almost as if they're waiting for someone to come out and meet with them."

"Captain … should we disembark?"

"No John, watch them for awhile."

"Hey, check what's comin' down the river dudes!" Garrett's tense warning changed everyone's perspective. "It just came out from behind the waterfall! There must be a passageway through the cliffs."

The thought made my mind whirl; a hidden settlement back in the mountains seemed far-fetched. But given what we'd been through on this journey I was ready to accept anything. Everyone's attention was riveted now on the vessel approaching us. I could see it was a kind of hybrid construction of what we'd seen underground and the early Rognvald longboat design. When it was close enough we could see there were no oarsmen, or sails, and the main mast was folded down towards the prow; we could also hear the churning of a motor.

"Can it be true," Garrett chuckled; "Vikings on motorboats?"

"We've heard rumors the culture was modernizing," the professor turned towards the Captain. "Although there was no proof, I have accepted for months now that some degree of retrofitting had to have happened for them to survive against what the Mortiken and their global associates were accomplishing."

"Its interesting professor," the Captain chuckled with some reserve, "they certainly would be able to get around easier and faster. I wonder to what degree though, and why, if they choose to remain sequestered from modern society, would they need to?"

The Professor shrugged. The directness of the question seemed to bedevil him. A moment later he turned back to what he was doing on the computer. Returning my attention to the scene I watched as one of the men, just inside the doorway of one of the larger crannogs, began communicating on a radio. It was only a matter of seconds before the longboat approaching us vanished.

"Whaaa … them dudes have CSAT?" Garrett radioed.

"That or something similar," Rorek began laughing.

"This could present us with a problem sir," John suggested. "It may be the preliminaries to their mounting an offensive against us."

"No, this is something else brother, I'm sure of it!" Anders interjected. "Gabriel, what does your gut tell you?"

"Speak it out son," the Captain encouraged.

"Ccccaptain," I stammered, not being comfortable with being put on the spot, "I'm sure it's a signal. I'm sure they're trying to ascertain whether or not we're the Ghost Vessel."

"What do you suggest then Gabriel?"

Something started burning in me, a thing I didn't understand, and for a moment I hesitated answering the Captain. A soothing light was filling my spirit with warmth and clarity and I felt a kind of wisdom and courage being poured into me. With boldness and authority I turned and responded to the Captain's question: "I suggest that we cloak for a short time and then uncloak sir. It would be our response to what they've shown us here, and when we do uncloak we should all be on deck and greet these men together."

"Make it so!" the Captain ordered immediately. "Three minutes Helga and then uncloak. Alright people, on deck and no weapons."

"I hope Gabriel's right about this," Rorek grumbled.

"Faith brother," Olaf responded with a twinkle in his eye.

As soon as the CSAT had adapted us to the environment the two men standing along the shoreline called to the others and pointed; all of them began laughing hilariously. Soon the rest of the men were jabbering excitedly. The longboat appeared again suddenly; twenty yards off our stern, and all aboard began waving and laughing. Every one of us, except Helga, was spread out along the port rails waiting. Slinking quietly across the deck, Rolf sat down beside me and placed his head against my leg.

"Waiting on you Captain," Helga radioed from the control room.

For several moments the Captain hesitated. I could see he was deep in thought about something.

"What am I missing here," he muttered.

"Is there anything I can do to help sir?"

Suddenly the Captain's eyes opened wide.

"Yes Gabriel there is!" He whispered with both fists clenched. "Greet them; something eloquent maybe. I'm sure they've been expecting us; I can feel this whole thing in my bones now. You *are* the chosen one Gabriel. The time has come for you to put on that mantle Floki passed to you. Speak to them before we uncloak."

Bolstered now I asked the Holy Spirit to enlighten me to what He wanted me to do and say. Immediately I envisioned Floki Vildarsen lying near the steps of the castle in the valley and I remembered the words he'd spoken just before he'd passed: *"I know that the Christ has sent you to me. You are here because the Holy One willed it. Take Rolf, he is yours now; this is the Christ's will. He will be your friend. He will recognize the First Tribe when you find them, and he will take part in the revealing of the Tempest during the day of many collisions. You are now the chosen one Gabriel, my mantle is yours, remember son, Christ before all else."*

Nervously I bent down and whispered: "Rolf, are these men from the First Tribe?" Rolf met my gaze intently for several seconds and then turned back towards the shoreline. Staring intently through the rails he began growling and his hackles went up. A moment later the sky erupted in a grand display of lightning and after that Rolf barked several times and sat down. Rolf's barking was clearly audible to the men on shore; all the talking and laughing stopped. Something inside me shifted and I felt as if something warm was being poured on my head once again; these men *were* of the First Tribe.

"You can do it son," the Captain nodded with eyes ablaze.

Grabbing the rails I cried out in the ancient language: *"honored men and warriors of the First Tribe of Rognvald's, we, being the men and women of the Ghost Vessel, rejoice in this glorious meeting, and we greet thee with respect and exultation in the blessings of our most Holy Christ."*

Nothing happened; all of them stared stone-faced; it was not the reaction I had anticipated.

"Let's say the ancient phrase together then sir," I stammered.

Captain Olaf nodded. When we were visible all of us stood in a single line and shouted together in unison: *"CHRIST BEFORE ALL ELSE!"* Great joy broke forth along the shoreline. Something amazing happened after that. Each one of them turned towards us, snapped to attention and, with their right hands fully extended above their heads, and their finger extended, they all responded back clearly in the English language: *"WE SALUTE YOU MEN AND WOMEN OF THE GHOST VESSEL, CHRIST BEFORE ALL ELSE!"*

Fifty-Six

An Alliance is Born

A long-haired muscular man moved forward. I got goose-pimples when he pulled himself erect, and bowed, and the other men moved back. His bearing was strong and he appeared visibly determined in the presence of strangers. I knew something meaningful was about to be conveyed and, when he began speaking, all of them lowered their heads in respect. His elocution was impassioned, and unwavering, but I was bewildered with the rigid formalness of how he communicated; it was so dissimilar to the way we did. Captain raised both hands and began shaking his head and the man stopped speaking. Turning to me he whispered: "I can't understand a word he's saying Gabriel. I know you're going to have to teach me the language someday, but for now son I have to fully understand what he's telling us."

"No problem sir, I'll take care of it," I promised.

After assuring the man on shore that I could interpret, so that both parties would understand, he nodded and declared: "A mighty gift you possess young warrior, and we all thank you." The men behind him applauded and saluted with a loud shout.

"And thank *you* for your patience my friend," the Captain began with both hands extended. The leader moved forward smiling. Again the men behind him applauded and saluted.

"Sheesh, what's with these dillweeds?" Garrett muttered.

"I am not as gifted, or as eloquent, as my young ward here." The Captain pointed and laughed with gusto. "But I *am* very interested in fully understanding every word you share sir."

The man bowed politely and smiled. At once a dialogue began. He introduced himself as Gunnar, and also as their clan leader.

"We bid thee welcome leader of the ghost men," Gunnar spread his arms out like the Captain had. Once again all the men applauded. "We have been expecting you, but had no idea that our paths would cross at this time or in this place."

"It is a mystery Gunnar, yes, but thanks to the Holy Christ, and Rolf here, we have finally found each other." Rolf yipped several times and then put his paws on the top rail. Gunnar's men shouted in unison.

"Yes, we are indeed relieved now that the many stories about the legendary Ghost Vessel are real."

"Indeed they are my friend, indeed they are," the Captain smiled.

"There are rumors Captain that the son of a legendary Vildarsen is aboard your vessel. A warrior son, a swordsman, a longboat builder, and one gifted with strange uttering's and the creatures of the sea. If it be true we would be honored to meet him."

"Anders ..." the Captain motioned.

Anders moved swiftly to the forefront and spoke: "I am Anders, Gunnar, son of Utgard, of the clan Vildarsen. I greet thee and all thy valiant people in respect and honor."

Every man ashore, and on the longboat, snapped to attention and saluted him with a loud vocalization. This time Anders responded in like fashion and remained at attention until Gunnar had acknowledged him. At Gunnar's behest two men jumped off the longboat and, after wading ashore, they ran up next to him.

"These are of your clan Anders, son of Utgard." Gunnar turned and pointed with pride. "These are Goren and Ingmar Vildarsen; both fine men with fine families. They are skilled in the construction of longboats and in the installation of diesel engines."

Both men snapped to attention. Anders responded in like fashion and both parties saluted one another. Once again all of Gunnar's men saluted and shouted. For me this behavior was beginning to get humorous. Why were they so formal?

"Captain Olaf," Gunnar continued with the same air of formality, "we bid thee join us here in the village that we may feast together and drink of the horn in celebration of this new alliance."

Garrett was beside himself now. Seeing this, Anders motioned for him to come over and stand with him in, what I could only understand as, a show of solidarity and friendship. But it was much more than that. Anders had seen something that no one else had and when I realized that I cringed inside at what would soon be shared.

"Get it off your chest little brother," Anders encouraged him.

"Drink a' the horn Gunnar?" Garrett chuckled low and sinister. "Ya'll mean honey liquor; spirits; booze; John Barleycorn; imbibing a little hair-a-the-dog together? Dig it man, a little wine is pretty fine at the right time, but we don't get crocked on this crew. No sir! Me and the Norse here is homey's;" he motioned with his thumb, "the whole crew is homey's dude, familia all of us. Did you know that we've fought wars against nature, and the Mortiken, and seen things, and done things, in the realm of the Ancients that'd freak you dudes out! I mean I'm just sayin' dude..."

There was no applause, or saluting, or shouting. Gunnar's men had gathered into groups and were whispering and pointing. Just as I was about to protest having to interpret this, the Captain turned and assured me: "It's OK Gabriel, don't worry, this is who we are, who Garrett is; there's nothing wrong with being ourselves."

Frustrated with Gunnar's men Anders whispered something in Garrett's ear and they both slapped high fives.

"This should be good," the Captain and Rorek chuckled.

Anders winked at us. Turning and facing each other they both stripped off their shirts, threw them on the deck, and then they flexed their muscles and began roaring wildly and stomping the deck. It got everyone's attention. When they'd finished their ritual both stood meek as nuns gazing at one another. You could have heard a pin drop. All the men on shore, and on the longboat, stared disbelievingly. Now Garrett and Anders turned towards Gunnar with toothy smiles and snapped to attention and saluted him the way his men had done us. Gunnar stood wide-eyed and wordless.

"Friends Gunnar, family," Garrett spoke in their language and then he and Anders opened their arms wide. "Can you dig it?"

A look of satisfaction formed on Gunnar's face and he started laughing in big belly guffaws. When he had explained to his men all of them broke into belly laughs and began flexing their muscles too. Somehow a bond had taken place, which quickly eased the formalness between both parties, and changed the chemistry of how we related to one another; it was a moment to be savored. It was like we'd been lifelong friends, now, and part of a brotherhood given to the same cause. Smiling toothily now, too, Gunnar motioned with both hands and said: "Captain Olaf, please join us in celebration, tonight we roast the pig in your honor."

The Captain nodded eagerly and answered: "We are honored, Gunnar, to join you in a feast of celebration. And we would also be willing to help you in any way; we have very skilled cooks."

"Yes Captain, the extra help would be a blessing."

When orders had been issued the longboat turned in the river and vanished someplace near the waterfall. Two hours later they returned with supplies and half a dozen women. I could only guess, given this short turnaround, that their settlement was quite close. Was this what Rolf had caught wind of? When Betsy and Helga had been introduced, a bond formed immediately between the women and work began. A makeshift kitchen, made of stumps and rough planks, was constructed and then a fire was kindled.

"Can you believe this?" Anders whispered to us. "We're gonna break bread with part of the First Tribe dude. Rolf did well man, he really did well."

"I'll never doubt the mutt again, I swear." Garrett groaned.

A short distance away Rolf was watching. He seemed to smile when our eyes met, and then he barked a few times and shook nonchalantly. Today he was the undisputed hero.

Fifty-Seven

The Joyous Influences of Viking Cuisine

Friday morning- September 8th

I couldn't help thinking that the Viking food the evening before (roasted pig, fresh vegetables, flat bread, and a most delightful sweet corn porridge; a specialty inclusive to the women of this particular tribe) had changed my whole outlook on life for the better. It was one of the best meals we'd had in months. The fellowship was excellent and the horn, Gunnar had mentioned sharing, was not hard liquor at all. It was a kind of wine made from a secret blend of raspberries and pears and, as we were informed, the making of it was a tradition the First Tribe had followed proudly for centuries. So we imbibed with these people, in deference to a centuries old tradition, and did so with gusto, but not to our detriment; who were we to say no to something that tasted so exquisite and made everyone so joyously expressive.

Before dinner there was prayer, first Olaf, and then Gunnar, and when they were finished the Viking women sang a traditional song about Frey the god of sunshine and earthly fruits, and Freya who loved music and spring flowers, and Bragi the god of poetry, and his wife Iduna whose special apples made those feeling old and worthless young and vibrant again. The music touched me deeply. And as I listened, enchanted with the harmonies and the mythological stories, my college years flooded back to me, (the highs and lows, the joys and sorrows) and I recalled my old friends and sweet Ingrid. Tears came to my eyes as I visualized the places we'd discovered, the pizza parties, the walks along the beach, and the many discussions we'd had about our beloved poetry, and literature, and music. We had been so full of ourselves back then, somehow convincing one another, in the cecity of our passions, that we were destined to become the new clerisy, young idealists confident in their ability to change old thinking and, with stellar literary creations, expand the bounds of consciousness. Oh how tireless we'd been, and what passion defined our days, but oh how easily the fancies of youth had deluded our impressible minds. How well I knew this now. The drive I'd had to excel in school, and to graduate, and to stand on my own, and apart from my Father's influences had been exceptional. And all the restlessness, and the ineffable yearning in me to move on in search of mysteries, and faraway places, and the answers to the questions that churned in me about the world and life, had only happened during those magical years. How very far we'd come since leaving the harbor, and how much we'd learned about what life really was about.

After the meal the Vikings sang songs; beautiful melodies with stories of past exploits, the heartache of loss, and the challenges and joys of knowing the one true God. Accompanied by the sound of small drums, uniquely constructed wooden flutes, and hard round sticks beat together rhythmically, we danced around the fire lost in the moment, the sound, and the warmth of the wine. Tonight our hearts were ablaze with the miracle of being found by a faction of the First Tribe that *we* had been searching for for so long.

Not all of us were overjoyed. The professor pecked at his meal and had moved away when the festivities began. I caught glimpses of his face, at times, in the reddish glow of the fire; stoic and worn, forehead etched with stress lines, a chase of recondite expressions coming and going, and the heaviness in his eyes, all made my heart ache. Quietly uninvolved and distant he watched us. At one point I approached him, to see if there was anything that I might do for him, but he brusquely waved me off. Something had changed in him; something deep in his spirit that was beyond the touch of anyone except the Holy Spirit. He'd come so close to death aboard the Red Dragon, and his effort to save Eloise must have been very trying. Giving up his beloved GVIN in a ploy to save his only real friends, (Hector and the others) and to keep us out of harm's way was something I had trouble imagining.

At long last the professor stood up and approached the Viking leader. Gunnar stood and bowed politely. After formalities were exchanged he spoke briefly to Captain Olaf and then boarded the *Heimdall*. Watching as he shuffled below decks I prayed that God would fill his heart with peace, and give him the strength and focus necessary to accomplish the challenges still before us.

Fifty-Eight

An Interesting Conversation

Much was discussed between Gunnar and Olaf, and having the opportunity to sit with them, and interpret their special conversation, was truly an honor for me. Betsy sat near and took down everything on my laptop for our records.

What Gunnar knew about us was very surprising. As he recounted it; the First Tribe had been, for many decades, anticipating the legendary Ghost Vessel's arrival before the prophesied Viking Armageddon between the Rognvalds and Baaldurians, now known to the crew as 'the day of many collisions'. How could that be, and where had information like that come from? During the conversation Gunnar never made any mention of the Tempest Sword or of the blood rubies. Asking the Captain to see if I should tell them - given the fact that I was the chosen one and, at some point, would be presenting the treasure to them personally - he shook his head no. Perhaps the sword and rubies were a legend that was too sacred to talk about, or maybe these people knew absolutely nothing about them. How strange it was that God had chosen us, and a Vildarsen, to retrieve their long lost legacy for them. Notwithstanding the irony I knew, at some point that, we would be presenting the First Tribe with, undoubtedly, the greatest Rognvald symbolic treasure ever created.

Gunnar went on to tell us that many of the scattered Viking settlements had been summoned by the King to take part in a once a century ceremony commencing this year in early October and that someone on Montague Island had been instrumental, to some degree, in the engineering of this momentous endeavor.

When Gunnar was called away to resolve a dispute I turned to the Captain: "Do you think it was Regan Pendleton sir?"

"Could be son; could very well be. He's by far intelligent enough to orchestrate something that complicated."

"He sure is," Betsy agreed, "he's good at what he does. Remember how instrumental he was in getting the lost tribes back to Montague Island? I can see him involved in this for sure."

"But how did he know where everyone was sir?"

"I don't know Gabriel. But you wanna know something, I'm

realizing tonight that there's a lot that we don't know about what's going on. It's a big complicated puzzle that we're only a piece of."

"I agree sir, a whole lot. But we can sure be proud that we did our part and accomplished what we did."

"Amen to that son," the Captain smiled.

When Gunnar returned he explained that his clan had been sent back, the previous week, to retrieve what was left behind during the transition. He said that beyond the waterfall was the main settlement for eight hundred people for close to one hundred and fifty years. The settlement our Rolf had discovered had been added only a few years previous as a way of handling the influx of newcomers and the clans coming back.

About two hours into their conversation Captain Olaf probed the Viking leader about their relationship with the Haida. Reticent at first, Gunnar finally opened up and told us that there had been a great battle between them in the early years. It was a riveting recount that kept Betsy typing feverishly. He began his story saying the battle was short-lived. The occupants (of the settlement) along the shoreline and several other tribes, further south, had joined together but had been defeated overwhelmingly by the Northmen in only one day. Fear of annihilation was rampant after that but the Vikings had no interest in such things. In an effort to broker a lasting peace a covenant was entered into between both nations. Instead of concentrating now only on their differences, guidelines were laid down that gave each of them topographical boundary, personal autonomy, and established a celebration between the leaders once a year at summer solstice. For decades the Vikings and the Haida prospered peacefully under this simple but binding covenant and became friends.

During the years of Haida conquest, when they were raiding along the western coastline, at times all the way to the California's, trade continued and never a word was whispered about the Vikings even when the majority of the Haida had been diminished from alcohol and scattered by the encroachment of modern society. The Indians honored the alliance they had with the Norsemen (till their demise) and the Norsemen were always generous and apportioned much wisdom to their children, during their glory years, about longboat construction, sea travel, and navigation. I began to see now why the anthropologist Diamond Jenness had referred to them as the "Indian Vikings" of the northwest coast.

When the fire was waning and people had begun yawning and dispersing, Gunnar started to open up a bit. As he'd told it the Haida had venerated the Rognvald clan for almost a century. This, he hailed, was because of bravery in battle, celestial navigation, farming skill, boat construction, and also something that once had happened, an unexpected gathering between the Indians and, what Gunnar referred to as, the *ancient ones.* Something inside me stood at attention when I heard that. He went on to tell us a story about a group of strangely dressed visitors that had appeared on the shoreline one day, apparently from the woods, who had met with the Haida chiefs. The Haida, as Gunnar gestured with emotion, were struck with a kind of reverential fear at the appearing of these strangers. The holy men of the tribe were brought out to meet them and after a short discussion, during which the strangers mysteriously communicated in the Haida language, they were allowed access to the inner council. Here they were fed with the finest foods and allowed to stand above the elder chiefs and speak. At some point the strangers presented an ornate leather satchel to them. Out of the satchel came a single talisman made of turquoise and gold that was offered to the Haida chief as a gift. There was also a scroll of six prophesies meant specifically for the holy men, which they accepted, and also a list of exact instructions for how the Haida must co-exist, and do business, with the Northmen. The Captain's eyes pierced through me as Gunnar spoke. I knew exactly what he was thinking. This story was uncannily similar to the one about Brynhild Busla just before she'd been taken from Torfar-Kolla.

As he was about to share the content of the scroll two of Gunnar's men approached him. When one of them whispered something in his ear Gunnar's face tensed and the conversation shifted immediately. I felt my face flushing with anger. Betsy's eyes were burning, too, and I sensed the Captain was galled. Why had he suddenly become reticent? Trying to remain cool I forced myself to see something good in what had just happened. Then it came to me that Gunnar's willingness to share the content of the scrolls with us was a kind of validation that the Haida had once shared the prophecies with the Northmen and that the content had been passed down for generations between clans. Even though this was a good thing, in my opinion, why did they deem us unworthy of hearing it now? Anger began boiling up in me; what an insult this was. Apparently having sensed my intentions to protest vehemently the Captain grabbed my arm and whispered: "We'll discuss this later! Don't say a word; I don't want to offend the man!"

"Alright sir," I nodded back. "But it's bloody unfair!"

"We'll inform Jonah tomorrow son. E-mail him what Betsy has taken down. He needs to know what we've learned. I think maybe the mystery about the Anasazi has been resolved. Maybe we'll be blessed enough to find out how they did it. Keep your ears open for clues."

"I will sir, promise." I assured him.

Fifty-Nine

Investigating the Settlement, Rolf Acquires a Taste for Pig Shank and Raspberry Pear Wine, Garrett is invited to play Drums

Wednesday – September 13th

The others had been in Pine Valley now for three days. Jonah was involved in long overdue maintenance on their property, and Roxanne was taking care of last minute preparations her courses required at the University of San Diego. The Vildarsen's rustic log home was completed, and Angelina had hired a contractor to stain and seal the exterior, and also to build them a barn. At the behest of the Captain and Rorek's friend, Captain Janus of the Magdalena, she'd agreed to chartering the Raptor two times a week for day trips down to Mexico to help rebuild Captain Janus' dwindling business and to append the Vildarsen's income. After expenses they would be clearing $650.00 a week as supplemental profit to what they were already earning.

Eloise was on the mend. According to Lizzy's update she was recovering but had not regained any memory of her deeds, or of her nefarious alliance with Amalek Baaldur. Because her appetite had returned Lizzy was allowing her to take short jaunts in the hills and also help Roxanne and Angelina with their shared gardening. It was an amazing thing getting Eloise aboard the *Heimdall* the way we had. No one could have foreseen the professor's involvement in her rescue, or the chain of events that led up to getting her off the Red Dragon before it sank. Who, in the wildest stretch of thought, would ever have imagined that the onetime Mortiken high witch, and our deadly sworn enemy, was now helping our ladies with their gardens in Pine Valley? I was convinced now it was Gods will for Eloise to be exonerated from the Baaldurian ethos and given a second chance at a normal life.

While the Vikings were removing the last vestiges of their lives from their homes, for the last five days, we'd been busy investigating both settlements and taking as many pictures as possible. There was an air of finality, now, in what we were doing together. Everyone felt it but no one wanted to talk about it. Change was in the offing and I was convinced that very soon we would all be moving into another season. I clung to the notion that someday all that we'd been through would make sense, and that the work we'd accomplished would reap some kind of a tangible reward we could all enjoy. In the meantime, being filled with purpose, and happy, was something everyone had been missing for a long while. As I worked something one of my favorite professors had written came back to me: *"high spirits flow along with hope as we watch for what was once envisioned to bear witness to a reality that we were successful in what we saw ourselves accomplishing, and that we had become who we envisioned ourselves becoming."*

We ate with the Vikings each evening and celebrated in song and dance together. During this time Rolf had acquired a taste for roasted pig shank and raspberry pear wine. Watching him gnaw the meat and bones and lap up the elixir and, afterwards, bark and chase his tail filled everyone with unbridled joy. Gunnar's people loved Rolf and he loved them. Kinships were being forged now between the crew and the tribe. The Viking ladies were thrilled with Betsy's adept culinary skills and they invited her each night to help with meal preparations. The results were incredible and we ate like pigs.

As soon as the musicians and singers found out that Garrett was a drummer they pressed him to perform with them each night after the meal. At first Garrett balked, but then, after a private pep talk from Anders, he accepted their invitation graciously. After considering what instruments the musicians had to offer, he chose the specific drums he wanted, and then put together a make-shift kit. The first time he played an expression came over his face that I'd never seen before. I was convinced he had discovered a part of himself that he'd been looking for all his life. Garrett's expertise sparked something in the Viking musicians and they began to improvise together as never before. They loved his passionate interpretations, as well as his energy, and the powerful rhythms he employed soon had taken their beloved traditions to another level of expression. Even Gunnar, usually reserved and stoic, (according to several of his men) got up one evening during a riveting rhythmic performance and began dancing with abandon. By the end of the fourth evening we were in awe. On the last night the leader asked Garrett if he would teach the clans what he'd shown them, and if he would consider playing with them at the King and Queens's great celebration in several weeks.

"If the boss lets me I'll give it a shot, you bet." Garrett smiled toothily. Captain nodded tearfully at his talented ward. He was aware of the emotional purging happening inside him and he was gladdened because of it. During the week Garrett's optimism was at an all time high, and his spirit, for the first time since I'd known him, had become peaceful and quiet. Something, at long last, had been set right in his heart.

Sixty

We Depart the Canadian Settlement, Dealing with Gunnar's Trust issues, and Arrangements are made to deliver the Treasure to Kitkatla

Our work here was finally at an end. Both settlements had been photographed, and documented, and the files had been uploaded to Roxanne for analysis and interpretation. Five longboats carrying the women and musicians, and whatever valuables had been retrieved, had departed the previous morning in the low-lying early mists. No one heard a sound when they left and there were no goodbyes.

Today the remaining longboats would head north in the Queen Charlotte Sound and we would be following. Protocol required now that vessels remain cloaked. We'd be shadowing the ferry route from Seattle, past Prince Rupert, north through the Hecate Strait, and then inland through a convoluted series of waterways to some passageway hidden northeast of Revilligigado Island. We had no coordinates to navigate by, and upon reaching our anchorage we'd be completely dependent on Gunnar for any more involvement. Anders was furious with Gunnar's disinclination to trust us and openly considered breaking ties with them because of it.

"Don't they understand how much we've endured getting here," Anders fumed, "don't they understand what we've given up, what we've accomplished, and what we're about to present them?"

"Let's try and stay professional and do our jobs," the Captain encouraged, "much is out of our hands now crew, our phase of the journey is almost complete. These people are allies, whether it seems like it or not. Let's stay focused, please. Let me say this so there will be no doubt about my intentions, my main interest is to do what's best for us. Our priority is to protect the vessel and our people."

Rolf barked sharply.

"Oh, sorry buddy, and Rolf's priority too," Captain added. Rolf trotted over and licked his hand.

Even though I knew the Captain's reasoning was spot-on I still couldn't help wondering how Floki Vildarsen would have reacted to this. Gunnar told us there were hidden routes the Vikings had used for centuries that no outsider had ever been privy to. I could understand that, but why were we seen as outsiders? We'd been written about in their prophecies and they'd anticipated our arrival. Even Anders, a direct Vildarsen descendent, was considered an outsider at present. Exasperated, we stayed in the galley after breakfast to discuss this development and to pray for wisdom and guidance. As always praying changed everyone's dismal mindset. Captain announced, after having considered the earnestness of our involvement objectively, that though he respected Gunnar's bullheadedness about the safety of the hidden settlements, this prescript would be ignored for the safety and welfare of the *Heimdall* crew. The crew cheered wildly. Captain instructed Helga and Garrett, that once we'd re-entered the Pacific Ocean, to begin tracking the *Heimdalls* GPS from the VEW satellites and download the streaming data so we could chart the precise route we'd be taking. It was a plan that not only protected us; it also offered us leverage for any eventuality that may threaten the vessel or our lives. We were satisfied with the Captain's ruling and the anger quickly dissipated in all of us.

Praying had clearly given us the wisdom and the peace needed to rise above our own petty opinions. We understood now that we had entered the final phase of our journey and that it was requiring us to take a step back and embrace a more diverse scenario. It was not a time to get egotistical about our accomplishments, nor was it a time to pass judgment on what was not fully understood. We couldn't allow ourselves to get insulted because the Vikings were preoccupied with protecting their own interests and didn't fully trust us. We would be meeting many characters from here on out, unknown to us, who had been on journeys of their own in various parts of the world towards the same goal. We were only one part of an elaborate puzzle, working together with those we'd never met, and we must embrace these willing adventurers as compeers and rejoice in what they had accomplished. As a crew we were playing a part in something much greater than we would probably ever know. As Rorek had reminded us, our only remaining duty now was for me to present the Tempest Sword and Rubies to the First Tribe before the day of many collisions. After that our involvement was officially done.

Mysterious passages and hidden settlements were certainly reminiscent to me of what Garrett and I had discovered atop the escarpment in the Pontevedra Province on our first year out. It was intriguing to me knowing that the many widespread clans of the First Tribe were right under the noses of everyone in southeastern Alaska, and western Canada, and no one even knew it. Given satellites and modern technology, and all the fishermen in the waterways and tributaries each day, keeping the comings and goings of the clans so remarkably cloistered had to have been a monumental work anointed of the Holy Spirit. Perhaps the First Tribe's mistrust of everyone in modern society was a good thing.

After departure the Captain contacted Jonah for an update. He was enthused to hear the Captain's voice and once again bemoaned that he couldn't be with us for so significant an occasion. He was emotional still about everything he'd learned earlier concerning the Anasazi and assured us he was pursuing what needed to be done with his friend at the Modis Project. Sadly nothing, as yet, had been ascertained. After praying both men decided that the time had finally come to transport the Tempest sword and the rubies to the *Heimdall*.

"They may play out as our 'ace in the hole' Olaf," Jonah went on somewhat pensively, "It's possible that once we present the King and Queen with the sword and rubies we may very well have access to the inner council of the whole Viking Nation. This could prove invaluable as far as them trusting us. Besides, what a blessing that would be for us to be part of." The Captain and I both agreed.

Near the end of the conversation Jonah mentioned that Lizzy was going to return shortly and that he would be back aboard the *Heimdall* within two weeks. A great hoopla erupted when the crew found out.

Because of Jonah's foresight, the rubies and the Tempest had been packaged and made ready for transportation many months previous. He advised the professor be given the responsibility for developing a foolproof plan for delivery. The Captain agreed. Jonah suggested then that the package first be picked up by Hector near San Clemente. He said they had a friend there who owned seven hundred acres, just east of the city, and an operation such as ours could remain safe on the vastness of his property. After running this by the professor he assured Jonah, and the Captain, that all arrangements would be made post haste. He wasn't fooling. That very afternoon every detail of a complicated transportation puzzle had been stitched together into a tangible plan. We were all stunned at his skillfulness in assembling a thing so challenging in so short a time. It seemed now to me, and to everyone else aboard, that the professor was back on his game.

The plan was laid out as such.

Lizzy and the package were slated to be taken up to San Clemente the following day. Roxanne would be dealing with all the preliminary details and driving. Hector had been notified to rendezvous with her at their friend's ranch in a rented helicopter. As soon as the package was loaded they would fly up to San Marcos Pass north of Santa Barbara. There, at a private airstrip, Hector would transfer the package (as cargo) aboard a small jet, my Father had somehow arranged for and then he and Lizzy would fly (this time as passengers) up near Port Alberni on Vancouver Island. A truck, equipped with a camper and stocked with food, would be waiting for them to transport the package to a secluded landing strip used by the forest service and the National Guard in times of emergency. The professor's sole remaining HH-60 helicopter would be waiting for them at this landing strip fully fueled. From that point on Hector and Lizzy would be traveling alone and, after spending the night in the ranger's cabin, they would be flying the package up near a deserted mining town just north of Kitkatla. We would be meeting up with them there to transfer the package and Lizzy aboard the *Heimdall*. Arrangements for anonymity would be made with someone my father knew in the Royal Canadian Mounted Police in Kitkatla. A top secret mission, requiring the greatest of discretion, would be taking place in the outskirts of their township which no one could be privy to. The Captain in the RCMP acceded to my father's wishes and no questions were asked. He assured him that all would be as he wished it. After Hector was finished with the mission he'd be flying the HH-60 back down to San Diego. There it would be stored in Pine Valley, on Jonah's property, until he was ready to make the journey north to us.

Sixty-One

Biding our Time, and a Most Incredible E-mail from Elwin Proudmore

<u>*Sunday – September 28th*</u>

Two weeks had passed since we'd departed the settlement in Canada. Aside from the trip to Kitkatla, we'd been biding our time, and had remained anchored in a secluded bay. Lizzy and Jonah were back with us and the Tempest Sword and rubies were safely aboard.

Gunnar came to visit, towards the end of the first week, to let us know that the high council was still deliberating about our future with the First Tribe. I could feel my blood pressure rising. He mentioned, too, that all the musicians were still enthusiastic about Garrett playing with them at the yearly celebration in October. Garrett was unmoved with the request and both he and the Captain shook their heads no.

As easily as it could have been to get demoralized during this time we chose, instead, to be as productive as possible. Lizzy resolved to give everyone head to toe, and all points in-between, physicals. Notwithstanding the awkwardness during certain procedures, we were all pleased to learn that everyone was in splendid health and that there were no physical anomalies or cancers in anyone.

We were still all disciplined to the physical training we'd begun when the Norseman had joined the crew. This rigorous sixty minute daily regimen had changed us dramatically and was imparting in all of us the courage and fortitude necessary to deal with anything that beset or challenged us. In addition to our regular duties we found time each day to scuba dive, and fish, and finish those things that we'd put aside because of time constraints. Captain and I cleaned up the charts and our journals, Rorek fine-tuned all the new systems, Garrett and Helga incorporated and organized every file amassed above and below the surface, and dear Betsy delighted everyone at the evening meal with her newly acquired skills in Viking gastronomy.

An encrypted e-mail came in the middle of the third week from my Father. The followed is what he wrote us: *"Hello Gabriel, please make sure that you read this to the crew. I've found Gudrun and Ulrik*

Bjornson. My tanker 'Sac Doyle' intercepted radio transmissions in the Sea of Cortez. I've been in contact with both of them. They've been hiding out on Cedros Island. They told me they survived the war with Amalek's troops and that they've been running a few trips back and forth to the mainland for money and supplies. They are both quite eager to be back together with all of you. They send their love."

Tears began forming in Anders eyes but he remained silent.

"Now son brace up, I'm retiring from professional life. I've sold Proudmore Energy Inc. Another UK oil company I've been doing business with the last few months expressed interest in us and they'll be merging PEI with the second largest oil conglomerate in Europe to create a global supertanker company. It was time son. Besides, the world market is changing radically and we just do not have any desire to deal with the unscrupulous cut-throat celebrities clamoring for profit in the energy business now. Mother and I've had enough; we both want something different now, so here's what we've done. We've purchased Isla Socorro and San Benedicto Island; they'll both be ours next week."

All of us stared stone-faced; it was difficult assimilating what father had written. For awhile we discussed this most incredible news and when we'd settled down I continued.

"Son, we'll be sole owners of the land, all the buildings, and we'll have water rights twenty-four miles out around each of the islands. I had a dream several months ago that I shared with Mother. She understood and agreed it was time. We've been discussing ideas about building a resort for fishermen and divers. Cottages or cabins

perhaps with a restaurant near the airstrip. Maybe Betsy would be interested in managing it. She could develop her own menu and choose her own staff. I would fund everything until it got going. I'm also going to build a bay on the eastern side. The Heimdall can anchor there and any other vessels that visit. I talked to Ulrik and Gudrun briefly about running the airport and their own air business from Socorro. They were very interested. I told them that I could give them a place to live – it might be profitable for them. Things are happening rather quickly now so I've decided to hire a Mexican company to demolish the military complex on Socorro and replant the land. I'm also going to install new electrical generators, wind generators on the western side of the island, a desalinization plant for drinking water, and storage towers for the resort. We'll own the Viking settlement and graveyard, and also the "Boiler" on San Benedicto Island. I'm sure Anders will love to hear that. Can you understand what I'm starting to see with this now? Let me know what you guys think. Negotiations for the purchase have been completed. The papers have been drafted and notarized and are slated to be signed the beginning of next week in Edinburgh. Oh, by the way, tell the professor I arranged with a three star general in the Army, who owed me a huge favor, to airlift the SES out of the Caldera and transport it up to Montague Island. It's going to be stored at Cape Cleare with Anders longboat for the time being. Maybe at some point we can bring both down to Socorro and store them there ..."

Father encouraged us to stay diligent and focused and to do what was needed to bring our journey to an honorable conclusion. Much was going on around us now and fathers e-mail had opened our eyes to things we would never have dreamed of. Plans were being made, friendships were being forged, pieces were being moved, loose ends were being tied up, Anders cousins were alive, and much that had remained unresolved was finding a most remarkable fruition.

Sixty-Two

Summoned to the Eiderdrake Settlement, Three Symbols in the Middle of the Forest, Jonah's Insights resolve the Anasazi Conundrum

Monday - October 7th

I was awakened early by the low rumbling of a diesel motor; because of a particular frequency, I'd become familiar with, I knew Gunnar's longboat was approaching. After alerting everyone on the intercom I bolted up on deck.

"Why aren't they cloaked," Anders whispered as he approached me by the rails, "I wonder what's goin' on?"

"Helga, uncloak us," Olaf ordered.

"Right away Captain," she answered.

The men aboard the longboat were smiling and their behavior seemed less formal than it had been in the settlement. Gunnar raised his hand as they neared, his men fell silent, the diesel was switched off, and, when they were alongside, Anders threw out a rope. Moseying up next to me Rolf sat down quietly to watch and listen. These people were his friends now and he was comfortable around them. After moving up to the prow Gunnar stood tall and began speaking. He told us that we had been accepted by the Rognvald's as peers and that the King and Queen had proclaimed blessings upon us. Rolf nuzzled my leg happily and woofed once.

"Awaken from thy slumbers thou blessed of heaven." Gunnar's impassioned voice continued. "Shake off the dross of thy impatience and confusion, for life is about to blossom in unending colors. Your works are known to the clans and you have been accepted by all. You have been granted audience with the great King Eyvindr and his Queen Æsa, they hath declared the Ghost Warriors outsiders no more. Arise men and women of *Heimdall*; arise and embrace this day of grace. Shake off all sullenness of spirit and lift up a song to the Christ who is before all and above all. Great is His name and the gift that will be bestowed upon thee. For no person, since the beginning, has been granted entrance into the Eiderdrake Settlement, and no one, since the beginning, given audience to any ruler of the Rognvalds.

You are the first! Rejoice thou blessed of heaven and of the First Tribe. Our clans will sing and play together boldly in celebration of your great victories. We will sing an epic poem of Heroes, and we will share the exploits of the legendary Ghost Vessel which hath changed the destiny for all Rognvald descendants. Blessed of the Holy Christ are you brothers and sisters."

"Gunnar, what should we do," the Captain seemed flabbergasted as he shouted down from the wheelhouse door.

"Follow us!" Gunnar's eyes were ablaze with excitement. "Use the diesel Captain. Today heaven is smiling upon thee."

So we followed them along pristine fjords and an intricate and hidden system of narrow deep watercourses. All were no less than thirty feet wide and the depth accommodated the keel of the *Heimdall* without mishap. We must have been a curiosity to the wildlife here. Otters began following us, playfully frolicking nearer the shoreline, and Sockeye salmon, Chinook, Coho's, and brown speckled trout were teeming around the vessel just below the surface. Above us no less than fifty Eagles had begun circling near the center mast and some were landing on the crow's nest and the satellite dish. The men on the longboat were pointing and laughing as if this behavior was novel.

"We've never seen this before," Gunnar affirmed. "They usually stay above the trees and away from the longboats."

"It's probably the height of the mast Gunnar," the Captain grimaced, "Garrett, disperse them! I don't want um crappin' on the equipment."

"On it boss," Garrett waved and began climbing the mast.

The shoreline was verdant with wildflowers and an occasional patch of wild strawberries pushing down to the water's edge. The valleys, and mountainsides, for as far as we could see, were defined by healthy dense stands of Sitka Spruce, Western Hemlock, Alder, Paper Birch, and Willows.

"Check it out guys," Betsy laughed and pointed.

Just off the starboard bow a pod of dolphins had surfaced and were crisscrossing in front of the schooner. The sight of them filled me with wonderment, and joy, and the crew started laughing hilariously.

"Oh John this is so great," Helga bubbled joyfully.

"Yah, but where did all the fish go?" John moaned. "I was just about to get our poles honey."

"It is a miracle sign Captain, we haven't seen the dolphins for years," Gunnar shouted from the stern again.

For a moment I contemplated these creatures. Without giving any credence to where they'd come from, or why, I wondered if the dolphins had always been swimming with us, and watching, and if they had reappeared at precisely the right moment to take part in the final celebrations of our Monumental Journey. Gunnar's booming voice redirected our attention to the longboat; they'd begun slowing down and were motioning for us to do the same. Directly in front of them a huge wall, woven tight with willow branches and covered with green vines, was blocking the waterway.

"It's a gate," John cried out, "like in the Pontevedra."

After a long blast on a wooden horn the gate slowly swung open. Before us a magnificent expanse of water was being swallowed in the far horizon. And as we were passing through I noticed a dozen or more islands, like strangely formed creatures, rising up from the perfectly mirrored surface of the lake. Each was uniquely shaped and enshrouded by a milky diaphanous mist. Another dolphin pod surfaced suddenly twenty yards off the port bow. They were making clacking noises and clowning around for attention and handouts. Still tagging along with us, the others, we'd encountered earlier, mingled with them and soon all were cavorting together. After awhile, as they splashed and played, you couldn't tell one pod from the other. After awhile they all jumped up, at the same moment, and disappeared beneath the surface. It was the last we saw of the dolphins. I was convinced, seeing this, that God had shown us a sign of two similar forces joining together and becoming one, to confirm what was about to happen in our lives. On we went enraptured with our magnificent surroundings. Taking it all in, the isolation, the pure air and pristine water, the beauty and serenity, the miracle of how the wildlife was interacting with us, we continued heading southeast following the longboat. After about thirty minutes I began catching glimpses of smoke plumes near the base of the cliffs in the distance.

"Captain, I think we're approaching the Eiderdrake Settlement," John shouted back from the bow.

"Kinda' reminds me of the settlement in the Pontevedra," the Captain shouted back.

"The way the cliffs are formed here is similar to how they are in

Canyon de Chele in northeastern Arizona," Jonah mentioned when he'd joined John at the bow. "The Anasazi built their dwellings under the cliffs there; it seems they've done the same here too."

Gunnar pointed towards a narrow inlet and motioned to follow. After several hundred yards we passed into a deep bay. Around us I counted no less than twenty longboats and dozens of fishing vessels, (of varying size) with bows up on the shore or tied off to one of half a dozen piers. It appeared to be a hub of commerce. As far as I could see, in either direction, there were hundreds of structures built under the overhangs of the cliffs. Many people were congregating now along the shores, watching, as Gunnar motioned us towards the dock. When we were alongside John lowered the gangplank and several of us went ashore to secure lines to pilings. There was no pomp, no fanfare, and there weren't any heralds; I sensed only curiosity in these people. Gunnar delivered a short speech to those along the shoreline. When he'd finished the crowd applauded and, in unison, shouted: "Christ before all else!" After that they dispersed to resume their activities.

Never once had I envisioned the home of the First Tribe being like this. What I'd imagined had more allure, and was more like a mythological city than this was. Granted, the Eiderdrake was pristine and untouched, but from what I'd seen (thus far) this was even more rustic than the Pontevedra Settlement was. I could only assume that keeping it well hidden had compelled the original architects to blend the constructions with the terrain, which in turn had kept them invisible to all air traffic centuries later. God's intervention was obvious to me in this. From where I was I could see that most of the constructions were hidden from plain view. Because of this fact I returned to the bridge and entered the last satellite coordinates into the VEW software. I wanted to understand why better. After a few moments an immense lake came into view with many dozens of islands scattered across the surface. Around the periphery timberland pushed down to water's edge and spread out hundreds of miles in all four directions; it appeared that the Eiderdrake was out in the middle of a vast unclaimed wilderness. The nearest civilization was sixty miles northwest and we were separated from all public waterways, many miles to the west, by a labyrinth of tangled watersheds. After investigating the lake's periphery I realized that nothing at all was visible; not one structure, plume of smoke, vessels, or people; it was truly a miracle. Now, with my curiosity really piqued, I pulled up the program Betsy and Helga had developed for viewing down through the magma vents into the underground realm. But even this sensitive program offered little more than I'd already discovered. I could only make out what appeared as dwellings on several of the largest, more mountainous, wooded islands several miles west of us, and also what may be vessels on the lake in the same area. I could also make out plumes of smoke wafting to the north of us, but those could easily be construed as volcanic vents. Anyone flying over, even as low as two thousand feet, would view nothing here but a pristine wilderness free from mans influences. It was amazing, in this modern age, that this place had remained so isolated from adventurers, and hunters, and fishermen. To further my understanding I spread the parameters of my search out to include the forests around the settlement. Panning southeast I chanced upon something that startled me.

"Gabriel," the Captain barked, "I want you to stop what you're doing right now and come ashore."

"Coming sir!"

After protecting my work I ran ashore. Gunnar was pointing the others towards a grouping of huts in a stand of trees near the shore.

"These will be yours my friends," he smiled. "Please enjoy the food and drink inside that has been prepared for you. I will send someone for you in the morning. Know that a great prophecy has been fulfilled with your arrival. There are few details we know other than that the appearance of the Ghost Vessel will open a door for the chosen one and the gifts he will present."

Even hearing that affirmation couldn't offset the excitement that was burning in me from my discovery. I had to get back to figure out what I'd seen without making a big fuss about it.

"Sir, please, I *have* to get back to my work." I whispered to the Captain. "I found something southeast of us of great interest."

"Alright son - keep me informed."

"I will sir - can Jonah come with me?"

"Of course he can," the Captain motioned for Jonah.

There were three distinct symbols in the midst of the forest. Two of them were touching and the third was several hundred yards closer to us. None of them were overtly conspicuous but they were prominent, when viewed directly, and meticulously made. All three were half a mile from the southern edge of the Eiderdrake Settlement.

"Jonah, look at this," I pointed at the screen. "What are they?"

"Oh my gracious ... Gabriel this is incredible, all three are Anasazi symbols – good job son." Jonah's eyes were as bright as I'd ever seen them.

"Do they mean anything Jonah?"

"Of course they do! First, it proves the Anasazi are up here. The Vikings didn't do this Gabriel, only the Anasazi could have done this. The half circles – radius up, means islands or land, radius down means body of water, and the square on end, like a diamond, with a circle inside touching all the planes, and a solid circle in the center of that circle means Great Spirit."

"What do you make of it Jonah?"

"I see it as a message and an affirmation. Son, you've discovered it exactly when you were supposed to, and the fact that I understand it says a lot to me about who was supposed to see it and exactly when. I've been reminded of something here Gabriel, our timetable is not God's. God's timing is perfect, ours is flawed. It seems we weren't the only ones called to find the First Tribe."

"I don't understand Jonah."

"Something's begun churning in me son; oh man, I feel like oil is being poured on my head."

"I know that feeling, it happened to me in the Eastern Mountains Jonah. I never really understood it, but I know my mind and heart were opened to a lot of things I would never have been able to think on my own."

"I think the Anasazi may be living on some of the islands on this body of water." Jonah said as he hugged me.

"What? But how, there were thousands of them? How did they get all the way up to Alaska?"

"We don't know that there *were* thousands Gabriel. I'm thinking now there were many less."

"Jonah, even if there were only a hundred they couldn't have traveled this far unnoticed. There's no way!"

"Alrek Stormwrack Gabriel, do you remember him?"

"Uh huh I do," I nodded.

"He negotiated with the Anasazi privately. Even the King wasn't privy to all that was discussed or agreed on between them. What we know is that Vadrun rewarded Stormwrack with four longboats, gold and textiles, and that he departed Torfar-Kolla two weeks after he was finished and sailed northwest. Then, two and a half months later, on a foreordained day, the Anasazi left with a splinter group of Vikings.

"But why four longboats Jonah, and why did he go northwest?"

"Good questions. The King probably told him he could have anything he wanted, and going *northwest*, well, I have a theory. Hear me out Gabriel. Let's say Stormwrack was Christian, and the majority of the Anasazi had been converted to Christianity, and let's presuppose that this was the main reason that Vadrun, an Odinist, wanted them purged from Torfar-Kolla. Let's say Stormwrack was not actually summoned by the King, but he had come, at another's behest, to get the Anasazi get out of the Underground Realm. Let's say there were outsiders – Christians – in the underground realm

446

that had helped with this subterfuge to protect the Anasazi from being exterminated. When Vadrun heard that Stormwrack was in the neighborhood, because of his reputation, he sent for him to resolve his problem. Stormwrack played into this and got exactly what he wanted from it to make his plan work. He negotiated behind closed doors to keep everything between him and the Anasazi; this was part of his plan. He established the exact day the Anasazi would leave the city; he did the same for when he left the city. In order for this subterfuge to work they would have to have someplace inconspicuous and safely hidden from all the activity on the great sea to go to.

"Himminglaeva, they went up to Himminglaeva Jonah, and that's where the four longboats picked them up."

"Yes! Stormwrack was waiting in Himminglaeva for them. He didn't cross the sea at all – he made it appear that way and doubled back. The Anasazi needed guides to get to Himminglaeva, they'd never been there before; that's why a splinter group of Christian allies went with them. Whatever was left along the coast had to have been wiped out in the sea storms. It's why we never found any evidence of the Indians anywhere in the Eastern Mountains or in any other place we explored.

"Oh Jonah, I can totally see this, and I totally agree."

"Let's consider Gabriel that Sky Wolf was a passage to the surface Stormwrack had discovered; another river, perhaps, that he'd used to ingress and egress the underground realm. What if in the negotiations Stormwrack revealed to the Anasazi that if they complied with the King's wishes to leave Torfar-Kolla that he could get them to the First Tribe? They could have made it up to Alaska in the longboats easily a hundred years ago. And the gold and textiles could have been used to buy supplies, or barter with, if they ever encountered the Haida during their raids."

"Exactly, the Haida raided as far south as the California's in those days so it totally makes sense. We never did explore the far northwest underground very thoroughly. There probably *was* another entrance.

"I agree! Now, the strangers that met with the Haida, in the Canadian Settlement, were the Anasazi Gabriel, I'm convinced of it. The talisman, the prophecies, and the rules they were given, about how they should deal with the Northmen (I think it) was so the Haida would introduce them to the Canadian Viking Settlement so they could get passage up to the Eiderdrake Settlement."

"But how did they know about the Canadian Settlement?"

"Alrek Stormwrack must have been there before. He must have known about the Eiderdrake Settlement too, he must have lived there, or had dealings with them. There is no other way he could have offered the Anasazi so much specifically? Remember Gabriel, the First Tribe was as much revered by the Anasazi as they were by the Vikings."

"Gosh Jonah, I think the Holy Spirit just gave you most of the missing pieces in the puzzle. Did I tell you that I found a grouping of large mountainous islands several miles from here?"

"No you didn't."

"Yah ... they all appeared to have dwellings on them, too, and vessels on the water around them. It could corroborate what you've postulated here."

"Do you remember the coordinates?"

"I do, here they are," I pointed at the screen.

Jonah held a magnifying glass up to the screen and gasped.

"The Anasazi *are* here! Don't say a thing about this. I want to research this some more - you and me - and save it for a surprise. We better get outside. I don't want to offend anyone."

"Yah, ok, but is there anything I should do before?"

"Yes, encrypt a file and send images of the symbols to Roxanne. Give her the coordinates of these islands, too, and tell her what you saw. I'll tell her tonight what we discussed. Here's her personal address. When you're done I'll see you outside."

"Sure Jonah, I'll be there ASAP."

Sixty-Three

A Great Viking Prophecy is fulfilled, Mystery Guests arrive, Preparing for the Great Ceremony, Garrett Performs with the Viking Musicians, Anders and the Crew are embraced by the Rognvald Warriors and People

A great prophecy had been fulfilled with the *Heimdall's* arrival. Gunnar had been quite clear when he'd declared this to us. According to him they already knew of the 'chosen one' and, though they had no specifics, they knew also of the gifts this person would be offering to the reigning King and Queen. Their prophecies were correct; there was a great treasure awaiting them.

Aside from a hum of activity along the shoreline, the day was still and peaceful. Around 2 pm eight wooden smacks departed near where we were docked; all were rigged like small sloops. At 5 pm all eight returned laden with fish. Near our huts a group of workers cleaned the catch, filleted them, and then, whatever was left was thrown out to a pod of dolphins waiting near the pier. Workers arrived within minutes and, after filling their wooden carts with the fresh fillets, they headed out to make their deliveries. Shortly after that Gunnar's longboat departed.

After showering and changing clothes we gathered outside one of the huts and ate what had been prepared. We discussed many things during the meal; where the prophecies had come from about us, how many others had been following similar paths towards the same goal as ours, and if we would ever meet them. How could it be that people with no knowledge of us, and little understanding of what we'd accomplished, had been given wisdom about what would transpire.

The sun had dipped below the far horizon and all of us were meditating on chairs outside the huts. The meal had been excellent and was sitting well. In the twilight, shadows had lengthened across the bay, and colors were deepening along the shoreline. Erratic breezes were blowing in now from across the lake and the air had a musty fragrance of night jasmine. When the moon had finally edged up over the cliffs, and was creating mysterious shadows dancing through the trees, Gunnar's longboat returned; they were escorting a gorgeously constructed smaller vessel. Standing near the bow together a petite woman, and a burly man, with a beard halfway down his chest, were the only passengers; both were wrapped in cloaks that hid their identity. Fully intrigued we all watched quietly. As soon as he'd disembarked Gunnar turned and motioned for us to remain where we were. Captain nodded our compliance. As the woman was being helped from the vessel the lake breezes picked up suddenly again and her cloak was blown from her head and fell back over her shoulders. The woman's skin glowed with a milky opaline luster in the radiant moonlight; she appeared as a goddess and I was utterly transfixed with her beauty. Another sudden gust caught her long flaxen lochs and whipped them around in front of her. After complaining to her escort, he reached around at once and gently pulled the hair back over her shoulders. Patiently he waited until she had it clasped in both her hands before he let go. When it was secured again she turned towards us and smiled and then pulled the cloak back over her head. The scene was intoxicating.

"What a babe, I wonder who they are?" Garrett murmured as they were whisked into the large wooden building.

"Who knows," John answered, "they weren't gone very long."

"Maybe they picked them up from one of the islands," Anders pondered.

"Could be," Rorek nodded, "the ones in the north were pretty big."

"I saw a plume of smoke on one of them when we first came in," Olaf mentioned. "Did anyone see that?"

"I did sir, right after we entered the channel," John confirmed.

"She was so striking, goodness," Betsy marveled. "It seemed as if she was a queen in a story."

"You noticed that too huh?" Garrett chuckled.

As easy as it could have been to find fault with what had been imposed on us, no one could muster any animosity to do so. There was a kind of peace of mind here that we'd experienced only once before on our journey affecting us as deeply as it had then. Gunnar told us, when we arrived in the Eiderdrake, that we were not allowed to explore or go near the large wooden structure they'd just escorted the mysterious couple into. We were allowed to explore the shoreline, and, though we could exchange greetings with passersby's, no in-depth conversations were allowed. We were also instructed to keep the wolfhound aboard the schooner or tied up outside the huts. Certainly Rolf was unhappy with this ruling but he seemed to understand and quietly acquiesced. The citizenry avoided talking with us as well but they were polite and smiled, or waved, as they passed. Such was our first day in the Eiderdrake Settlement. We were here but disconnected on many levels. The gloaming and the night passed uneventfully and our sleep was deep and restful.

6 am Tuesday Oct 8th

We were summoned early. Servants arrived with deliciously prepared breakfast trays and to encourage us that, after we'd eaten, we prepare for the commencement of the great observance and feast.

They instructed us that we, and Rolf, would be escorted into the large hall and given seats of distinction very near the thrones at 3pm. We were all given a piece of white embroidered cloth (which resembled a narrow kind of tunic) and were instructed to wear it in the presence of the council, and of the King and Queen.

"It is a show of respect," one servant explained, "and will indicate your willingness to be part of a time honored tradition."

"It also establishes that you are of the Ghost Vessel," another servant continued, "venerated warriors, written of in legends and prophecies - ones who have fought and won great battles against our sworn enemies, the Baaldurians - that have come so far to honor the Rognvald Nation."

Before they departed we were also given shoulder bags for whatever trinkets or gifts we wanted to present the Queen.

"The Queen doth love trinkets," one servant laughed. "She has collected many over the years, all sizes and shapes, and shows them occasionally in the great celebration."

Bowing politely all three scurried away.

"Captain," Anders began, "we can easily carry the rubies in these bags. When it's time to offer our gifts wouldn't it be something if we poured out the blood rubies instead of some cheesy trinkets?"

"Dude ..." Garrett slapped high fives, "a most excellent idea."

"It is an excellent idea Norse," the Captain raved, "is everyone in agreement?" The idea was sensational and everyone agreed.

"Let's pray before we get ready," Jonah suggested, "it's really important that we have Gods timing from here on out."

The morning went by quickly. We all showered, and put on our best clothes, and the ladies did their hair and helped Anders with his. We were a sight indeed when we'd finished. Everyone looked so unlike themselves – so handsome and beautiful. During prayer the idea to let Rolf carry the Tempest Sword on his back (in the silken bag we'd found it in) was agreed upon. Around two pm Jonah nudged me and motioned to follow him to the bridge.

"Look Gabriel," he pointed at the computer screen. "Three vessels have departed those islands you discovered. They're all headed in this direction."

"Oh Jonah, is it the Anasazi?"

"It is son, it is, and they're in full regalia too," he sighed as tears formed in his eyes. "It seems they'll be part of the celebration too."

"Are we ever going to know how they did it?"

"My heart is at peace Gabriel. For now let's rejoice in this miracle, son, and embrace what we've been given.

The servants arrived at 3pm and, with no ostentation, we were escorted to the wooden castle. It was larger than what we'd seen from the *Heimdall*, or the huts, and extended back several hundred yards under the cliffs. A feeling of rapture whelmed us as the large wooden doors opened and we passed through. Just inside was an elaborate antechamber lined with wooden statues and bustling with hundreds of people. Each of them stopped what they were doing, as we passed, and bowed with a great show of respect. Along the length of the vestibule were three large archways; each with the same Rognvald symbol over it that we'd become so familiar with on our travels.

We were escorted through the passage on our far right. Inside was another enormous room, with a heavily beamed ceiling, lined with long work tables and looms for making tapestries. Around the upper periphery was a narrow catwalk and sizeable openings that allowed light and air into the area.

"We will enter the royal hall from one of the side entrances," one of the older servants informed us. "They are preparing for the jubilation. Please do not speak until you have been seated. When the guards enter, they will climb the staircases to the balcony and position themselves around the entire hall. At that time you may get up to look around if you wish. When you hear trumpets please sit back down. The musicians will begin playing at that time and young Garrett will be invited to join them. His instruments will be available as he made them in the Sandrake Settlement."

The royal hall was a bustle of activity and the warm sound of laughter filled my heart with joy. An assortment of exquisite tapestries, artifacts, and weapons hung on the walls and, deftly fitted into the timbers above us, sculptures depicting battles, and warriors, and frightful sea creatures, were clearly visible. In dozens of niches, around the perimeter of the hall, life sized wooden statues loomed with fixed stares; these must have been effigies to their heroes and kings. We passed very near one of them. In it was a statue of an impressive looking man with a long beard and fiercely intelligent eyes. I could hardly believe it. At the base was a plaque that read: ALREK STORMWRACK.

"Jonah, look," I pointed in disbelief.

"Oh lord!" he whispered shaking his head.

Hung around the neck was a replication of the talisman we'd discovered in the mysterious wooden box. It was an exact copy of the very talisman that Anders had carried through the Eastern Mountains and presently was wearing around his neck.

"I wonder what it means," I whispered back.

"I have no idea son," Jonah looked at me mystified.

Two large wooden thrones were set high in the rear center of the room and six others were evenly dispersed on each side in a semi-circle; everything was uncannily similar here to what we'd found in the Pontevedra castle. Twelve staircases led up to a wooden balcony encircling the entire room. On the bottom floor I counted twelve doorways around the perimeter; all were in line with doorways directly above them along the balcony. Everywhere around us servants were setting up tables and bringing in food. As soon as we were seated I removed the silken bag from Rolf and we removed the shoulder bags, filled with rubies, and put them under our seats. No one noticed; it was as if what we were doing was invisible to them and for this I thanked God. Several dozen guards entered and took up their positions; all were dressed in traditional garb and bore short swords and spears. Others began drifting in. They all politely acknowledged us and then joined together in small cliques and began talking. It felt to me as if they knew who we were but had been instructed to remain separated from us as we had them. The room was blossoming so we all sat quietly and watched. Next all the musicians and singers appeared from one of the doorways on the far side of the room. Applause rippled throughout the hall as they filed in and I could feel excitement intensifying as they set up their instruments. Many of the younger people left their groups and began congregating near where the musicians would be playing. When the setup was finished the leader motioned at Garrett to come and join them. Standing and smiling, Garrett smoothed his clothes and looked at the Captain.

"Knock um dead son," the Captain smiled warmly.

"You got it Caps," Garrett laughed, "I'm gonna show these First Tribe dudes something 'bout the youth a California – dig it!"

We all applauded as he sat down at his kit and began twirling his drumsticks. Several of the younger girls immediately expressed their appreciation and moved nearer him. At first he didn't notice them but then, because they all were hopelessly intrigued with his hair, each of them in turn reached out to touch it.

"Diggin' on that do ladies?" Garrett laughed. The girls began giggling and touched his hair again. Garrett smiled toothily and then flexed his muscles. Other girls gathered around and began chattering and pointing. Suddenly the festivities began. The single drums started, then the hand instruments came in, then the stringed instruments and clapping, and when the leader pointed at Garrett a rousing rhythmic song took off. Garrett's girls began dancing and laughing hilariously. Many others were filing in now. And all of them began dancing and making merry. Seemingly out of nowhere warriors and beautifully clad blonde women appeared along the balcony above us; there were younger children running up and down the stairs, and older men, and women, finding seats to watch from. The room had become animated with laughter and rejoicing.

"Can you believe this?" Anders jumped up and began dancing.

After awhile a regal looking elder man, with long flowing hair, stepped forward on the balcony behind the thrones. When he raised his hand the music came to an abrupt stop and the warriors and guards snapped to attention. The crowd was hushed when he pointed down at Anders. Opening both his arms wide the elder man began speaking: "We are honored by your presence, Anders, son of Utgard, of the clan Vildarsen. Your father's bravery and skill has been known to us for many decades. We honor his life. We honor his accomplishments. We honor his memory. We honor you his son. In respect we salute you Anders Vildarsen, and the crew of the Ghost Vessel, for the work you have accomplished to rid us of the scourge of Baaldurian filth."

The crowd roared its approval and began applauding. When the warriors along the balcony drew their swords the crowd fell silent. Thrusting them up, all shouted in unison loudly: "Christ before all else!" Anders stood at attention and saluted the leader. After that Anders turned and pointed at the crew. When we stood the whole room got up and began cheering and clapping. This time the reaction was so irresistibly energetic that Rolf got up on his hind legs and danced. The audience seemed to love this and applauded even more. Overwhelmed with emotion Anders genuflected with tears on his cheeks. It was a poignant moment that touched all of us very deeply. Out of respect Anders remained where he was, for awhile, but as soon as he had pulled himself erect the music began anew and the room burst out again with liveliness and feasting.

For two hours we danced and ate and laughed. Never had I seen festivities like these. The hall was pulsing with laughter and gaiety and love. There was warmth of purpose here that I had very rarely experienced anywhere in my life except with the crew. At one point, during one of the songs, the trumpets began a majestic fanfare and all activity came to a halt. Unsure about what would be transpiring next we returned to our seats to watch. From behind the thrones a warm golden swath of light was creeping along the floor from an opening door. The King and Queen had entered and were being escorted into the hall by handmaidens and personal guards. Not a sound was heard as they mounted up the stairs to their thrones. Out of respect the crew stood and Rolf moved in next to me. The hall remained quiet until the King and Queen had been seated and then, all the warriors and guards snapped to attention, all the men in the audience bowed deeply, and all the ladies curtsied.

Sixty-Four

We present the Blood Rubies and Tempest Sword, to King Eyvindr and Queen AEsa of the First Tribe of Rognvald's - Our Journey Ends

"What a magnificent hound you have." The Queen stood again unexpectedly and motioned for Rolf to come to her. Being unsure what to do Rolf whined uneasily and remained by my side.

"What is his name?" she asked with an inquisitive smile.

"His name is Rolf highness," I answered politely.

"Well then, Rolf, would you come and sit with us during the ceremonies?" Rolf looked up at me.

"Be nice dude and don't fart," I instructed him.

Barking once he trotted over and sat down between the King and Queen. Everyone began applauding when the queen gave him a treat. The King stood next and faced us.

"Captain Olaf ..." the King raised both hands and motioned towards him. The Captain moved closer. "Welcome Captain Olaf and friends of the Rognvald's ..."

Applause filled the hall and, when the warriors stood at attention and raised their swords, all manner of joyfulness broke out. I was amazed at the intensity of the response. We were being honored by these people. I felt a flood of emotion rising up in me, and a strange burning in my soul. And then, when Betsy took hold of my hand, and I felt her trembling; I praised God aloud because I somehow knew that our mandate was just about to find its fruition. We had finally made it.

"Oh honey, I am so proud of you," she whispered. "Everything we've worked so hard for is just about to be fulfilled."

When the King held up his hands the applause ended and he continued: "Ever wild and mysterious are the wandering paths that have brought the Ghost Vessel to us. As the sun, shining forth with warmth and life, have you come to us from a far country. Through tempestuous great waters, and Odin's buffeting, and though leviathan tried to devour you, you were victorious against the vile Baaldurians that rose against you to kill and steal and destroy. Strong and unbending you forged against all that would try and prevail against thee, and now as towering strong trees you stand honored as brothers and sisters before us in this assembly. I pray that you will accept this Captain Olaf as a token of our appreciation."

The King stepped down and stood before the Captain. In his hands was a beautifully crafted golden talisman that he placed around the Captain's neck. Olaf bowed and took a step back.

"Thankyou King Eyvindr." The Captains eyes were glistening.

"The smoke of your great journey is fading," the King went on, "and your fearless deeds have offered all of the First Tribe the hope of victory over our sworn enemies and a brighter tomorrow. We rejoice in your appearing brothers and sisters of *Heimdall*, and also in our many friends who have, in the past, taken their own paths to find us."

The King motioned up at the balconies and in dramatic parlance proclaimed: "Many years hence they came, these ancient ones. From the bowels of the earth, out from the great Torfar-Kolla, escaping the oppression of Vadruns tyranny, up through Sky Wolf, our father, Alrek Stormwrack, led them over great waters to be with the Rognvald Nation, and here now they live in peace with us. Let them join us now, these honored allies and friends."

The musicians started a simple rhythm and from all twelve doors dozens of Anasazi, dressed in full regalia, entered the room and distanced themselves between the guards along the balcony. I was astonished and Betsy began sobbing. The proof, now, of Jonah's many years of work was standing in the hall celebrating the First Tribe with us. I could feel Jonah's heart finally was at ease. And with his eyes glistening he smiled and put his arm around my shoulder. As the applause lessened the King motioned back towards the thrones.

"People of Eiderdrake, much has been rumored, and many tears have been shed wondering and waiting, but now with joyous heart I give you the true queen of Torfar-Kolla, her majesty, Brynhild Busla."

The King's voice was cracking with emotion and tears were streaming down AEsa's cheeks. Approaching them she curtsied gracefully and then turned towards the room and did the same. She was the very same woman we'd seen the evening before.

"We welcome her to us and the safety of this place," The King continued. "for she has endured much misery at the hands of the Baaldurians and we thank the Holy Christ for sparing her life and bringing her to us so that she may be joined with the Rognvald's on this wondrous and blessed occasion."

We were all speechless. Applause thundered in the hall for her and all on the floor, and on the balconies, honored her with an outpouring of love that touched my soul. Garrett stared love struck from behind his drums. Never before had I seen an expression like the one on his face. Brynhild was genteel and graceful and the most beautiful woman that I'd ever seen besides Betsy. We were both in awe and the crew bowed deeply as she passed. She nodded demurely towards us and then, after smiling warmly at Garrett, she ascended with her burly escort behind her, scratched Rolf on the head, and then sat down next to Queen AEsa.

The King motioned next for everyone to be seated and, after unrolling a parchment given him from one of the servants, he began reading: "Embracing this vision of words given of our father, the Mighty Agar, and his servant Gamelin, the Most High Christ smiles upon those who are willing to pursue the unknown paths in faith. From a far distant land the Ghost Vessel will appear with one chosen to quench the thirst of longing and to reanimate purpose for the scattered tribes. Awaken thou enshrouded, still, in this time of revealing, for wide is the light that illumes the path of one empowered in language, and thought, and pure of heart. He rides over leviathan to the hidden realm upon the winds of the great oceans, with ghost warriors, at the appointed time, with news of great accomplishment and to offer a remembrance of souls lost on the great journey."

"Of course, I understand now, it makes sense," I heard Anders whispering; "the blood rubies represent to these people the souls of all those that were lost on the Shallows of Three Rocks."

The King placed the prophetic parchment down and stepped to the floor. Half a dozen guards moved closer to him. For several moments he seemed lost in thought and stood silently. No one moved or spoke. Suddenly, with his arms outstretched, he asked: "who I pray among you is the chosen?"

"It is I great King, I am the chosen one," I spoke out with authority. "I am Gabriel Baaldur Proudmore of Aberdeen Scotland, and I come with the ghost warriors bearing a magnificent treasure for Eyvindr and AEsa of the First Tribe of Rognvalds."

An earthquake shook the settlement for a moment and then one rolling clap of thunder boomed. Instinctively the others picked up the bags from underneath their seats and moved next to me. No one spoke a word. Never had I felt so sure of myself.

"We offer you this treasure of souls lost on the great voyage."

All of us, at the same moment, poured the blood rubies onto the floor in front of the thrones. Brynhild cried out when we did, AEsa began weeping, everyone in the hall gasped, and the King, seemingly in a swoon, stumbled backwards and was caught, before he fell, by his guards. All of the rubies somehow rolled into one unbroken circle. Not one was left apart from the other. It was a miracle. Now feeling a kind of strength I'd never experienced before I reached down, drew the sword from its sheath, and thrust it high above my head.

"King Eyvindr, we present the Tempest Sword, envisioned and called forth by King Agar, forged and brought into existence by Gamelin the Wizard, once lost on the Shallows of Three Rocks, now, after centuries, found, and returned to the First Tribe of Rognvald's."

All in the hall, and on the balcony, knelt with their eyes to the floor. The guards and warriors removed their weapons and laid them down. The Anasazi covered their eyes with their hands. Not a sound was heard as I moved towards the King and knelt before him with the sword in both my outstretched arms.

"It is yours majesty," I proclaimed to the King, "yours and the First Tribe of Rognvald's. We of the schooner *Heimdall* offer it to you in gratitude and love."

With trembling hands the King took hold of the Tempest and

clutched it firmly to his breast. A warm glow had begun emanating from the circle of rubies and was filling the hall. Around us I could feel angels singing and praising God. A glorious look of satisfaction was on the Kings face as he sank back into his throne. Brynhild and AEsa rose up and stood next to King Eyvindr with their eyes lifted up to Heaven. Something very powerful was happening. Standing and bowing I moved back to where Betsy was. After hugging her I heard the same voice whispering in me that had given me instructions since the beginning: *"she is yours Gabriel to wed and to love."* At that moment something in my heart fell into place and I was suddenly freed from all my many fears and dysfunctions. Taking Betsy in my arms I looked in her eyes and asked: "I love you so much Betsy, would you marry me?"

"I would love to be your wife," she whispered back.

Instantly the wings of my heart unfurled and I soared into all the possibilities of our life together; much was racing through me now. Despite all the wars and dangers and detours the Holy Spirit had, at last, safely brought us to the First Tribe of Rognvald's alive and healthy. All we had purposed together had been accomplished. My calling was completed and, because of that; I could feel a great burden had finally been lifted from the crew. Garrett got up from his drums and made his way over to us. Rolf came down from the thrones and sat down next to me. All of us lined up together and joined hands. We had been successful in what God had called us to do and now it was time to move on. After bowing to the royals we faced the people in the hall and, with great satisfaction for all that God had allowed us to accomplish, we raised our hands, and our voices, and shouted in unison: CHRIST BEFORE ALL ELSE. Everyone responded and stood and began applauding. We had run the course, fought the good fight, and we had completed our mission; our journey was now at an end.

The End

About the Author

Richard began creating in his teens, first as a classical trumpet player, then as a guitarist and lyricist, and then as a writer of poetry and short-stories. He is presently an internationally published poet and has authored four books. As a novelist his primary motivations integrate Jules Verne, Edgar Rice Burroughs, Robert Lewis Stevenson, C.S. Lewis and a host of other gifted writers into a uniquely crafted compelling blend of adventure, mystery, historical fiction, and spirituality.